OMERTA

OMERTA

Mario Puzo

R A N D O M   H O U S E
LARGE PRINT

A Division of Random House, Inc.
Published in association with Random House.
New York 2000

Library of Congress Cataloging-in-Publication Data
Puzo, Mario, 1920–1999
Omerta / by Mario Puzo.—1st large print ed.
p.   cm.
ISBN 0-375-43058-X
1. Mafia—Fiction.   2. Criminals—Fiction.
3. Organized crime—Fiction.   4. Large type books.
I. Title.
PS3566.U9 O46 2000
813'.54—dc21   00-021660

FIRST LARGE PRINT EDITION

This Large Print Edition published in
accord with the standards of N.A.V.H.

To
Evelyn Murphy

Omerta:

a Sicilian code of honor which forbids informing about crimes thought to be the affairs of the persons involved

World Book Dictionary

OMERTA

PROLOGUE
1967

IN THE STONE-FILLED VILLAGE of Castellammare del Golfo, facing the dark Sicilian
Mediterranean, a great Mafia Don lay dying.
Vincenzo Zeno was a man of honor, who all his
life had been loved for his fair and impartial judgment, his help to those in need, and his implacable
punishment of those who dared to oppose his will.

Around him were three of his former followers,
each of whom had gone on to achieve his own
power and fame: Raymonde Aprile from New
York in America, Octavius Bianco from Palermo,
and Benito Craxxi from Chicago. Each owed
him one last favor.

Don Zeno was the last of the true Mafia chiefs,
having all his life observed the old traditions. He
extracted a tariff on all business, but never on
drugs or prostitution. And never did a poor man
come to his house for money and go away
empty-handed. He corrected the injustices of the

law—the highest judge in Sicily could make his ruling, but if you had right on your side, Don Zeno would veto that judgment with his own force of will, and arms.

No philandering youth could leave the daughter of a poor peasant without Don Zeno persuading him into holy matrimony. No bank could foreclose on a helpless farmer without Don Zeno interfering to put things right. No young lad who hungered for a university education could be denied it for lack of money or qualification. If they were related to his *cosca,* his clan, their dreams were fulfilled. The laws from Rome could never justify the traditions of Sicily and had no authority; Don Zeno would overrule them, no matter what the cost.

But in the last few years his power had begun to wane, and he'd had the weakness to marry a very beautiful young girl, who had produced a fine male child. She had died in childbirth, and the boy was now two years old. The old Mafia don, knowing that the end was near and that without him his *cosca* would be pulverized by the more powerful *coscas* of Corleone and Clericuzio, pondered the future of his son.

He had called his three friends to his bedside because he had an important request, but first he thanked them for the courtesy and respect they had shown in traveling so many miles. Then he told them that he wanted his young son, Astorre, to be taken to a place of safety and brought up under different circumstances. And yet to be brought up in the tradition of a man of honor, like himself.

"I can die with a clear conscience," he said, though his friends knew that in his lifetime he had decided the deaths of hundreds of men, "if I can see my son to safety. For in this two-year-old I see the heart and soul of a true Mafioso, a rare and almost extinct quality."

He told them he would choose one of them to act as guardian to this unusual child, and with this responsibility would come great rewards.

"It is strange," Don Zeno said, staring through clouded eyes. "According to tradition, it is the first son who is the true Mafioso. But in my case it took until I reached my eightieth year before I could make my dream come true. I'm not a man of superstition, but if I were, I could believe this child grew from the soil of Sicily itself. His eyes are as green as olives that spring from my best trees. And he has the Sicilian sensibility—romantic, musical, happy. Yet if someone offends him, he doesn't forget, as young as he is. But he must be guided."

"And so what do you wish from us, Don Zeno?" Craxxi asked. "For I will gladly take this child of yours and raise him as my own."

Bianco stared at Craxxi almost resentfully. "I know the boy from when he was first born. He is familiar to me. I will take him as my own."

Raymonde Aprile looked at Don Zeno but said nothing.

"And you, Raymonde?" Don Zeno asked.

Aprile said, "If it is me that you choose, your son will be my son."

The Don considered the three of them, all worthy men. He regarded Craxxi the most intelligent. Bianco was surely the most ambitious and forceful. Aprile was a more restrained man of virtue, a man closer to himself. But he was merciless.

Don Zeno, even while dying, understood that it was Raymonde Aprile who most needed the child. He would benefit most from the child's love, and he would make certain his son learned how to survive in their world of treachery.

Don Zeno was silent for a long moment. Finally he said, "Raymonde, you will be his father. And I can rest in peace."

THE DON'S FUNERAL was worthy of an emperor. All the *cosca* chiefs in Sicily came to pay their respects, along with cabinet ministers from Rome, the owners of the great latifundia, and hundreds of subjects of his widespread *cosca*.

Atop the black horse-drawn hearse, Astorre Zeno, two years old, a fiery-eyed baby attired in a black frock and black pillbox hat, rode as majestically as a Roman emperor.

The cardinal of Palermo himself conducted the service and proclaimed memorably, "In sickness and in health, in unhappiness and despair, Don Zeno remained a true friend to all." He then intoned Don Zeno's last words: "I commend myself to God." he said. "He will forgive my sins, for I have tried every day to be just."

And so it was that Astorre Zeno was taken to America by Raymonde Aprile and made a part of his own household.

CHAPTER 1
1995

WHEN THE STURZO TWINS, Franky and Stace, pulled into Heskow's driveway, they saw four very tall teenagers playing basketball on the small house court. Franky and Stace got out of their big Buick, and John Heskow came out to meet them. He was a tall, pear-shaped man; his thin hair neatly ringed the bare top of his skull, and his small blue eyes twinkled. "Great timing," he said. "There's someone I want you to meet."

The basketball game halted. Heskow said proudly, "This is my son, Jocko." The tallest of the teenagers stuck out his huge hand to Franky.

"Hey," Franky said. "How about giving us a little game?"

Jocko looked at the two visitors. They were about six feet tall and seemed in good shape. They both wore Ralph Lauren polo shirts, one red and the other green, with khaki trousers and rubber-soled shoes. They were amiable-looking, handsome men, their craggy features set with a graceful confidence. They were obviously brothers, but Jocko could not know they were twins. He figured them to be in their early forties.

"Sure," Jocko said, with boyish good nature.

Stace grinned. "Great! We just drove three thousand miles and have to loosen up."

Jocko motioned to his companions, all well over six feet, and said, "I'll take them on my side against you three." Since he was the much better player, he thought this would give his father's friends a chance.

"Take it easy on them," John Heskow said to the kids. "They're just old guys futzing around."

It was midafternoon in December, and the air was chilly enough to spur the blood. The cold Long Island sunlight, pale yellow, glinted off the glass roofs and walls of Heskow's flower sheds, his front business.

Jocko's young buddies were mellow and played to accommodate the older men. But suddenly Franky and Stace were whizzing past them for layup shots. Jocko stood amazed at their speed; then they were refusing to shoot and passing him the ball. They never took an outside shot. It seemed a point of honor that they had to swing free for an easy layup.

The opposing team started to use their height

to pass around the older men but astonishingly
enough got few rebounds. Finally, one of the boys
lost his temper and gave Franky a hard elbow in
the face. Suddenly the boy was on the ground.
Jocko, watching everything, didn't know exactly
how it happened. But then Stace hit his brother
in the head with the ball and said, "Come on.
Play, you shithead." Franky helped the boy to his
feet, patted him on the ass, and said, "Hey, I'm
sorry." They played for about five minutes more,
but by then the older men were obviously tuck-
ered out and the kids ran circles around them.
Finally, they quit.

Heskow brought sodas to them on the court,
and the teenagers clustered around Franky, who
had charisma and had shown pro skills on the
court. Franky hugged the boy he had knocked
down. Then, he flashed them a man-of-the-world
grin, which set pleasantly on his angular face.

"Let me give you guys some advice from an
old guy," he said. "Never dribble when you can
pass. Never quit when you're twenty points down
in the last quarter. And never go out with a
woman who owns more than one cat."

The boys all laughed.

Franky and Stace shook hands with the kids
and thanked them for the game, then followed
Heskow inside the pretty green-trimmed house.

Jocko called after them, "Hey, you guys are good!"

Inside the house, John Heskow led the two brothers upstairs to their room. It had a very heavy door with a good lock, the brothers noticed as Heskow let them in and locked the door behind them.

The room was big, a suite really, with an attached bathroom. It had two single beds—Heskow knew the brothers liked to sleep in the same room. In a corner was a huge trunk banded with steel straps and a heavy metal padlock. Heskow used a key to unlock the trunk and then flung the lid open. Exposed to view were several handguns, automatic weapons, and munitions boxes, in an array of black geometric shapes.

"Will that do?" Heskow asked.

Franky said, "No silencers."

"You won't need silencers for this job."

"Good," Stace said. "I hate silencers. I can never hit anything with a silencer."

"OK," Heskow said. "You guys take a shower and settle in, and I'll get rid of the kids and cook supper. What did you think of my kid?"

"A very nice boy," Franky said.

"And how do you like the way he plays basketball?" Heskow said with a flush of pride that made him look even more like a ripened pear.

"Exceptional," Franky said.

"Stace, what do you think?" Heskow asked.

"Very exceptional," said Stace.

"He has a scholarship to Villanova," Heskow said. "NBA all the way."

WHEN THE TWINS came down to the living room a little while later, Heskow was waiting. He had prepared sautéed veal with mushrooms and a huge green salad. There was red wine on the table.

The three of them sat down. They were old friends and knew each other's history. Heskow had been divorced for thirteen years. His ex-wife and Jocko lived a couple of miles west in Babylon. But Jocko spent a lot of time here, and Heskow had been a constant and doting father.

"You were supposed to arrive tomorrow morning," Heskow said. "I would have put the kid off if I knew you were coming today. By the time you phoned, I couldn't throw him and his friends out."

"That's OK," Franky said. "What the hell."

"You guys were good out there with the kids," Heskow said. "You ever wonder if you could have made it in the pros?"

"Nah," Stace said. "We're too short, only six feet. The eggplants were too big for us."

"Don't say things like that in front of the kid," Heskow said, horror-stricken. "He has to play with them."

"Oh, no," Stace said. "I would never do that."

Heskow relaxed and sipped his wine. He always liked working with the Sturzo brothers. They were both so genial—they never got nasty like most of the scum he had to deal with. They had an ease in the world that reflected the ease between them. They were secure, and it gave them a pleasant glow.

The three of them ate slowly, casually. Heskow refilled their plates direct from the frying pan.

"I always meant to ask," Franky said to Heskow. "Why did you change your name?"

"That was a long time ago," Heskow said. "I wasn't ashamed of being Italian. But you know, I look so fucking German. With blond hair and blue eyes and this nose. It looked really fishy, my having an Italian name."

The twins both laughed, an easy, understanding laugh. They knew he was full of shit, but they didn't mind.

When they finished their salad, Heskow served double espresso and a plate of Italian pastries. He offered cigars but they refused. They stuck to their Marlboros, which suited their rugged western faces.

"Time to get down to business," Stace said.

"This must be a big one, or why did we have to drive three thousand fucking miles? We could have flown."

"It wasn't so bad," Franky said. "I enjoyed it. We saw America, firsthand. We had a good time. The people in the small towns were great."

"Exceptional," Stace said. "But still, it was a long ride."

"I didn't want to leave any traces at the airports," Heskow said. "That's the first place they check. And there will be a lot of heat. You boys don't mind heat?"

"Mother's milk to me," Stace said. "Now, who the fuck is it?"

"Don Raymonde Aprile." Heskow nearly choked on his espresso saying it.

There was a long silence, and then for the first time Heskow caught the chill of death the twins could radiate.

Franky said quietly, "You made us drive three thousand miles to offer us this job?"

Stace smiled at Heskow and said, "John, it's been nice knowing you. Now just pay our kill fee and we'll be moving on." Both twins laughed at this little joke, but Heskow didn't get it.

One of Franky's friends in L.A., a freelance writer, had once explained to the twins that though a magazine might pay him expenses to do an article, they would not necessarily buy it. They would just pay a small percentage of the agreed-upon fee to kill the piece. The twins had adopted that practice. They charged just to listen to a proposition. In this case, because of the travel time and there were two of them involved, the kill fee was twenty thousand.

But it was Heskow's job to convince them to take the assignment. "The Don has been retired for three years," he said. "All his old connections are in jail. He has no power anymore. The only one who could make trouble is Timmona Portella, and he won't. Your payoff is a million bucks, half when you're done and the other half in a year. But for that year, you have to lay low. Now everything is set up. All you guys have to be is the shooters."

"A million bucks," Stace said. "That's a lot of money."

"My client knows it's a big step to hit Don Aprile," Heskow said. "He wants the best help. Cool shooters and silent partners with mature heads. And you guys are simply the best."

Franky said, "And there are not many guys who would take the risk."

"Yeah," Stace said. "You have to live with it the rest of your life. Somebody coming after you, plus the cops, and the feds."

"I swear to you," Heskow said, "the NYPD won't go all out. The FBI will not take a hand."

"And the Don's old friends?" Stace asked.

"The dead have no friends." Heskow paused for a moment. "When the Don retired, he cut all ties. There's nothing to worry about."

Franky said to Stace, "Isn't it funny, in all our deals, they always tell us there's nothing to worry about?"

Stace laughed. "That's because they're not the shooters. John, you're an old friend. We trust you. But what if you're wrong? Anybody can be wrong. What if the Don still has old friends? You know how he operates. No mercy. We get nailed, we don't just get killed. We'll spend a couple of hours in hell first. Plus our families are at stake under the Don's rule. That means your son. Can't play for the NBA in his grave. Maybe we should know who's paying for this."

Heskow leaned toward them, his light skin a scarlet red as if he were blushing. "I can't tell you that. You know that. I'm just the broker. And I've thought of all that other shit. You think I'm fucking stupid? Who doesn't know who the Don is? But he's defenseless. I have assurances of that from the top levels. The police will just go through the motions. The FBI can't afford to investigate. And the top Mafia heads won't interfere. It's foolproof."

"I never dreamed that Don Aprile would be one of my marks," Franky said. The deed appealed to his ego. To kill a man so dreaded and respected in his world.

"Franky, this is not a basketball game," Stace warned. "If we lose, we don't shake hands and walk off the court."

"Stace, it's a million bucks," Franky said. "And John never steered us wrong. Let's go with it."

Stace felt their excitement building. What the hell. He and Franky could take care of themselves. After all, there was the million bucks. If the truth were told, Stace was more mercenary than Franky, more business-oriented, and the million swung him.

"OK," Stace said, "we're in. But God have mercy on our souls if you're wrong." He had once been an altar boy.

"What about the Don being watched by the FBI?" Franky asked. "Do we have to worry about that?"

"No," Heskow said. "When all his old friends went to jail, the Don retired like a gentleman. The FBI appreciated that. They leave him alone. I guarantee it. Now let me lay it out."

It took him a half hour to explain the plan in detail.

Finally Stace said, "When?"

"Sunday morning," Heskow said. "You stay here for the first two days. Afterward the private jet flies you out of Newark."

"We have to have a very good driver," Stace said. "Exceptional."

"I'm driving," Heskow said, then added, almost apologetically, "It's a very big payday."

FOR THE REST of the weekend, Heskow baby-sat for the Sturzo brothers, cooking their meals, running their errands. He was not a man easily impressed, but the Sturzos sometimes sent a chill to his heart. They were like adders, their heads constantly alert, yet they were congenial and even helped him tend to the flowers in his sheds.

The brothers played basketball one-on-one just before supper, and Heskow watched fascinated by how their bodies slithered around each other like snakes. Franky was faster and a deadly shooter. Stace was not as good but more clever. Franky could have made it to the NBA, Heskow thought. But this was not a basketball game. In a real crisis, it would have to be Stace. Stace would be the primary shooter.

CHAPTER 2

THE GREAT 1990s FBI blitz of the Mafia families in New York left only two survivors. Don Raymonde Aprile, the greatest and most feared, remained untouched. The other, Don Timmona Portella, who was nearly his equal in power but a far inferior man, escaped by what seemed to be pure luck.

But the future was clear. With the 1970 RICO laws so undemocratically framed, the zeal of special FBI investigating teams, and the death of the belief in omerta among the soldiers of the American Mafia, Don Raymonde Aprile knew it was time for him to retire gracefully from the stage.

The Don had ruled his Family for thirty years and was now a legend. Brought up in Sicily, he had none of the false ideas or strutting arrogance of the American-born Mafia chiefs. He was, in fact, a throwback to the old Sicilians of the nineteenth century who ruled towns and villages with their personal charisma, their sense of honor, and their deadly and final judgment of any suspected enemy. He also proved to have the strategic genius of those old heroes.

Now, at sixty-two, he had his life in order. He had disposed of his enemies and accomplished his duties as a friend and a father. He could enjoy old age with a clear conscience, retire from the disharmonies of his world, and move into the more fitting role of gentleman banker and pillar of society.

His three children were safely ensconced in successful and honorable careers. His oldest son, Valerius, was now thirty-seven, married with children, and a colonel in the United States Army and lecturer at West Point. His career had been determined by his timidity as a child; the Don had secured a cadet appointment at West Point to rectify this defect in his character.

His second son, Marcantonio, at the early age of thirty-five, was, out of some mystery in the variation of his genes, a top executive at a national TV network. As a boy he had been moody and lived in a make-believe world and the Don thought he would be a failure in any serious enterprise. But now his name was often in the papers as some sort of creative visionary, which pleased the Don but did not convince him. After all, he was the boy's father. Who knew him better?

His daughter, Nicole, had been affectionately called Nikki as a young child but at the age of six demanded imperiously that she be called by her proper name. She was his favorite sparring partner. At the age of twenty-nine, she was a corporate lawyer, a feminist, and a pro bono advocate of those poor and desperate criminals who otherwise could not afford an adequate legal defense. She was especially good at saving murderers from the electric chair, husband killers from prison confinement, and repeat rapists from being given life terms. She was absolutely opposed to the death penalty, believed in the rehabilitation of any criminal, and was a severe critic of the economic structure of the United States. She believed a country as rich as America should not be so indifferent to the poor, no matter what their faults. Despite all this she was a very skilled and tough negotiator in corporate law, a striking and forceful woman. The Don agreed with her on nothing.

As for Astorre, he was part of the family, and closest to the Don as a titular nephew. But he seemed like a brother to the others because of his intense vitality and charm. From the age of three to sixteen he had been their intimate, the beloved youngest sibling—until his exile to Sicily eleven years before.

THE DON planned his retirement carefully. He distributed his empire to placate potential enemies but also rendered tribute to loyal friends, knowing that gratitude is the least lasting of virtues and that gifts must always be replenished. He was especially careful to pacify Timmona Portella. Portella was dangerous because of his eccentricity and a passionate murderousness that sometimes had no relationship to necessity.

How Portella escaped the FBI blitz of the 1990s was a mystery to everyone. For he was an American-born don without subtlety, a man incautious and intemperate, with an explosive temper. He had a huge body with an enormous paunch and dressed like a Palermo picciotto, a young apprentice killer, all colors and silk. His power was based in the distribution of illegal drugs. He had never married and still at age fifty was a careless womanizer. He only showed true affection for his younger brother, Bruno, who seemed slightly retarded but shared his older brother's brutality.

Don Aprile had never trusted Portella and rarely did business with him. The man was dangerous through his weakness, a man to be neutralized. So now he summoned Timmona Portella for a meeting.

Portella arrived with his brother, Bruno. Aprile met them with his usual quiet courtesy but came to the point quickly.

"My dear Timmona," he said. "I am retiring from all business affairs except my banks. Now you will be very much in the public eye and you must be careful. If you should ever need any advice, call on me. For I will not be completely without resources in my retirement."

Bruno, a small replica of his brother who was awed by the Don's reputation, smiled with pleasure at this respect for his older brother. But Timmona understood the Don far better. He knew that he was being warned.

He nodded respectfully to the Don. "You have always showed the best judgment of us all," he said. "And I respect what you are doing. Count on me as your friend."

"Very good, very good," the Don said. "Now, as a gift to you, I ask you to heed this warning. This FBI man, Cilke, is very devious. Do not trust him in any way. He is drunk with his success, and you will be his next target."

"But you and I have already escaped him," Timmona said. "Though he brought all our friends down. I don't fear him but I thank you."

They had a celebratory drink, and the Portella brothers left. In the car Bruno said, "What a great man."

"Yes," Timmona said. "He was a great man."

As for the Don, he was well satisfied. He had seen the alarm in Timmona's eyes and was assured there would no longer be any danger from him.

DON APRILE REQUESTED a private meeting with Kurt Cilke, the head of the FBI in New York City. Cilke, to the Don's own surprise, was a man he admired. He had sent most of the East Coast Mafia chiefs to jail and almost broken their power.

Don Raymonde Aprile had eluded him, for the Don knew the identity of Cilke's secret informer, the one who made his success possible. But the Don admired Cilke even more because the man always played fair, had never tried frame-ups or power-play harassments, had never given publicity pin marks on the Don's children. So the Don felt it was only fair to warn him.

THE MEETING was at the Don's country estate in Montauk. Cilke would have to come alone, a violation of the Bureau rules. The FBI director himself had given approval but insisted Cilke use a special recording device. This was an implant in his body, below his rib cage, which would not show on the outer walls of his torso; the device was not known to the public, and its manufacture was strictly controlled. Cilke realized that the real purpose of the wire was to record what he said to the Don.

They met on a golden October afternoon on the Don's verandah. Cilke had never been able to penetrate this house with a listening device, and a judge had barred constant physical surveillance. This day he was not searched in any way by the Don's men, which surprised him. Obviously Don Raymonde Aprile was not going to make him an illicit proposal.

As always, Cilke was amazed and even disturbed by the impression that the Don made on him. Despite knowing that the man had ordered a hundred murders, broken countless laws of society, Cilke could not hate him. And yet he believed such men evil, hated them for how they destroyed the fabric of civilization.

Don Aprile was clad in a dark suit, dark tie, and white shirt. His expression was grave and yet understanding, the lines in his face the gentle ones of a virtue-loving man. How could such a humane face belong to someone so merciless, Cilke wondered.

The Don did not offer to shake hands out of a sensibility not to embarrass Cilke. He gestured for his guest to be seated and bowed his head in greeting.

"I have decided to place myself and my family under your protection—that is, the protection of society," he said.

Cilke was astonished. What the hell did the old man mean?

"For the last twenty years you have made yourself my enemy. You have pursued me. But I was always grateful for your sense of fair play. You never tried to plant evidence or encourage perjury against me. You have put most of my friends in prison, and you tried very hard to do the same to me."

Cilke smiled. "I'm still trying," he said.

The Don nodded in appreciation. "I have rid myself of everything doubtful except a few banks, surely a respectable business. I have placed myself under the protection of your society. In return I will do my duty to that society. You can make it much easier if you do not pursue me. For there is no longer any need."

Cilke shrugged. "The Bureau decides. I've been after you for so long, why stop now? I might get lucky."

The Don's face became graver and even more tired. "I have something to exchange with you. Your enormous success of the past few years influenced my decision. But the thing is, I know your prize informant, I know who he is. And I have told no one."

Cilke hesitated for only seconds before he said impassively, "I have no such informant. And again, the Bureau decides, not me. So you've wasted my time."

"No, no," the Don said. "I'm not seeking an advantage, just an accommodation. Allow me, because of my age, to tell you what I have learned. Do not exercise power because it is easy to your hand. And do not get carried away with a certainty of victory when your intellect tells you there is even a hint of tragedy. Let me say I regard you now as a friend, not an enemy, and think to yourself what you have to gain or lose by refusing this offer."

"And if you are truly retired, then of what use is your friendship?" Cilke said, smiling.

"You will have my goodwill," the Don said. "That is worth something even from the smallest of men."

LATER CILKE PLAYED the tape for Bill Boxton, his deputy, who asked, "What the hell was that all about?"

"That's the stuff you have to learn," Cilke told him. "He was telling me that he's not completely defenseless, that he was keeping an eye on me."

"What bullshit," Boxton said. "They can't touch a federal agent."

"That's true," Cilke said. "That's why I kept after him, retired or not. Still, I'm wary. We can't be absolutely sure . . ."

HAVING STUDIED the history of the most prestigious families in America, those robber barons who had ruthlessly built their fortunes while breaking the laws and ethics of human society, Don Aprile became, like them, a benefactor to all. Like them, he had his empire—he owned ten private banks in the world's largest cities. So he gave generously to build a hospital for the poor. And he contributed to the arts. He established a chair at Columbia University for the study of the Renaissance.

It was true that Yale and Harvard refused his twenty million dollars for a dormitory to be named for Christopher Columbus, who was at the time in disrepute in intellectual circles. Yale did offer to take the money and name the dorm after Sacco and Vanzetti, but the Don was not interested in Sacco and Vanzetti. He despised martyrs.

A lesser man would have felt insulted and nursed a grievance, but not Raymonde Aprile. Instead, he simply gave the money to the

Catholic Church for daily masses to be sung for his wife, now twenty-five years in Heaven.

He donated a million dollars to the New York Police Benevolent Association and another million to a society for the protection of illegal immigrants. For the three years after his retirement, he showered his blessings on the world. His purse was open to any request except for one. He refused Nicole's pleas to contribute to the Campaign Against the Death Penalty—her crusade to stop capital punishment.

It is astonishing how three years of good deeds and generosity can almost wipe out a thirty-year reputation of merciless acts. But great men also buy their own goodwill, self-forgetfulness and forgiveness of betraying friends and exercising lethal judgment. And the Don too had this universal weakness.

For Don Raymonde Aprile was a man who had lived by the strict rules of his own particular morality. His protocol had made him respected for over thirty years and generated the extraordinary fear that had been the base of his power. A chief tenet of that protocol was a complete lack of mercy.

This sprang not from innate cruelty, some psychopathic desire to inflict pain, but from an absolute conviction: that men always refused to obey. Even Lucifer, the angel, had defied God and had been flung from the heavens.

So an ambitious man struggling for power had no other recourse. Of course there were some persuasions, some concessions to another man's self-interest. That was only reasonable. But if all that failed, there was only the punishment of death. Never threats of other forms of punishment that might inspire retaliation. Simply a banishment from this earthly sphere, no more to be reckoned with.

Treachery was the greatest injury. The traitor's family would suffer, as would his circle of friends; his whole world would be destroyed. For there are many brave, proud men willing to gamble their lives for their own gain, but they would think twice about risking their loved ones. And so in this way Don Aprile generated a vast amount of terror. He relied on his generosity in worldly goods to win their less necessary love.

But it must be said, he was as merciless to himself. Possessed of enormous power, he could not prevent the death of his young wife after she had given him three children. She died a slow and horrible death from cancer as he watched over her for six months. During that time he came to believe that she was being punished for all the mortal sins he had committed, and so it was that he decreed his own penance: He would never remarry. He would send his children away to be educated in the ways of lawful society, so they would not grow up in his world so full of hate and danger. He would help them find their way, but they would never be involved in his activities. With great sadness he resolved that he would never know the true essence of fatherhood.

So the Don arranged to have Nicole, Valerius, and Marcantonio sent to private boarding schools. He never let them into his personal life. They came home for the holidays, when he played the role of a caring but distant father, but they never became part of his world.

And yet despite everything and though they were aware of his reputation, his children loved him. They never talked about it among themselves. It was one of those family secrets that was not a secret.

No one could call the Don sentimental. He had very few personal friends, no pets, and he avoided holiday and social gatherings as much as possible. Only once, many years before, he had committed an act of compassion that astounded his colleagues in America.

Don Aprile, when he returned from Sicily with the child, Astorre, found his beloved wife dying of cancer and his own three children desolate. Not wanting to keep the impressionable infant in such a circumstance for fear it would harm him in some way, the Don decided to place him in the care of one of his closest advisors, a man named Frank Viola, and his wife. This proved to be an unwise choice. At the time, Frank Viola had ambitions to succeed the Don.

But shortly after the Don's wife died, Astorre Viola, at the age of three, became a member of the Don's personal family when his "father" committed suicide in the trunk of his car, a curious circumstance, and his mother died of a brain hemorrhage. It was then that the Don had taken Astorre into his household and assumed the title of uncle.

When Astorre was old enough to begin asking about his parents, Don Raymonde told him that he had been orphaned. But Astorre was a curious and tenacious young boy, so the Don, to put an end to all his questions, told him that his parents had been peasants, unable to feed him, and had died, unknown, in a small Sicilian village. The Don knew this explanation didn't completely satisfy the boy, and he felt a twinge of guilt over deceiving him, but he knew it was important while the child was still young to keep his Mafia roots a secret—for Astorre's own safety and for the safety of the Aprile children.

• • •

DON RAYMONDE was a farseeing man and knew that his success could not last forever—it was too treacherous a world. From the beginning he planned to switch sides, to join the safety of organized society. Not that he was truly conscious of his purpose, but great men have an instinct for what the future will demand. And in this case, truly, he acted out of compassion. For Astorre Viola, at the age of three, could have made no impression, could have given no hint of what he would later become as a man. Or how important a part he would play in the Family.

The Don understood that the glory of America was the emergence of great families, and that the best social class sprang from men who had at first committed great crimes against that society. It was such men who in the search for fortune had also built America and left evil deeds to crumble into forgotten dust. How else could it be done? Leave the Great Plains of America to those Indians who could not conceive of a three-story dwelling? Leave California to Mexicans who had no technical ability, no vision of great aqueducts to feed water to lands that would allow millions to enjoy a prosperous life? America had the genius to attract millions of laboring poor from all over the world, to entice them to the necessary hard work of building the railroads, the dams, and the sky-scratching buildings. Ah,

the Statue of Liberty had been a stroke of promo-
tional genius. And had it not turned out for the
best? Certainly there had been tragedies, but that
was part of life. Was not America the greatest
cornucopia the world had ever known? Was not a
measure of injustice a small price to pay? It has
always been the case that individuals must sacrifice to further the advance of civilization and
their particular society.

But there is another definition of a great man.
Primarily that he does not accept that burden. In
some way, criminal, immoral, or by sheer
cunning, he will ride the crest of that wave of
human progress without sacrifice.

Don Raymonde Aprile was such a man. He
generated his own individual power by his intelligence and by his complete lack of mercy. He
generated fear; he became a legend. But his children, when they were grown, never believed in
the most atrocious stories.

There was the legend of the beginning of his
rule as Family chief. The Don controlled a
construction company run by a subordinate,
Tommy Liotti, whom the Don had made rich at
an early age with city building contracts. The
man was handsome, witty, a thorough charmer,
and the Don always enjoyed his company. He had
only one fault: He drank to excess.

Tommy married the Don's wife's best friend,

Liza, an old-fashioned handsome woman with a sharp tongue, who felt it her duty to curb her husband's obvious pleasure with himself. This led to some unfortunate incidents. He accepted her barbs well enough when he was sober, but when drunk he would slap her face hard enough to make her bite her tongue.

It was also unfortunate that the husband had a massive strength, due to working hard and long on construction sites during his youth. Indeed, he always wore short-sleeved shirts to display his magnificent forearms and his great biceps.

Sadly, the incidents escalated over a period of two years. One night Tommy broke Liza's nose and knocked out a few teeth, which required expensive surgical repair. The woman did not dare ask Don Aprile's wife for protection, since such a request would probably make her a widow, and she still loved her husband.

It was not Don Aprile's desire to interfere in the domestic squabbles of his underlings. Such things could never be solved. If the husband had killed the wife, he would not have been concerned. But the beatings posed a danger to his business relationship. An enraged wife could make certain testimonies, give damaging information. For the husband kept large quantities of cash in his house for those incidental bribes so necessary to the fulfillment of city contracts.

So Don Aprile summoned the husband. With the utmost courtesy, he made it plain he interfered in the man's personal life only because it affected business. He advised the man to kill his wife outright or divorce her or never to ill-treat her further. The husband assured him it would never happen again. But the Don was mistrustful. He had noticed that certain gleam in the man's eyes, the gleam of free will. He considered this one of the great mysteries of life, that a man will do what he feels like doing with no regard to the cost. Great men have allied themselves with the angels at a terrible price to themselves. Evil men indulge their slightest whim for small satisfactions while accepting the fate of burning in Hell.

And so it turned out with Tommy Liotti. It took nearly a year, and Liza's tongue grew sharper with her husband's indulgence. Despite the warning from the Don, despite his love for his children and his wife, Tommy beat her in the most violent fashion. She ended up in the hospital with broken ribs and a punctured lung.

With his wealth and political connections, Tommy bought one of the Don's corrupt judges with an enormous bribe. Then he talked his wife into coming back to him.

Don Aprile observed this with some anger and regretfully took charge of the affair. First, he attended to the practical aspects of the matter. He obtained a copy of the husband's will and learned that like a good family man, he had left all his worldly goods to his wife and children. She would be a rich widow. Then he sent out a special team with specific instructions. Within the week the judge received a long box wrapped in ribbons, and in it, like a pair of expensive long silk gloves, were the two massive forearms of the husband, one wearing on its wrist the expensive Rolex watch the Don had given him years before as a token of his esteem. The next day the rest of the body was found floating in the water around the Verrazano Bridge.

Another legend was chilling because of its ambiguity, like some childish ghost story. While the Don's three children were attending boarding school, an enterprising and talented journalist noted for his witty exposure of the frailties of famous people tracked them down and enticed them into what seemed like harmless verbal exchange. The writer had great fun with their innocence, their preppy clothes, their juvenile idealism about how to make a better world. The journalist contrasted it with their father's reputation while admitting that Don Aprile had never actually been convicted of a crime.

The piece became famous, circulated in newsrooms throughout the country even before publication. It was the kind of success a writer dreams about. Everybody loved it.

The journalist was a nature lover, and every year he took his wife and two children to a cabin in upstate New York for hunting and fishing and living simply. They were there one long Thanksgiving weekend. On Saturday the cabin, ten miles from the nearest town, caught fire. There was no rescue for about two hours. By then the house had burned to smoking logs and the journalist and his family were merely charred and brittle sticks. There was an enormous outcry and a massive investigation, but no evidence of foul play could be found. The conclusion was that the family had been overcome by smoke before they could escape.

Then a curious thing happened. A few months after the tragedy, whispers and rumors began to circulate. Anonymous tips came in to the FBI, the police, the press. They all suggested that the fire was an act of vengeance by the infamous Don Aprile. The press, hot for a story, clamored for the case to be reopened. It was, but again there was no indictment. Yet, despite any proof, this became another legend of the Don's ferocity.

But that was the general public; the authorities were satisfied, in this instance, that the Don was beyond reproach. Everybody knew journalists were exempt from any retaliation. You would have to kill thousands, so what was the point? The Don was too intelligent to take such a risk. Still, the legend never died. Some FBI teams even thought the Don himself had inspired the rumors to fulfill his legend. And so it grew.

But there was another side to the Don: his generosity. If you served him loyally, you became rich and had a formidable protector in times of travail. The rewards given by the Don were enormous but the punishments final. That was his legend.

AFTER HIS MEETINGS with Portella and Cilke, Don Aprile had details to tidy up. He set in motion the machinery to bring Astorre Viola back home after his eleven-year exile.

He needed Astorre, indeed had prepared him for this moment. Astorre was the Don's favorite, even above his own children. As a child Astorre was always a leader, precocious in his sociability. He loved the Don, and he did not fear him as his own children sometimes did. And though Valerius and Marcantonio were twenty and eighteen years old, when Astorre was ten, he established his independence from them. Indeed, when Valerius, somewhat of a military martinet, tried to chastise him, he fought back. Marcantonio was much more affectionate to him and bought him his first banjo to encourage his singing. Astorre accepted this as the courtesy of one adult to another.

The only one Astorre took orders from was Nicole. And though she was two years older, she treated him as a suitor, as he demanded even as a small boy. She made him run her errands and listened soulfully to the Italian ballads he sang her. And she slapped his face when he tried to kiss her. For even as a small boy, Astorre was enraptured by feminine beauty.

And Nicole was beautiful. She had large dark eyes and a sensual smile; her face revealed every emotion she felt. She challenged anyone who tried to insinuate that as a female she was not as important as any man in her world. She hated the fact that she was not as physically strong as her brothers and Astorre, that she could not assert her will by force but only by her beauty. All this made her absolutely fearless, and she taunted them all, even her father, despite his dread reputation.

AFTER HIS WIFE'S DEATH, when the children were still young, Don Aprile made it a practice to spend one summer month in Sicily. He loved the life in his native village, near the town of Montelepre, and he still owned property there, a house that had been the country retreat of a count, called Villa Grazia.

After a few years he hired a housekeeper, a Sicilian widow named Caterina. She was a very handsome woman, strong with a rich peasant beauty and a keen sense of how to run a property and command respect from the villagers. She became his mistress. All of this he kept secret from his family and friends, though now he was a man of forty and a king in his world.

Astorre Viola was only ten years old the first time he accompanied Don Raymonde Aprile to Sicily. The Don had been requested to mediate a great conflict between the Corleonesi *cosca* and the Clericuzio *cosca*. And it was also his pleasure to spend a quiet month of tranquillity at Villa Grazia.

Astorre, at ten, was affable—there was no other word. He was always cheerful, and his handsome round face with its olive skin radiated love. He continually sang in a sweet tenor voice. And when he was not singing, he offered lively conversation. Yet he had the fiery qualities of a born rebel, and he terrorized the other boys his age.

The Don brought him to Sicily because he was the best of company for a middle-aged man, which was a curious commentary on both, as well as a reflection on how the Don had brought up his own three children.

Once the Don settled his business affairs, he mediated the dispute and brought about temporary peace. Now he enjoyed his days reliving his childhood in his native village. He ate lemons, oranges, and olives from their briny barrels, and he took long walks with Astorre under the sullen deadly light of the Sicilian sun that reflected all the stone houses and countless rocks with a stunning heat. He told the small boy long-ago stories of the Robin Hoods of Sicily, their fights against the Moors, the French, the Spaniards, the pope himself. And tales of a local hero, the Great Don Zeno.

At night, together on the terrace of the Villa Grazia, they watched the azure sky of Sicily lit with a thousand shooting stars and the flashes of lightning hurling through the mountains just a short distance away. Astorre picked up the Sicilian dialect immediately and ate the black olives from the barrel as if they were bits of candy.

In just a few days Astorre established his leadership in a gang of young village boys. It was a wonder to the Don that he could do so, for Sicilian children were full of pride and feared no one. Many of these ten-year-old cherubs were already familiar with the *lupara,* the ever-present Sicilian shotgun.

Don Aprile, Astorre, and Caterina spent long summer nights eating and drinking alfresco in the luxuriant garden, the orange and lemon trees saturating the air with their citrus perfume. Sometimes old boyhood friends of the Don were invited to dinner and a game of cards. Astorre helped Caterina serve them drinks.

Caterina and the Don never showed public signs of affec-tion, but all was understood in the village, so no man dared to present any gallantries to Caterina and all showed her the respect the female head of the house was due. No time in his life was more pleasant to the Don.

It was just three days before the end of the visit that the unimaginable happened: The Don was kidnapped while walking the streets of the village.

IN THE NEIGHBORING province of Cinesi, one of the most remote and undeveloped in Sicily, the head of the village *cosca*, the local Mafioso, was a ferocious, fearless bandit by the name of Fissolini. Absolute in his local power, he really had no communication with the rest of the Mafia *coscas* on the island. He knew nothing of Don Aprile's enormous power, nor did he think it could penetrate his own remote and secure world. He decided to kidnap the Don and hold him for ransom. The only rule he knew he was breaking was that he was encroaching onto the territory of the neighboring *cosca*, but the American seemed a rich enough prize to warrant the risk.

The *cosca* is the basic unit of what is called the Mafia and is usually composed of blood relatives. Law-abiding citizens such as lawyers or doctors attach themselves to a *cosca* for protection of their interests. Each *cosca* is an organization in and of itself but may ally itself to a stronger and more powerful one. It is this interlinking that is commonly called the Mafia. But there is no overall chief or commander.

A *cosca* usually majors in a particular racket in its particular territory. There is the *cosca* that controls the price of water and prevents the central government from building dams to lower the price. In that way it destroys the government's monopoly. Another *cosca* will control the food and produce markets. The most powerful ones in Sicily at this time were the Clericuzio *cosca* of Palermo, which controlled the new construction in all of Sicily, and the Corleonesi *cosca* of Corleone, which controlled the politicians in Rome and engineered the transportation of drugs all over the world. Then there were the piddling *coscas* who demanded tribute from romantic youths to sing to the balconies of their beloveds. All *coscas* regulated crime. They would not tolerate lazy good-for-nothings burglarizing innocent citizens who paid their *cosca* dues. Those who stabbed for wallets or raped women were summarily punished by death. Also, there was no tolerance of adultery within the *coscas*. Both men and women were executed. That was understood.

Fissolini's *cosca* made a poor living. It controlled the sale of holy icons, was paid to protect a farmer's livestock, and organized the kidnapping of careless wealthy men.

And so it was that Don Aprile and little Astorre, strolling along the streets of their village, were picked up in two vintage American army trucks by the ignorant Fissolini and his band of men.

The ten men in peasant clothes were armed with rifles. They plucked Don Aprile off the ground and threw him into the first truck. Astorre, without hesitation, jumped into the open bed of the truck to stay with the Don. The bandits tried to throw him out, but he clung to the wooden posts. The trucks traveled an hour to the base of the mountains around Montelepre. Then everyone switched to horseback and donkey and climbed the rocky terraces toward the horizon. Throughout the trip, the boy observed everything with large green eyes but never spoke a word.

Near sunset, they reached a cave set deep in the mountains. There they were fed a supper of grilled lamb and homemade bread and wine. On the campsite was a huge statue of the Virgin Mary enclosed in a hand-carved dark wooden shrine. Fissolini was devout in spite of his ferocity. He also had a natural peasant courtesy and presented himself to the Don and the boy. There was no doubt he was chief of the band. He was short and built powerfully as a gorilla, and he carried a rifle and two guns on his body belt. His face was as stony as Sicily, but there was a merry twinkle in his eyes. He enjoyed life and its little jokes, especially that he held in his power a rich American worth his weight in gold. And yet there was no malice in him.

"Excellency," he said to the Don, "I don't want you to worry about this young lad. He will carry the ransom note to town tomorrow morning."

Astorre was eating lustily. He had never tasted anything so delicious as this grilled lamb. But he finally spoke up with cheerful bravery. "I'm staying with my Uncle Raymonde," he said.

Fissolini laughed. "Good food gives courage. To show my respect for His Excellency I prepared this meal myself. I used my mother's special spices."

"I'm staying with my uncle," Astorre said, and his voice rang out clear, defiant.

Don Aprile said to Fissolini sternly yet kindly,

"It's been a wonderful night—the food, the mountain air, your company. I look forward to the fresh dew in the country. But then I advise you to bring me back to my village."

Fissolini bowed to him respectfully. "I know that you are rich. But are you that powerful? I am only going to ask for one hundred thousand dollars in American money."

"That insults me," the Don said. "You will injure my reputation. Double it. And another fifty for the boy. It will be paid. But then your life will be an eternal misery." He paused for a moment. "I'm astonished you could be so rash."

Fissolini sighed. "You must understand, Excellency, I am a poor man. Certainly I can take what I want in my province, but Sicily is such a cursed country that the rich are too poor to support men like myself. You must understand that you are the chance to make my fortune."

"Then you should have come to me to offer your services," the Don said. "I always have use for a talented man."

"You say that now because you are weak and helpless," Fissolini said. "The weak are always so generous. But I will follow your advice and ask double. Though I feel a little guilty about that. No human is worth so much. And I will let the boy go free. I have a weakness for children—I have four of my own whose mouths I must feed."

Don Aprile looked at Astorre. "Will you go?"

"No," Astorre said, lowering his head. "I want to be with you." He raised his eyes and looked at his uncle.

"Then let him stay," the Don said to the bandit.

Fissolini shook his head. "He goes back. I have a reputation to keep. I will not be known as a kidnapper of children. Because after all, Your Excellency, though I have the utmost respect, I will have to send you back piece by piece if they do not pay. But if they do, I give you the word of honor of Pietro Fissolini, not a hair of your mustache will be touched."

"The money will be paid," the Don said calmly. "And now let us make the best of things. Nephew, sing one of your songs for these gentlemen."

Astorre sang to the bandits, who were enchanted and complimented him, ruffling his hair affectionately. Indeed it was a magical moment for all of them, the child's sweet voice filling the mountains with songs of love.

Blankets and sleeping bags were brought out of a nearby cave.

Fissolini said, "Your Excellency, what would you like for breakfast tomorrow? Some fish, fresh from the water perhaps? Then some spaghetti and veal for lunch? We are at your service."

"I thank you," the Don said. "A bit of cheese and fruit will be enough."

"Sleep well," Fissolini said. He was softened by the boy's look of unhappiness, and he patted Astorre on the head. "Tomorrow you will rest in your own bed."

Astorre closed his eyes to fall asleep immediately on the ground next to the Don. "Stay beside me," the Don said, as he reached his arms around the boy.

Astorre slept so soundly that the rising cinderred sun was over his head when a clatter awoke him. He rose and saw that the hollow was filled with fifty armed men. Don Aprile, gentle, calm, and dignified, was sitting on a great ledge of stone, sipping from a mug of coffee.

Don Aprile saw Astorre and beckoned to him. "Astorre, do you want some coffee?" He pointed a finger at the man before him. "This is my good friend, Bianco. He has rescued us."

Astorre saw a huge man who, though he was well encased in fat, wore a suit and tie, and seemed to be unarmed, was far more frightening than Fissolini. He had a curly head of white hair and large pink eyes, and he radiated power. But he seemed to blanket that power when he spoke with a soft, gravelly voice.

Octavius Bianco said, "Don Aprile, I must

apologize for being so late and that you had to sleep like a peasant on the ground. But I came as soon as I got the news. I always knew Fissolini was a dunce, but I never expected him to do this."

There began the sound of hammering, and some men moved out of Astorre's vision. He saw two young boys, nailing together a cross. Then, lying on the far side of the hollow, he saw Fissolini and his ten bandits trussed on the ground and tethered to trees. They were encased by a web of wire and rope, their limbs entwined. They looked like a mound of flies on a lump of meat.

Bianco asked, "Don Aprile, which of these scum do you wish to judge first?"

"Fissolini," the Don said. "He is the leader."

Bianco dragged Fissolini before the Don; he was still tightly bound, like a mummy. Bianco and one of his soldiers lifted him and forced him to stand. Then Bianco said, "Fissolini, how could you be so stupid? Didn't you know the Don was under my protection or I would have kidnapped him myself? Did you think you were just borrowing a flask of oil? Some vinegar? Have I ever entered your province? But you were always headstrong, and I knew you would come to grief. Well, since like Jesus you must hang from the cross, make your apologies to Don Aprile and his little boy. And I will give you mercy and shoot you before we hammer in the nails."

"So," the Don said to Fissolini. "Explain your disrespect."

Fissolini stood upright and proud. "But the disrespect was not for your person, Excellency. I did not know how important and dear you were to my friends. That fool, Bianco, might have kept me fully informed. Excellency, I have made a mistake and I must pay." He stopped for a moment and then shouted angrily and scornfully at Bianco, "Stop those men from hammering those nails. I'm going deaf. And you can't scare me to death before you kill me!"

Fissolini paused again and said to the Don, "Punish me, but spare my men. They followed my orders. They have families. You will destroy an entire village if you kill them."

"They are responsible men," Don Aprile said sarcastically. "I would insult them if they did not share your fate."

At this moment Astorre, even in his child's mind, realized that they were talking life and death. He whispered, "Uncle, don't hurt him." The Don made no sign of having heard.

"Go on," he said to Fissolini.

Fissolini gave him a questioning look, at once proud and wary. "I will not beg for my life. But those ten men lying there are all in my blood family. If you kill them, you destroy their wives and their children. Three of them are my sons-in-law. They had absolute faith in me. They trusted my judgment. If you let them go, I would make them swear their undying loyalty to you before I die. And they will obey me. That is something, to have ten loyal friends. That is not nothing. I am told you are a great man, but you cannot be truly great if you do not show mercy. You shouldn't make a habit of it, of course, but just this once." He smiled at Astorre.

For Don Raymonde Aprile this was a familiar moment, and he was in no doubt as to his decision. He had always distrusted the power of gratitude, and he believed that no one could direct the influence of free will in any man, except by death. He regarded Fissolini impassively and shook his head. Bianco moved forward.

Astorre strode to his uncle and looked him square in the eyes. He had understood everything. He put out his hand to protect Fissolini.

"He didn't hurt us," Astorre said. "He just wanted our money."

The Don smiled and said, "And that's nothing?"

Astorre said, "But it was a good reason. He wanted the money to feed his family. And I like him. Please, Uncle."

The Don smiled at him and said, "Bravo." Then he remained silent for a long time, ignoring Astorre tugging at his hand. And for the first time in many years the Don felt the urge to show mercy.

Bianco's men had lit up small cigars, very strong, and the smoke wafted through the dawn air carried on the mountain breezes. One of the men came forward and from his hunting jacket took out a fresh cigar and offered it to the Don. With a child's clarity, Astorre understood this was not only a courtesy but a demonstration of respect. The Don took the cigar, and the man lit it for him within cupped hands.

The Don puffed his cigar slowly and deliberately, then said, "I will not insult you by showing you mercy. But I will offer you a business arrangement. I recognize you had no malice and you showed the utmost regard for my person and the boy. So this is the arrangement. You live. Your comrades live. But for the rest of your lives, you will be at my command."

Astorre felt an enormous relief, and he smiled at Fissolini. He watched Fissolini kneel to the ground and kiss the Don's hand. Astorre noticed that the surrounding armed men puffed furiously on their cigars, and even Bianco, grand as a mountain, trembled with pleasure.

Fissolini murmured, "Bless you, Your Excellency."

The Don put his cigar down on a nearby rock. "I accept your blessing, but you must understand. Bianco came to save me, and you are expected to do the same duty. I pay him a sum of money, and I will do the same for you every year. But one act of disloyalty and you and your world will be destroyed. You, your wife, your children, your nephews, your sons-in-law will cease to exist."

Fissolini rose from his knees. He embraced the Don and burst into tears.

And so it was that the Don and his nephew became most formally united. The Don loved the boy for persuading him to show mercy, and Astorre loved his uncle for giving him the lives of Fissolini and his ten men. It was a bond that lasted the rest of their lives.

THE LAST NIGHT in Villa Grazia, Don Aprile had espresso in the garden and Astorre ate olives from their barrel. Astorre was very pensive, not his usual sociable self.

"Are you sorry to leave Sicily?" the Don asked.

"I wish I could live here," Astorre said. He put the pits of his olives in his pocket.

"Well, we will come every summer together," the Don said.

Astorre looked at him like a wise old friend, his youthful face troubled.

"Is Caterina your girlfriend?" he asked.

The Don laughed. "She is my good friend," he said.

Astorre thought about this. "Do my cousins know about her?"

"No, my children do not know." Again the Don was amused by the boy and wondered what would come next.

Astorre was very grave now. "Do my cousins know you have such powerful friends like Bianco who will do anything you tell them they must do?"

"No," the Don said.

"I won't tell them about anything," Astorre said. "Not even about the kidnapping."

The Don felt a surge of pride. Omerta had been bred into his genes.

Late that night, alone, Astorre went to the far corner of the garden and dug a hole with his bare hands. In that hole he put the olive pits he had secreted in his pocket. He looked up at the pale night blue of the Sicilian sky and dreamed of himself as an old man like his uncle, sitting in this garden on a similar night, watching his olive trees grow.

AFTER THAT, everything was fate, the Don believed. He and Astorre made the yearly trip to Sicily until Astorre was sixteen. In the back of the

Don's mind, a vision was forming, a vague outline of the boy's destiny.

It was his daughter who created the crisis that moved Astorre into that destiny. At the age of eighteen, two years older than Astorre, Nicole fell in love with him and with her fiery temperament did little to conceal the fact. She completely overwhelmed the susceptible boy. They became intimate with all the hot furiousness of youth.

The Don could not allow this, but he was a general who adjusted his tactics to the terrain. He never gave any hint he knew of the affair.

One night he called Astorre into his den and told him he would be sent to England for his schooling and to serve an apprenticeship in banking with a certain Mr. Pryor of London. He did not give any further reason, knowing the boy would realize he was being sent away to end the affair. But he had not reckoned with his daughter, who had listened outside the door. She came storming into the room, her passionate outrage making her even more beautiful.

"You're not sending him away," she screamed at her father. "We'll run away together."

The Don smiled at her and said placatingly, "You both have to finish school."

Nicole turned to Astorre, who was blushing with embarrassment. "Astorre, you won't go?" she said. "Will you?"

Astorre did not answer, and Nicole burst into tears.

It would be hard for any father not to be moved by such a scene, but the Don was amused. His daughter was splendid, truly Mafioso in the old sense, a prize in any form. Despite that, for weeks afterward she refused to speak to her father and locked herself away in her room. But the Don did not fear she would be brokenhearted forever.

It amused him even more to see Astorre in the trap of all maturing adolescents. Certainly Astorre loved Nicole. And certainly her passion and her devotion made him feel like the most important person on earth. Any young man can be seduced by such attention. But just as certainly, the Don understood that Astorre wanted an excuse to be free of any encumbrance on his march to the glories of life. The Don smiled. The boy had all the right instincts, and it was time for his real schooling.

SO NOW, three years after his retirement, Don Raymonde Aprile felt the security and satisfaction of a man who has made the right choices in life. Indeed the Don felt so secure that he began to develop a closer relationship with his children, finally enjoying the fruits of fatherhood—to some degree.

Because Valerius had spent most of the last twenty years in foreign army posts, he had never been close to his father. Now that he was stationed at West Point, the two men saw each other more often and began to speak more openly. Yet it was difficult.

With Marcantonio, it was different. The Don and his second son enjoyed some kind of rapport. Marcantonio explained his work in TV, his excitement over the dramatic process, his duty to his viewers, his desire to make the world a better place. The lives of such people were like fairy tales to the Don. He was fascinated by them.

Over family dinners, Marcantonio and his father could quarrel in a friendly way for the entertainment of the others. Once the Don told Marcantonio, "I have never seen people so good or so evil as your characters in those dramas."

Marcantonio said, "That is what our audience believes. We have to give it to them."

At one family gathering, Valerius had tried to explain the rationale for the war in the Persian Gulf, which in addition to protecting important economic interests and human rights had also been a ratings bonanza for Marcantonio's TV network. But to all of this the Don just shrugged. These conflicts were refinements in power that did not interest him.

"Tell me," he said to Valerius. "How do nations really win wars? What is the deciding factor?"

Valerius considered this. "There is the trained army, brilliant generals. There are the great battles, some lost, some won. When I worked in intelligence, and we analyzed everything, it comes to this: The country that produces the most steel wins the war, simply that."

The Don nodded, finally satisfied.

His warmest and most intense relationship was with Nicole. He was proud of her accomplishments, her physical beauty, her passionate nature, and her intelligence. And, true, young as she was, just thirty-two, she was a powerful up-and-coming lawyer with good political connections, and she had no fear of anyone in a suit who represented entrenched power.

Here the Don had helped her secretly; her law firm was deeply indebted to him. But her brothers were wary of her for two reasons: she was unmarried, and she did a great deal of pro bono work. Despite his admiration for her, the Don could never take Nicole seriously in the world. She was, after all, a woman. And one with troubling taste in men.

At family dinners the father and daughter argued constantly, like two great cats frolicking dangerously, occasionally drawing blood. They had one serious bone of contention, the only thing that could affect the Don's constant affability. Nicole believed in the sacredness of human life, that capital punishment was an abomination. She had organized and led the Campaign Against the Death Penalty.

"Why?" the Don asked.

And Nicole would become infuriated all over again. Because she believed capital punishment would eventually destroy humanity. That if killing was condoned under any circumstances, then it could be justified by another set of circumstances, another set of beliefs. Eventually, it would not serve evolution or civilization. And believing that brought her into constant conflict with her brother Valerius. After all, what else did the army do? The reasons didn't matter to her. Killing was killing and would set us all back to cannibalism or worse. At every opportunity, Nicole fought in courts all over the country to save condemned murderers. Although the Don considered this the sheerest nonsense, he nonetheless proposed a toast to her at a family dinner following her victory in a famous pro bono case. She had secured commutation of the death sentence of one of the decade's most notorious criminals, a man who had killed his best friend and sodomized the newly made widow. In his getaway, he had executed two gas station attendants while he robbed them. He had gone on to rape and murder a ten-year-old girl. His career was brought to a close only when he attempted to kill two policemen in their cruiser. Nicole had won the case on grounds of insanity, and on the assurance that he would live the rest of his life in an institution for the criminally insane without the hope of release.

The next family dinner was a celebration to honor Nicole for winning another case—this time her own. In a recent trial she had championed a difficult principle of law at great personal risk. And she had been brought before the Bar Association for unethical practice and had been acquitted. Now she was exuberant.

The Don, in a cheerful mood, showed an uncharacteristic interest in this case. He congratulated his daughter on the acquittal but was somewhat confused, or pretended to be, by the circumstances. Nicole had to explain it to him.

She had defended a man, thirty years of age, who had raped, sodomized, and killed a twelve-year-old girl, then secretly hidden her body so that it could not be found by the police. Circumstantial evidence against him had been strong, but without a *corpus,* the jury and judge would be reluctant to give him the death penalty. The parents of the victim were in anguish in their frustrated desire to find the body.

The murderer confided to Nicole, as his attorney, where the body was buried and authorized her to negotiate a deal—he would reveal the body's whereabouts in exchange for a life sentence rather than execution. However, when Nicole opened negotiations with the prosecutor, she was faced with a threat of prosecution herself if she did not immediately reveal the whereabouts of the body. She believed it mattered to society to protect the confidentiality between attorney and client. Therefore, she refused, and a prominent judge declared her in the right.

The prosecutor, after consulting with the parents of the victim, finally consented to the deal.

The murderer told them that he had dismembered the body, placed it in a box filled with ice, and buried it in a nearby marshland in New Jersey. And so the body was found and the murderer sentenced to life imprisonment. But then the Bar Association brought her up on charges of unethical negotiation. And today she had won her acquittal.

The Don toasted to all of his children and then asked Nicole, "And you behaved honorably in all this?"

Nicole lost her exuberance. "It was the principle of the thing. The government cannot be allowed to breach the lawyer/client privilege in any one situation, no matter how grave, or it is no longer sacrosanct."

"And you felt nothing for the victim's mother and father?" the Don asked.

"Of course I did," Nicole said, annoyed. "But how could I let this affect a basic principle of the law? I suffered for that, I really did; why wouldn't I? But unfortunately, in order to set precedents for future law sacrifices have to be made."

"And yet the Bar Association put you on trial," the Don said.

"To save face," Nicole said. "It was a political move. Ordinary people, unschooled in the complexities of the legal system, can't accept these principles of law, and there was an uproar. So my trial diffused everything. Some very prominent judge had to go public and explain that I had the right under the Constitution to refuse to give that information."

"Bravo," the Don said jovially. "The law is always full of surprises. But only to lawyers, of course."

Nicole knew he was making fun of her. She said sharply, "Without a body of law, no civilization can exist."

"That is true," the Don said as if to appease his daughter. "But it seems unfair that a man who commits a terrible crime escapes with his life."

"That's true," Nicole said. "But our system of

law is based on plea bargaining. It is true that each criminal gets less punishment than he deserves. But in a way that's a good thing. Forgiveness heals. And in the long run, those who commit crimes against our society will be more easily rehabilitated."

So it was with a good-humored sarcasm that the Don proposed his toast. "But tell me," he said to Nicole. "Did you ever believe the man innocent by reason of his insanity? After all, he did exercise his free will."

Valerius looked at Nicole with cool, measuring eyes. He was a tall man, forty years of age with a bristly short mustache and hair already turning to steel gray. As an intelligence officer, he had himself made decisions that overlooked human morality. He was interested in her reasoning.

Marcantonio understood his sister, that she aspired to a normal life partly out of shame for their father's life. He was more worried that she would say something rash, something that her father could never forgive her for.

As for Astorre, he was dazzled by Nicole—her flashing eyes, the incredible energy with which she responded to her father's goading. He remembered their lovemaking as teenagers and felt her still obvious affection for him. But now he was transformed, no longer what he was when they were lovers. That was understood. He wondered if her brothers knew about that long-ago affair. And he too worried that a quarrel would break the bonds of family, a family that he loved, that was his only refuge. He hoped Nicole would not go too far. But he had no sympathy for her views. His years in Sicily had taught him differently. But it amazed him that the two people he cared most about in the world could be so different. And it occurred to him that even if she were right, he could never side with Nicole against her father.

Nicole looked boldly into her father's eyes. "I don't believe he had free will," she said. "He was forced by the circumstances of his life—by his own distorted perceptions, his genetic heritage, his biochemistry, the ignorance of medicine—he was insane. So of course I believe it."

The Don pondered this for a moment. "Tell me," he said. "If he admitted to you all his excuses were false, would you still have tried to save his life?"

"Yes," Nicole said. "Each individual life is sacred. The state has no right to take it."

The Don smiled at her mockingly. "That's your Italian blood. Do you know that modern Italy has never had the death penalty? All those human lives saved." His sons and Astorre flinched at his sarcasm, but Nicole was unabashed.

She said to him sternly, "It is barbaric for the

state under the mantle of justice to commit premeditated murder. I would think that you of all people would agree with that." It was a challenge, a reference to his reputation. Nicole laughed, then said more soberly, "We have an alternative. The criminal is locked away in an institution or a prison for life without hope of release or parole. Then he is no longer a danger to society."

The Don looked at her coolly. "One thing at a time," he said. "I do approve of the state taking a human life. And as for your lifetime without parole or release, that's a joke. Twenty years pass and supposedly new evidence is found, or rehabilitation is assumed and the criminal has made a new person of himself, so now spills the milk of human kindness. The man goes free. But no one cares for the dead. That's not really important . . ."

Nicole frowned. "Dad, I didn't imply that the victim isn't important. But taking a life will not get the victim's life back. And the longer we condone killing, under any circumstances, the longer it will go on."

Here the Don paused and drank his wine as he looked around the table at his two sons and Astorre. "Let me tell you the reality," he said, and turned to his daughter. He spoke with an intensity rare for him. "You say human life is sacred?

From what evidence? Where in history? The wars that have killed millions are endorsed by all governments and religions. The massacres of thousands of enemies in a political dispute, over economic interests, are recorded through time. How many times has the earning of money been placed above the sanctity of human life? And you yourself condone the taking of a human life when you get your client off."

Nicole's dark eyes flashed. "I have not condoned it," she said. "I have not excused it. I think it's barbaric. I have just refused to lay the ground for more of it!"

Now the Don spoke more quietly but more sincerely. "Above all this," he said, "the victim, your loved one, lies beneath the earth. He is forever banished from this world. We will never see his face, we will never hear his voice, we will never touch his flesh. He is in darkness, lost to us and our world."

They all listened silently as the Don took another sip of wine. "Now, my Nicole. Hear me. Your client, your murderer, is sentenced to life imprisonment. He will be behind bars or in an institution for the rest of his life. So you say. But each morning he will see the rising sun, he will taste hot food, he will hear music, the blood will run in his veins and interest him in the world. His loved ones can still embrace him. I understand he can even study books, learn carpentry to build a table and chairs. In short, he lives. And that is unjust."

Nicole was resolute. She did not flinch. "Dad, to domesticate animals, you don't let them eat raw meat. You don't let them get a taste of it or they want more. The more we kill, the easier it gets to kill. Can't you see that?" When he didn't answer her, she asked, "And how can you decide what's just or unjust? Where do you draw the line?" It had been meant as a defiance but was more of a plea to understand all her years of doubt in him.

They all expected an outburst of fury by the Don at her insolence, but suddenly he was in a good humor. "I have had my moments of weakness," he said, "but I never let a child judge his or her parents. Children are useless and live by our sufferance. And I consider myself beyond reproach as a father. I have raised three children who are pillars in society, talented, accomplished, and successful. And not completely powerless against fate. Can any of you reproach me?"

At this point Nicole lost her anger. "No," she said. "As a parent no one can reproach you. But you left something out. The oppressed are the ones who hang. The rich wind up escaping the final punishment."

The Don looked at Nicole with great seriousness. "Why, then, do you not fight to change the laws so that the rich hang with the poor? That is more intelligent."

Astorre murmured, smiling cheerfully. "There would be very few of us left." And that remark cut the tension.

"The greatest virtue of humanity is mercy," Nicole said. "An enlightened society does not execute a human being, and it refrains from punishment as much as common sense and justice allows."

It was only then that the Don lost his customary good humor. "Where did you get such ideas?" he asked. "They are self-indulgent and cowardly—more, they are blasphemous. Who is more merciless than God? He does not forgive, He does not ban punishment. There is a Heaven and there is a Hell by His decree. He does not banish grief and sorrow in His world. It is His Almighty duty to show no more than the necessary mercy. So who are you to dispense such marvelous grace? It's an arrogance. Do you think that if you are so saintly, you can create a better world? Remember, saints can only whisper prayers to God's ear and only when they have earned the right to do so by their own martyrdom. No. It is our duty to pursue our fellowman.

Or what great sins he could be capable of committing. We would deliver our world to the devil."

This left Nicole speechless with anger and Valerius and Marcantonio smiling. Astorre bowed his head as if in prayer.

Finally Nicole said, "Daddy, you are just too outrageous as a moralist. And you certainly are no example to follow."

There was a long silence at the table as each one sat with memories of their strange relationship with the Don. Nicole never quite believing the stories she'd heard about her father and yet fearing they were true. Marcantonio remembering one of his colleagues at the network asking slyly, "How does your father treat you and the other kids?"

And Marcantonio, considering the question carefully, knowing the man was referring to his father's reputation, had said quite seriously, "My father is very cordial to us."

Valerius was thinking how much his father was like some generals he had served under. Men who got the job done without any moral scruples, without any doubts as to their duty. Arrows that sped to their mark with deadly swiftness and accuracy.

For Astorre it was different. The Don had always shown him affection and trust. But he was also the only one at the table who knew that the reputation of the Don was true. He was remembering three years before when he had returned from his years of exile. The Don had given him certain instructions.

The Don had told him, "A man my age can die from stubbing his toe on a door, or from a black mole on his back, or from a break in the beating of his heart. It is strange that a man does not realize his mortality every second of his life. No matter. He need not have enemies. But still one must plan. I have made you a majority heir to my banks; you will control them and share the income with my children. And for this reason: Certain interests want to buy my banks, one headed by the consul general of Peru. The federal government continues to investigate me under the RICO laws so they can seize my banks. What a nice piece of business for them. They will find nothing. Now, my instructions to you are never sell the banks. They will be more profitable and powerful as time goes on. In time the past will be forgotten.

"If something unexpected happens, call Mr. Pryor, to assist you as controller. You know him well. He is extremely qualified, and he too profits from the banks. He owes me his loyalty. Also, I will introduce you to Benito Craxxi in Chicago. He is a man of infinite resources and also profits from the banks. He too is trustworthy. Meanwhile, I will give you a macaroni business simply to run and give you a good living. For all this I charge you with the safety and prosperity of my children. It is a harsh world, and I have brought them up as innocents."

Three years later, Astorre was pondering these words. Time had passed, and it seemed now that his services would not be needed. The Don's world could not be shattered.

But Nicole was not quite finished with her arguments. "What about the quality of mercy?" she said to her father. "You know, what Christians preach?"

The Don replied without hesitation. "Mercy is a vice, a pretension to powers we do not have. Those who give mercy commit an unpardonable offense to the victim. And that is not our duty here on earth."

"So you would not want mercy?" Nicole asked.

"Never," the Don said. "I do not seek it or desire it. If I must, I will accept the punishment for all my sins."

It was at this dinner that Colonel Valerius Aprile invited his family to attend the confirmation of his twelve-year-old son, in New York City, two months hence. His wife had insisted on a big celebration at her family's old church. It was in the Don's newly transformed character to accept this invitation.

AND SO ON a cold December Sunday noon, bright with a lemon-colored light, the Aprile family went to Saint Patrick's on Fifth Avenue, where the brilliant sunshine etched the image of that great cathedral into the streets around it. Don Raymonde Aprile, Valerius and his wife, Marcantonio, anxious for a quick getaway, and Nicole, beautiful in black, watched the cardinal himself, red-hatted and sipping wine, give Communion and administer Heaven's admonitory ceremonial slap on the cheek.

It was a sweet and mysterious pleasure to see the boys on the brink of puberty, girls ripening into nubility in their white gowns with the red silk scarves draped around, marching down the aisles of the cathedral, stone angels and saints watching over them. Confirming that they would serve God for the rest of their lives. Nicole had tears in her eyes, though she didn't believe a word the cardinal was saying. She laughed to herself.

Out on the steps of the cathedral, the children shed their robes and showed off their hidden finery. The girls in frail cobwebby white lace dresses, the boys in their dark suits, glaring white shirts, and traditional red neckties knitted at their throats to ward off the Devil.

Don Aprile emerged from the church, Astorre on one side, Marcantonio on the other. The children milled around in a circle, Valerius and his wife proudly holding their son's gown as a photographer snapped their picture. Don Aprile began to descend the steps alone. He breathed in the air. It was a glorious day; he felt so alive and alert. And when his newly confirmed grandson came over to hug him, he patted his head affectionately and put a huge gold coin in the boy's palm—the traditional gift on a child's confirmation day. Then with a generous hand he reached into his jacket pocket and pulled out a handful of smaller gold coins to give to the other boys and girls. He was gratified by their shouts of joy and indeed by being in the city itself, its tall gray stone buildings as sweet as the trees. He was quite alone, only Astorre a few paces behind. He looked down at the stone steps in front of him, then paused a moment as a huge black car pulled up as if to receive him.

IN BRIGHTWATERS that Sunday morning Heskow got up early and went to get baked goods and the newspapers. He stored the stolen car in the garage, a huge black sedan packed with the guns and masks and boxes of ammunition. He checked the tires, the gas and oil, and the braking lights. Perfect. He went back into the house to wake up Franky and Stace, but of course they were already up and Stace had the coffee ready.

They ate breakfast in silence and read the Sunday papers. Franky checked the college basketball scores.

At ten o'clock Stace said to Heskow, "The car ready?" and Heskow said, "All set."

They got into the car and left, Franky sitting up front with Heskow, Stace in the back. The trip to the city would take an hour, so they would have an extra hour to kill. The important thing was to be on time.

In the car Franky checked the guns. Stace tried on one of the masks, little white shells attached to side strings, so that they could hang them around their necks until they had to put them on at the last moment.

They drove into the city listening to opera on the radio. Heskow was an excellent driver, conservative, steady-paced, no disturbing acceleration or deceleration. He always left a good space in front and back. Stace gave a little grunt of approval, which lifted part of the strain; they were tense but not jittery. They knew they had to be perfect. They couldn't miss the shot.

Heskow weaved slowly through the city; he

seemed to catch every red light. Then he turned onto Fifth Avenue and waited half a block from the cathedral's great doors. The church bells began to ring, the sound clanging against the surrounding steel skyscrapers. Heskow started up the motor again. All three men watched the children swirling out into the streets. It worried them.

Stace murmured, "Franky, the head shot." Then they saw the Don come out, walk ahead of the men on either side of him, and begin to descend the steps. He seemed to look directly at them.

"Masks," Heskow said. He accelerated slightly, and Franky put his hand on the door handle. His left hand cradled the Uzi, ready to come out onto the sidewalk.

The car speeded up and stopped as the Don reached the last step. Stace jumped out of the backseat onto the street, the car between him and his target. In one quick move he rested his gun on the roof. He shot two-handed. He only fired twice.

The first bullet hit the Don square in the fore-head. The second bullet tore out his throat. His blood spurted all over the sidewalk, showering yellow sunlight with pink drops.

At the same time Franky, on the sidewalk, fired a long burst of his Uzi over the heads of the crowd.

Then both men were back in the car and

Heskow screeched down the avenue. Minutes later they were driving through the tunnel and then onto the little airport, where a private jet took them aboard.

AT THE SOUND of the first shot Valerius hurled his son and wife to the ground and covered them with his body. He actually saw nothing that happened. Neither did Nicole, who stared at her father with astonishment. Marcantonio looked down in disbelief. The reality was so different from the staged fiction of his TV dramas. The shot to the Don's forehead had split it apart like a melon so that you could see a slosh of brains and blood inside. The shot in the throat had hacked away the flesh in a jagged chunk so that he looked as if he had been hit with a meat cleaver. And there was an enormous amount of blood on the pavement around him. More blood than you could imagine in a human body. Marcantonio saw the two men with eggshell masks over their faces; he also saw the guns in their hands, but they seemed unreal. He could not have given any details about their clothing, their hair. He was paralyzed with shock. He could not even have said if they were black or white, naked or clothed. They could have been ten feet tall or two.

But Astorre had been alert as soon as the black sedan stopped. He saw Stace fire his gun and thought the left hand pulled the trigger. He saw Franky fire the Uzi, and that was definitely left-handed. He caught a fleeting glance at the driver, a round-headed man, obviously heavy. The two shooters moved with the grace of well-conditioned athletes. As Astorre dropped to the sidewalk, he reached out to pull the Don down with him, but he was a fraction of a second too late. And now he was covered with the Don's blood.

Then he saw the children move like a whirl-wind of terror, a huge red dot at the center of it. They were screaming. He saw the Don splayed over the steps as if death had disjointed his skeleton itself. And he felt an enormous dread of what all this would do to his life and the lives of those dearest to him.

Nicole came to stand over the Don's body. Her knees folded against her will, and she kneeled next to him. Silently, she reached out to touch her father's bloody throat. And then she wept as if she would weep forever.

CHAPTER 3

THE ASSASSINATION of Don Raymonde Aprile was an astounding event to the members of his former world. Who would dare to risk killing such a man, and to what purpose? He had given away his empire; there was no realm to steal. Dead, he could no longer lavish his beneficent gifts or use his influence to help someone unfortunate with the law or fate.

Could it be some long-postponed revenge? Was there some hidden gain that would come to light? Of course, there might be a woman, but he had been a widower for close to thirty years and had never been seen with a woman; he was not regarded as an admirer of female beauty. The Don's children were above suspicion. Also, this was a professional hit, and they did not have the contacts.

So his killing was not only a mystery but almost sacrilegious. A man who had inspired so much fear, who had gone unharmed by the law and jackals alike while he ruled a vast criminal empire for over thirty years—how could he be brought so to death? And what an irony, when he had finally found the path of righteousness and placed himself under the protection of society, that he would live for only three short years.

What was even more strange was the lack of any longtime furor after the Don's death. The media soon deserted the story, the police were secretive, and the FBI shrugged it off as a local matter. It seemed as if all the fame and power of Don Aprile had been washed away in his mere three years of retirement.

The underground world showed no interest. There were no retaliatory murders—all the Don's friends and former loyal vassals seemed to have forgotten him. Even the Don's children seemed to have put the whole affair behind them and accepted their father's fate.

No one seemed to care—no one except Kurt Cilke.

KURT CILKE, FBI agent in charge in New York, decided to take a hand in the case, though it was strictly a local homicide for the NYPD. He decided to interview the Aprile family.

A month after the Don's funeral, Cilke took his

deputy agent, Bill Boxton, with him to call on Marcantonio Aprile. They had to be careful of Marcantonio. He was head of programming of a major TV network and had a lot of clout in Washington. A polite phone call arranged an appointment through his secretary.

Marcantonio received them in his plush office suite at the network's midtown headquarters. He greeted them graciously, offering them coffee, which they refused. He was a tall, handsome man with creamy olive skin, exquisitely dressed in a dark suit and an extraordinary pink-and-red tie manufactured by a designer whose ties were favored by TV anchors and hosts.

Cilke said, "We're helping out with the investigation of your father's death. Do you have knowledge of anyone who would bear him ill will?"

"I really wouldn't know," Marcantonio said, smiling. "My father kept us all at a distance, even his grandchildren. We grew up completely outside his circle of business." He gave them a small apologetic wave of his hand.

Cilke didn't like that gesture. "What do you think was the reason for that?" he asked.

"You gentlemen know his past history," Marcantonio said seriously. "He didn't want any of his children to be involved in his activities. We were sent away to school and to college to make our own place in the world. He never came to our homes for dinner. He came to our graduations; that was it. And of course, when we understood, we were grateful."

Cilke said, "You rose awfully fast to your position. Did he maybe help you out a little?"

For the first time Marcantonio was less than affable.

"Never. It's not unusual in my profession for young men to rise quickly. My father sent me to the best schools and gave me a generous living allowance. I used that money to develop dramatic properties, and I made the right choices."

"And your father was happy with that?" Cilke asked. He was watching the man closely, trying to read his every expression.

"I don't think he really understood what I was doing, but yes," Marcantonio said wryly.

"You know," Cilke said, "I chased your father for twenty years and could never catch him. He was a very smart man."

"Well, we never could either," Marcantonio said. "My brother, my sister, or me."

Cilke said, laughing as if at a joke, "And you have no feeling of Sicilian vengeance? Would you pursue anything of that kind?"

"Certainly not," Marcantonio said. "My father brought us up not to think that way. But I hope you catch his killer."

"How about his will?" Cilke asked. "He died a very rich man."

"You'll have to ask my sister, Nicole, about that," Marcantonio said. "She's the executor."

"But you do know what's in it?"

"Sure," Marcantonio said. His voice was steely.

Boxton broke in. "And you can't think of anyone at all who might wish to do him harm?"

"No," Marcantonio said. "If I had a name, I'd tell you."

"OK," Cilke said. "I'll leave you my card. Just in case."

BEFORE CILKE went on to talk to the Don's two other children, he decided to pay a call on the city's chief of detectives. Since he wanted no official record, he invited Paul Di Benedetto to one of the fanciest Italian restaurants on the East Side. Di Benedetto loved the perks of the high life, as long as he didn't have to dent his wallet.

The two of them had often done business over the years, and Cilke always enjoyed his company. Now he was watching Paul sample everything.

"So," Di Benedetto said, "the feds don't often spring for such a fancy meal. What is it that you want?"

Cilke said, "That was a *great* meal. Right?"

Di Benedetto shrugged with heavy shoulders,

like the roll of a wave. Then he smiled a little maliciously. For such a tough-looking guy, he had a great smile. It transformed his face into that of some beloved Disney character.

"Kurt," he said, "this place is full of shit. It's run by aliens from outer space. Sure, they make the food look Italian, they make it smell Italian, but it tastes like goo from Mars. These guys are aliens, I'm telling you."

Cilke laughed. "Hey, but the wine is good."

"It all tastes like medicine to me unless it's guinea red mixed with cream soda."

"You're a hard man to please," Cilke said.

"No," Di Benedetto said. "I'm easy to please. That's the whole problem."

Cilke sighed. "Two hundred bucks of government money shot to shit."

"Oh, no," Di Benedetto replied. "I appreciate the gesture. Now, what's up?"

Cilke ordered espresso for both of them. Then he said, "I'm investigating the Don Aprile killing. A case of yours, Paul. We kept tabs on him for years and nothing. He retires, lives straight. He has nothing anybody wants. So why the killing? A very dangerous thing for anybody to do."

"Very professional," Di Benedetto said. "A beautiful piece of work."

Cilke said, "So?"

"It doesn't make any sort of sense," Di

Benedetto said. "You wiped out most of the Mafia bigwigs, a brilliant job too. My hat's off to you. Maybe you even forced this Don to retire. So the wiseguys that are left have no reason to knock him off."

"What about the string of banks he owns?" Cilke asked.

Di Benedetto waved his cigar. "That's your line of work. We just go after the riffraff."

"What about his family?" Cilke said. "Drugs, women chasing, anything?"

"Absolutely not," Di Benedetto said. "Upstanding citizens with big professional careers. The Don planned it that way. He wanted them to be absolutely straight." He paused now, and he was deadly serious. "It's not a grudge. He squared everything with everybody. It's not random. There has to be a reason. Somebody gains. That's what we're looking for."

"What about his will?" Cilke asked.

"His daughter files it tomorrow. I asked. She told me to wait."

"And you stood still for it?" Cilke asked.

"Sure," Di Benedetto said. "She's a top-notch lawyer, she has clout, and her law firm is a political force. Why the hell would I try to get tough with her? I just ate out of her hand."

"Maybe I can do better," Cilke said.

"I'm sure you can."

• • •

KURT CILKE had known the assistant chief of detectives, Aspinella Washington, for over ten years. She was a six-foot-tall African-American with close-cropped hair and finely chiseled features. She was a terror to the police she commanded and the felons she apprehended. By design, she acted as offensively as possible, and she really wasn't too fond of Cilke or the FBI.

She received Cilke in her office by saying, "Kurt, are you here to make one of my black brethren wealthy again?"

Cilke laughed. "No, Aspinella," he said. "I'm here looking for information."

"Really," she said. "For free? After you cost the city five million dollars?"

She was wearing a safari jacket and tan trousers. Beneath her jacket he could see the holstered gun. On her right hand was a diamond ring that looked as if it could cut through facial tissue like a razor.

She still bore a grudge against Cilke because the FBI had proven a brutality case against her detectives and on the basis of civil rights the victim had won a huge judgment—and also sent two of her detectives to jail. The victim, who had gotten rich, had been a pimp and drug pusher whom Aspinella herself had once severely beaten. Although she had been appointed assistant chief as a political sop to the black vote, she functioned much more toughly on black felons than on whites.

"Stop beating innocent people," Cilke said, "and I'll stop."

"I never framed anyone who wasn't guilty," she said, grinning.

"I'm just checking in on the Don Aprile murder," Cilke said.

"What's it your business? It's a local gang hit. Or are you making that another fucking civil rights case?"

"Well, it could be related to currency or drugs," Cilke said.

"And how do you know that?" Aspinella asked.

"We have our informers."

Suddenly Aspinella was in one of her rages. "You fucking FBI guys come in for info and then you won't give me any? You guys are not even honest-to-god cops. You float around arresting white-collar pricks. You never get into the dirty work. You don't know what the hell that is. Get the fuck out of my office."

CILKE WAS PLEASED with the interviews. Their pattern was clear to him. Both Di Benedetto and Aspinella were going to go into the tank on the Don Aprile murder. They would not cooperate with the FBI. They would just go through the motions. In short, they had been bribed.

There was a reason for his beliefs. He knew that traffic in drugs could only survive if police officials were paid off, and he had word, not good in court, that Di Benedetto and Aspinella were on the drug lord's payroll.

BEFORE CILKE interviewed the Don's daughter, he decided to take his chances with the older son, Valerius Aprile. For that he and Boxton had to drive up to West Point, where Valerius was a colonel in the United States Army and taught military tactics—whatever the hell that meant, Cilke thought.

Valerius received them in a spacious office that looked down upon the parade grounds where cadets were practicing marching drills. He was not as affable as his brother had been, though he was not discourteous. Cilke asked him if he knew his father's enemies.

"No," he said. "I've served out of the country for most of the last twenty years. I attended family celebrations when I could. My father was only concerned that I get promoted to general. He wanted to see me wearing that star. Even brigadier would have made him happy."

"He was a patriot, then?" Cilke asked.

"He loved this country," Valerius said curtly.

"He got you your appointment as a cadet?" Cilke pressed.

"I suppose so," Valerius said. "But he could never get me made a general. I guess he had no influence in the Pentagon, or at any rate I just wasn't good enough. But I love it anyway. I have my place."

"You're sure you can't give us a lead on any of your father's enemies?" Cilke asked.

"No, he didn't have any," Valerius said. "My father would have made a great general. When he retired he had everything covered. When he used power, it was always with preemptive force. He had the numbers and the materials."

"You don't seem to be that concerned that somebody murdered your father. No desire for vengeance?"

"No more than for a fellow officer fallen in battle," Valerius said. "I'm interested, of course. Nobody likes to see his father killed."

"Do you know anything about his will?"

"You'll have to ask my sister about that," Valerius said.

LATE THAT AFTERNOON Cilke and Boxton were in the office of Nicole Aprile, and here they received a completely different reception.

Nicole's office could be reached only by going through three secretarial barriers and after passing what Cilke recognized as a personal security aide, who looked as though she could take both him and Boxton apart in two seconds. He could tell by the way she moved that she had trained her body to the strength of a male. Her muscles showed through her clothing. Her breasts were strapped down, and she wore a linen jacket over her sweater and black slacks.

Nicole's greeting was not warm, though she looked very attractive, dressed in a haute couture suit of deep violet. She wore huge gold hoop earrings, and her black hair was shiny and long. Her features were finely cut and stern but were betrayed by huge soft brown eyes.

"Gentlemen, I can give you twenty minutes," she said.

She was wearing a frilly blouse beneath the violet jacket, and its cuffs almost covered her hands as she extended one for Cilke's ID. She looked it over carefully and said, "Special agent in charge? That's pretty high up for a routine inquiry."

She spoke in a tone that was familiar to Cilke, one that he had always resented. It was the slightly scolding tone of the federal attorneys when they dealt with the investigative arm they oversaw.

"Your father was a very important man," Cilke said.

"Yes, until he retired and placed himself under the protection of the law," Nicole said bitterly.

"Which makes his killing even more mysterious," Cilke said. "We were hoping you might give us some idea about the people who might have a grudge against him."

"It's not so mysterious," Nicole said. "You know his life much better than I do. He had plenty of enemies. Including you."

"Even our worst critics would never accuse the FBI of a hit on the steps of a cathedral," Cilke said dryly. "And I wasn't his enemy. I was an enforcer of the law. After he retired he had no enemies. He bought them off." He paused for a moment. "I find it curious that neither you nor your brothers seem interested in finding out who the man was who murdered your father."

"Because we're not hypocrites," Nicole said. "My father was no saint. He played the game and paid the price." She paused. "And you're wrong about my not being interested. In fact I'm going to petition for my father's FBI file under the Freedom of Information Act. And I hope you don't cause any delay because then we will be enemies."

"That's your privilege," Cilke said. "But maybe

you can help me by telling me the provisions of your father's will."

"I didn't draw up the will," Nicole said.

"But you are the executor, I hear. You must know the provisions by now."

"We're filing for probate tomorrow. It will be public record."

"Is there anything you can tell me now that may help?" Cilke asked.

"Just that I won't be taking early retirement."

"So why won't you tell me anything today?"

"Because I don't have to," Nicole said coolly.

"I knew your father pretty well," Cilke said. "He would have been reasonable."

For the first time Nicole looked at him with respect that he knew her father so well. "That's true," she said. "OK. My father gave away a lot of money before he died. All he left us was his banks. My brothers and I get forty-nine percent, and the other fifty-one percent goes to our cousin, Astorre Viola."

"Can you tell me anything about him?" Cilke asked.

"Astorre is younger than me. He was never in my father's business, and we all love him because he's such a charming nut. Of course, I don't love him as much now."

Cilke searched his memory. He could not recall a file on Astorre Viola. Yet there would have to be.

"Could you give me his address and phone number?" Cilke asked.

"Sure," Nicole said. "But you're wasting your time. Believe me."

"I have to clean up the details," Cilke said apologetically.

"And what gives the FBI an interest?" Nicole asked. "This is a local homicide."

Cilke said coolly, "The ten banks your father owned were international banks. There could be currency complications."

"Oh, really," Nicole said. "Then I better ask for his file right away. After all, I own part of those banks now." She gave him a suspicious glance. He knew he would have to keep an eye on her.

THE NEXT DAY Cilke and Boxton drove out to Westchester County to meet with Astorre Viola. The wooded estate included a huge house and three barns. There were six horses in the meadow, which was enclosed by a waist-high split-rail fence and wrought-iron gates. Four cars and a van were parked in the lot in front of the house. Cilke memorized two of the license-plate numbers.

A woman of about seventy let them in and led them to a plush living room jammed with recording equipment. Four young men were reading sheet music on stands, and one was seated at the piano—a professional combo on sax, bass, guitar, and drums.

Astorre stood at the microphone opposite them singing in a hoarse voice. Even Cilke could tell that this was the kind of music that would find no audience.

Astorre stopped vocalizing and said to the visitors, "Can you wait just five minutes until we finish recording? Then my friends can pack up and you can have all the time you want."

"Sure," Cilke said.

"Bring them coffee," Astorre told the maid. Cilke was pleased. Astorre didn't just make a polite offer; he commanded it for them.

But Cilke and Boxton had to wait longer than five minutes. Astorre was recording an Italian folk song—while strumming a banjo—and he sang in a coarse dialect Cilke did not understand. It was enjoyable to listen to him, like hearing your own voice in the shower.

Finally they were alone and Astorre was wiping his face. "That wasn't so bad," he said, laughing. "Was it?"

Cilke found himself immediately liking the man. About thirty, he had a boyish vitality and did not seem to take himself seriously. He was tall and well built, with a boxer's grace. He had a dark-skinned beauty and the kind of irregular but sharp features you might see in fifteenth-century portraits. He did not seem vain, but around his neck he wore a collar of gold two inches wide, to which was attached an etched medallion of the Virgin Mary.

"It was great," Cilke said. "You're cutting a record for distribution?"

Astorre smiled, a wide, good-natured grin. "I wish. I'm not that good. But I love these songs, and I give them to friends as presents."

Cilke decided to get to work. "This is just routine," he said. "Do you know of anyone who would have wanted to harm your uncle?"

"No one at all," Astorre said, straight-faced. Cilke was tired of hearing this. Everyone had enemies, especially Raymonde Aprile.

"You inherit controlling interest in the banks," Cilke said. "Were you that close?"

"I really don't understand that," Astorre said. "I was one of his favorites when I was a kid. He set me up in my business and then sort of forgot about me."

"What kind of business?" Cilke asked.

"I import all the top-grade macaroni from Italy,"

Cilke gave him a skeptical look. "Macaroni?"

Astorre smiled; he was used to this reaction. It was not a glamorous business. "You know how Lee Iacocca never says *automobiles,* he always says *cars?* Now, in my business, we never say *pasta* or *spaghetti,* we always say *macaroni.*"

"And now you'll be a banker?" Cilke said.

"I'll give it a whirl," Astorre said.

AFTER THEY LEFT, Cilke asked Bill Boxton, "What do you think?" He liked Boxton enormously. The man believed in the Bureau, as he did—that it was fair, that it was incorruptible and far superior to any other law-enforcement agency in its efficiency. These interviews were partly for his benefit.

"They all sound pretty straight to me," Boxton said. "But don't they always?"

Yes, they always did, Cilke thought. Then something struck him. The medallion hanging from Astorre's gold collar had never moved.

THE LAST INTERVIEW was the most important to Cilke. It was with Timmona Portella, the reigning Mafia boss in New York, the only one besides the Don who had escaped prosecution after Cilke's investigations.

Portella ran his enterprises from the huge penthouse apartment of a building he owned on the West Side. The rest of the building was occupied by subsidiary firms that he controlled. The security was as tight as Fort Knox, and Portella himself traveled by helicopter—the roof was equipped with a landing pad—to his estate in New Jersey. His feet rarely touched the pavement of New York.

Portella greeted Cilke and Boxton in his office with its overstuffed armchairs and bulletproof walls of glass that gave a wonderful view of the city skyline. He was a huge man, immaculately dressed in a dark suit and gleaming white shirt.

Cilke shook Portella's meaty hand and admired the dark tie hanging from his thick neck.

"Kurt, how can I help you?" Portella said in a voice that rang through the room. He ignored Bill Boxton.

"I'm just checking out the Aprile affair," Cilke said. "I thought you might have some information that could help me."

"What a shame, his death," Portella said. "Everybody loved Raymonde Aprile. It's a mystery to me who could have done this. In the last years of his life Aprile was such a good man. He became a saint, a real saint. He gave away his money like a Rockefeller. When God took him his soul was pure."

"God didn't take him," Cilke said dryly. "It was an extremely professional hit. There has to be a motive." Portella's eye twitched, but he said nothing, so Cilke went on. "You were his colleague for many years. You must know something. What about this nephew of his who inherits the banks?"

"Don Aprile and I had some business together many years ago," Portella said. "But when Aprile retired he could just as easily have killed me. The fact that I'm alive proves we were not enemies. About his nephew I knew nothing except that he is an artist. He sings at weddings, at little parties, even in some small nightclubs. One of those young men that old folks like myself are fond of. And he sells good macaroni from Italy. All my restaurants use it." He paused and sighed. "It is always a mystery when a great man is killed."

"You know your help will be appreciated," Cilke said.

"Of course," Portella said. "The FBI always plays fair. I know my help will be appreciated."

He gave Cilke and Boxton a warm smile, which showed square, almost perfect teeth.

On the way back to the office, Boxton said to Cilke, "I read that guy's file. He's big into porn and drugs, and he's a murderer. How come we could never get him?"

"He's not as bad as most of the others," Cilke said. "And we'll get him someday."

KURT CILKE ordered an electronic surveillance on the homes of Nicole Aprile and Astorre Viola.

A domesticated federal judge issued the necessary order. Not that Cilke was really suspicious—he just wanted to be certain. Nicole was born a troublemaker, and Astorre looked too good to be true. It was out of the question to bug Valerius, since his home was on the West Point grounds.

Cilke had learned that the horses in Astorre's meadow were his passion. That he brushed and groomed one stallion each morning before he took it out. Which was not so bad, except that he rode dressed in full English regalia, red coat and all, including a black suede hunting cap.

He found it hard to believe that Astorre was so helpless a target that three muggers in Central Park had taken a pass at him. He had escaped, it seemed—but the police report was foggy about what had happened to the muggers.

TWO WEEKS LATER Cilke and Boxton were able to listen to the tapes he had planted in the house of Astorre Viola. The voices were those of Nicole, Marcantonio, Valerius, and Astorre. On tape they became human to Cilke; they had taken off their masks.

"Why did they have to kill him?" Nicole asked, her voice breaking with grief. There was none of the coldness she had shown to Cilke.

"There has to be a reason," Valerius said quietly.

His voice was much gentler when talking to his family. "I never had any connection to the old man's business, so I'm not worried about myself. But what about you?"

Marcantonio spoke scornfully; obviously he did not like his brother. "Val, the old man got you an appointment to West Point because you were a wimp. He wanted to toughen you up. Then he helped in your intelligence work overseas. So you're in this. He loved the idea you could be a commander. General Aprile—he loved the sound of it. Who knows what strings he pulled." His voice sounded far more energetic, more passionate on tape than in person.

There was a long pause, and then Marcantonio said, "And of course he got me started. He bankrolled my production company. The big talent agencies gave me a break on their stars. Listen, we were not in his life, but he was always in ours. Nicole, the old man saved you ten years of dues paying by getting you that job at the law firm. And Astorre, who do you think got your macaroni shelf space in the supermarkets?"

Suddenly Nicole was furious. "Dad may have helped me get through the door, but the only one responsible for my success in my career is me. I had to fight those sharks at the firm for everything I got. I'm the one who put in eighty-hour weeks reading the fine print." She paused, her voice cold now. She must have turned to Astorre then. "And what I want to know is why Dad put you in charge of the banks. What the hell do you have to do with anything?"

Astorre's voice sounded helpless with apology. "Nicole, I have no idea. I didn't ask for this. I have a business, and I love my singing and riding. Besides, there's a bright side for you. I have to do all the work, and the profits are divided equally among the four of us."

"But you have control and you're only a cousin," Nicole said. She added sarcastically, "He sure must have loved your singing."

Valerius said, "Are you going to try to run the banks yourself?"

Astorre's voice was filled with mock horror. "Oh, no, no, Nicole will give me a list of names, a CEO to do that."

Nicole sounded tearful with frustration. "I still don't understand. Why didn't Dad appoint me? Why?"

"Because he didn't want any one of his children to have leverage over the others," Marcantonio said.

Astorre said quietly, "Maybe it was to keep you all out of danger."

"How do you like that FBI guy coming on to us like he's our best friend?" Nicole said. "He hounded Dad for years. And now he thinks we're going to spill all our family secrets to him. What a creep."

Cilke felt a flush coming to his cheeks. He hadn't deserved that.

Valerius said, "He's doing his duty, and that's not an easy job. He must be a very intelligent man. He sent a lot of the old man's friends to jail. And for a long time."

"Traitors, informers," Nicole said scornfully. "And those RICO laws they enforce very selectively. They could send half of our political leaders to jail under those laws, and most of the Fortune Five Hundred."

"Nicole, you're a corporate lawyer," Marcantonio said. "Cut the crap."

Astorre said thoughtfully, "Where do the FBI agents get those snazzy suits? Is there a special 'Tailor to the FBI'?"

"It's the way they wear them," Marcantonio said. "That's the secret. But on TV we can never get a guy like Cilke right. Perfectly sincere, perfectly honest, honorable in every way. Yet you never trust him."

"Marc, forget your phony TV shows," Valerius said. "We are in a hostile situation, and there are two significant intelligence aspects. The why, then the who. Why was Dad killed? Then, who could it possibly be? Everyone says he had no enemies and nothing that anyone wanted."

"I have a petition to see Dad's file at the Bureau," Nicole said. "That may give us a clue."

"What for?" Marcantonio said. "We can't do anything about it. Dad would want us to forget it. This should be left to the authorities."

Nicole sounded scornful. "So we don't give a crap who killed our father? How about you, Astorre? Do you feel like that too?"

Astorre's voice was soft, reasonable. "What can we do? I loved your father. I'm grateful he was so generous to me in his will. But let's wait and see what happens. Actually, I like Cilke. If there's anything to find, he'll find it. We all have good lives, so why twist them out of shape?" He paused and then said, "Look, I have to call one of my suppliers, so I have to go. But you can stay here and talk things out."

There was a long silence on the tape. Cilke couldn't help feeling goodwill toward Astorre and resentment against the others. Still, he was satisfied. These were not dangerous people; they would cause him no trouble.

"I love Astorre," Nicole's voice said now. "He was closer to our father than any of us. But he's such a flake. Marc, can he possibly go anywhere with that singing?"

Marcantonio laughed. "We see thousands of guys like him in our business. He's like a football star in a small high school. He's fun, but he hasn't really got the goods. But he's got a good business and he enjoys it, so what the hell?"

"He has control of multibillion-dollar banks—everything we have, and what really interests him is singing and horseback riding," said Nicole.

Valerius said ruefully and with humor, "Sartorially splendid, but he has a lousy seat."

Nicole said, "How could Dad do that?"

"He made something very good out of that macaroni business," Valerius said.

"We have to protect Astorre," Nicole said. "He's too nice to run banks and too trusting to deal with Cilke."

At the end of the tape Cilke turned to Boxton. "What do you think?" he asked.

"Oh, like Astorre, I think you're a splendid fellow," Boxton said.

Cilke laughed. "No, I mean, are these people possible suspects in the murder?"

"No," Boxton said. "First, they are his kids, and second, they don't have the expertise."

"They are smart though," Cilke said. "They ask the right question. Why?"

"Well, it's not our question," Boxton said. "This is local, not federal. Or do you have a connection?"

"International banks," Cilke said. "But no sense wasting any more of the Bureau's money; cancel all the phone taps."

• • •

KURT CILKE liked dogs because they could not conspire. They could not hide hostility, and they were not cunning. They did not lie awake at night planning to rob and murder other dogs. Treachery was beyond their scope. He had two German shepherds to help guard his home, and he walked with them through the nearby woods at night with complete harmony and trust.

When he went home that night, he was satisfied. There was no danger in the situation, not from the Don's family. There would be no bloody vendetta.

Cilke lived in New Jersey with a wife he truly loved and a ten-year-old daughter he adored. His house was wrapped up with a tight security-alarm system plus the two dogs. The government paid. His wife had refused training to use a gun, and he relied on remaining anonymous. His neighbors thought he was a lawyer (which he was), as did his daughter. Cilke always kept his gun and bullets locked up with his Bureau ID when he was at home.

He never took his car to the railroad station for his commute to the city. Petty thieves might steal the car radio. When he arrived back in New Jersey, he called his wife on his cell phone and she came to pick him up. It was a five-minute ride home.

Tonight Georgette gave him a cheerful kiss on the mouth, a warm touch of flesh. His daughter, Vanessa, so boundlessly alive, bowled into him for a hug. The two dogs frolicked around him but were restrained. They all fitted easily into the big Buick.

It was this part of his life that Cilke treasured. With his family he felt secure, at peace. His wife loved him, he knew that. She admired his character, that he did his work without malice or trickery, with a sense of justice to his fellowman no matter how depraved. He valued her intelligence and trusted her enough to talk to her about his work. But of course he could not tell her everything. And she was busy with her own work, writing about famous women in history, teaching ethics at a local college, fighting for her social causes.

Now Cilke watched his wife as she prepared dinner. Her beauty always enchanted him. He watched Vanessa setting the table, imitating her mother, even trying to walk with that graceful balletlike movement. Georgette did not believe in having household help of any kind, and she had raised her daughter to be self-reliant. At the age of six, Vanessa was already making her own bed, cleaning her room, and helping her mother cook. As always, Cilke wondered why his wife loved him, felt blessed that she did.

Later, after they put Vanessa to bed (Cilke checked the bell she could ring if she needed them), they went into their own bedroom. And as always, Cilke felt the thrill of almost religious fervor when his wife undressed. Then her huge gray eyes, so intelligent, became smoky with love. And afterward, falling into sleep, she held his hand to guide them through her dreams.

Cilke had met her when he was investigating radical college organizations suspected of minor terrorist acts. She was a political activist who taught history at a small New Jersey college. His investigation showed she was simply a liberal and had no connection with a radical extremist group. And so Cilke wrote in his report.

But when he interviewed her as part of the investigation, he had been struck by her absolute lack of prejudice or hostility toward him as an FBI agent. In fact, she seemed curious about his work, how he felt about it, and oddly enough he answered her frankly: simply that he was one of the guardians of a society that could not exist without some regulation. He added half-jokingly that he was the shield between people like her and those who would devour her for their own agenda.

The courtship was short. They married quickly, really so that their common sense would not interfere with their love, for they both recognized they were opposites in almost every way. He shared none of her beliefs; when it came to the world he lived in, she was an innocent. She definitely shared none of his reverence for the Bureau. But she listened to his complaints, how he resented the character assassination of the Bureau saint, J. Edgar Hoover. "They paint him as a closet homosexual and reactionary bigot. What he really was was a dedicated man who simply did not develop a liberal conscience." He told her, "Writers deride the FBI as the Gestapo or KGB. But we have never resorted to torture, and we have never framed anybody—unlike the NYPD, for instance. We have never planted false evidence. The kids in college would lose their freedom if it wasn't for us. The right wing would destroy them, they are so dumb politically."

She smiled at his passion, was touched by it.

"Don't expect me to change," she told him, smiling. "If what you say is true, we have no quarrel."

"I don't expect you to change," Cilke said. "And if the FBI affects our relationship, I'll just get another job." He didn't have to tell her what a sacrifice that would be for him.

But how many people can say that they are perfectly happy, that they have one human being they can absolutely trust? He took such comfort in his guardianship and faithfulness to her spirit and her body. She could sense his alertness every second of the day for her safety and survival.

Cilke missed her terribly when he was away on training courses. He never was tempted by other women because he never wanted to be a conspirator against her. He cherished his return to her, to her trusting smile, her welcoming body, as she waited for him in the bedroom, naked, vulnerable, pardoning him for his work, a benediction to his life.

But his happiness was haunted by the secrets he had to keep from her, the serious complications of his job, his knowledge of a world that festered with the pus of evil men and women, the stains of humanity that spilled over into his own brain. Without her, it was simply not worth living in the world.

At one time, early, still shaky with fear of happiness, he had done the one thing he was truly ashamed of. He had bugged his own home to record his wife's every word, then listened in the basement to the tapes. He had listened to every inflection. And she had passed the test; she was never malicious, never petty or traitorous. He had done that for a year.

That she loved him despite his imperfections, his feral cunning, his need to hunt down fellow human beings seemed to Cilke a miracle. But he was always afraid that she would discover his true nature and then abhor him. And so in his work, he also became as fastidious as possible and acquired his reputation for fairness.

Georgette never doubted him. She had proved that one night when they were dinner guests at the director's house, along with twenty other guests, a semiofficial affair and a signal honor.

At one point during the evening the director managed to secure a moment alone with Cilke and his wife. He said to Georgette, "I understand you are involved in many liberal causes. I respect your right to do so, of course. But perhaps you don't truly comprehend that your actions could damage Kurt's career in the Bureau?"

Georgette smiled at the director and said gravely, "I do know that, and that would be the Bureau's mistake and misfortune. Of course, if it became too much of a problem, my husband would resign."

The director turned to Cilke, a look of surprise on his face. "Is that true?" he asked. "Would you resign?"

Cilke didn't hesitate. "Yes, it's true. I'll turn in the papers tomorrow if you like."

The director laughed. "Oh, no," he said. "We don't come by men like you often." Then he gave

Georgette his steely aristocratic eye. "Uxorious-ness may be the last refuge of the honest man," he said.

They all laughed at the laborious witticism to show their goodwill.

CHAPTER 4

FOR FIVE MONTHS after the Don's death, Astorre was busy conferring with some of the Don's old retired colleagues, taking measures to protect the Don's children from harm and investigating the circumstances of his murder. Most of all he had to find a reason for such a daring and outrageous act. Who would give the order to kill the great Don Aprile? He knew he had to be very careful.

Astorre had his first meeting with Benito Craxxi in Chicago.

Craxxi had retired from all illegal operations ten years before the Don. He was the man who had been the great consiglieri of the National Mafia Commission itself and had an intimate knowledge of all Family structures in the United States. He had been the first to spot the decay in the power of the great Families, foreseeing their decline. And so he had prudently retired to play

the stock market, where he was pleasantly surprised that he could steal as much money with no
risk of legal punishment whatsoever. The Don
had given Craxxi's name to Astorre as one of the
men he must consult, if necessary.

Craxxi, at seventy, lived with two bodyguards,
a chauffeur, and a young Italian woman who
served as cook and housekeeper and was ru-
mored to be his sexual companion. He was
in perfect health, for he had lived a life of
moderation; he ate prudently and drank only
occasionally. For breakfast a bowl of fruit and
cheese; for lunch an omelet or vegetable soup,
mostly beans and escarole; for dinner a simple
cutlet of beef or lamb and a great salad of onions,
tomatoes, and lettuce. He smoked only one cigar
a day, directly after dinner with his coffee and
anisette. He spent his money generously and
wisely. He was also careful to whom he gave
advice. For a man who gives the wrong counsel is
as hated as any enemy.

But with Astorre, he was generous, for Craxxi
was one of the many men who was greatly in the
debt of Don Aprile. It was the Don who had
protected Craxxi when he retired, always a dangerous move in the business.

It was a breakfast meeting. There were bowls of
fruit—glossy yellow pears, russet apples, a bowl of
strawberries almost as large as lemons, white

grapes, and dark red cherries. A huge crag of cheese was laid out on a wooden board like a sliver of gold-crated rock. The housekeeper served them coffee and anisette and disappeared.

"So, my young man," Craxxi said. "You are the guardian Don Aprile has chosen."

"Yes," Astorre said.

"I know he trained you for this task," Craxxi said. "My old friend always looked ahead. We consulted on it. I know you are qualified. The question remains, do you have the will?"

Astorre's smile was engaging, his countenance open. "The Don saved my life and gave me everything I have," he said. "I am what he made me. And I vowed I would protect the family. If Nicole isn't made a partner in the law firm, if Marcantonio's TV network fails, if something happens to Valerius, they still have the banks. I've had a happy life. I regret the reason I have the task. But I gave the Don my word, and I must keep it. If not, what can I believe in the rest of my life?"

There were moments of his childhood that flashed through his mind, moments of great joy for which he felt gratitude. Scenes of himself as a boy in Sicily with his uncle, walking through the vast mountainous terrain, listening to the Don's stories. He dreamed then of a different time, when justice was served, loyalty valued, and great deeds accomplished by kind and powerful men. And at that moment he missed both the Don and Sicily.

"Good," Craxxi said, interrupting Astorre's reverie and bringing him back to the present. "You were at the scene. Describe everything to me."

Astorre did so.

"And you are certain that both shooters were left-handed?" Craxxi asked.

"At least one, and probably the other," Astorre said.

Craxxi nodded slowly and seemed lost in thought. After what seemed long moments, he looked directly at Astorre and said, "I think I know who the shooters were. But not to be hasty. It is more important to know who hired them and why. You must be very careful. Now, I have thought very much of this matter. The most probable suspect is Timmona Portella. But for what reasons and to please who? Now, Timmona was always rash. But the killing of Don Aprile had to be a very risky enterprise. Even Timmona feared the Don, retirement or not.

"Now, here is my thought about the shooters. They are brothers who live in Los Angeles, and they are the most highly qualified men in the country. They never talk. Few people even know they are twins. And they are both left-handed.

They have courage, and they are born fighters. The danger would appeal to them, and the reward must have been great. Also, they must have had some reassurances—that the authorities would not pursue the case with conviction. I find it strange that there was no official police or federal surveillance of the confirmation at the cathedral. After all, Don Aprile was still an FBI target even after he retired.

"Now, understand, everything I've said is theory. You will have to investigate and confirm. And then, if I am correct, you must strike with all your might."

"One thing more," Astorre said. "Are the Don's children in danger?"

Craxxi shrugged. He was carefully peeling the skin off a golden pear. "I don't know," he said. "But don't be too proud to ask them to help. You yourself are undoubtedly in some peril. Now, I have a final suggestion for you. Bring your Mr. Pryor from London to run your banks. He is a supremely qualified man in every way."

"And Bianco in Sicily?" Astorre asked.

"Leave him there," Craxxi said. "When you are further along, we will meet again."

Craxxi poured anisette into Astorre's coffee. Astorre sighed. "It seems strange," he said. "I never dreamed I would have to act for the Don, the great Don Aprile."

"Ah, well," Craxxi said. "Life is cruel and hard for the young."

FOR TWENTY YEARS Valerius had lived in the military-intelligence world, not a fictional world like his brother's. He seemed to anticipate everything Astorre said and reacted without any surprise.

"I need your help," Astorre said. "You may have to break some of your strict rules of conduct."

Valerius said dryly, "Finally you're showing your true colors. I wondered how long it would take."

"I don't know what that means," Astorre said, somewhat surprised. "I think your father's death was a conspiracy that involved the NYPD and the FBI. You may think I'm fantasizing, but that's what I hear."

"It's not impossible," Valerius said. "But I don't have access to secret documents in my job here."

"But you must have friends," Astorre said. "In the intelligence agencies. You can ask them certain questions."

"I don't have to ask questions," Valerius said, smiling. "They gossip like magpies. That 'need to know' is all bullshit. Have you any idea what you're after?"

"Any information about the killers of your father," Astorre said.

Valerius leaned back in his chair, puffing on a cigar, his only vice. "Don't bullshit me, Astorre," he said. "Let me tell you something. I did an analysis. It could be a gangland act of retaliation or revenge. And I thought about you being in control of the banks. The old man always had a plan. I figure it like this. The Don made you his point man for the family. What follows from that? That you are trained, that you were his agent in place to be activated only at a crucial moment in time. There is an eleven-year gap in your life, and your cover is too good to be true—an amateur singer, a sporting horseman? And the gold collar you always wear is suspicious." He stopped, took a deep breath, and said, "How's that for analysis?"

"Very good," Astorre said. "I hope you kept it to yourself."

"Certainly," Valerius said. "But then it follows that you are a dangerous man. And that therefore there is an extreme action you will take. But some advice: Your cover is thin; it will be blown before much longer. As for my help, I live a very good life and I'm opposed to everything I think you are. So for now my answer is no. I won't help. If things change, I'll get in touch."

A WOMAN came out to guide Astorre into Nicole's office. Nicole gave him a hug and a kiss.

She was still fond of him; their teen romance had left no bitter scars.

"I have to speak to you in private," Astorre said.

Nicole turned to her bodyguard. "Helene, can you leave us alone? I'm safe with him."

Helene gave Astorre a long look. She was impressing herself on his consciousness, and she succeeded. Like Cilke, Astorre noted her extreme confidence—the kind of confidence shown by a card player with an ace in the hole or a person holding a concealed weapon. He looked to see where it could be hidden. The tight trousers and jacket molded her impressive physique—no gun there. Then he noted the slit in her trouser leg. She was wearing an ankle holster, which wasn't really that smart. He smiled at her as she left, exerting his charm. She looked back at him blankly.

"Who recruited her?" Astorre asked.

"My father," Nicole said. "It worked out very well. It's amazing how she can handle muggers and mashers."

"I'll bet," Astorre said. "Did you manage to get the old man's file from the FBI?"

"Yes," Nicole said. "And it's the most horrible list of allegations I've ever read. I simply don't believe it, and they could never prove any of it."

Astorre knew that the Don would want him to deny the truth. "Will you let me have the file for a couple of days?" he asked.

Nicole gave her blank-faced lawyer stare. "I don't think you should see it right now. I want to write an analysis of it, underline what's important, then give it to you. Actually, there's nothing that will help you. Maybe you and my brothers shouldn't see it."

Astorre looked at her thoughtfully, then smiled. "That bad?"

"Let me study it," Nicole said. "The FBI are such shits."

"Whatever you say is OK with me. Just remember, this is a dangerous business. Look after yourself."

"I will," Nicole said. "I have Helene."

"And I'm here if you need me." Astorre placed his hand on Nicole's arm to reassure her, and for a moment she looked at him with such longing he felt uncomfortable. "Just call."

Nicole smiled. "I will. But I'm OK. I am." In fact, she was really looking forward to her evening with an incredibly charming and attractive diplomat.

IN HIS ELABORATE office suite lined with six TV screens, Marcantonio Aprile was having a meeting with the head of the most powerful advertising agency in New York. Richard Harrison was a tall, aristocratic-looking man, perfectly dressed, with the appearance of a former model but the intensity of a paratrooper.

On Harrison's lap was a small case of video-tapes. With absolute assurance, without asking permission, he went to a TV set and inserted one of the tapes.

"Watch this," he said. "It's not one of my clients, but I think it's just astounding."

The videotape played a commercial for Ameri-can pizza, and the pitchman was Mikhail Gorbachev, the former president of the Soviet Union. Gorbachev sold with quiet dignity, never saying a word, just feeding his grandchildren pizza while the crowd voiced its admiration.

Marcantonio smiled at Harrison. "A victory for the free world," he said. "So what?"

"The former leader of the Soviet Republic, and now he's clowning around doing a commer-cial for an American pizza company. Isn't that astonishing? And I hear they only paid him half a million."

"OK," Marcantonio said. "But why?"

"Why does anyone do anything so humiliat-ing?" Harrison said. "He needs the money desperately."

And suddenly Marcantonio thought of his father. The Don would feel such contempt for a man who had ruled a great country and did not provide financial security for his family. Don Aprile would think him the most foolish of men.

"A nice lesson in history and human psychology," Marcantonio said. "But again, so what?"

Harrison tapped his box of videos. "I have more, and I anticipate some resistance. These are a little more touchy. You and I have done business for a long time. I want to make sure you let these commercials run on your network. The rest will necessarily follow."

"I can't imagine," Marcantonio said.

Harrison inserted another tape and explained. "We have purchased the rights to use deceased celebrities in our commercials. It is such a waste that the famous dead cease to have a function in our society. We want to change that and restore them to their former glory."

The tape began to play. There was a succession of shots of Mother Teresa ministering to the poor and sick of Calcutta, her nun's habit draping over the dying. Another shot of her receiving the Nobel Peace Prize, her homely face shining, her saintly humility so moving. Then a shot of her ladling out soup from a huge pot to the poor in the streets.

Suddenly the picture blazes with color. A richly dressed man comes to a pot with an empty bowl. He says to a beautiful young woman, "Can

I have some soup? I hear it's wonderful." The young woman gives him a radiant smile and ladles some soup into his bowl. He drinks, looking as if he's in ecstasy.

Then the screen dissolves to a supermarket and a whole shelf of soup cans labeled "Calcutta." A voice-over proclaims, "Calcutta Soup, a life giver to rich and poor alike. Everyone can afford the twenty varieties of delicious soup. Original recipes by Mother Teresa."

"I think that's done in pretty good taste," Harrison said.

Marcantonio raised his eyebrows.

Harrison inserted another video. A brilliant shot of Princess Diana in her wedding dress filled the screen, followed by shots of her in Buckingham Palace. Then dancing with Prince Charles, surrounded by her royal entourage, all in frenetic motion.

A voice-over intones, "Every princess deserves a prince. But this princess had a secret." A young model holds up an elegant crystal bottle of perfume, the product label clear. The voice-over continues, "With one small spray of Princess perfume, you too can capture your prince—and never have to worry about vaginal odor."

Marcantonio pressed a button on his desk and the screen went black.

Harrison said, "Wait, I have more."

Marcantonio shook his head. "Richard, you are amazingly inventive—and insensitive. Those commercials will never play on my network."

Harrison protested, "But some of the proceeds go to charity—and they are in good taste. I hoped you would lead the way. We're good friends, after all."

"So we are," Marcantonio said. "But still, the answer is no."

Harrison shook his head and slowly put his videos back in the box.

Marcantonio, smiling, asked, "By the way, how did the Gorbachev spot do?"

Harrison shrugged. "Lousy. The poor son of a bitch couldn't even sell *pizza*."

MARCANTONIO CLEARED UP other work and prepared for his evening duties. Tonight he had to attend the Emmys. His network had three big tables for its executives and stars and several nominations. His date was Matilda Johnson, an established newscaster.

His office had a bedroom suite with a bathroom and shower attached and a closet full of clothes. He often stayed there overnight when he had to work late.

At the ceremony he was mentioned by some of

his winners as being important to their success. This was always pleasant. But while he was clapping and kissing cheeks, he thought of all the awards celebrations and dinners he had to attend during the year: the Oscars, the People's Choice Awards, the AFI tributes, and other special awards to aging stars, producers, and directors. He felt like a teacher awarding homework stars to elementary schoolchildren who would run home to show their mothers. And then he felt a momentary shame for his malice—these people deserved their honors, needed the approval as much as they needed the money.

After the ceremony he amused himself by watching actors with slight credentials trying to impress their personalities on people like himself who had clout, and an editor of a successful magazine being courted by some freelance writers—he noted the wariness on her face, the careful and cold cordiality, as if she were Penelope waiting for a more famous suitor.

Then there were the anchors, the heavyweights, men and women of intelligence, charisma, and talent who had the exquisite dilemma of wooing stars they wanted for interviews while discouraging those not yet quite important enough.

The star actors were sparkling with hope and

desire. They were already successful enough to make the jump from TV to the movie screens, never to return—or so they thought.

Finally Marcantonio was exhausted; the continual grinning with enthusiasm, the cheery voice he must use to losers, the note of exuberance with his winners all wore him out. Matilda whispered to him, "Are you coming to my place tonight, a little later?"

"I'm tired," Marcantonio said. "Tough day, tough night."

"That's OK," she said with sympathy. They both had tight schedules. "I'll be in town for a week."

They were good friends because they didn't have to take advantage of each other. Matilda was secure. She didn't need a mentor or a patron. And Marcantonio never took part in negotiations with news talent; that was a job for the chief of Business Affairs. The lives they led could not possibly result in marriage. Matilda traveled extensively; he worked fifteen hours a day. But they were buddies who sometimes spent the night together. They made love, gossiped about the business, and appeared together at some social functions. And it was understood that theirs was a secondary relationship. The few times Matilda fell in love with some new man, their nights were cut out. Marcantonio never fell in love, so this was not a problem for him.

Tonight he suffered a certain fatigue with the world he lived in. So he was almost delighted to find Astorre waiting for him in the lobby of his apartment building.

"Hey, great to see you," Marcantonio said. "Where have you been?"

"Busy," Astorre said. "Can I come up and have a drink?"

"Sure," Marcantonio said. "But why the cloak and dagger? Why didn't you call? You could have been hanging out in this lobby for hours; I was supposed to go to a party."

"No problem," Astorre said. He'd had his cousin under surveillance all evening.

In the apartment Marcantonio fixed them both drinks.

Astorre seemed a little embarrassed. "You can initiate projects at your network, right?"

"I do it all the time," Marcantonio said.

"I have one for you," Astorre said. "It has to do with your father being killed."

"No," Marcantonio said. It was his famous *no* in the industry that barred all further discussion. But it didn't seem to intimidate Astorre.

"Don't say no to me like that," Astorre said. "I'm not selling you something. This concerns the safety of your brother and sister. And you." Then he gave a huge grin. "And me."

"Tell me," Marcantonio said. He saw his cousin in an astonishing new light. Could that happy-go-lucky kid have something in him after all?

"I want you to do a documentary on the FBI," Astorre said. "Specifically how Kurt Cilke managed to destroy most of the Mafia Families. There would be a huge audience for that, right?"

Marcantonio nodded. "What's your purpose?"

"I just can't get any data on Cilke," Astorre told him. "It would be too dangerous to try. But if you're doing a documentary, no government agency will dare to step on your toes. You can find out where he lives, his history, how he operates, and where he stands in the power structure of the Bureau. I need all that info."

"The FBI and Cilke would never cooperate," Marcantonio said. "That would make a show difficult." He paused. "It's not like the old days when Hoover was director. These new guys play their cards very close."

"You can do it," Astorre said. "I need you to do it. You have an army of producers and investigative reporters. I have to know all about him. Everything. Because I think he may be part of a conspiracy against your father and our family."

"That's a really crazy theory," Marcantonio said.

"Sure," Astorre said. "Maybe it's not true. But I know it was no simple gangland killing. And that Cilke does a funny kind of inquiry. Almost like he's smoothing over tracks, not uncovering them."

"So I help you get the information. Then what can you do?"

Astorre spread his hands and smiled. "What can I do, Marc? I just want to know. Maybe I can make some kind of a deal. And I just have to look at the documentation. I won't make a copy of it. You won't be compromised."

Marcantonio stared at him. His mind was making the adjustment to the pleasant, charming face of Astorre. He said thoughtfully, "Astorre, I'm curious about you. The old man left you in control. Why? You're a macaroni importer. I always thought of you as a charming eccentric with your scarlet riding jacket and your little music group. But the old man would never trust the man you seem to be."

"I don't sing anymore," Astorre said, smiling. "I don't ride much either. The Don always had a good eye; he had faith in me. You should have the same." He paused for a moment and then said with utmost sincerity, "He picked me so that his children wouldn't have to take the heat. He chose me and taught me. He loved me but I was expendable. It's that simple."

"You have the ability to fight back?" Marcantonio said.

"Oh, yes," Astorre said, and he leaned back and smiled at his cousin. It was a deliberately sinister smile that a TV actor would give to show that he was evil, but it was done with such mocking high spirits that Marcantonio laughed.

He said, "That's all I have to do? I won't be involved further?"

"You're not qualified to go further," Astorre said.

"Can I think it over for a few days?"

"No," Astorre said. "If you say no, it will be me against them."

Marcantonio nodded. "I like you, Astorre, but I can't do it. It's just too much risk."

THE MEETING with Kurt Cilke in Nicole's office proved a surprise for Astorre. Cilke brought Bill Broxton and insisted that Nicole be present. He was also very direct.

"I have information that Timmona Portella is trying to establish a billion-dollar fund in your banks. Is that true?" Cilke asked.

"That's private information," Nicole said. "Why should we tell you?"

"I know he made the same offer he made your father," Cilke said. "And your father refused."

"Why should all this interest the FBI?" Nicole asked in her "go fuck yourself" voice.

Cilke refused to be irritated. "We think he is laundering drug money," he said to Astorre. "We want you to cooperate with him so we can monitor his operation. We want you to appoint some of our federal accountants to positions in your bank." He opened his briefcase. "I have some papers for you to sign, which will protect both of us."

Nicole took the papers out of his hand and read the two pages very quickly.

"Don't sign," she warned Astorre. "The banks customers have a right to privacy. If they want to investigate Portella, they should get a warrant."

Astorre took the papers and read them. He smiled at Cilke. "I trust you," he said. He signed the papers and handed them to Cilke.

"What's the quid pro quo?" Nicole asked. "What do we get for cooperating?"

"Performing your duty as good citizens," Cilke said. "A letter of commendation from the president, and the stopping of an audit of all your banks that could cause you a lot of trouble if you're not absolutely clean."

"How about a little information on my uncle's murder?" Astorre said.

"Sure," Cilke said. "Shoot."

"Why was there no police surveillance at the confirmation service?" Astorre asked.

"That was the decision of the chief of detectives, Paul Di Benedetto," Cilke said. "And also his right hand. A woman named Aspinella Washington."

"And how come there were no FBI observers?" Astorre asked.

"I'm afraid that was my decision," Cilke said. "I didn't feel there was any need."

Astorre shook his head. "I don't think I can go through with your proposition. I need a few weeks to think it over."

"You've already signed the papers," Cilke said. "This information is now classified. You can be prosecuted if you reveal this conversation."

"Why would I do that?" Astorre asked. "I just don't want to be in the banking business with the FBI or Portella."

"Think it over," Cilke said.

When the two FBI men left, Nicole turned on Astorre with fury. "How dare you veto my decision and sign those papers! That was just stupid."

Astorre was glaring at her; it was the first time she had ever seen any trace of anger in him. "He feels secure with that piece of paper I signed," Astorre said. "And that's what I want him to feel."

CHAPTER 5

MARRIANO RUBIO was a man with a finger in a dozen pies, all of which had fillings of pure gold. He held the post of consul general for Peru, though he spent much of his time in New York. He also was international representative of big-business interests for many South American countries and for Communist China. He was a close personal friend of Inzio Tulippa, the leader of the primary drug cartel in Colombia.

Rubio was as fortunate in his personal life as he was in business. A forty-five-year-old bachelor, he was a respectable womanizer. He kept only one mistress at a time, all suitable and generously supported when they were replaced by a younger beauty. He was handsome, an interesting conversationalist, a marvelous dancer. He had a truly great wine cellar and an excellent three-star chef.

But like many fortunate men, Rubio believed in pushing fate. He enjoyed pitting his wits against dangerous men. He needed risk to flavor the exotic dish that was his life. He was involved in the illegal shipping of technology to China; he established a line of communication on the highest levels for the drug barons; and he was the bagman who paid off American scientists to emigrate to South America. He even had dealings with Timmona Portella, who was as eccentrically dangerous as Inzio Tulippa.

Like all high-risk gamblers, Rubio prided himself on an ace in the hole. He was safe from all legal peril because of his diplomatic immunity, but he knew there were other dangers, and in those areas he was careful.

His income was enormous, and he spent lavishly. There was such power in being able to buy anything he wanted in the world, including the love of women. He enjoyed supporting his ex-mistresses, who remained valued friends. He was a generous employer and intelligently treasured the goodwill of people dependent on him.

Now, in his New York apartment, which was very fortunately part of the Peruvian consulate, Rubio dressed for his dinner date with Nicole Aprile. The engagement was as usual with him, part business and part pleasure. He had met Nicole at a Washington dinner given by one of her prestigious corporate clients. At first sight he had been intrigued by her not-quite-regular beauty, the sharp, determined face with intelligent eyes and mouth, her small, voluptuous body, but also by her being the daughter of the great Mafia chief Don Raymonde Aprile.

Rubio had charmed her, but not out of her senses, and he was proud of her for that. He admired romantic intelligence in a woman. He would have to win her respect with deeds, not words. Which he had immediately set about doing by asking her to represent one of his clients in a particularly rich deal. He had learned that she did a great deal of pro bono work to abolish the death penalty and had even defended some notorious convicted murderers to put off their executions. To him she was the ideal modern woman—beautiful, with a highly professional career, and compassionate in the bargain. Barring some sort of sexual dysfunction, she would make a most agreeable companion for a year or so.

All this was before the death of Don Aprile.

Now the main purpose of his courtship was to learn if Nicole and her two brothers would put their banks at the disposal of Portella and Tulippa. Otherwise there would be no point in killing Astorre Viola.

INZIO TULIPPA had waited long enough. More than nine months after the killing of

Raymonde Aprile, he still had no arrangement with the inheritors of the Don's banks. A great deal of money had been spent; he had given millions to Timmona Portella to bribe the FBI and the police in New York, and to procure the services of the Sturzo brothers, and yet he was no further in his plans.

Tulippa was not the vulgar impersonation of a high-powered drug dealer. He came from a reputable and wealthy family and had even played polo for his native land of Argentina. He now lived in Costa Rica, and he had a diplomatic Costa Rican passport, which gave him immunity from prosecution in any foreign land. He handled the relations with the drug cartels in Colombia, with the growers in Turkey, refineries in Italy. He made arrangements for transport, the necessary bribing of officials from the highest rank to the lowest. He planned the smuggling of huge loads into the United States. He was also the man who lured American nuclear scientists to South American countries and supplied the money for their research. In all ways he was a prudent, capable executive, and he had amassed an enormous fortune.

But he was a revolutionary. He furiously defended the selling of drugs. Drugs were the salvation of the human spirit, the refuge of those damned to despair by poverty and mental illness.

They were the salve for the lovesick, for the lost souls in our spiritually deprived world. After all, if you no longer believed in God, society, your own worth, what were you supposed to do? Kill yourself? Drugs kept people alive in a realm of dreams and hope. All that was needed was a little moderation. After all, did drugs kill as many people as alcohol and cigarettes, as poverty and despair? No. On moral grounds, Tulippa was secure.

Inzio Tulippa had a nickname all over the world. He was known as "the Vaccinator." Foreign industrialists and investors with enormous holdings in South America—whether oil fields, car manufacturing plants, or crops, necessarily had to send top executives there. There were many from the United States. Their biggest problem was the kidnapping of their executives on foreign soil, for which they had to pay ransoms in the millions of dollars.

Inzio Tulippa headed a company that insured these executives against kidnapping, and every year he visited the United States to negotiate contracts with these corporations. He did this not only for money but because he needed some of the industrial and scientific resources of these companies. In short, he performed a vaccinating service. This was important to him.

But he had a more dangerous eccentricity. He

viewed the international persecution of the illegal drug industry as a holy war against himself,
and he was determined to protect his empire. So
he had ridiculous ambitions. He wanted to
possess nuclear capabilities as a lever in case disaster ever struck. Not that he would use it except as
a last resort, but it would be an effective bargaining weapon. It was a desire that would seem
ridiculous to everyone except the New York FBI
agent in charge, Kurt Cilke.

AT ONE POINT in his career, Kurt Cilke had
been sent to an FBI antiterrorist school. His
selection for the six-month course had been a
mark of his high standing with the director.
During that time he had access (complete or not,
he didn't know) to the most highly classified
memoranda and case scenarios on the possible
use of nuclear weapons by terrorists from small
countries. The files detailed which countries had
weapons. To public knowledge there was Russia,
France, and England, possibly India and Pakistan.
It was assumed that Israel had nuclear capability.
Kurt read with fascination scenarios detailing
how Israel would use nuclear weapons if an Arab
bloc were at the point of overwhelming it.

For the United States there were two solutions
to the problem. The first was that if Israel were so

attacked, the United States would side with Israel before it had to use nuclear weapons. Or, at the crucial point, if Israel could not be saved, the United States would have to wipe out Israel's nuclear capability.

England and France were not seen as problems; they could never risk nuclear war. India had no ambitions, and Pakistan could be wiped out immediately. China would not dare; it did not have the industrial capacity short-term.

The most immediate danger was from small countries like Iraq, Iran, and Libya, where leaders were reckless, or so the scenarios claimed. The solution here was almost unanimous. Those countries would be bombed to extinction with nuclear weapons.

The greatest short-term danger was that terrorist organizations secretly financed and supported by a foreign power would smuggle a nuclear weapon into the United States and explode it in a large city. Probably Washington, D.C., or New York. This was inevitable. The proposed solution was the formation of task forces to use counterintelligence and then the utmost punitive measures against these terrorists and whoever backed them. It would require special laws that would abridge the rights of American citizens. The scenarios acknowledged the impossibility of these laws until somebody finally succeeded at blowing up a good portion of an American metropolis. Then the laws would pass easily. But until then, as one scenario airily remarked, "It was the luck of the draw."

There were only a few scenarios depicting criminal use of nuclear devices. This was almost absolutely discounted on the grounds that the technical capacity, the procurement of material, and the broad scope of people involved would inevitably lead to informers. One solution to this was that the Supreme Court would condone a death warrant without any judicial process on any such criminal mastermind. But this was fantasy, Kurt Cilke thought. Mere speculation. The country would have to wait until something happened.

But now, years later, Cilke realized it was happening. Inzio Tulippa wanted his own little nuclear bomb. He lured American scientists to South America and built them labs and supplied money for their research. And it was Tulippa who wanted access to Don Aprile's banks to establish a billion-dollar war chest for the purchase of equipment and material—so Cilke had determined in his own investigation. What was he to do now?

He would discuss it soon with the director on his next trip to FBI headquarters in Washington. But he doubted they would be able to solve the problem. And a man like Inzio Tulippa would never give up.

INZIO TULIPPA ARRIVED in the United States to meet with Timmona Portella and to pursue the acquisition of Don Aprile's banks. At the same time, the head of the Corleonesi *cosca* of Sicily, Michael Grazziella, arrived in New York to work out with Tulippa and Portella the details on the distribution of illegal drugs all over the world. Their arrivals were very different.

Tulippa arrived in New York on his private jet, which also carried fifty of his followers and bodyguards. These men wore a certain uniform: white suits, blue shirts, and pink ties, with floppy yellow Panama hats on their heads. They could have been members of some South American rhumba band. Tulippa and his entourage all carried Costa Rican passports; Tulippa, of course, had Costa Rican diplomatic immunity.

Tulippa and his men moved into a small private hotel owned by the consul general in the name of the Peruvian consulate. And Tulippa did not slink around like some shady drug dealer. He was, after all, the Vaccinator, and the representatives of the large American corporations vied to make his stay a pleasant one. He attended the openings of Broadway shows, the ballet at Lincoln Center, the

Metropolitan Opera, and concerts given by famous South American artists. He even appeared on talk shows in his role as president of the South American Confederation of Farm Workers and used the forums to defend the use of illegal drugs. One of these interviews—with Charlie Rose on PBS—became notorious.

Tulippa claimed it was a disgraceful form of colonialism that the United States fought against the use of cocaine, heroin, and marijuana all over the world. The South American workers depended on the drug crops to keep themselves alive. Who could blame a man whose poverty entered his dreams to purchase a few hours of relief by using drugs? It was an inhumane judgment. And what about tobacco and alcohol? They did much more damage.

At this, fifty followers in the studio, Panama hats in laps, applauded vigorously. When Charlie Rose asked about the damage drugs wreaked, Tulippa was especially sincere. His organization was pouring huge sums of money into research to modify drugs so that they would not be harmful; in short, they would be prescription drugs. The programs would be run by reputable doctors rather than pawns of the American Medical Association, who were so unreasonably antinarcotics and lived in dread of the United States Drug Enforcement Agency. No, narcotics could be the next great blessing for humanity. The fifty yellow Panama hats went flying into the air.

Meanwhile, the Corleonesi *cosca* chief, Michael Grazziella, made an altogether different entry into the United States. He slipped in unobtrusively, with only two bodyguards. He was a thin and scrawny man with a faunlike head and a knife scar across his mouth. He walked with a cane, for a bullet had shattered his leg when he was a young Palermo *picciotto*. He had a reputation for diabolical cunning—and it was said that he had planned the murder of the two greatest anti-Mafia magistrates in Sicily.

Grazziella stayed at Portella's estate as his guest. He had no qualms about his own safety, for Portella's entire drug-dealing business depended on him.

The conference had been arranged to plan a strategy to control the Aprile banks. This was of the utmost importance in order to launder the billions of dollars of black-market money from drugs and also to acquire power in the financial world of New York. And for Inzio Tulippa, it was crucial not only to launder his drug money but to finance his nuclear arsenal. It would also make his role as the Vaccinator safer.

They all met at the Peruvian consulate, which was security-proof in addition to supplying the cloak of diplomatic immunity. The consul general, Marriano Rubio, was a generous host. Since he received a cut of all their revenues and he would head their legitimate interests in the States, he was full of goodwill.

Gathered around the small oval table, they made an interesting scene.

Grazziella looked like an undertaker in his black shiny suit, white shirt, and thin black tie, for he was still in mourning for his mother, who had died six months before. He spoke in a low, doleful voice with a thick accent, but he was clearly understood. He seemed such a shy, polite man to have been responsible for the death of a hundred Sicilian law-enforcement officials.

Timmona Portella, the only one of the four whose native tongue was English, spoke in a loud bellow, as if all the others were deaf. His attire too seemed to shout: He wore a gray suit and lime green shirt with a shiny blue silk tie. The perfectly tailored jacket would have hidden his huge belly if it was not unbuttoned to show blue suspenders.

Inzio Tulippa looked classically South American, with a white, loose-draped silk shirt and scarlet handkerchief around his neck. He carried his yellow Panama hat in his hand reverently. He spoke a lilting accented English, and his voice had the charm of a nightingale. But today he had a forbidding frown on his sharp Indian face; he was a man not pleased with the world.

Marriano Rubio was the only man who seemed pleased. His affability charmed them all. His voice was well bred in the English style, and he was dressed in a style he called *en pantoufle:* pajamas of green silk and a bathrobe of a darker forest green. He wore soft brown slippers lined with white wool fur. After all, it was his building and he could relax.

Tulippa opened the discussion, speaking directly to Portella with a deadly politeness. "Timmona, my friend," he said, "I paid handsomely to get the Don out of the way, and we still do not own the banks. This after waiting almost a year."

The consul general spoke in his lubricating, calming way. "My dear Inzio," he said, "I tried to buy the banks. Portella tried to buy the banks. But we have an obstacle we did not foresee. This Astorre Viola, the Don's nephew. He has been left in control, and he refuses to sell."

"So?" Inzio said. "Why is he still alive?"

Portella laughed, a huge bellow. "Because he is not so easy to kill," he said. "I put a four-man surveillance team on his house, and they disappeared. Now I don't know where the hell he is, and he has a cloud of bodyguards whenever he moves."

"Nobody is that hard to kill," Tulippa said, the charming lilt of his voice delivering the words like a lyric to a popular song.

Grazziella spoke for the first time. "We knew
Astorre back in Sicily, years ago. He is a very
lucky man, but then, he is also extremely Qualified. We shot him in Sicily and thought him dead.
If we strike again, we must be sure. He is a
dangerous man."

Tulippa said to Portella, "You claim you have
an FBI man on the payroll? Use him, for the sake
of God."

"He's not that bent," Portella said. "The FBI is
classier than the NYPD. They would never do a
straight-out hit job."

"OK," Tulippa said. "So we snatch one of the
Don's kids and use them to bargain with Astorre.
Marriano, you know his daughter." He winked.
"You can set her up."

Rubio did not warm to this proposal. He
puffed on his thin after-breakfast cigar and then
said stormily, without courtesy, "No." He paused.
"I'm fond of the girl. I won't put her through
anything like that. I veto any of you doing so."

At this the other men raised their eyebrows.
The consul general was inferior to them in actual
power. He saw their reaction and smiled at them,
again becoming his affable self.

"I know I have this weakness. I fall in love. But
indulge me. I'm on strong and correct political
ground. Inzio, I know kidnapping is your métier,
but it doesn't really work in America. Especially a

woman. Now, if you take one of the brothers and make a quick deal with Astorre, you have a chance."

"Not Valerius," Portella said. "He is army intelligence and has CIA friends. We don't want to bring down that load of shit."

"Then it will have to be Marcantonio," the consul general said. "I can do a deal with Astorre."

"Make a bigger offer for the banks," Grazziella said softly. "Avoid violence. Believe me, I've been through this kind of thing. I've used guns instead of money, and it's always cost me more."

They looked at him with astonishment. Grazziella had a fearsome reputation for violence.

"Michael," the consul general said, "you're talking about billions of dollars. And Astorre still won't sell."

Grazziella shrugged. "If we must take action, so be it. But be very careful. If you can get him out in the open during negotiations, then we can get rid of him."

Tulippa gave them all a huge grin. "That's what I like to hear. And Marriano," he said, "don't keep falling in love. That is a very dangerous vice."

MARRIANO RUBIO finally persuaded Nicole and her brothers to sit down with his syndicate and discuss the sale of the banks. Of course, Astorre Viola also had to be present, though Nicole could not guarantee this.

Before the meeting Astorre briefed Nicole and her brothers on what to say and exactly how to behave. They understood his strategy: that the syndicate was to think he alone was their opponent.

This meeting was held in a conference room of the Peruvian consulate. There were no caterers, but a buffet had been prepared and Rubio himself poured their wine. Due to scheduling differences, the meeting took place at ten in the evening.

Rubio made the introductions and led the meeting. He handed Nicole a folder. "This is the proposition in detail. But to put it very briefly, we offer fifty percent over the market price. Though we will have complete control, the Aprile interest will receive ten percent of our profits over the next twenty years. You can all be rich and enjoy your leisure without the terrible strains that such a business life entails."

They waited while Nicole glanced briefly through the papers. Finally she looked up and said, "This is impressive, but tell me why such a generous offer?"

Rubio smiled at her fondly. "Synergy," he said. "All business now is synergy; as with computers and aviation, books and publishing, music and drugs, sports and TV. All synergy. With the Aprile banks, we will have a synergy in international finance, we will control the building of cities, the election of governments. This syndicate is global and we need your banks, so our offer is generous."

Nicole spoke to the other members of the syndicate. "And you gentlemen are all equal partners?"

Tulippa was quite taken with Nicole's dark good looks and stern speech, so he was at his most charming when he answered. "We are legally equal in this purchase, but let me assure you I consider it an honor to be in association with the Aprile name. No one admired your father more."

Valerius, stone-faced, spoke out coolly, directly to Tulippa. "Don't misunderstand me, I want to sell. But I prefer an outright sale without the percentage. On a personal level, I want to be completely out of this thing."

"But you are willing to sell?" Tulippa asked.

"Certainly," Valerius said. "I want to wash my hands of it."

Portella started to speak, but Rubio cut him off.

"Marcantonio," he said, "how do you feel about our offer? Does it appeal to you?"

Marcantonio said in a resigned voice, "I'm with Val. Let's make the deal without the percentages. Then we can all say good-bye and good luck."

"Fine, we can make the deal that way," Rubio said.

Nicole said coolly, "But then of course you have to increase the premium. Can you handle that?"

Tulippa said, "No problem," and gave her a dazzling smile.

Grazziella, his face concerned, his voice polite, asked, "And what about our dear friend Astorre Viola? Does he agree?"

Astorre gave an embarrassed laugh. "You know I've come to like the banking business. And Don Aprile made me promise I would never sell. I hate to go against my whole family here, but I have to say no. And I control a majority of voting stock."

"But the Don's children have an interest," the consul general said. "They could sue in a court of law."

Astorre laughed aloud.

Nicole said tightly, "We would never do that."

Valerius smiled sourly, and Marcantonio seemed to find the idea hilarious.

Portella muttered, "The hell with this," and started to rise to leave.

Astorre said in a voice of conciliation, "Be patient. I may get bored with being a banker. In a few months we can meet again."

"Certainly," Rubio said. "But we may not be able to hold the financial package together for that long. You may get a lower price."

There was no shaking of hands when they parted.

AFTER THE APRILES left with Astorre, Michael Grazziella said to his colleagues, "He is just buying time. He will never sell."

Tulippa sighed, "Such a simpatico man. We could become good friends. Maybe I should invite him to my plantation in Costa Rica. I could show him the best time of his life."

The others laughed. Portella said coarsely, "He's not going on a honeymoon with you, Inzio. I have to take care of him up here."

"With better success than before, I hope," Tulippa said.

"I underestimated him," Portella said. "How could I tell? A guy who sings at weddings? I did the job on the Don right. No complaints there."

The consul general, his handsome face beaming in appreciation, said, "A magnificent job,

Timmona. We have every confidence in you. But this new job should be done as soon as possible."

WHEN THEY LEFT the meeting, the Aprile family and Astorre went for a late supper to the Partinico restaurant, which had private dining rooms and was owned by an old friend of the Don's.

"I think you all did very well," Astorre told them. "You convinced them you were against me."

"We are against you," Val said.

"Why do we have to play this game?" Nicole said. "I really don't like it."

"These guys may be involved in your father's death," Astorre said. "I don't want them to think they can get anyplace by hurting any of you."

"And you're confident you can handle anything they throw at you," Marcantonio said.

"No, no," Astorre protested. "But I can go into hiding without ruining my life. Hell, I'll go to the Dakotas and they'll never find me." His smile was so broad and convincing that he would have fooled anyone but the children of Don Aprile. "Now," he said. "Let me know if they contact any of you directly."

"I've gotten a lot of calls from Detective Di Benedetto," Valerius said.

Astorre was surprised. "What the hell is he calling you for?"

Valerius smiled at him. "When I was in field intelligence, we got what was labeled 'What do you know' calls. Somebody wanted to give you information or help in some deal. What they really wanted was information on how your investigation was doing. So Di Benedetto calls me as a courtesy to keep me up to date on his case. Then he pumps me for info on you, Astorre. He has a great interest in you."

"That's very flattering," Astorre said with a grin. "He must have heard me sing someplace."

"No chance," Marcantonio said dryly. "Di Benedetto has been calling me too. He says he has an idea for a cop series. There's always room for another cop show on TV, so I've been encouraging him. But the stuff he's sent me is just bullshit. He's not serious. He just wants to keep track of us."

"Good," Astorre said.

"Astorre, you want them to target you instead of us?" Nicole said. "Isn't that too dangerous? That Grazziella guy gives me the creeps."

"Oh, I know about him," Astorre said. "He's a very reasonable man. And your consul general is a true diplomat; he can control Tulippa. The only one I have to worry about right now is Portella. The guy is just dumb enough to start real trouble." He said all this as though it were just an everyday business dispute.

"But how long does this go on?" Nicole asked.

"Give me another few months," Astorre told her. "I promise that we will all be in agreement by then."

Valerius gave him a disdainful look. "Astorre, you were always an optimist. If you were an intelligence officer under my command, I'd transfer you to the infantry just to wake you up."

It was not a happy dinner. Nicole kept studying Astorre as if she were trying to learn some secret. Valerius obviously had no confidence in Astorre, and Marcantonio was reserved. Finally Astorre raised a glass of wine and said cheerfully, "You are a gloomy crew, but I don't care. This is going to be a lot of fun. Here's to your father."

"The great Don Aprile," Nicole said sourly.

Astorre smiled at her and said, "Yes, to the great Don."

ASTORRE ALWAYS RODE in the late afternoon. It relaxed him, gave him a good appetite for dinner. If he was courting a woman, he always made her ride with him. If the woman couldn't ride, he gave her lessons. And if she didn't like horses, he would cease to pursue her.

He had built a special riding trail on his estate

that led through the forest. He enjoyed the chattering of the birds, the rustle of small animals, the occasional siting of a deer. But most of all he enjoyed dressing up for riding. The bright red jacket, the brown riding boots, the whip in his hand that he never used. The black suede hunting cap. He smiled at himself in the mirror, fancying himself an English lord of the manor.

He went down to the stables, where he kept six horses, and was pleased to see that the trainer, Aldo Monza, had already fitted out one of his stallions. He mounted and slowly cantered onto the forest trail. Picking up speed, he rode through a tattered canopy of red and gold leaves that made a lace curtain against the sinking sun. Only slender sheaves of gold lit the trail. The horse's hooves kicked up the smell of decaying leaves. He saw the fragrant pile of wheaty manure and spurred his horse past it, then rode onto a split in the trail, which gave him a different route to circle home. The gold on the trail disappeared.

He reined in the horse. At that moment two men appeared before him. They were dressed in the floppy clothes of farm laborers. But they wore masks, and metal gleamed silver in their hands. Astorre spurred his horse and put his head down along its flank. The forest filled with light and the sound of exploding bullets. The men were very close, and Astorre felt the bullets hit him in the side and back. The horse panicked into a wild gallop as Astorre concentrated on keeping his seat. He galloped on down the trail, and then two other men appeared. They were not masked or armed. He lost consciousness and slid off the horse and into their arms.

WITHIN AN HOUR Kurt Cilke received a report from the surveillance team that had rescued Astorre Viola. What really surprised him was that Astorre, beneath all his foppish dress, wore a bulletproof vest that covered his torso the length of his red riding jacket. And not just your ordinary Kevlar, but one specially handmade. Now, what the hell was a guy like Astorre doing wearing armor? A macaroni importer, a club singer, a flaky horse rider. Sure, the impact of the bullets had stunned him, but they had not penetrated. Astorre was already out of the hospital.

Cilke started writing a memo to have Astorre's life investigated from childhood on. The man might be the key to everything. But he was sure of one thing: He knew who had attempted to murder Astorre Viola.

ASTORRE MET with his cousins at Valerius's home. He told them of the attack, how he had been shot. "I've asked you for help," he said. "And you refused and I understood. But now I think you should reconsider. There is some sort of a threat to all of you. I think it could be solved by selling off the banks. That would be a win-win situation. Everybody gets what they want. Or we can go for a win-lose situation. We keep the banks and fight off and destroy our enemies, whoever they are. Then there is the lose-lose situation, which we must be careful not to fall into. That we fight our enemies and win but the government gets us anyway."

"That's an easy choice," Valerius said. "Just sell the banks. The win-win."

Marcantonio said, "We're not Sicilians; we don't want to throw everything away for the sake of vengeance."

"We sell the banks and we're throwing away our future," Nicole said calmly. "Marc, someday you'd like your own network. Val, with big political donations you could become an ambassador or a secretary of defense. Astorre, you could sing with the Rolling Stones." She smiled at him. "OK, that's a little far-fetched," she said, changing her tone. "Forget the jokes. Is killing our father nothing to us? Do we reward them for murder? I think we should help Astorre as much as we can."

"Do you know what you're saying?" Valerius said.

"Yes," Nicole said quietly.

Astorre said to them gently, "Your father taught me that you can't let other men impose their will on you or life's not worth living. Val, that's what war is, right?"

"War is a lose-lose decision," Nicole said sharply.

Valerius showed his irritation. "No matter what the liberals say, war is a win–lose situation. You are much better off to win a war. Losing is an unthinkable horror."

"Your father had a past," Astorre said. "That past now has to be reckoned with by all of us. So now I ask you for your help again. Remember, I am under your father's orders, and my job is to protect the family, which means holding on to the banks."

Valerius said, "I'll have some information for you within a month."

Astorre said, "Marc?"

Marcantonio said, "I'll get to work on that program right away. Let's say two months, three."

Astorre looked at Nicole. "Nicole, have you completed the analysis of the FBI file on your father?"

"No, not yet." She seemed upset. "Shouldn't we get Cilke's help on this?"

Astorre smiled. "Cilke is one of my suspects,"

he said. "When I have all the information we can decide what to do."

IN A MONTH Valerius came through with some information—unexpected, unwelcome. Through his CIA contacts, he had learned the truth about Inzio Tulippa. He had contacts in Sicily, Turkey, India, Pakistan, Colombia, and other Latin American countries. He even had a relationship with the Corleonesi in Sicily and was more than their equal.

According to Valerius, it was Tulippa who was financing certain nuclear-research labs in South America. Tulippa who was desperately trying to set up a huge fund in America to buy equipment and material. Who, in his dreams of grandeur, wanted to possess an awful weapon of defense against the authorities if worse ever came to worst. It therefore followed that Timmona Portella was a front for Tulippa. This was happy news for Astorre. This was another player in the game, another front on which to have to fight.

"Is what Tulippa plans possible?" Astorre asked.

"He certainly thinks it is," Valerius said. "And he has the protection of government officials where he's located the labs."

"Thanks, Val," Astorre said, patting his cousin on the shoulder affectionately.

"Sure," Valerius said. "But that's all the help you get from me."

IT TOOK SIX WEEKS for Marcantonio to research the network profile on Kurt Cilke. A huge file of information was given to Astorre by Marcantonio, hand to hand. Astorre kept it for twenty-four hours and returned it.

It was only Nicole who worried him. She'd lent him a copy of the FBI file on Don Aprile, but there was a whole section that was completely blacked out. When he questioned her about this she said, "That's how I received it."

Astorre had studied the document carefully. The blacked-out section seemed to be about the period of time when he was only two years old. "That's OK," he told Nicole. "It's too long ago to be important."

Now Astorre could no longer be put off. He had enough information to begin his war.

NICOLE HAD BEEN dazzled by Marriano Rubio and his courtship. She had never really recovered from Astorre's betrayal of her when she was a young girl, when he had elected to obey her father. Though she had had some prudent short affairs with powerful men, she knew that men would always conspire against women.

But Rubio seemed an exception. He never got angry with her when her schedule interfered with their plans to be together. He understood her career came first. And he never indulged in that ridiculous, insulting emotion of many men who thought their jealousy was proof of true love.

It helped that he was generous in his gifts; it was even more important that she found him interesting and enjoyed listening to him talk about literature and the theater. But his greatest virtue was that he was an enthusiastic lover, expert in bed, and aside from that did not take up too much of her time.

ONE EVENING Rubio took Nicole to dinner at Le Cirque with some of his friends: a world-famous South American novelist who charmed Nicole with his sly wit and extravagant ghost stories; a renowned opera singer who at every dish hummed an aria of delight and ate as though he were going to the electric chair; and a conservative columnist, the reigning oracle on world affairs for *The New York Times* who took great pride in being hated by liberals and conservatives alike.

After dinner Rubio took Nicole home to his opulent apartment in the Peruvian consulate. There he made love to her passionately, both physically and with whispered words. Afterward, he lifted her naked from his bed and danced with her while reciting poetry in Spanish. Nicole had a wonderful time. Especially when they were quiet and he poured them champagne and said sincerely, "I do love you." His magnificent nose and brow shone with truthfulness. How brazen men were. Nicole felt a quiet satisfaction that she had betrayed him. Her father would have been proud of her. She had acted in a truly Mafioso fashion.

AS HEAD of the New York FBI office, Kurt Cilke had far more important cases than the murder of Don Raymonde Aprile. One was the broad investigation of six giant corporations that conspired illegally to ship banned machinery, including computer technology, to Red China. Another was the conspiracy of the major tobacco companies perjuring themselves before a congressional investigating committee. The third was the emigration of middle-level scientists to South American countries such as Brazil, Peru, and Colombia. The director wanted to be briefed on these cases.

On the flight down to Washington, Boxton said, "We have the tobacco guys nailed; we have the China shipments nailed—internal documents, informers saving their asses. The only thing we don't have is those scientists. But I guess you become a deputy director after this. They can't deny your record."

"That's up to the director," Cilke said. He knew why the scientists were down in South America, but he didn't correct Boxton.

In the Hoover Building, Boxton was barred from the meeting.

IT WAS ELEVEN MONTHS after the killing of Don Aprile. Cilke had prepared all his notes. The Aprile case was dead, but he had better news on even more important cases. And this time there was a real chance that he would be offered one of the key deputy director's jobs in the Bureau. He had made his mark with good work, and he had put in his time.

The director was a tall, elegant man whose descendants came to America on the *Mayflower*. He was extremely wealthy in his own right and had entered politics as a public duty. And he had laid down strict rules at the beginning of his tenure. "No hanky-panky," he said good-humoredly in his Yankee twang. "By the book.

No loopholes in the Bill of Rights. An FBI agent is always courteous, always fair. He is always correct in his private life." Any bit of scandal—wife beating, drunkenness, too close a relationship with a local police official, any third-degree antics—and you were out on your ass even if your uncle was a senator. These had been the rules for the last ten years. Also, if you got too much press, even good, you were on your way to surveillance of igloos in Alaska.

The director invited Cilke to sit down in an extremely uncomfortable chair on the other side of his massive oak desk.

"Agent Cilke," he said, "I called you down for several reasons. Number one: I have placed in your personal file a special commendation for your work against the Mafia in New York. Due to you we have broken their backs. I congratulate you." He leaned over to shake Cilke's hand. "We don't make it public now because the Bureau takes credit for its individual achievements. And also, it might place you in some danger."

"Only from some crazy," Cilke said. "The criminal organizations understand they cannot harm an agent."

"You're implying that the Bureau carries out personal vendettas," the director said.

"Oh, no," Cilke said. "It's just that we would pay more attention."

The director let that pass. There were boundaries. Virtue always had to tread a very thin line. "It's not fair to keep you on the hook," the director said. "I've decided not to appoint you one of my deputies here in Washington. Not at the present time. For these reasons. You are enormously street-smart, and there is still work to be done in the field. The Mafia, for lack of a better word, is still operational. Number two: Officially you have an informant whose name you refuse to divulge even to the top supervising personnel of the Bureau. Unofficially, you have told us. That is classified AFLAX. So you're OK, unofficially. Third: Your relationship with a certain New York chief of detectives is too personal."

The director and Cilke had other items on their meeting agenda. "And how is our operation 'Omerta'?" the director asked. "We must be very careful that we have legal clearance on all our operations."

"Of course," Cilke said, straight-faced. The director knew damn well that corners would have to be cut. "We've had a few obstacles. Raymonde Aprile refused to cooperate with us. But of course that obstacle no longer exists."

"Mr. Aprile was very conveniently killed," the director said sardonically. "I won't insult you by asking if you had any prior knowledge. Your friend Portella, perhaps?"

"We don't know," Cilke said. "Italians never go to authorities. We just have to look for dead bodies turning up. Now, I approached Astorre Viola as we discussed. He signed the confidentiality papers but refused to cooperate. He won't do business with Portella, and he won't sell the banks."

"So what do we do now?" the director asked. "You know how important this is. If we can indict the banker under RICO, we can get the banks for the government. And that ten billion would go to fight crime. It would be an enormous coup for the Bureau. And then we can put an end to your association with Portella. He's outlived his usefulness. Kurt, we are in a very delicate situation. Only my deputies and myself know of your cooperation with Portella. That you receive payments from him, that he thinks of you as his confederate. Your life could be in danger."

"He wouldn't dare harm a federal agent," Cilke said. "He's crazy, but he's not that crazy."

"Well, Portella has to go down in this operation," the director said. "What are your plans?"

"This guy Astorre Viola is not the innocent everyone says he is," Cilke said. "I'm having his past checked out. Meanwhile, I'm going to ask Aprile's children to override him. But I worry, can we make RICO stick all the way back ten years for something they do now?"

"That's the job of our attorney general," the director said. "We just have to get our foot in the door, and then a thousand lawyers will go all the way back. We're bound to come up with something the courts can uphold."

"About my secret Cayman account that Portella puts money into," Cilke said. "I think you should draw some out so that he thinks I'm spending it."

"I'll arrange that," the director said. "I must say, your Timmona Portella is not frugal."

"He really believes I sold out," Cilke said, smiling.

"Be careful," the director said. "Don't give them the grounds that would make you a true confederate, an accomplice to a crime."

"I understand," Cilke said. And thought, easier said than done.

"And don't take unnecessary risks," the director said. "Remember, drug people in South America and Sicily are linked with Portella, and they are reckless fellows."

"Shall I keep you advised day by day orally or in writing?" Cilke asked.

"Neither," the director said. "I have absolute confidence in your integrity. And besides, I don't want to have to lie to some congressional committee. To become one of my deputies, you will have to clear these things up." He waited expectantly.

Cilke never dared even to think his real thoughts in the presence of the director, as if the man could read his mind. But still, the rebellion flashed. Who the fuck did the director think he was, the American Civil Liberties Union? With his memos to emphasize that the Mafia was not Italian, Muslims were not terrorists, that blacks were not the criminal class. Who the fuck did he think committed the street crimes?

But Cilke said quietly, "Sir, if you want my resignation, I've built up enough time for an early retirement."

"No," the director said. "Answer my question. Can you clean up your relationships?"

"I have given the names of all the informants to the Bureau," Cilke said. "As for cutting corners, that's a matter of interpretation. As for being friends with the local police force, that's PR for the Bureau."

"Your results speak for your work," the director said. "Let's try another year. Let's go on." He paused for a long moment and sighed. Then he asked almost impatiently, "Have we got enough on the tobacco-company executives for perjury in your judgment?"

"Easily," Cilke said, and wondered why the director even asked. He had all the files.

"But it could be their personal beliefs," the director said. "We have polls that show that half the American people agree with them."

"That's not relevant to the case," Cilke said. "The people in the poll did not commit perjury in their testimony to Congress. We have tapes and internal documents that prove the tobacco executives knowingly lied. They conspired."

"You're right," the director said with a sigh. "But the attorney general has made a deal. No criminal indictments, no prison time. They will pay fines of hundreds of billions of dollars. So close that investigation. It's out of our hands."

"Fine, sir," Cilke said. "I can always use the extra manpower on other things."

"Good for you," the director said. "I'll make you even happier. On that shipping of illegal technology to China, that's very serious business."

"There's no option," Cilke said. "Those companies deliberately broke a federal law for financial gain and breached the security of the United States. The heads of those companies conspired."

"We do have the goods on them," the director said, "but you know conspiracy is a catchall. Everybody conspires. But that's another case you can close and save the manpower."

Cilke said incredulously, "Sir, are you saying a deal has been made on that?"

The director leaned back in his chair and frowned at Cilke's implied insolence, but he made allowances. "Cilke, you are the best field man in the Bureau. But you have no political sense. Now listen to me, and never forget this: You cannot send six billionaires to prison. Not in a democracy."

"And that's it?" Cilke asked.

"The financial sanctions will be very heavy," the director said. "Now, on to other things, one very confidential. We're going to exchange a federal prisoner for one of our informers who is being held hostage in Colombia, a very valuable asset in our war on the drug trade. This is a case you're familiar with." He referred to a case four years ago in which a drug dealer took five hostages, a woman and four children. He killed them and also killed a Bureau agent. He was given life without parole. "I remember that you were adamant on the death penalty," the director said. "Now we are going to let him go, and I know you won't be too happy. Remember, all this is secret, but the papers will probably dig it up and there will be an enormous fuss. You and your office will never comment. Is that understood?"

Cilke said, "We can't let anyone kill our agents and get away with it."

"That attitude is not acceptable in a federal officer," the director said.

Cilke tried not to show his outrage. "Then all our agents will be endangered," Cilke said. "That's how it is on the streets. The agent was killed trying to save the hostages. It was a cold-blooded execution. Setting the killer free is an insult to the life of that agent."

"There can be no vendetta mentality in the Bureau," the director said. "Otherwise we're no better than they are. Now, what do you have about those scientists who've emigrated?"

At that moment Cilke realized he could no longer trust the director. "Nothing new," he lied. He had decided from now on he would not be part of the agency's political compromises. He would play a lone hand.

"Well, now you have a lot of manpower, so work on it," the director said. "And after you nail Timmona Portella, I'd like to bring you up here as one of my deputies."

"Thank you," Cilke said. "But I've decided after I clear up Portella, I'm taking my retirement."

The director gave a deep sigh. "Reconsider it. I know how all this deal making must distress you.

But remember this: The Bureau is not only responsible for protecting society against law-breakers, but we must also take only the actions that, in the long run, benefit our society as a whole."

"I remember that from school," Cilke said. "The end justifies the means."

The director shrugged. "Sometimes. Anyway, reconsider your retirement. I'm putting a letter of recommendation in your file. Whether you stay or go, you will receive a medal from the president of the United States."

"Thank you, sir," Cilke said. The director shook his hand and escorted him to the door. But he had one final question. "What happened to that Aprile case? It's been months and it seems nothing has been done."

"It's NYPD, not ours," Cilke said. "Of course, I looked into it. So far no motive. No clues. I would think there's no chance of it being solved."

THAT NIGHT Cilke had dinner with Bill Boxton.

"Good news," Cilke told him. "The tobacco and the China machine cases are closed. The attorney general is going after financial sanctions, not criminal. That frees a lot of manpower."

"No shit," Boxton said. "I always thought the director was straight. A square shooter. Will he resign?"

"There are square shooters and there are square shooters with little nicks on the edges," Cilke said.

"Anything else?" Boxton asked.

"When I bring Portella down, I get to be the director's deputy. Guaranteed. But by then I'll be retired."

"Yeah," Boxton said. "Put in a word for me for that job."

"No chance. The director knows you use four-letter words." He laughed.

"Shit," Boxton said, in mock disappointment. "Or is it *fuck*?"

THE NEXT NIGHT Cilke walked home from the railroad station. Georgette and Vanessa were in Florida visiting Georgette's parents for a week, and he hated taking a taxi. He was surprised not to hear the dogs barking when he walked up the driveway. He called out for them but nothing happened. They must have wandered off into the neighborhood or the nearby woods.

He missed his family, especially at mealtimes. He had eaten dinner alone or with other agents in too many cities all over America, always alert to any kind of danger. He prepared a simple meal for himself as his wife had taught him to do— a vegetable, a green salad, and a small steak. No coffee, but a brandy in a small thimble of a glass. Then he went upstairs to shower and call his wife before reading himself to sleep. He loved books, and he was always made unhappy when the FBI was portrayed as heavy villains in detective novels. What the hell did they know?

When he opened the bedroom door he could smell the blood instantly and his whole brain fell into a chaotic jumble; all the hidden fears of his life came rushing in on him.

The two German shepherds lay on his bed. Their brown and white fur was mottled red, their legs tied together, their muzzles wrapped in gauze. Their hearts had been cut out and rested on their bellies.

With great effort, his mind came together. Instinctively, he called his wife to make sure she was OK. He told her nothing. Then he called the FBI duty officer for a special forensic team and a cleanup squad. They would have to get rid of all the bedclothes, the mattress, the rug. He did not notify the local authorities.

Six hours later the FBI teams had left and he wrote a report to the director. He poured himself a regular-sized glass of brandy and tried to analyze the situation.

For a moment he considered lying to Georgette, concocting a story about the dogs running away. But there were the missing rug and bedsheets to be explained. And besides, it wouldn't be fair to her. She had a choice to make. More than anything, she would never forgive him if he lied. He would have to tell her the truth.

THE NEXT DAY Cilke flew first to Washington to confer with the director and then down to Florida, where his wife and daughter were vacationing with his in-laws.

There, after having lunch with them, he took Georgette for a walk along the beach. As they watched the glimmering blue water he told her about the dogs being killed, that it was an old Sicilian Mafia warning used to intimidate.

"According to the papers you got rid of the Mafia in this country," Georgette said musingly.

"More or less," Cilke said. "We have a few of the drug organizations left, and I'm pretty sure who did this."

"Our poor dogs," Georgette said. "How can people be so cruel? Have you talked to the director?"

Cilke felt a surge of irritation that she was so concerned about the dogs. "The director gave me three options," he said. "That I resign from the Bureau and relocate. I refused that option. The second was that I relocate my family under Bureau protection until this case is over. The third is that you remain in the house as if nothing has happened. We would have a twenty-four-hour security team guarding us. A woman agent would live in the house with you, and you and Vanessa will be accompanied by two bodyguards wherever you go. There will be security posts set up around the house with the latest alarm equipment. What do you think? In six months this will all be over."

"You think it's a bluff," Georgette said.

"Yes. They don't dare harm a federal agent or his family. It would be suicide for them."

Georgette gazed out at the calm blue water of the bay. Her hand clasped his more tightly.

"I'll stay," she said. "I'd miss you too much, and I know you won't leave this case. How can you be certain you'll finish in six months?"

"I'm certain," Cilke said.

Georgette shook her head. "I don't like you being so certain. Please don't do anything awful. And I want one promise. When this case is over, you'll retire from the Bureau. Start your own law practice or teach. I can't live this way the rest of my life." She was in deadly earnest.

The phrase that stuck in Cilke's head was that she would miss him too much. And as he so often did, he wondered how a woman like her could possibly love a man like him. But he had always known that someday she would make this demand. He sighed and said, "I promise."

They continued their walk along the beach and then sat in a little green park that protected them against the sun. A cool breeze from the bay ruffled his wife's hair, making her look very young and happy. Cilke knew he could never break his promise to her. And he was even proud of her cunning in extracting his promise at the exact proper moment, when she risked her life to stay on his side. After all, who would want to be loved by an unintelligent woman? At the same time Agent Cilke knew his wife would be horrified, humiliated by what he was thinking. Her cunning was probably innocent. Who was he to judge it? She had never judged him, never suspected his own not-so-innocent cunning.

CHAPTER 6

FRANKY AND STACE STURZO owned a huge sporting-goods store in L.A. and a house in Santa Monica that was only five minutes from the Malibu beach. Both of them had been married once, but their marriages didn't take, so now they lived together.

They never told any of their friends they were twins, although they had the same easygoing confidence and extraordinary athletic suppleness. Franky was the more charming and temperamental. Stace was the more levelheaded, just a little stolid, but they were both noted for their amiability.

They belonged to one of the large classy gyms that dotted L.A., a gym filled with digital body-building machines and wide-screen wall TV's to watch while working out. It had a basketball court, a swimming pool, and even a boxing ring. Its staff of trainers were good-looking, sculptured men and pretty, well-toned women. The brothers used the gym to work out and also to meet women who trained there. It was a great hunting ground for men like them, surrounded by hopeful actresses trying to keep their bodies beautiful and bored, neglected wives of high-powered movie people.

But mostly Franky and Stace enjoyed pickup basketball games. Good players came to the gym—sometimes even a reserve on the L.A. Lakers. Franky and Stace had played against him and felt they had held their own. It brought back fond memories of when they had been high school all-stars. But they had no illusions that in a real game they would have been so fortunate. They had played all out, and the Laker guy had just been having a good time.

In the gym's health-food restaurant, they struck up friendships with the female trainers and gym members and even sometimes a celebrity. They always had a good time, but it was a small part of their lives. Franky coached the local grade-school basketball team, a job he took very seriously. He always hoped to discover a superstar in the making, and he radiated a stern amiability that made the kids love him. He had a favorite coaching tactic. "OK," he would say, "you're twenty points down, it's the last quarter. You come out and score the first ten points. Now you got them where you want them—you can win. It's just nerve and confidence. You can always win. You're ten points down, then five, then you're even. And you've got them!"

Of course, it never worked. The kids were not developed enough physically or tough enough mentally. They were just kids. But Franky knew the really talented ones would never forget the lesson and that it would help them later on.

Stace concentrated on running the store, and he made the final decision on which hit jobs they would take. There had to be minimum risk and maximum price. Stace believed in percentages all the way and also had a gloomy temperament. What the brothers had going for them was that they rarely disagreed on anything. They had the same tastes and they were almost always evenly matched in physical skills. They sometimes sparred against each other in the boxing ring or played each other one-on-one on the basketball court. This cemented their relationship. They trusted each other absolutely.

They were now forty-three years old and their lives suited them, but they often talked about getting married again and having families. Franky kept a mistress in San Francisco, and Stace had a girlfriend in Vegas, a showgirl. Both women had shown no inclination for marriage, and the brothers felt they were just treading water, hoping for someone to show up.

Since they were so genial, they made friends
easily and had a busy social life. Still, they spent
the year after killing the Don with some appre-
hension. A man like the Don could not be killed
without some danger.

Around November, Stace made the necessary
call to Heskow about picking up the second five
hundred grand of the payment. The phone call
was brief and seemingly ambiguous.

"Hi," Stace said. "We're coming in about a
month from now. Everything OK?"

Heskow seemed glad to hear from him. "Everything's perfect," he said. "Everything's ready. Could
you be more specific on time? I don't want you
coming when I'm out of town somewhere."

Stace laughed and said casually, "We'll find you.
OK? Figure a month." Then he hung up.

The money pickup in a deal like this always
had an element of danger. Sometimes people
hated to pay up for something already done. That
happened in every business. Then sometimes
people had delusions of grandeur. They thought
they were as good as the professionals. The danger
was minimal with Heskow—he had always been
a reliable broker. But the Don's case was special,
as was the money. So they didn't want Heskow to
have a fix on their plans.

The brothers had taken up tennis the past year,
but it was the one sport that defeated them. They

were so athletically gifted that they could not accept this defeat, though it was explained to them that tennis was a sport where you had to acquire the strokes early in life by instruction, that it really depended on certain mechanics, like learning a language. So they had m ade arrangements to stay for three weeks at a tennis ranch in Scottsdale, Arizona, for an introductory course. From there they would travel to New York to meet Heskow. Of course, during these weeks at the tennis ranch they could pass some of their evenings in Vegas, which was less than an hour from Scottsdale by plane.

THE TENNIS RANCH was superluxurious. Franky and Stace were given a two-bedroom adobe cottage with air-conditioning, an Indian-motif dining room, a balconied living room, and a small kitchen. They had a superb view of the mountains. There was a built-in bar, a big refrigerator, and a huge TV.

But the three weeks started off on a sour note. One of the instructors gave Franky a hard time. Franky was easily the best in the group of beginners, and he was especially proud of his serve, which was completely unorthodox and wild. But the instructor, a man named Leslie, seemed particularly irritated by it.

One morning Franky hit the ball to his opponent, who couldn't come near it, and he said
proudly to Leslie, "That's an ace, right?"

"No," Leslie said coldly. "That's a foot fault.
Your toe went over the serving line. Try again,
with a proper serve. The one you have will more
often be out than in."

Franky hit another serve, fast and accurate.
"Ace, right?" he said.

"That is a foot fault," Leslie said slowly. "And that
serve is a bullshit serve. Just get the ball in. You're a
very decent player for a hacker. Play the point."

Franky was annoyed but controlled himself.
"Match me up with somebody who's not a
hacker," he said. "Let's see how I do." He paused.
"How about you?"

Leslie looked at him with disgust. "I don't play
matches with hackers," he said. He pointed to a
young woman in her late twenties or early thir-
ties. "Rosie?" he said. "Give Mr. Sturzo a one-set
match."

The girl had just come to the court. She had
beautiful tanned legs coming out of white shorts,
and she wore a pink shirt with the tennis-ranch
logo. She had a mischievous pretty face, and her
hair was pulled back in a ponytail.

"You have to give me a handicap," Frank said
disarmingly. "You look too good. Are you an
instructor?"

"No," Rosie said. "I'm just here to get some serving lessons. Leslie is a champ trainer for that."

"Give him a handicap," Leslie said. "He's way below you in the levels."

Franky said quickly, "How about two games in each four-game set?" He would bargain down to less.

Rosie gave him a quick, infectious smile. "No," she said, "that won't do you any good. What you should ask for is two points in each game. Then you would have a chance. And if we get to deuce, I have to win by four instead of two."

Franky shook her hand. "Let's go," he said. They were standing close together, and he could smell the sweetness of her body. She whispered, "Do you want me to throw the match?"

Franky was thrilled. "No," he said. "You can't beat me with that handicap."

They played with Leslie watching, and he didn't call the foot faults. Franky won the first two games, but after that Rosie rolled over him. Her ground strokes were perfect, and she had no trouble at all with his serve. She was always standing where Franky had to hit the ball, and though several times he got to deuce, she put him away 6–2.

"Hey, you're very good for a hacker," Rosie said. "But you didn't start playing until you were over twenty, right?"

"Right." Franky was beginning to hate the word *hacker.*

"You have to learn the strokes and serve when you're a kid," she said.

"Is that right?" Franky teased. "But I'll beat you before we leave here."

Rosie grinned. She had a wide, generous mouth for such a small face. "Sure," she said. "If you have the best day of your life and I have my worst." Franky laughed.

Stace came up and introduced himself. Then he said, "Why don't you have dinner with us tonight? Franky won't invite you because you beat him, but he'll come."

"Ah, that's not true," Rosie said. "He was just about to ask me. Is eight o'clock OK?"

"Great," Stace said. He slapped Franky with his racquet.

"I'll be there," Franky said.

They had dinner at the ranch restaurant, a huge vaulting room with glass walls that let in the desert and mountains. Rosie proved to be a find, as Franky told Stace later. She flirted with both of them, she talked all the sports and knew her stuff, past and present—the great championship games, the great players, the great individual moments. And she was a good listener; she drew them out. Franky even told her about coaching the kids and how his store provided them with the best equipment, and Rosie said warmly, "Hey, that's great, that's just great." Then they told her they had been high school basketball all-stars in their youth.

Rosie also had a good appetite, which they approved of in a woman. She ate slowly and daintily, and she had a trick of lowering her head and tilting it to the side with an almost mock shyness when she talked about herself. She was studying for a Ph.D. in psychology at New York University. She came from a moderately wealthy family, and she had already toured Europe. She had been a tennis star in high school. But she said all this with a self-deprecating air that charmed them, and she kept touching their hands to maintain contact with them as she spoke.

"I still don't know what to do when I graduate," she said. "With all my book knowledge, I can never figure people out in real life. Like you two guys. You tell me your history, you are two charming bastards, but I have no idea what makes you tick."

"Don't worry about that," Stace said. "What you see is what you get."

"Don't ask me," Franky said to her. "Right now my whole life is centered on how to beat you at tennis."

After dinner the two brothers walked Rosie down the red clay path to her cottage. She gave them each a quick kiss on the cheek, and they were left alone in the desert air. The last image they took with them was Rosie's pert face gleaming in the moonlight.

"I think she's exceptional," Stace said.

"Better than that," Franky said.

FOR THE REST of Rosie's two weeks at the ranch, she became their buddy. In late afternoons after tennis they went golfing together. She was good, but not as good as the brothers. They could really whack the ball far out and had nerves of steel on the putting green. A middle-aged guy at the tennis ranch came with them to the golf course to make up a foursome and insisted on being partnered with Rosie and playing for ten dollars a hole, and though he was good, he lost. Then he tried to join them for dinner that night at the tennis ranch. Rosie rebuffed him, to the delight of the twins. "I'm trying to get one of these guys to propose to me," she said.

It was Stace who got Rosie into bed by the end of the first week. Franky had gone down to Vegas for the evening to gamble and to give Stace a clear shot. When he returned at midnight, Stace wasn't in the room. The next morning when he appeared Franky asked him, "How was she?"

"Exceptional," Stace said.

"You mind if I take a shot?" Franky asked.

This was unusual. They had never shared a woman; it was one area where their tastes differed. Stace thought it over. Rosie fitted in perfectly with both of them. But the three couldn't keep hanging out together if Stace was getting Rosie and Franky was not. Unless Franky brought another girl into the combo—and that would spoil it.

"It's OK," Stace said.

So the next night Stace went down to Vegas and Franky took his shot with Rosie. Rosie made no trouble at all, and she was delightful in bed— no fancy tricks, just good-hearted fun and games. She didn't seem uncomfortable about it at all.

But the next day when the three of them had breakfast, Franky and Stace didn't know quite how to act. They were a little too formal and polite. Deferential. Their perfect harmony was gone. Rosie polished off her eggs and bacon and toast and then leaned back and said with amusement, "Am I going to have trouble with you two guys? I thought we were buddies."

Stace said sincerely, "It's just that we're both crazy about you, and we don't know exactly how to handle this."

Rosie said, laughing, "I'll handle it. I like you both a lot. We're having a good time. We're not getting married, and after we leave the tennis ranch, we'll probably never see each other again. I'll go back to New York, and you guys will go back to L.A. So let's not spoil it now unless one of you is the jealous type. Then we can just cut out the sex part."

The twins were suddenly at ease with her. "Fat chance," Stace said.

Franky said, "We're not jealous, and I'm going to beat you at tennis one time before we leave here."

"You haven't got the strokes," Rosie said firmly, but she reached out and clasped both their hands.

"Let's settle it today," Franky said.

Rosie tilted her head shyly. "I'll give you three points a game," she said. "And if you lose, you won't give me any more of that macho crap."

Stace said, "I'll put a hundred bucks on Rosie."

Franky smiled wolfishly at both of them. There was no way he would let himself lose to Rosie with a three-point handicap. He said to Stace, "Make that bet five."

Rosie had a mischievous smile on her face. "And if I win, Stace gets tonight with me."

Both brothers laughed aloud. It gave them pleasure that Rosie was not that perfect, that she had a touch of malice in her.

Out on the tennis court, nothing could save Franky—not his whirlwind serve, not his acrobatic returns or the three-point spot. Rosie had a top spin she had never used before that completely baffled Franky. She zipped him 6–0. When the set was over, Rosie gave Franky a kiss on the cheek and whispered, "I'll make it up to you tomorrow night." As promised, she slept with Stace after the three of them had dinner. This alternated for the rest of the week.

The twins drove Rosie to the airport the day she left. "Remember, if you ever get to New York, give me a ring," she said. They had already given her an open invitation to stay with them anytime she came to L.A. Then she surprised them. She held out two small gift-wrapped boxes. "Presents," she said, and smiled happily. The twins opened the boxes, and each found a Navajo ring with a blue stone. "To remember me by."

Later, when the brothers went shopping in town, they saw the rings on sale for three hundred bucks.

"She could have bought us a tie each or one of those funny cowboy belts for fifty bucks," Franky said. They were extraordinarily pleased.

They had another week to spend at the ranch, but they spent little of it playing tennis. They golfed and flew to Vegas in the evenings. But they made it a rule not to spend the night there. That's how you could lose big—take a shellacking in the early-morning hours when your energy was down and your judgment was impaired.

Over dinner they talked about Rosie. Neither would say a disloyal word about her, though in their hearts they held her in lower esteem because she had fucked both of them.

"She really enjoyed it," Franky said. "She never got mean or moody after."

"Yeah," Stace said. "She was exceptional. I think we found the perfect broad."

"But they always change," Franky said.

"Do we call her when we get to New York?" Stace asked.

"I will," Franky said.

A WEEK AFTER they left Scottsdale they registered at the Sherry-Netherland in Manhattan. The next morning they rented a car and drove out to John Heskow's house on Long Island. When they pulled into the driveway, they saw Heskow sweeping his basketball court clean of a thin skin of snow. He raised his hand in welcome. Then he motioned them to pull into the garage attached to the house. His own car was parked outside. Franky jumped out of the car before Stace pulled in, to shake Heskow's hand but really to put him in close range if anything happened.

Heskow unlocked the door and ushered them inside.

"It's all ready," he said. He led them upstairs to the huge trunk in the bedroom and unlocked it. Inside were stacks of money rubber-banded into six-inch bundles, along with a folded leather bag, almost as big as a suitcase. Stace threw the bundles onto the bed. Then the brothers rifled through each stack to make sure they were all hundreds and that there were no counterfeits. They only counted the bills in one stack and multiplied it by one hundred. Then they loaded the money into the leather bag. When they were finished, they looked up at Heskow. He was smiling. "Have a cup of coffee before you go," he said. "Take a leak or whatever."

"Thanks," Stace said. "Is there anything we should know? Any fuss?"

"None at all," Heskow said. "Everything's perfect. Just don't be too flashy with the dough."

"It's for our old age," Franky said, and the brothers laughed.

"What about his kids?" Franky asked. "They didn't make any noise?"

"They were brought up straight," Heskow said. "They're not Sicilians. They are very successful professionals. They believe in the law. And they're lucky they're not suspects."

The twins laughed and Heskow smiled. It was a good joke.

"Well, I'm just amazed," Stace said. "Such a big man and so little fuss."

"Well, it's been a year now and not a peep," Heskow said.

The brothers finished their coffee and shook hands with Heskow. "Keep well," Heskow said. "I may be calling you again."

"You do that," Franky said.

BACK IN THE CITY the brothers dumped the money into a joint security safe-deposit box. Actually, two. They didn't even dip any casual spending money. Then they went back to the hotel and called Rosie.

She was surprised and delighted to hear from them so soon. Her voice was eager as she urged them to come to her apartment at once. She would show them New York, her treat. So that evening they arrived at her apartment and she served them drinks before they all left for dinner and the theater.

Rosie took them to Le Cirque, which she told them was the finest restaurant in New York. The food was great, and even though it was not on the menu, at Franky's request they cooked him up a plate of spaghetti that was the best he'd ever tasted. The twins could not get over the fact that a fancy restaurant could serve the food they liked so much. They also noted that the maître d' treated Rosie in a very special way, and that impressed them. They had their usual great time, Rosie urging them to tell their stories. She looked especially beautiful. It was the first time they had seen her dressed formally.

Over coffee, the brothers gave Rosie their present. They had bought it at Tiffany's that afternoon and had it wrapped in a maroon velvet box. It had cost five grand, a simple gold chain with a diamond-encrusted locket of white platinum.

"From me and Stace," Franky said. "We chipped in."

Rosie was stunned. Her eyes became watery and gleaming. She put the chain over her head so that the locket rested between her breasts. Then she leaned over and kissed both of them. It was a simple sweet kiss on the lips that tasted of honey.

THE BROTHERS had once told Rosie they had never gone to a Broadway musical, so the next night she was taking them to see *Les Misérables*. She promised them they would really love it. And they did, but with a few reservations. Later, in her apartment, Franky said, "I don't believe he didn't kill the cop Javert when he had the chance."

"It's a musical," Stace said. "Musicals don't make sense even in the movies. It's not their job."

But Rosie disputed this. "It shows Jean Valjean

has become a really good man," she said. "It's about redemption. A man who sins and steals and then reconciles with society."

This irritated even Stace. "Wait a minute," he said. "The guy started off a thief. Once a thief, always a thief. Right, Franky?"

Now Rosie took fire. "What would you two guys know about a man like Valjean?" And that broke the brothers up. Rosie smiled her good-humored smile. "Which of you is staying tonight?" she asked.

She waited for the answer and finally said, "I don't do threesomes. You have to take turns."

"Who do you want to stay?" Franky asked.

"Don't start that," Rosie warned. "Or we'll have a beautiful relationship like in the movies. No screwing. And I'd hate that," she said, smiling to take the edge off. "I love you both."

"I'll go home tonight," Franky said. He wanted her to know she didn't have power over him.

Rosie kissed Franky good night and accompanied him to the door. She whispered, "I'll be special tomorrow night."

THEY HAD SIX DAYS to spend together. Rosie had to work on her dissertation during the day, but she was available in the evenings.

One night the twins took her to a Knicks game

at the Garden when the Lakers were in town, and they were delighted that she appreciated all the fine points of the game. Afterward they went toore Christmas Eve, she had to leave town for the week. The brothers had assumed she would spend Christmas with her family. But now they noticed that for the first time since they had known her, she looked a little depressed.

"No, I'm spending Christmas alone in a house my family owns upstate. I wanted to duck all that phony Christmas stuff, to just study and sort out my life."

"So just cancel and spend Christmas with us," Franky said. "We'll change our flight back to L.A."

"I can't," Rosie said. "I have to study, and that's the best place."

"All alone?" Stace asked.

Rosie ducked her head. "I'm such a dope," she said.

"Why don't we go up with you for just a few days?" Franky asked. "We'll leave the day after Christmas."

"Yeah," Stace said, "we could use some peace and quiet."

Rosie's face was glowing. "Would you really?" she said happily. "That's so great. We could go skiing on Christmas. There's a resort just thirty minutes from the house. And I'll cook a Christmas dinner." She paused for a moment and then said unconvincingly, "But promise you'll leave after Christmas; I really have to work."

"We have to get back to L.A.," Stace said. "We have a business to run."

"God, I love you guys," Rosie said.

Stace said casually, "Franky and me were talking. You know we've never been to Europe, and we thought when you're finished with school this summer, we could all go together. You be our guide. Top of the line in everything. Just a couple of weeks. We could have a great time if you were with us."

"Yeah," Franky said. "We can't go alone." They all laughed.

"That is just a wonderful idea," Rosie said. "I'll show you London and Paris and Rome. And you will absolutely adore Venice. You may never leave. But hell, summer is a long time away, you guys. I know you, you'll be chasing other women by then."

"We want you," Franky said almost angrily.

"I'll be ready when I get the call," Rosie said.

ON THE MORNING of December 23, Rosie pulled up to their hotel to pick up the twins. She was driving a huge Cadillac whose trunk held her big suitcases and a few gayly wrapped presents and still had room for their more modest ones.

Stace took the backseat and let Franky ride up front with Rosie. The radio was playing, and none of them talked for about an hour. That was what was great about Rosie.

While waiting for Rosie to pick them up, the brothers had had a conversation over breakfast. Stace could see Franky was uneasy with him, which was rare between the twins.

"Spit it out," Stace said.

"Don't take this wrong," Franky said. "I'm not jealous or anything. But could you lay off Rosie while we're up there?"

"Sure," Stace said. "I'll tell her I caught the clap in Vegas."

Franky grinned and said, "You don't have to go that far. I'd just like to try having her for myself. Otherwise, I'll lay off and you can have her."

"You're a jerk," Stace said. "You'll ruin everything. Look, we didn't muscle her, we didn't con her. This is what she wants to do. And I think it's great for us."

"I'd just like to try it by myself," Franky said again. "Just for a little while."

"Sure," Stace said. "I'm the older brother, I have to watch out for you." It was their favorite joke, and indeed it always did seem Stace was a few years older than Franky instead of ten minutes.

"But you know she'll be wise to you in two

seconds," Stace said. "Rosie is smart. She'll know you're in love with her."

Franky looked at his brother with astonishment. "I'm in love with her?" he said. "Is that it? Jesus fucking Christ." And they both laughed.

NOW THE CAR was out of the city and rolling through the farmland of Westchester County. Franky broke the silence. "I never saw so much snow in my life," he said. "How the hell can people live here?"

"Because it's cheap," Rosie said.

Stace asked, "How much longer?"

"About an hour and a half," Rosie said. "You guys need to stop?"

"No," Franky said, "let's get there."

"Unless you have to stop," Stace said to Rosie.

Rosie shook her head. She looked very determined, hands tight on the wheel, peering intently at the slow-falling snowflakes.

About an hour later they went through a small town, and Rosie said, "Just another fifteen minutes."

The car went up a steep incline, and on top of a small hill was a house, gray as an elephant, surrounded by snow-covered fields, the snow absolutely pure white and unmarked, no footprints, no car tracks.

Rosie pulled to a stop at the front-porch entrance, and they got out. She loaded them down with suitcases and the Christmas boxes. "Go on in," she said. "The door is open. We don't lock up out here."

Franky and Stace crunched up the steps of the porch and opened the door. They were in an enormous living room decorated with animal heads on the walls, and there was a huge fire in a hearth as big as a cave.

Outside suddenly, they could hear the roar of the Cadillac's motor, and at that moment six men appeared from the two entryways of the house. They were holding guns, and the leader, a huge man with a great mustache, said in a slightly accented voice, "Don't move. Don't drop the packages." Then the guns were pressed against their bodies.

Stace understood at once, but Franky was worried about Rosie. It took him about thirty seconds to put it together—the roar of the engine and Rosie not being there. Then with the worst feeling he had ever had in his life, he realized the truth. Rosie was bait.

CHAPTER 7

ON THE NIGHT before Christmas Eve
Astorre attended a party given by Nicole at
her apartment. She had invited professional
colleagues and members of her pro bono groups,
including her favorite, the Campaign Against the
Death Penalty.

Astorre liked parties. He loved to chat with
people he would never see again and who were
so different from him. Sometimes he met interesting women with whom he had brief affairs.
And he always hoped to fall in love; he missed it.
Tonight Nicole had reminded him of their
teenage romance, not coy or flirting but with
good humor.

"You broke my heart when you obeyed my
father and went to Europe," she said.

"Sure," Astorre said. "But that didn't stop you
from meeting other guys."

For some reason Nicole was very fond of him

tonight. She held his hand in an intimate school-girl way, she kissed him on the lips, she clung to him as if she knew that he was about to escape her once again.

This confused him because all his old tender-ness was aroused, but he understood starting up again with Nicole would be a terrible mistake at this junction of his life. Not with the decisions he had to make. Finally she led him to a group of people and introduced him.

Tonight there was a live band, and Nicole asked Astorre to sing in his now gravelly but warm lilt-ing voice, which he always loved doing. They sang an old Italian love ballad together.

When he serenaded Nicole, she clung to him and looked into his eyes searching for something in his soul. Then, with a final sorrowful kiss, she let him go.

Afterward Nicole had a surprise for him. She led him to a guest, a quietly beautiful woman with wide intelligent gray eyes. "Astorre," she said, "this is Georgette Cilke, who chairs the Campaign Against the Death Penalty. We often work together."

Georgette shook his hand and complimented him on his singing. "You remind me of a young Dean Martin," she said.

Astorre was delighted. "Thank you," he said.

"He's my hero. I know his entire catalogue of songs by heart."

"My husband is a big fan, too," Georgette said. "I like his music, but I don't like the way he treats women."

Astorre sighed, knowing he was on the losing end of an argument, but one he had to make anyway as a certified soldier to the cause. "Yes, but we must separate the artist from the man."

Georgette was amused by the gallantry of Astorre's defense. "Must we?" she asked with a wry smile. "I don't think we should ever condone that kind of behavior."

Astorre could see Georgette wasn't going to give in on this point, so all he did was begin to sing a few bars of one of Dino's most famous Italian ballads. He looked deeply into her green eyes, swaying to the music, and he saw her beginning to smile.

"OK, OK," she said. "I'll admit the songs are good. But I'm still not ready to let him off the hook."

She touched him gently on the shoulder before drifting away. Astorre spent the rest of the party observing her. She was a woman who did nothing to enhance her beauty but had a natural grace and a gentle kindness that took away any threat that beauty makes. And Astorre, like every-

body in the room, fell a little bit in love with her.
Yet she seemed genuinely unaware of the affect
she had on people. She had not an ounce of the
flirt in her.

By this time Astorre had read Marcantonio's
documentary notes on Cilke, a stubborn ferret
on the trail of human flaws, coldly efficient in his
work. And he also had read that his wife truly
loved him. There was the mystery.

Halfway through the party, Nicole came up to
him and whispered that Aldo Monza was in the
reception room.

"I'm sorry, Nicole," Astorre said. "I have to go."

"OK," Nicole said. "I was hoping you'd get to
know Georgette better. She is absolutely the
brightest and best woman I've ever met."

"Well, she is beautiful," Astorre said, and he
thought to himself how foolish he still was about
women—already he was building such fantasy on
one meeting.

When Astorre went into the reception room,
he found Aldo Monza sitting uncomfortably in
one of Nicole's fragile but beautiful antique
chairs. Monza rose and whispered to him, "We
have the twins. They await your pleasure."

Astorre felt his heart sink. Now it would begin.
Now he would be tested, again. "How long will
it take to drive up there?" he asked.

"Three hours at least. We have a blizzard."

Astorre looked at his watch. It was ten-thirty P.M. "Let's get started," he said.

When they left the building the air was white with snow and the parked cars were half buried in drifts. Monza had a huge dark Buick waiting.

Monza drove, Astorre beside him. It was very cold, and Monza turned on the heater. Gradually the car turned into an oven smelling of tobacco and wine.

"Sleep," Monza said to Astorre. "We have a long ride ahead of us, and a night of labor."

Astorre let his body relax and his mind slip into dreams. Snow blurred the road. He remembered the burning heat of Sicily and the eleven years during which the Don had prepared him for this final duty. And he knew how inevitable was his fate.

ASTORRE VIOLA was sixteen years old when Don Aprile ordered him to study in London. Astorre was not surprised. The Don had sent all his children to private schools and made them grow up in college; it was not only because he believed in education but to keep them isolated from his own business and way of life.

In London Astorre stayed with a prosperous couple who had emigrated many years before from Sicily and who seemed to have a very comfortable life in England. They were middle-aged and childless, and they had changed their name from Priola to Pryor. They looked extremely English, their skins bleached by English weather, their dress and movement serenely un-Sicilian. Mr. Pryor went off to work wearing a bowler hat and carrying a furled umbrella; Mrs. Pryor dressed in the flowered dresses and swooping bonnets of dowdy English matrons.

In the privacy of their home they reverted to their origins. Mr. Pryor wore patched baggy pants and collarless black shirts, while Mrs. Pryor dressed in a very loose black dress and cooked in the old Italian style. He called her Marizza and she called him Zu.

Mr. Pryor worked as the chief executive of a private bank that was a subsidiary of a huge Palermo bank. He treated Astorre as a favorite nephew yet kept his distance. Mrs. Pryor indulged him with food and affection as if he were a grandson.

Mr. Pryor gave Astorre a car and a handsome living allowance. Schooling had already been arranged at a small obscure university just outside London that specialized in business and banking but also had a good reputation in the arts. Astorre enrolled in the required curriculum, but his real interest was in his acting and singing classes. He filled his schedule with electives in music and history. It was during this stay in London that he fell in love with the imagery of fox hunting—not the killing and the chase but the pageantry—the red coats, the brown dogs, the black horses.

In one of his acting classes Astorre met a girl his own age, Rosie Conner. She was extremely pretty, with that air of innocence that can be devastating to young men and provocative to older ones. She was also talented and played some of the leading roles in the plays staged by the class. Astorre, on the other hand, was relegated to smaller parts. He was handsome enough, but something in his personality prevented him from sharing himself with an audience. Rosie had no such problem. It was as if she were inviting every audience to seduce her.

They took vocal classes together too, and Rosie admired Astorre's singing. It was evident the teacher did not share her admiration; in fact, he advised Astorre to drop his music courses. He did not really have more than a pleasant voice, but even worse, he had no musical comprehension.

After only two weeks Astorre and Rosie became lovers. This was more by her initiation than by his, though by this time he was madly in love with her—as madly in love as any sixteen-year-old can be. He almost completely forgot

Nicole. Rosie seemed more amused than passionate. But she was so vibrantly alive, she adored him when she was with him; she was ardent in bed and always generous in every way. A week after they became lovers, she bought him an expensive present: a red hunting jacket with a black suede hunting cap and fine leather whip. She presented them as something of a joke.

As young lovers do, they told each other their life stories. Rosie told him her parents owned a huge ranch in South Dakota and that she had spent her childhood in a dreary Plains town. She finally escaped by insisting she wanted to study drama in England. But her childhood had not been a total loss. She had learned to ride, hunt, and ski, and in high school she had been a star in the drama club as well as on the tennis court.

Astorre poured his heart out to her. He told her how he longed to be a singer, how he loved the English way of life with its old medieval structures, its royal pageantry, its polo matches and fox hunts. But he never told her about his uncle, Don Raymonde Aprile, and his childhood visits to Sicily.

She made him dress in his hunting garb and then undressed him. "You are so handsome," she said. "Maybe you were an English lord in a past life."

This was the only part of her that made Astorre

uncomfortable. She truly believed in reincarnation. But then she made love to him and he forgot everything else. It seemed that he had never been so happy, except in Sicily.

But at the end of one year, Mr. Pryor took him into his den to give him some bad news. Mr. Pryor was wearing pantaloons and a peasant knit jacket, his head covered with a checkered, billed cap whose shadow hid his eyes.

He said to Astorre, "We have enjoyed your stay with us. My wife loves your singing. But now regretfully we must say our good-byes. Don Raymonde has sent orders for you to go to Sicily to live with his good friend Bianco. There is some business you must learn there. He wants you to grow up a Sicilian. You know what that means."

Astorre was shocked by the news but never questioned that he must obey. And though he yearned to be in Sicily again, he could not bear the thought of never seeing Rosie again. He said to Mr. Pryor, "If I visit London once a month, can I stay with you?"

"I would be insulted if you did not," Mr. Pryor said. "But for what reason?"

Astorre explained about Rosie, professed his love for her.

"Ah," Mr. Pryor said, sighing with pleasure. "How fortunate you are to be parted from the woman you love. True ecstasy. And that poor girl, how she will suffer. But go, don't worry. Leave me her name and address so I can look after her."

Astorre and Rosie had a tearful farewell. He swore he would fly back to London each month to be with her. She swore she would never look at another man. It was a delicious separation. Astorre would worry about her. Her appearance, her cheerful manner, her smile always invited seduction. The very qualities he loved her for were always a danger. He had seen it many times, as lovers always do, believing that all the men in the world must desire the woman he loved, that they too must be attracted to her beauty, her wit and high spirits.

Astorre was on the plane to Palermo the very next day. He was met by Bianco, but a drastically changed Bianco. The huge man now wore a tailored silk suit and white broad-brimmed hat. He dressed to fit his status, for now Bianco's *cosca* ruled most of the construction business in war-ravaged Palermo. It was a rich living but far more complicated than in the old days. Now he had to pay off all the city and ministry officials from Rome and defend his territory from rival *coscas* like the powerful Corleonesi.

Octavius Bianco embraced Astorre and recalled the long-ago kidnapping and then told him of Don Raymonde's instruction. Astorre was to be trained to be Bianco's bodyguard and pupil in business deals. This would take at least five years, but at the end of that time, Astorre would be a true Sicilian and so worthy of his uncle's trust. He had a head start: Because of his childhood visits he could speak the Sicilian dialect like a native.

Bianco lived in an enormous villa just outside Palermo, staffed with servants and a platoon of guards around the clock. Because of his wealth and power he was now connected intimately with the high society of Palermo. During the day Astorre was trained in shooting and explosives and instruction with the rope. In the evenings Bianco took him to meet friends in their homes and in the coffee bars. Sometimes they attended society dances, where Bianco was the darling of the rich conservative widows and Astorre sang gentle love songs to their daughters.

What amazed Astorre the most was the open bribery of high-placed officials from Rome.

One Sunday the national minister of reconstruction came to visit and cheerfully, without any trace of shame, took a suitcase full of cash, thanking Bianco effusively. He explained almost apologetically that half of it had to go to the prime minister of Italy himself. Later, when Astorre and Bianco were back home, Astorre asked if that was possible.

Bianco shrugged. "Not half, but I would hope

some. It's an honor to give His Excellency a little pocket money."

During the following year Astorre visited Rosie in London, flying in for just one day and night at a time. These were nights of bliss for him.

Also, that year he had his baptism of fire. A truce had been arranged between Bianco and the Corleonesi *cosca*. A leader of the Corleonesi was a man named Tosci Limona. A small man with a terrible cough, Limona had a striking hawklike profile and deep-socketed eyes. Even Bianco voiced some fear of him.

The meeting between the two leaders was to take place on neutral ground and in the attendance of one of the highest-ranking magistrates in Sicily.

This judge, called the Lion of Palermo, took great pride in his absolute corruption. He reduced the sentences of Mafia members convicted of murder, and he refused to allow prosecutions to go forward. He made no secret of his friendship with the Corleonesi *cosca* and that of Bianco. He had a great estate ten miles from Palermo, and it was here that the meeting was to take place in order to ensure that no violence would be done.

The two leaders were permitted to bring four bodyguards each. They also shared the Lion's fee for arranging the meeting and presiding over it and, of course, the rent of his home.

With his huge mane of white hair almost obscuring his face, the Lion was the picture of respectable jurisprudence.

Astorre commanded Bianco's group of bodyguards, and he was impressed by the affection shown between the two men. Limona and Bianco showered each other with embraces, kissing cheeks and clasping hands stoutly. They laughed and whispered intimately over the elaborate dinner the Lion presented to them.

So he was surprised when, once the party was over and he and Bianco were alone, Bianco said to him, "We have to be very careful. That bastard Limona is going to kill us all."

And Bianco proved to be right.

A week later an inspector of police on Bianco's payroll was murdered as he left the home of his mistress. Two weeks after that one of the society swells of Palermo, a partner in Bianco's construction business, was killed by a squad of masked men invading his house and riddling him with bullets.

Bianco responded by increasing the number of his bodyguards and taking special pains to secure the vehicles he traveled in. The Corleonesi were known for their skill with explosives. Bianco also stuck very close to his villa.

But there came a day when he had to go into Palermo to pay off two high-ranking city officials and decided to dine in his favorite restaurant there. He chose a Mercedes and a top driver/guard. Astorre sat in the backseat with him. A car preceded him and a car followed, both with two armed men in addition to the drivers.

They were driving along a broad boulevard when suddenly a motorcycle with two riders zoomed out of a side street. The passenger had a Kalashnikov rifle and pumped bullets toward the car. But Astorre had already shoved Bianco to the floor and then returned fire as the cyclists zoomed away. The motorcycle went down another side street and vanished.

Three weeks later, under cover of night, five men were captured and brought to Bianco's villa, where they were tied up and hidden in the cellar. "They are Corleonesi," Bianco said to Astorre. "Come down the cellar with me."

The men were bound in Bianco's old peasant style, their limbs interlocked. Armed guards stood over them. Bianco took one of the guard's rifles and without saying a word shot all five men in the back of the head.

"Throw them in the streets of Palermo," he commanded. Then he turned to Astorre. "After you decide to kill a man, never speak to him. It makes things embarrassing for both of you."

"Were they the cyclists?" Astorre asked.

"No," Bianco said. "But they will serve."

And it did. From then on peace reigned between the Palermo *cosca* and the Corleonesi.

ASTORRE HAD NOT been back to London to see Rosie for almost two months. Early one morning he received a call from her. He had given her his number, to be used only in an emergency.

"Astorre," she said in a very calm voice. "Can you fly back right away? I'm in terrible trouble."

"Tell me what it is," Astorre said.

"I can't, over the phone," Rosie said. "But if you really love me, you'll come."

When Astorre asked Bianco's permission to leave, Bianco said, "Bring money." And he gave him a huge bundle of English pounds.

WHEN ASTORRE arrived at Rosie's apartment, she let him in quickly and then carefully locked the door. Her face was dead white, and she was huddled in a bulky bathrobe he had never seen before. She gave him a quick grateful kiss. "You're going to be angry with me," she said sadly.

In that moment Astorre thought she was pregnant, and he said quickly, "Darling, I can never be angry at you."

She held him tightly. "You've been gone over a year, you know. I tried so hard to be faithful. But that's a long time."

Suddenly Astorre's mind was clear, icy. Here again was betrayal. But there was something more. Why had she wanted him to come so quickly? "OK," he said, "why am I here?"

"You have to help me," Rosie said, and led him into the bedroom.

There was something in the bed. Astorre threw back the sheet to find a middle-aged man lying on his back, completely naked, yet with a dignified look. This was partly due to the small silver goatee or perhaps more to the delicate carvings of his face. His body was spare and thin, with a great mat of fur across his chest; oddest of all, he wore gold-rimmed spectacles over his open eyes. Though his head was large for his body, he was a handsome man. He was about as dead a man as Astorre had ever seen, despite the fact that there were no wounds. The spectacles were crooked, and Astorre reached to straighten them.

Rosie whispered, "We were making love and he went into this horrible spasm. He must have had a heart attack."

"When did this happen?" Astorre asked. He was in minor shock.

"Last night," Rosie said.

"Why didn't you just call the emergency medical team?" Astorre said. "It's not your fault."

"He's married and maybe it is my fault. We used amyl nitrate. He had trouble climaxing." She said it without any embarrassment.

Astorre was genuinely astonished by her self-possession. Looking at the corpse, he had the strange feeling that he should dress the man and remove his spectacles. He was too old to be naked, at least fifty—it didn't seem right. He said to Rosie without malice but with the incredulity of the young, "What did you see in this guy?"

"He was my history professor," Rosie said. "Really very sweet, very kind. It was a spur-of-the-moment thing. This was only the second time. I was so lonely." She paused for a moment and then, looking directly into his eyes, said, "You've got to help me."

"Does anyone know he was seeing you?" Astorre asked.

"No."

"I still think we should call the police."

"No," Rosie said. "If you're afraid, I'll take care of it myself."

"Get dressed," Astorre said with a stern look. He pulled the sheet back over the dead man.

An hour later they were at Mr. Pryor's house; he answered the door himself. Without a word, he took them to the den and listened to their story. He was very sympathetic to Rosie and patted her hand in consolation, at which point Rosie burst into tears. Mr. Pryor took off his cap and actually clucked with sympathy.

"Give me the keys to your apartment," he said to Rosie. "Stay the night here. Tomorrow you can return to your home and everything will be in order. Your friend will have disappeared. You will then stay here a week before you go back to America."

Mr. Pryor showed them to their bedroom as if he assumed that nothing had happened to spoil their love affair. And then he took leave of them to take care of business.

Astorre always remembered that night. He lay on the bed with Rosie, comforting her, wiping her tears. "It was only the second time," she whispered to him. "It didn't mean anything, and we were such close friends. I missed you. I admired him for his mind, and then one night it just happened. He couldn't climax, and I hate to say this about him, but he couldn't even keep an erection. So he asked to use the nitrate."

She seemed so vulnerable, so hurt, so broken by her tragedy that all Astorre could do was comfort her. But one thing stuck in his mind. She had stayed in her home with a dead body for over twenty-four hours until he arrived. That was a mystery, and if there was one mystery, there could be others. But he wiped away her tears and kissed her cheeks to comfort her.

"Will you ever see me again?" she asked him, digging her face into his shoulder, making him feel the softness of her body.

"Of course I will," Astorre said. But in his heart he wasn't so sure.

The next morning Mr. Pryor reappeared and told Rosie she could return to her flat. Rosie gave him a grateful hug, which he accepted warmly. He had a car waiting for her.

After she left, Mr. Pryor, correct in bowler hat and umbrella, took Astorre to the airport. "Don't worry about her," Mr. Pryor said. "We will take care of everything."

"Let me know," Astorre said.

"Of course. She is a marvelous girl, a Mafioso woman. You must forgive her little trespass."

CHAPTER 8

DURING THOSE YEARS in Sicily, Astorre was trained to be a Qualified Man. He even led a squad of six of Bianco's cosca men into Corleone itself to execute their premier bombardier, a man who had blown up an Italian Army general and two of the most able anti-Mafia magistrates in Sicily. It was a daring raid that established his reputation in the upper levels of the Palermo cosca led by Bianco.

Astorre also led an active social life and frequented the cafés and nightclubs of Palermo— mostly to meet beautiful women. Palermo was full of the young Mafia picciotti, or foot soldiers, of different coscas, all insistent on their manhood, all careful to cut a fine figure with their tailored suits, their manicured nails, and hair slicked back like skin. All looking to make their mark—to be feared and to be loved. The youngest of them were in their teens, sporting finely groomed mustaches, their lips red as coral. They never gave an inch to another male, and Astorre avoided them. They were reckless, killing even those of high rank in their world and thus ensuring their own almost immediate death. For the killing of a fellow Mafia member was like the seduction of his wife, punished by murder. To assuage their pride, Astorre always showed these picciotti an amiable deference. And he was popular with them. It helped that he fell half in love with a club dancer called Buji and so avoided their ill will in matters of the heart.

ASTORRE SPENT several years as Bianco's right-hand man against the Corleonesi *cosca*. Periodically he received instructions from Don Aprile, who no longer made his annual visit to Sicily.

The great bone of contention between the Corleonesi and Bianco's cosca was a matter of long-term strategy. The Corleonesi cosca had decided on a reign of terror against the authorities. They assassinated investigating magistrates and blew up generals sent to suppress the Mafia in Sicily. Bianco believed that this was harmful in the long run despite some immediate benefits. But his objections led to his own friends being killed. Bianco retaliated, and the carnage became so pervasive that both sides again sought a truce.

• • •

DURING HIS years in Sicily, Astorre made one close friend. Nello Sparra was five years older than Astorre and played with a band in a Palermo nightclub where the hostesses were very pretty and some did duty as high-class prostitutes.

Nello did not lack for money—he seemed to have various sources of income. He dressed beautifully in the Palermo Mafioso style. He was always high-spirited and ready for adventure, and the girls in the club loved him because he gave them small presents on their birthday and holidays. And also because they suspected he was one of the secret owners of the club, which was a nice safe place to work thanks to the strict protection of the Palermo *cosca* that controlled all the entertainment in the province. The girls were only too glad to accompany Nello and Astorre to private parties and excursions into the countryside.

Buji was a tall, striking, and voluptuous brunette who danced at Nello Sparra's nightclub. She was famous for her temper and her independence in taking lovers. She never encouraged a *picciotto:* The men who courted her had to have money and power. She had a reputation for being mercenary in a frank and open way that was considered Mafioso. She required expensive gifts, but her beauty and ardor made the rich men of Palermo eager to satisfy her needs.

Over the years Buji and Astorre established a liaison on the hazardous brink of true love. Astorre was Buji's favorite, though she did not hesitate to abandon him for an especially remunerative weekend with a rich Palermo businessman. When she first did this Astorre tried to reproach her, but she overwhelmed him with her common sense.

"I'm twenty-one years old," she said. "My beauty is my capital. When I'm thirty I can be a housewife with a bunch of kids or be independently wealthy with my own little shop. Sure, we have good times, but you will return to America, where I have no wish to go—and where you have no wish to take me. Let's just enjoy ourselves as free human beings. And despite everything, you will get the best of me before I get tired of you. So stop this nonsense. I have my own living to make." Then she added slyly, "And besides, you have too dangerous a trade for me to count on you."

Nello owned an enormous villa outside Palermo, on the seashore. With ten bedrooms, it easily accommodated their parties. On the grounds was a swimming pool shaped like the island of Sicily and two clay tennis courts, which were rarely used.

On weekends the villa would fill up with Nello's extended family, who came to visit from the countryside. The children who did not swim were penned into the tennis courts with their toys and old racquets to play with the small yellow tennis balls, which they kicked around like soccer balls until they were strewn on the clay like small yellow birds.

Astorre was included in this family life and accepted as a darling nephew. Nello became like a brother to him. At night Nello even invited him up to the club bandstand and they sang Italian love ballads to the audience, which cheered them enthusiastically and to the delight of the hostesses.

THE LION of Palermo, that eminently corruptible judge, again offered his house and his presence for a meeting between Bianco and Limona. Again, they were each allowed to bring four bodyguards. Bianco was even willing to give up a small piece of his Palermo construction empire to secure peace.

Astorre was taking no chances. He and his three guards were heavily armed for the meeting.

Limona and his entourage were waiting at the magistrate's home when Bianco, Astorre, and the guards arrived. A multi-course dinner had been prepared. None of the bodyguards sat down to the meal, only the magistrate—his full white mane tied out of the way with a pink ribbon—and Bianco and Limona. Limona ate very little but was extremely amiable and receptive to Bianco's expressions of affection. He promised that there would be no more assassination of officials, especially the ones in Bianco's pocket.

At the end of the dinner, as they prepared to go into the living room for a final discussion, the Lion excused himself and said he would be back in five minutes. He did so with a deprecatory smile that made them understand he was answering a call of nature.

Limona opened another bottle of wine and filled Bianco's glass. Astorre went to a window and glanced down into the huge driveway. A lone car was waiting, and as he watched, the great white head of the Lion of Palermo appeared in the driveway. The magistrate got into the car, which quickly sped away.

Astorre did not hesitate one moment. His mind instantly pieced things together. His gun was in his hand without his even thinking. Limona and Bianco had their arms entwined, drinking from their glasses. Astorre stepped close to them, brought up his gun, and fired into Limona's face. The bullet hit the glass first before entering Limona's mouth, and shards of glass flew like diamonds over the table. Astorre immediately turned his gun on Limona's four bodyguards and started firing. His own men had their guns out shooting. The bodies fell to the floor.

Bianco looked at him dumbfounded.

Astorre said, "The Lion has left the villa," and Bianco immediately understood that it had been a trap.

"You must be careful," Bianco told Astorre, gesturing at Limona's corpse. "His friends will be after you."

IT IS POSSIBLE for a headstrong man to be loyal, but it is not so easy for him to keep himself out of trouble. And so it proved with Pietro Fissolini. Following Don Raymonde's rare show of mercy toward him, Fissolini never betrayed the Don, but he betrayed his own family. He seduced the wife of his nephew Aldo Monza. And this was many years after his promise to the Don, when he was sixty years old.

This was extraordinarily foolhardy. When Fissolini seduced his nephew's wife, he destroyed his leadership of the *cosca*. Because in the Mafia's separate clusters, to maintain power, one must put family above all. What made the situation even more dangerous was that the wife was the niece of Bianco. Bianco would not tolerate any vengeance on his niece by the husband. The husband inevitably had to kill Fissolini, his favorite uncle and the leader of the *cosca*. Two provinces would engage in bloody strife, and it would decimate the countryside. Astorre sent word to the Don asking for his instructions.

The reply came: "You saved him once; you must decide again."

Aldo Monza was one of the most valued members of the *cosca* and the extended family. He had been one of the men spared death by the Don years earlier. So when Astorre summoned him to the Don's village, he came willingly. Astorre barred Bianco from the conference with assurances that he would protect the daughter.

Monza was tall for a Sicilian, nearly six feet. He was magnificently built, his body molded by hard labor since he was a child. But his eyes were cavernous and his face barely covered with flesh pulled so tight his head looked like a skull. It made him seem particularly unattractive and dangerous—and, in some sense, tragic. Monza was the most intelligent and most educated of Fissolini's *cosca*. He had studied in Palermo to be a veterinarian, and he always carried his professional bag. He had a natural sympathy for animals and was always much in demand. Yet he was as fiercely dedicated to the Sicilian code of honor as any peasant. Next to Fissolini, he was the most powerful man in the *cosca*.

Astorre had made his decision. "I am not here to plead for Fissolini's life. I understand that your *cosca* has agreed to your vengeance. I understand your grief. But I am here to plead for the mother of your children."

Monza stared at him. "She was a traitor, to me and my children. I cannot let her live."

"Listen to me," Astorre said. "No one will seek vengeance for Fissolini. But the woman is Bianco's niece. He will seek vengeance for her death. His *cosca* is stronger than yours. It will be a bloody war. Think of your children."

Monza gave a contemptuous wave of his hand. "Who knows even if they are mine? She is a whore." He paused. "And she will die a whore's death." His face became illumined with death. He was beyond rage. He was willing to destroy the world.

Astorre tried to imagine the man's life in his village, his wife lost, his dignity betrayed by his uncle and his wife.

"Listen very carefully," Astorre said. "Years ago Don Aprile spared your life. Now he asks this favor. Take your revenge on Fissolini as we know you must. But spare your wife, and Bianco will arrange to have her and the children go to relatives in Brazil. As for you personally, I make this offer with approval from the Don. Come with me as my personal assistant, my friend. You will live a rich and interesting life. And you will be spared the shame of living in your village. You will also be safe from the vengeance of Fissolini's friends."

It pleased Astorre that Aldo Monza made no gesture of anger or surprise. For five minutes he remained silent, thinking carefully. Then Monza said, "Will you continue payment to my family *cosca*? My brother will lead them."

"Certainly," Astorre said. "They are valuable to us."

"Then after I kill Fissolini, I will come with you. Neither you nor Bianco can interfere in any way. My wife does not go to Brazil until she sees the dead body of my uncle."

"Agreed," Astorre said. And remembering Fissolini's joyful, jolly face and roguish smile, he felt a pang of regret. "When will it happen?"

"On Sunday," Monza said. "I will be with you on Monday. And may God burn Sicily and my wife in a thousand eternal hells."

"I will go with you back to your village," Astorre said. "I will take your wife under my protection. I'm afraid you may be carried away."

Monza shrugged. "I cannot let my fate be decided by what a woman puts in her vagina."

• • •

THE FISSOLINI *cosca* met early that Sunday morning. The nephews and sons-in-law had to decide whether or not to kill Fissolini's younger brother also, to avoid his vengeance. Certainly, the brother must have known of the seduction and, by not speaking, condoned it. Astorre did not take any part in that discussion. He simply made clear that the wife and children could not be harmed. But his blood chilled at the ferocity of these men over what seemed to him not so grave an offense. He realized now how merciful the Don had been with him.

He understood it was not only a sexual matter. When a wife betrays her husband with a lover, she lets a possible Trojan horse into the political structure of the *cosca*. She can leak secrets and weaken defenses; she gives her lover power over her husband's Family. She is a spy in a war. Love is no excuse for such treachery.

So the *cosca* assembled Sunday morning for breakfast in the home of Aldo Monza, and then the women went to mass with the children. Three men of the *cosca* took Fissolini's brother out to the fields—and to his death. The others listened to Fissolini hold court with the rest of his *cosca* gathered around him. Only Aldo Monza

ing them drinks and food. But this did not relax their vigilance. For one thing, they enjoyed watching the lithe bodies of the two women in their bathing suits, speculating about which of them was better in bed, and all agreeing on Buji, whose vivacious speech and laughter gave evidence of a higher potential for arousal. Now they prepared for the walk on the beach in good humor, even rolling up their trouser legs.

But Astorre motioned for them. "We'll stay in sight," he told them. "Enjoy your drinks."

The four of them strolled down the beach just out of reach of the surf, Astorre and Nello in front and the two women behind them. When the women had gone fifty yards, they began to strip off their bathing suits. Buji took down her shoulder straps to show her breasts and cupped them to hold the sun.

They all jumped into the surf, which was mild and rippling. Nello was a first-class swimmer, and he dove underwater and came up between Stella's legs so that when he stood she was on his shoulders. He shouted to Astorre, "Come on out!!" and Astorre waded to where he could swim, Buji holding on to him from behind. He pushed her underwater, sinking with her below the surface, but instead of being frightened, Buji tugged at his shorts to uncover his behind.

Submerged, he felt a throbbing in his ears. At

the same time he saw Buji's exposed white breasts suspended in the green water below the sea and her laughing face close to his. Then the throbbing in his ears came to a roar, and he surfaced, Buji clinging to his bare hips.

The first thing he saw was a speedboat roaring toward him, its motor a thunderstorm churning up air and water. Nello and Stella were on the beach. How did they get there so fast? Far off, he could see his bodyguards, trousers rolled, starting to run toward the sea from the villa. He pushed Buji underwater and away from him and tried to wade to the beach. But he was too late. The speedboat was very close, and he saw a man with a rifle aiming carefully. The noise of the shots was muffled by the roar of the motor.

The first bullet spun Astorre around so that he was a broad target to the gunman. His body seemed to jump out of the water, then collapsed below the surface. He could hear the boat receding, and then he felt Buji tugging at him, dragging him, and trying to lift him onto the beach.

When the bodyguards arrived they found Astorre facedown in the surf, a bullet in his throat, Buji weeping at his side.

IT TOOK ASTORRE four months to recover from his wounds. Bianco had him hidden in a small private hospital in Palermo where he could be guarded and given the best treatment. Bianco visited him every day, and Buji came on her days off from the club.

It was near the end of his stay that Buji brought him a two-inch-wide gold neckband from the center of which hung a gold disk etched with an image of the Virgin Mary. She put it around his neck like a collar and positioned the medallion over his wound. It had been treated with adhesive that made it stick to the skin. The disk was no bigger than a silver dollar, but it covered the wound and looked like an adornment. Still, there was nothing effeminate about it.

"That does the job," Buji said affectionately. "I couldn't bear looking at it." She kissed him gently.

"You just wash off the adhesive once a day," Bianco said.

"I'll get my throat slit by somebody who wants gold," Astorre said wryly. "Is this really necessary?"

"Yes," Bianco said. "A man of respect cannot flaunt an injury inflicted by an enemy. Also, Buji is right. Nobody can bear the sight of it."

The only thing that registered with Astorre was that Bianco had called him a man of respect. Octavius Bianco, that ultimate Mafioso, had done him the honor. He was surprised and flattered.

After Buji left—for a weekend with the wealthiest wine merchant in Palermo—Bianco held a mirror up for Astorre. The band of gold was handsomely made. The Madonna, Astorre thought; she was all over Sicily, in roadside shrines, in cars and houses, on children's toys.

He said to Bianco, "Why is it the Madonna Sicilians worship, instead of the Christ?"

Bianco shrugged. "Jesus was, after all, a man, and so cannot be fully trusted. Anyway, forget all that. It's done. Before you go back to America, you will spend a year with Mr. Pryor in London to learn about the banking business. Your uncle's orders. There is another thing. Nello must be killed."

Astorre had gone over the whole affair many times in his mind and knew Nello was guilty. But what was the reason? They had been good friends for such a long time, and it had been a genuine friendship. But then there had come the killing of the Corleonesi. Nello must be related in some way to the Corleonesi *cosca* and he had no choice.

And there was the fact that Nello had never tried to visit him in the hospital. In fact, Nello had disappeared from Palermo. He played at the club no more. Still, Astorre hoped he might be wrong.

"Are you sure it was Nello?" Astorre said. "He was my dearest friend."

"Who else could they use?" Bianco said. "Your most bitter enemy? Of course, your friend. In any case you will have to punish him yourself as a man of respect. So get well."

On Bianco's next visit Astorre said to him, "We have no proof against Nello. Let the matter rest, and make your peace with the Corleonesi. Let the word go out that I died of my wounds."

At first Bianco argued furiously, but then he accepted the wisdom of Astorre's advice and thought him a clever man. He could make peace with the Corleonesi, and the score would be even. As for Nello, he was just a pawn and not worth killing. Until another day.

IT TOOK a week for arrangements to be made. Astorre would return to the United States through London, to be briefed by Mr. Pryor. Bianco told Astorre that Aldo Monza would be sent to America directly to stay with Don Aprile and would be waiting for him in New York.

Astorre spent a year with Mr. Pryor in London. It was an enlightening experience.

In Mr. Pryor's den, over a jug of wine with lemon, it was explained that there were extraordinary plans for him. That his stay in Sicily had been part of a specific plan by the Don to prepare him for a certain important role.

Astorre asked him about Rosie. He had never forgotten her—her grace, her pure joy in living, her generosity in all things, including lovemaking. He missed her.

Mr. Pryor raised his eyebrows. "That Mafioso girl," he said. "I knew you would not forget her."

"Do you know where she is?" Astorre asked.

"Certainly," Pryor said. "In New York."

Astorre said hesitantly, "I've been thinking about her. After all, I was gone a long time and she was young. What happened was very natural. I was hoping to see her again."

"Of course," Mr. Pryor said. "Why would you not? After dinner I will give you all the information you need."

So late that night in Mr. Pryor's den, Astorre got the full story on Rosie. Mr. Pryor played tapes of Rosie's phone conversations that revealed her meetings with men in her flat. These tapes made clear that Rosie had sexual liaisons with them, that they gave her expensive gifts and money. It was a shock for Astorre to hear her voice, using tones that he had thought were meant only for him—the clear laugh, the witty, affectionate quips. She was extremely charming and never coarse or vulgar. She made herself sound like a high school girl going on a prom date. Her innocence was a work of genius.

Mr. Pryor was wearing his cap low over his eyes, but he was watching Astorre.

Astorre said, "She's very good, isn't she?"

"A natural," Mr. Pryor said.

"Were these tapes made when I was going with her?" Astorre asked.

Mr. Pryor made a deprecating gesture. "It was my duty to protect you. Yes."

"And you never said anything?" Astorre said.

"You were really madly in love," Mr. Pryor said. "Why should I spoil your pleasure? She was not greedy, she treated you well. I was young myself once, and believe me, in love the truth is of no importance. And despite everything, she is a marvelous girl."

"A high-class call girl," Astorre said, almost bitterly.

"Not really," Mr. Pryor said. "She had to live by her wits. She ran away from home when she was fourteen, but she was highly intelligent and wanted an education. She also wanted to live a happy life. All perfectly natural. She could make men happy, a rare talent. It was fair that they should pay a price."

Astorre laughed. "You are an enlightened Sicilian. But what about spending twenty-four hours with the dead body of a lover?"

Mr. Pryor laughed with delight. "But that is the best part of her. Truly Mafioso. She has a warm heart but a cold mind. What a combination. Magnificent. But then, you must always be wary of her. Such a person is always dangerous."

"And the amyl nitrate?" Astorre asked.

"Of that she is innocent. Her affair with the professor had been going on before she met you, and he insisted on the drug. No, what we have here is a girl who straightforwardly thinks of her own happiness to the exclusion of everything else. She has no social inhibitions. My advice to you is stay in touch. You may want to make some professional use of her."

"I agree," Astorre said. He was surprised that he felt no anger toward Rosie. That her charm was all she needed to be forgiven. He would let it go, he told Mr. Pryor.

"Good," Mr. Pryor said. "After a year here, you will go to Don Aprile."

"And what will happen to Bianco?" Astorre asked.

Mr. Pryor shook his head and sighed. "Bianco must yield. The Corleonesi cosca is too strong. They will not pursue you. The Don made the peace. The truth is that Bianco's success has made him too civilized."

ASTORRE KEPT track of Rosie. Partly out of caution, partly out of fond remembrance of the

great love of his life. He knew that she had
returned to school and was working toward her
Ph.D. in psychology at New York University and
that she lived in a secure apartment building
nearby where she had finally become more
professional with older and richer men.

She was very clever. She ran three liaisons at a
time and apportioned her rewards among expensive gifts of money, jewelry, and vacations to the
spas of the rich—where she made further
contacts. No one could call her a professional
call girl, since she never asked for anything, but
she never refused a gift.

That these men fell in love with her was a fore-
gone conclusion. But she never accepted their
offers of marriage. She insisted that they were
friends who loved each other, that marriage was
not suitable for her or them. Most of the men
accepted this decision with grateful relief. She
was not a gold digger; she did not press for
money and showed no evidence of greed. All she
wanted was to live in a luxurious style, free of
encumbrance. But she did have an instinct to
squirrel money away for a rainy day. She had five
different bank accounts and two safe-deposit
boxes.

It was a few months after the Don's death that
Astorre decided to see Rosie again. He was
certain that it was only to get her help in his

plans. He told himself that he knew her secrets and she could not dazzle him again. And she was in his debt and he knew her fatal secret.

He knew also that in a certain sense she was amoral. That she put herself and her pleasure in an exalted realm, an almost religious belief. She believed with all her heart that she had a right to be happy and that this took precedence over everything else.

But more than anything, he wanted to see her again. Like many men, the passage of time had lessened her betrayals and heightened her charms. Now her sins seemed more a youthful carelessness, not some proof that she did not love him. He remembered her breasts, how they blotched with pink when she made love; the way she ducked her head in shyness; her infectious high spirits; her gentle good humor. The way she walked so effortlessly with her stiltlike legs and the incredible heat of her mouth on his lips. Despite all this, Astorre convinced himself that this visit was strictly business. He had a job for her to do.

Rosie was about to enter her apartment building when he stepped in front of her, smiled, and said hello. She was carrying books in her right arm and she dropped them on the pavement. Her face blushed with pleasure; her eyes sparkled. She threw her arms around him and kissed him on the mouth.

"I knew I'd see you again," she said. "I knew you'd forgive me." Then she pulled him into the building and led him up one flight of stairs to her apartment.

There she poured them drinks, wine for her, brandy for him. She sat next to him on the sofa. The room was luxuriously furnished, and he knew where the money came from.

"Why did you wait so long?" Rosie asked. As she spoke, she was removing the rings from her fingers, detaching her earrings, tugging at the lobes. She slipped off the three bracelets from her left arm, all gold and diamonds.

"I was busy," Astorre said. "And it took me a long time to find you."

Rosie gave him an affectionate, tender look. "Do you still sing? Do you still ride in that ridiculous red outfit?" She kissed him again, and Astorre felt a warmth in his brain, a hopeless response.

"No," he said. "Rosie, we can't go back."

Rosie pulled him to his feet. "It was the happiest time of my life," she said. Then they were in the bedroom, and in seconds they were naked.

Rosie took a bottle of perfume from her night table and sprayed first herself, then him. "No time for a bath," she said, laughing. And then they were in bed together and he saw the pink blotches grow slowly over her breasts.

For Astorre it was a disembodied experience. He enjoyed the sex but he could not enjoy Rosie. A vision arose in his mind of her keeping vigilance over the dead professor's body for a night and a day. Had he been alive, could he have been helped to live? What had Rosie done alone with death and the professor?

Lying on her back, Rosie reached out to touch his check. She ducked her head down and murmured softly, "That old black magic doesn't work anymore." She had been toying with the gold medallion on his neck, saw the ugly purple wound, and kissed it.

Astorre said, "It was fine."

Rosie sat up, her naked torso and breasts hanging over him. "You can't forgive me for the professor, that I let him die and stayed with him. Isn't that right?"

Astorre didn't answer. He would never tell her what he knew about her now. That she had never changed.

Rosie got out of bed and started to dress. He did the same.

"You're a much more terrible person," Rosie said. "The adopted nephew of Don Aprile." And your friend in London who helped clean up my mess. He did a very professional job for an English banker, but not when you know he immigrated from Italy. It wasn't hard to figure out."

They were in the living room, and she made them another drink. She looked earnestly into his eyes. "I know what you are. And I don't mind, I really don't. We're really soul mates. Isn't that perfect?"

Astorre laughed. "The last thing I want to find is a soul mate," he said. "But I did come to see you on business."

Rosie was impassive now. All the charm was gone from her face. She began to slip her rings back onto her fingers. "My price for a quickie is five hundred dollars," she said. "I can take a check." She smiled at him mischievously—it was a joke. He knew she only took gifts on holidays and birthdays, and those were far more substantial. In fact, the apartment they were in had been a birthday gift from an admirer.

"No, seriously," said Astorre. And then he told her about the Sturzo brothers and what he wanted her to do. And he put the closer on it. "I'll give you twenty thousand now for expenses," he said, "and another hundred thousand when you're done."

Rosie looked at him very thoughtfully. "And what happens afterward?" she asked.

"You don't have to worry," Astorre said.

"I see," Rosie said. "And what if I say no?"

Astorre shrugged. He didn't want to think about that. "Nothing," he said.

"You won't turn me in to the English authorities?" she said.

"I could never do that to you," Astorre said, and she could not doubt the sincerity in his voice.

Rosie sighed. "OK." And then he saw her eyes sparkle. She grinned at him. "Another adventure," she said.

NOW, RIDING out through Westchester, Astorre was awakened from his memories by Aldo Monza pressing his leg. "A half hour to go," Monza said. "You have to prepare yourself for the Sturzo brothers."

Astorre stared out the car window at the fresh snowflakes falling. They were in a countryside barren but for large, bare trees, whose sparkling branches stuck out like magician's wands. The blanket of luminescent snow made the covered stones seem like bright stars. At that moment Astorre felt a cold desolation in his heart. After this night, his world would change, he would change, and in some way his true life would begin.

• • •

ASTORRE REACHED the safe house in a landscape ghostly white, snow in huge drifts.

Inside, the Sturzo twins were handcuffed, their feet shackled, and special restraining jackets fitted onto their bodies. They were lying on the floor of one bedroom, guarded by two armed men.

Astorre regarded them with sympathy. "It's a compliment," he told them. "We appreciate how dangerous you are."

The two brothers were completely different in their attitudes. Stace seemed calm, resigned, but Franky glared at them with hatred that transfigured his face from its usual amiable look into a gargoyle.

Astorre sat on the bed. "I guess you guys have figured it out," he said.

Stace said quietly, "Rosie was bait. She was very good, right, Franky?"

"Exceptional," Franky said. He was trying to keep his voice from ranging hysterically high.

"That's because she really liked you guys," Astorre said. "She was crazy about you, especially Franky. It was tough for her. Very tough."

Franky said contemptuously, "Then why did she do it?"

"Because I gave her a lot of money," Astorre

said. "Really a lot of money. You know how that is, Franky."

"No, I don't," Franky said.

"I figure it took a big price for two smart guys like you to take the contract on the Don," Astorre said. "A million? Two million?"

Stace said, "You have it all wrong. We had no part in that. We're not that stupid."

Astorre said, "I know you're the shooters. You have a rep for having big balls. And I checked you out. Now, what I want from you is the name of the broker."

"You're wrong," Stace said. "There is no way you can put that on us. And who the hell are you, anyway?"

"I'm the Don's nephew," Astorre said. "His sweeper-upper. And I've been checking you two guys out for nearly six months. At the time of the shooting, you weren't in L.A. You didn't show for over a week. Franky, you missed two games coaching the kids. Stace, you never dropped in to see how the store went. You never even called. So just tell me where you were."

"I was in Vegas gambling," Franky said. "And we could talk better if you took off some of these restraints. We're not fucking Houdinis."

Astorre gave him a sympathetic smile. "In a bit," he said. "Stace, how about you?"

"I was up with my girlfriend in Tahoe," Stace said. "But who the hell can remember?"

Astorre said, "Maybe I'll have better luck talking to you separately."

He left them and went down to the kitchen, where Monza had coffee waiting for him. He told Monza to put the brothers into different bedrooms and keep two guards with each man at all times. Aldo was working with a six-man team.

"Are you sure you have the right fellows?" Monza said.

"I think so," Astorre said. "If not them, it's just their bad luck. I hate to ask you, Aldo, but you may have to help them talk."

"Well, they don't always talk," Monza said. "It's hard to believe, but people are willful. And these two look very hard to me."

"I just hate to go that low," Astorre said.

He waited an hour before going up to the room where Franky was. Night had fallen, but reflected in the lamplight outside he could see snowflakes swirling slowly down. He found Franky on the floor in full restraints.

"It's very simple," Astorre said to him. "Give us the name of the broker, and you may get out of here alive."

Franky looked at him with hatred. "I'll never fucking tell you anything, you asshole. You got the wrong guys. And I'll remember your face and I'll remember Rosie."

"That's absolutely the wrong thing to say," Astorre told him.

"Were you fucking her too?" Franky said. "You're a pimp?"

Astorre understood. Franky would never forgive the betrayal by Rosie. What a frivolous response to a serious situation.

"I think you're being stupid," Astorre said. "And you guys have a rep for being smart."

"I don't give a flying fuck what you think," Franky said. "You can't do anything if you have no proof."

"Really? So I'm wasting my time with you," Astorre said. "I'll go talk with Stace."

Astorre went down to the kitchen for more coffee before he went up to Stace. He pondered the fact that Franky could look so confident and speak so brashly while under such strict constraints. Well, he would have to do better with Stace. He found the man propped up uncomfortably in bed.

"Take his jacket off," Astorre said. "But check his cuffs and shackles."

"I figured it out," Stace said to him calmly. "You know we have a stash. I can arrange for you to pick it up and end this nonsense."

"I just had a talk with Franky," Astorre said. "I

was disappointed in him. You and your brother are supposed to be very smart guys. Now you talk to me about money, and you know this is about you hitting the Don."

"You have it wrong," Stace said.

Astorre said gently, "I know you weren't in Tahoe, and I know Franky wasn't in Vegas. You are the only two freelancers who had the balls to take the job. And the shooters were lefties like you and Franky. So all I want to know is, who was your broker?"

"Why should I tell you?" Stace said. "I know the story is over. You guys didn't wear masks, you exposed Rosie, so you are not going to let us out of here alive. No matter what you promise."

Astorre sighed. "I won't try to con you. That's about it. But you have one thing you can bargain for. Easy or hard. I have a very Qualified Man with me, and I'm going to put him to work on Franky." As he said this, Astorre felt a queasiness in his stomach. He remembered Aldo Monza working on Fissolini.

"You're wasting your time," Stace said. "Franky won't talk."

"Maybe not," Astorre said. "But he'll be taken apart piece by piece, and each piece will be brought to you to check. I figure you to talk to save him from that. But why even start down that road? And Stace, why would you want to protect that broker? He was supposed to cover you, and he didn't."

Stace didn't answer. Then he said, "Why don't you let Franky go?"

Astorre said, "You know better than that."

"How do you know I won't lie to you?" Stace said.

"Why the hell should you?" Astorre said. "What do you gain? Stace, you can keep Franky from going through something really terrible. You have to see it clear."

"We were just the shooters, doing a job," Stace said. "The guy higher is the one you want. Why can't you just let us go?"

Astorre was patient. "Stace, you and your brother took the job of killing a great man. Big price, big ego thing. Come on. It boosted you. You guys took your shot and lost, and now you have to pay or else the whole world is on a tilt. It has to be. Now, all you have is the choice, easy or hard. In an hour from now you can be looking at a very important piece of Franky on that table. Believe me, I don't want to do that, I really don't."

Stace said, "How do I know you're not full of shit?"

Astorre said, "Think, Stace. Think how I set you up with Rosie. A lot of time and patience. Think, I got you to this place and have seven armed men. A lot of expenses and a lot of trouble. And just before Christmas Eve. I'm a very serious fellow, Stace, you can see that. I'll give you an hour to think it over. I promise if you talk, Franky will never know it's coming."

ASTORRE WENT down to the kitchen again. Monza was waiting for him.

"So?" Monza said.

"I don't know," Astorre said. "But I have to be at Nicole's Christmas Eve party tomorrow, so we have to end this tonight."

"It won't take me over an hour," Monza said. "He'll either talk or be dead."

ASTORRE RELAXED by the roaring fire for a short time and then went upstairs again to see Stace. The man looked weary and resigned. He had thought it over. He knew Franky would never talk—Franky thought there was still hope. Stace believed Astorre had put all the cards on the table. And now Stace comprehended the fears of all the men he had killed, their last despairing and fruitless hopes for some fate to save them. Against all probabilities. And he didn't want Franky to die like that, piece by piece. He studied Astorre's face. It was stern, implacable despite his youth. He had the gravity of a high judge.

The heavily falling snow was coating the windowpanes like white fur. Franky, in his room, was daydreaming about being in Europe with Rosie, the snow coating the Paris boulevards, falling into the canals of Venice. The snow like magic. Rome like magic.

Stace lay on his bed worrying about Franky. They had taken the shot and lost. And it was the end of the story. But he could help Franky think they were only twenty points down.

"I'm OK with it now," Stace said. "Make sure Franky doesn't know what's happening, OK?"

"I promise," Astorre said. "But I'll know if you're lying."

"No," Stace said. "What's the point? The broker is a guy named Heskow, and he lives in a town called Brightwaters, just past Babylon. He's divorced, lives alone, and has a sixteen-year-old humongous kid who's a terrific basketball player. Heskow's hired us for some jobs over the years. We go back to when we were kids. The price was a million, but still me and Franky were leery about taking it. Too big a hit. We took it because he said we didn't have to worry about the FBI and we didn't have to worry about the police. That it was a great big fix. He also told us that the Don no longer had any juice connections. But he was obviously wrong on that. You're here. It was just too big a payday to turn down."

"That's a lot of info to give a guy you think is full of shit," Astorre said.

"I want to convince you I'm telling the truth," Stace said. "I figured it out. The story is over. I don't want Franky to know it."

"Don't worry," Astorre said. "I believe you."

He left the room and went down to the kitchen to give Monza his instructions. He wanted their IDs, licenses, credit cards, et cetera. He kept his word to Stace: Franky was to be shot in the back of the head without any warning. And Stace was also to be executed without pain.

Astorre left to drive back to New York. The snow had turned to rain, and it rinsed the countryside of snow.

IT WAS RARE that Monza disregarded an order, but as the executioner he felt he had the right to protect himself and his men. There would be no guns. He would use rope.

First he took four guards to help him strangle Stace. The man didn't even try to resist. But with Franky it was different. For twenty minutes he tried to twist away from the rope. For a terrible twenty minutes Franky Sturzo knew he was being murdered.

Then the two bodies were wrapped in blankets and carried through the heavy glades as the rain

changed back into snow. They were deposited in
the forest behind the house. A hole in a very
dense thicket was the hiding place, and they
would not be discovered until spring, if ever. By
that time the bodies would be so destroyed by
nature that, Monza hoped, the cause of death
could not be determined.

But it was not only for this practical reason that
Monza had disobeyed his chief. For like Don
Aprile, he felt deeply that mercy could only
come from God. He despised the idea of any
kind of mercy for men who hired themselves out
as killers of other men. It was presumptuous for
one man to forgive another. That was the duty of
God. For men to pretend such mercy was an idle
pride and a lack of respect. He did not desire any
such mercy for himself.

CHAPTER 9

KURT CILKE BELIEVED in the law, those rules man invented to live a peaceful life. He had always tried to avoid those compromises that undermine a fair society, and he fought without mercy against the enemies of the state. After twenty years of the struggle, he had lost a great deal of his faith.

Only his wife lived up to his expectations. The politicians were liars, the rich merciless in their greed for power, the poor vicious. And then there were the born con men, the swindlers, the brutes and murderers. The enforcers of the law were only slightly better, but he had believed with all his heart that the Bureau was the best of all.

Over the past year he'd had a recurring dream. In it he was a boy of twelve, and he had to take a crucial school exam that would last all day. When he left the house his mother was in tears, and in his dream he understood why. If he did not pass the exam, he would never see her again.

In the dream he understood murder had become so rampant that laws had been set up with the help of the psychiatric community to develop a protocol of mental-health tests that could predict which twelve-year-olds would grow up to become murderers. Those who failed the test simply vanished. For medical science had proved that murderers killed for the pleasure of killing. That political crimes, rebellion, terrorism, jealousy, and stealing were simply the surface excuses. So it was only necessary to weed out these genetic murderers at an early age.

The dream jumped to his return home after the exam, and his mother hugged and kissed him. His uncles and cousins had prepared a huge celebration. Then he was alone in his bedroom shaking with fear. For he knew there had been a mistake. He should never have passed the exam, and now he would grow up to be a murderer.

The dream had occurred twice, and he did not mention it to his wife because he knew what the dream meant, or thought he did.

Cilke's relationship with Timmona Portella was now over six years old. It had begun when Portella murdered an underling in a blind rage. Cilke had immediately seen the possibilities. He had made arrangements for Portella to be an informant on the Mafia in return for nonprosecution of the murder. The director had approved the plan, and the rest was history. With Portella's help, Cilke had crushed the New York Mafia but had had to turn a blind eye to Portella's operations, including his supervision of the drug trade.

But Cilke, with approval from the director, had plans to bring Portella down again. Portella was determined to acquire the use of the Aprile banks to launder the drug money. But Don Aprile had proved obstinate. At one fateful meeting Portella had asked Cilke, "Will the FBI be surveilling Don Aprile when he attends his grandson's confirmation?" Cilke understood immediately, but he hesitated before he answered. Then he said slowly, "I guarantee that they will not be. But what about the NYPD?"

"That's taken care of," Portella said.

And Cilke knew he would be an accomplice to murder. But didn't the Don deserve it? He had been a ruthless criminal most of his life. He had retired with enormous wealth, untouched by the law. And look at the gain. Portella would walk right into his trap by acquiring the Aprile banks. And of course, there was always Inzio in the background, with his dreams of his own nuclear arsenal. Cilke knew that with luck he could wrap it all up and the government could get ten billion dollars' worth of Aprile banks under RICO, for there was no doubt that the Don's heirs would sell the banks, make a deal with Portella's secret emissaries. And ten or eleven billion dollars would be a powerful weapon against crime itself.

But Georgette would despise him, so she must never know. After all, she lived in a different world.

But now he had to meet with Portella again. There was the matter of his butchered German shepherds and who was behind it. He would start with Portella.

TIMMONA PORTELLA was that rarity in Italian men of achievement: a bachelor in his fifties. But he was by no means celibate. Every Friday he spent most of the night with a beautiful woman from one of the escort services controlled by his underlings. The instructions were that the girl be young, not too long in the game, that she be beautiful and delicately featured. That she be jolly and upbeat but not a wise-ass. And that no kinkiness be proposed. Timmona was a straight-from-the-shoulder sex guy. He had his little quirks, but they were harmlessly avuncular. One of them being that the girls had to have a plain Anglo-Saxon name like Jane or Susan; he could cope with something like Tiffany or even Merle, but nothing with any ethnicity. Rarely did he have the same woman twice.

These assignations were always held in a relatively small East Side hotel owned by one of his companies, where he had the use of an entire floor, consisting of two interlocking suites. One had a fully stocked kitchen, for Portella was a gifted amateur chef, oddly enough of Northern Italian cuisine, though his parents had been born in Sicily. And he loved to cook.

Tonight the girl was brought to his suite by the owner of the escort service, who stayed for a drink and then disappeared. Then Portella whipped up supper for two while they chatted and got acquainted. Her name was Janet. Portella cooked with quick efficiency. Tonight he made his specialty: veal Milanese, spaghetti in a sauce with Gruyère cheese, tiny roasted eggplants on the side, and a salad of greens with tomatoes. Dessert was an assortment of pastries from a famous French patisserie in the neighborhood.

He served Janet with a courtliness that belied his exterior; he was a large, hairy man with a huge head and coarse skin, but he always ate in shirt, tie, and jacket. Over dinner, he asked Janet questions about her life with concern unexpected in so brutal a man. He delighted to hear her tales of misfortune, how she had been betrayed by her father, brothers, lovers, and the powerful men who led her into a sinful life through economic pressures and unwanted pregnancies so she could save her poverty-stricken family. He was amazed at the varieties of dishonorable behavior displayed by his fellow men and marveled at his own goodness with women. For he was extremely generous with them, not only by giving them huge sums of money.

After dinner he took the wine into the sitting room and showed Janet six boxes of jewelry: a gold watch, a ruby ring, diamond earrings, a jade necklace, a jeweled armband, and a perfect string of pearls. He told her she could choose one as a gift. They were all worth a few thousand dollars—the girls would usually have them appraised.

Years ago one of his crews had hijacked a jewelry truck, and he had warehoused the contents rather than have them fenced. So, actually, the gifts cost him nothing.

While Janet considered what she wanted, and finally chose the watch, he drew her a bath, carefully testing the temperature of the water and providing her with his favorite perfumes and powders. It was only then, after she had relaxed, that they retired to bed and had good normal sex, as any happily married couple would do.

If he was particularly amorous, he might keep a

girl until four or five in the morning, but he never went to sleep while she was in his suite. This night he dismissed Janet early.

He did it all for his health. He knew that he had a wild temper that could get him into trouble. These weekly sex trysts calmed him down. Women in general had a quieting effect on him, and he proved the efficacy of his strategy by going to his doctor every Saturday and hearing with satisfaction that his blood pressure had returned to normal. When he told this to his doctor, the man had only murmured, "Very interesting." Portella was very disappointed in him.

There was another advantage to this arrangement. Portella's bodyguards were isolated in front of the suite. But the back door led to the adjoining suite with its entrance into a separate hallway, and it was there that Portella had meetings he did not want his closest advisors to know about. For it is a very dangerous business for a Mafia chief to meet in private with an FBI special agent. He would be suspected as an informer, and Cilke might be suspected by the Bureau of being a bribe taker.

It was Portella who supplied the phone numbers to be tapped, named the weaklings who would cave under pressure, pointed to clues to racket murders, and explained how certain rackets worked. And it was Portella who did some dirty jobs that the FBI could not legally do.

Over the years they had developed a code for arranging meetings. Cilke had a key to the suite door in the opposite hallway so he could enter without being detected by Portella's bodyguards and wait in the minor suite. Portella would get rid of his girl, and their meeting would begin. On this particular night, Portella was waiting for Cilke.

Cilke was always a little nervous at these meetings. He knew that not even Portella would dare harm an FBI agent, but the man had a temperament that verged on insanity. Cilke was armed, but to hide the identity of his informant he couldn't bring bodyguards.

Portella had a wineglass in his hand, and his first words of greeting were "What the fuck's wrong now?" But he was smiling genially and gave Cilke a half hug. Portella's massive belly was hidden in an elegant Chinese robe over white pajamas.

Cilke refused a drink, sat on the sofa, and said calmly, "A few weeks ago, I went home after work and found my two dogs with their hearts cut out. I thought you might have a clue." He watched Portella closely.

Portella's surprise seemed genuine. He had

been sitting in an armchair and seemed galvanized out of his seat. His face filled with rage. Cilke was not impressed; in his experience the guilty could react with the purest innocence. He said, "If you're trying to warn me off something, why not tell me directly?"

At this Portella said almost tearfully, "Kurt, you come here armed; I felt your gun. I am not armed. You could kill me and claim I resisted arrest. I trust you. I've deposited over a million dollars in your Cayman Island account. We're partners. Why would I pull such an old Sicilian trick? Somebody is trying to split us up. You have to see that."

"Who?" Cilke said.

Portella was thoughtful. "It can only be that Astorre kid. He has delusions of grandeur because he got away from me once. Check him out, and meanwhile I'll put a contract on him."

Finally Cilke was convinced. "OK," he said, "but I think we have to be very careful. Don't underestimate this guy."

"Don't worry," Portella said. "Hey, did you eat? I have some veal and spaghetti, a salad and some good wine."

Cilke laughed. "I believe you. But I have no time for dinner."

The truth was he did not want to break bread with a man he would soon be sending to prison.

• • •

ASTORRE NOW had enough information to draw up a battle plan. He was convinced that the FBI had a hand in the Don's death. And that Cilke was in charge of the operation. He now knew who the broker was. He knew that Timmona Portella had put out the contract. And yet there remained some mysteries. The ambassador, through Nicole, had offered to buy the banks with foreign investors. Cilke had offered him a deal to betray Portella into a criminal situation. These were disturbing and dangerous variations. He decided to consult with Craxxi in Chicago and to bring Mr. Pryor with him.

Astorre had already requested that Mr. Pryor come to America to run the Aprile banks. Mr. Pryor had accepted the offer, and it was extraordinary how quickly he changed from English gentleman to American high-powered executive. He wore a homburg instead of the bowler; he discarded his furled umbrella and carried a folded newspaper, and he arrived with his wife and two nephews. His wife changed from English matron to a sleeker style of dress, quite in fashion. His two nephews were Sicilians who spoke perfect English and had degrees in accounting. Both were devoted hunters and kept their hunting gear in the trunk of a limousine, which one of the nephews drove. In fact, both of them served as Mr. Pryor's bodyguards.

The Pryors settled into an Upper West Side town house protected by security patrols from a private agency. Nicole, who had opposed the appointment, was soon charmed by Mr. Pryor, especially when he told her they were distant cousins. There was no doubt that Mr. Pryor had a certain fatherly charm with women; even Rosie had adored him. And there was no doubt he could run the banks—even Nicole was impressed by his knowledge of international banking. Just by trading currencies he had increased the profit margins. And Astorre knew that Mr. Pryor had been an intimate of Don Aprile. Indeed, it had been Pryor who had persuaded the Don to acquire the banks with an interlock run by Mr. Pryor in England and Italy. Mr. Pryor had described their relationship.

"I told your uncle," Mr. Pryor said, "that banks can acquire more wealth with less risk than the business he was in. Those old-time enterprises are passé; the government is too strong and they are too focused on our people. It was time to get out. Banks are the gateway to make money if you have the experience, personnel, and political contacts. Without boasting, I can say I have the goodwill of the politicians of Italy with money. Everybody gets rich, and nobody gets hurt or winds up in jail. I could be a university professor teaching people how to get rich without breaking the law and resorting to violence. You just have to make certain the correct laws are passed. After all, education is the key to a higher civilization."

Mr. Pryor was being playful, yet he was somewhat in earnest. Astorre felt a deep rapport with him and gave him his absolute trust. Don Craxxi and Mr. Pryor were men he could rely on. Not only from friendship: Both of them earned a fortune from the ten banks the Don owned.

WHEN ASTORRE and Mr. Pryor arrived at Don Craxxi's home in Chicago, Astorre was surprised to see Pryor and Craxxi embrace each other with great warmth. They obviously knew each other.

Craxxi provided a meal of fruit and cheese and chatted with Mr. Pryor while they ate. Astorre listened with intense curiosity; he loved to hear old men tell stories. Craxxi and Mr. Pryor agreed that the old ways of doing business had been fraught with peril. "Everybody had high blood pressure, everybody had heart problems," Craxxi said. "It was a terrible way to live. And the new element have no sense of honor. It's good to see them being wiped out."

"Ah," Mr. Pryor said. "But we all had to start somewhere. Look at us now."

All this talk made Astorre hesitate to bring up the business at hand. What the hell did these two old guys think they were doing now? Mr. Pryor chuckled at Astorre's look. "Don't worry, we are not yet saints, we two. And this situation challenges our own interests. So tell us what you need. We are ready to do business."

"I need your advice, nothing operational," Astorre said. "That's my job."

Craxxi said, "If it is solely for vengeance, I would advise you to go back to your singing. But I recognize, as I hope you do, that it is a matter of protecting your family from danger."

"Both," said Astorre. "Either reason would be sufficient. But my uncle had me trained for just this situation. I can't fail him."

"Good," Mr. Pryor said. "But recognize this fact: What you are doing is in your nature. Be careful about the risks you take. Don't be carried away."

Don Craxxi asked mildly, "How can I help you?"

"You were right about the Sturzo brothers," Astorre said. "They confessed to the hit, and they told me the broker was John Heskow, a man I've never heard of. So now I have to go after him."

"And the Sturzo brothers?" Craxxi asked.

"They are out of the picture."

The two old men were silent. Then Craxxi said, "Heskow I know. He has been a broker for twenty years. There are wild rumors about how he brokered some political assassinations, but I don't believe them. Now, whatever tactics you used to make the Sturzo brothers talk won't work with Heskow. He is a great negotiator, and he will recognize that he has to bargain his way out of death. He will know you must have information only he can give you."

"He has a son he adores," Astorre said. "A basketball player, and he is Heskow's life."

"That is an old card and he will trump it," Mr. Pryor said, "by withholding information that is crucial and giving you information that is not crucial. You have to understand Heskow. He has bargained with death all his life. Find another approach."

"There are a lot of things I want to know before I can go any further," Astorre said. "Who was behind the killing, and most of all, why? Now, here's my thought. It must be the banks. Somebody needs the banks."

"Heskow might know some of that," Craxxi said.

"It bothers me," Astorre said, "that there was no police or FBI surveillance at the cathedral for the confirmation. And the Sturzo brothers told me that they had been guaranteed there would be no surveillance. Can I believe that the police and the FBI had prior knowledge of the hit? Is that possible?"

"It is," Don Craxxi said. "And in that case you must be very careful. Especially with Heskow."

Mr. Pryor said coolly, "Astorre, your primary goal is to save the banks and protect Don Aprile's children. Vengeance is a minor goal that can be abandoned."

"I don't know," Astorre said, noncommittal now. "I'll have to think about that." He gave both men a sincere smile. "But we'll see how it works out."

The two old men did not believe him for a moment. In their lifetimes they had known and recognized young fellows like Astorre. They saw him as a throwback to the great Mafia leaders of the early days, men they had not become themselves because of a certain lack of charisma and will that only the great ones had: the men of respect who had dominated provinces, defied the rules of the state, and emerged triumphant. They recognized in Astorre that will, that charm, that single-mindedness that he himself was not aware of. Even his foolishness, his singing, his riding of horses were weaknesses that did not harm his destiny. They were merely youthful joys and showed his good heart.

Astorre told them about the consul general, Marriano Rubio, and about Inzio Tulippa trying to buy the banks. About Cilke trying to use him to trap Portella. The two old men listened carefully.

"Send them to me the next time," Mr. Pryor said. "From my information Rubio is the financial manager of the world drug trade."

"I won't sell," Astorre said. "The Don instructed me."

"Of course," Craxxi said. "They are the future and can be your protection." He paused and then went on. "Let me tell you a little story. Before I retired I had an associate, a very straight businessman, a credit to society. He invited me to lunch at his office building, in his private dining room. Afterward he took me on a tour and showed me these enormous rooms that held a thousand computer cubicles manned by young men and women.

"He said to me, 'That room earns me a billion dollars a year. There are nearly three hundred million people in this country, and we are devoted to making them buy our products. We plan special lotteries, prizes, and bonuses, we make extravagant promises, all legally defined to make them spend their money for all our companies. And you know what is crucial? We must have banks who will supply these three hundred million people credit to spend money they don't have.' Banks are the name of the game, you must have banks on your side."

"That's true," Mr. Pryor said. "And both sides profit. Though interest rates are high, those debts spur people on, make them achieve more."

Astorre laughed. "I'm glad that keeping the banks is smart. But it doesn't matter. The Don told me not to sell. That's enough for me. And that they killed him makes a difference."

Craxxi said to Astorre very firmly, "You cannot do harm to that man Cilke. The government is now too strong to take such ultimate action against. But I agree he is a danger of some kind. You must be clever."

"Your next step is Heskow," Pryor said. "He is crucial, but again you have to be careful. Remember, you can call on Don Craxxi for help, and I myself have resources. We are not fully retired. And we have an interest in the banks—not to mention our affection for Don Aprile, rest in peace."

"OK," Astorre said. "After I see Heskow, we can meet again."

ASTORRE WAS acutely aware of his dangerous position. He knew that his successes were small, despite his punishment of the assassins. They were only a thread pulled out of the mystery of Don Aprile's murder. But he relied on the infallible paranoia drilled into him during his years of training in Sicily's endless treacheries. He had to be especially careful now. Heskow seemed like an easy target, but he could also be booby-trapped.

One thing surprised him. He had thought himself happy in his life as a small businessman and amateur singer, but now he felt an elation that he had never experienced before. A feeling that he was back in a world in which he belonged. And that he had a mission. To protect the children of Don Aprile, to avenge the death of a man he had loved. He simply had to crack the will of the enemy. Aldo Monza had brought back ten good men from his village in Sicily. At Astorre's instructions he had ensured the livelihood of their families for life, no matter what happened to them.

"Do not count on the gratitude of deeds done for people in the past," he remembered the Don lecturing him. "You must make them grateful for things you will do for them in the future." The banks were the future for the Aprile family, Astorre, and his growing army of men. It was a future worth fighting for, no matter the cost.

Don Craxxi had supplied him with another six

men he absolutely vouched for. And Astorre had turned his home into a fortress with these men and the latest security detection devices. He had also set up a safe house to disappear to, if the authorities wanted to grab him for whatever reason.

He did not use close bodyguards. Instead, he relied on his own quickness and used his guards as advance scouts on the routes he would take.

He would let Heskow sit for a time. Astorre wondered about Cilke's reputation as an honorable man, as even Don Aprile had so described him.

"There are honorable men who spend all their lives preparing for a supreme act of treachery," Pryor had said to him. But despite all this, Astorre felt confident. All he would have to do was to stay alive as the puzzle pieces fit together.

The real test would come from men like Heskow, Portella, Tulippa, and Cilke. He would personally have to get his hands bloody once again.

IT TOOK a month for Astorre to figure out exactly how to handle John Heskow. The man would be formidable, tricky, easy to kill but difficult to extract information from. Using his son as leverage was too dangerous—it would force Heskow to plot against him while pretending to cooperate. He decided that he would not let Heskow know that the Sturzo brothers had told him Heskow was the driver on the hit. That might scare him too much.

Meanwhile, he amassed the necessary information on Heskow's daily habits. It seemed he was a temperate man whose primary love was growing flowers and selling them wholesale to florists and even personally from a roadside stand in the Hamptons. His only indulgence was attending the basketball games of his son's team, and he followed Villanova's basketball schedule religiously.

ONE SATURDAY NIGHT in January Heskow was going to the Villanova-Temple game at Madison Square Garden in New York. When he left his house he buttoned it up with his sophisticated alarm system. He was always careful in the everyday details of life, always confident that he had made provisions for every possible accident. And it was that confidence Astorre wanted to shatter at the very beginning of their interview.

John Heskow drove into the city and had a solitary dinner at a Chinese restaurant near the Garden. He always ate Chinese when he went out because it was the one thing he could not cook better at home. He liked the silver covers over each dish as if it contained some delightful surprise. He liked Chinese people. They minded their own business, didn't make small talk or show obsequious familiarity. And never, ever, had he found a mistake in his bill, which he always checked carefully because he ordered numerous dishes.

Tonight he went all out. He was particularly fond of Peking duck and crayfish in Cantonese lobster sauce. There was a special white fried rice and of course a few fried dumplings and spicy spareribs. He finished off with green-tea ice cream, an acquired taste, but one that showed he was a gourmet of Eastern food.

When he arrived at the Garden, the arena was only half full, though Temple had a high-ranked team. Heskow took his choice seat, provided by his son, near the floor and middle of the court. This made him proud of Jocko.

The game was not exciting. Temple crushed Villanova, but Jocko was the high scorer in the game. Afterward Heskow went back to the locker room.

His son greeted him with a hug. "Hey, Dad, I'm glad you came. You want to come out and eat with us?"

Heskow was enormously gratified. His son was

a true gentleman. Of course these kids didn't want an old geezer like him around on their night out in the city. They wanted to get drunk, have some laughs, and maybe get laid.

"Thanks," Heskow said. "I already had dinner, and I have a long drive home. You played great tonight. I'm proud of you. Now go out and have a good time." He gave his son a farewell kiss and wondered how he had gotten so lucky. Well, his son had a good mother, though she'd been a lousy wife.

It took Heskow only an hour to drive home to Brightwaters—the Long Island parkways were almost deserted at this hour. He was tired when he got there, but before going into the house he checked the flower sheds to make sure the temperature and moisture were OK.

In the moonlight reflected though the glass roof of the shed, the flowers had a wild, nightmarish beauty, the red almost black, the whites a ghostly vaporish halo. He loved looking at them, especially just before he went to sleep.

He walked the gravel driveway to his house and unlocked the door. Once inside he quickly pushed the numbers on the panel that would keep the alarm from going off, then went into the living room.

His heart took a giant leap. Two men stood waiting for him; he recognized Astorre. He knew enough about death to recognize it at a glance. These were the messengers.

But he reacted with the perfect defense mechanism. "How the fuck did you two guys get in here, and what the hell do you want?"

"Don't panic," Astorre said. He introduced himself, adding that he was the nephew of the deceased Don Aprile.

Heskow made himself get calm. He had been in tight spots before, and after the first rush of adrenaline, he had always been OK. He sat down on the sofa so that his hand was on the wooden armrest and reached for his hidden gun. "So what do you want?"

Astorre had an amused smiled on his face, which irritated Heskow, who had meant to wait for the right moment. Now he flipped open the armrest and reached for the gun. The hollow was empty.

At that moment three cars appeared in the driveway, headlights flashing into the room. Two more men entered the house.

Astorre said pleasantly, "I didn't underestimate you, John. We searched the house. We found the gun in the coffeepot, another taped underneath your bed, another in that fake letterbox, and the one in the bathroom taped behind the bowl. Did we miss any?"

Heskow didn't answer. His heart had started pounding again. He could feel it in his throat.

"What the hell are you growing in those flower sheds?" Astorre asked, laughing. "Diamonds, hemp, coke, what? I thought you'd never come in. By the way, that's a lot of firepower for someone who grows azaleas."

"Stop jerking me around," Heskow said quietly.

Astorre sat down in the chair opposite Heskow and then tossed two wallets—Gucci, one gold, one brown—on the coffee table between them. "Take a look," he said.

Heskow reached over and opened them. The first thing he saw was the Sturzo brothers' driver's licenses with their laminated photos. The bile in his throat was so sour he almost vomited.

"They gave you up," Astorre said. "That you were the broker on Don Aprile's hit. They also said you guaranteed there would be no NYPD or FBI surveillance at the church ceremony."

Heskow processed everything that had happened. They hadn't just killed him, though the Sturzo brothers were certainly dead. He felt one tiny pang of disappointment for that betrayal. But Astorre didn't seem to know he had been the driver. There was a negotiation here, the most important of his life.

Heskow shrugged. "I don't know what you're talking about."

Aldo Monza had been listening alertly, keeping a close eye on Heskow. Now he went into the kitchen and came back with two cups of black coffee, handing one to Astorre and one to Heskow. He said, "Hey, you got Italian coffee— great." Heskow gave him a contemptuous look.

Astorre drank his coffee and then said to Heskow, slowly, deliberately, "I hear you're a very intelligent man, that that's the only reason you're not dead. So listen to me and really think. I'm Don Aprile's cleanup man. I have all the resources he had before he retired. You knew him, you know what that means. You would never have dared to be the broker if he wasn't retired. Right?"

Heskow didn't say anything. Just kept watching Astorre, trying to judge him.

"The Sturzos are dead," Astorre continued. "You can join them. But I have a proposition, and you have to be very alert here. In the next thirty minutes you will have to convince me you're on my side, that you will act as my agent. If you don't, you will be buried beneath your flowers in the shed. Now let me tell you better news. I will never involve your son in this affair. I don't do that, and besides, such action would make you my enemy and ready to betray me. But you must realize that I am the one who keeps your son alive. My enemies want me dead. If they succeed, my friends will not spare your son. His fate rests on mine."

"So what do you want?" Heskow asked.

"I need information," Astorre said. "So you talk. If I'm satisfied, we have a deal. If I'm not, you're dead. So your immediate problem is staying alive tonight. Begin."

Heskow did not speak for at least five minutes. First he evaluated Astorre—such a nice-looking guy, not brutal or terrorizing. But the Sturzo brothers were dead. Then the breaking through the security of his house and the finding of the guns. Most ominous was Astorre waiting for him to reach for the nonexistent gun. So this was not a bluff, and certainly not a bluff he could call. Finally Heskow drank his coffee and made his decision, with reservations.

"I have to go with you," he said to Astorre. "I have to trust you to do the right thing. The man who hired me to broker the deal and gave me the money is Timmona Portella. The NYPD nonsurveillance I bought. I was Timmona's bagman and gave the NYPD chief of detectives, Di Benedetto, fifty grand and his deputy, Aspinella Washington, twenty-five. As for the FBI guarantee, Portella gave it to me. I insisted on credentials, and he told me he had this guy, Cilke, New York

Bureau chief, in his pocket. It was Cilke who gave the OK for the hit on the Don."

"You worked for Portella before?"

"Oh, yeah," Heskow said. "He runs the drugs in New York, so he has a lot of hits for me. None in the league of the Don. I never did get the connection. That's it."

"Good," Astorre said. His face was sincere. "Now I want you to be careful. For your own good. Is there anything more you can tell me?"

And suddenly Heskow knew he was seconds from death. That he had not done the job of convincing Astorre. He trusted his instincts. He gave Astorre a weak smile. "One more thing," he added, very slowly. "I have a contract with Portella right now. On you. I'm going to pay the two detectives a half million to knock you off. They come to arrest you, you resist arrest, and they shoot you."

Astorre seemed a little bemused. "Why so complicated and expensive?" he said. "Why not hire a straight hit man?"

Heskow shook his head. "They put you higher than that. And after the Don, a straight hit would draw too much attention. You being his nephew. The media would go wild. This way there's cover."

"Have you paid them yet?" Astorre asked.

"No," Heskow said. "We have to meet."

"OK," Astorre said. "Set up the meeting out of

traffic. Let me know the details beforehand. One thing. After the meeting, don't leave with them."

"Oh, shit," Heskow said. "Is that how it is? There will be enormous heat."

Astorre leaned back in his chair. "That's how it is," he said. He got up out of the chair and gave Heskow a half hug of friendship. "Remember," he said, "we have to keep each other alive."

"Can I hold out some of the money?" Heskow asked.

Astorre laughed. "No. That's the beauty of it. How do the cops explain the half million they have on them?"

"Just twenty," Heskow said.

"OK," Astorre said good-naturedly. "But no more. Just a little sweetener."

NOW IT WAS imperative for Astorre to have another meeting with Don Craxxi and Mr. Pryor for their advice on the wide operational plan he had to execute.

But circumstances had changed. Mr. Pryor insisted on bringing his two nephews to Chicago to act as bodyguards. And when they arrived in the Chicago suburb they found that Don Craxxi's modest estate had been turned into a fortress. The driveway leading to the house was blocked by little green huts manned by very tough-looking young men. A communications van was parked in the orchard. And there were three young men who answered doorbells and phones and checked visitors' IDs.

Mr. Pryor's nephews, Erice and Roberto, were lean and athletic, expert in firearms, and they clearly adored their uncle. They also seemed to know Astorre's history in Sicily and treated him with enormous respect, performing the smallest personal services for him. They carried his luggage. They poured his wine at dinner, brushing him off with their napkins; they paid his tips and opened doors, making it plain they regarded him as a great man. Astorre good-humoredly tried to put them at ease, but they would never descend to familiarity.

The men guarding Don Craxxi were not so polite. They were courteous but rigid, steady men in their fifties, completely focused on their job. And they were all armed.

That evening when Don Craxxi, Mr. Pryor, and Astorre had finished dinner and were eating fruit for their dessert, Astorre said to the Don, "Why all the security?"

"Just a precaution," his host answered calmly. "I've heard some disturbing news. An old enemy of mine, Inzio Tulippa, has arrived in America. He is a very intemperate man and very greedy, so it is always best to be prepared. He comes to meet

with our Timmona Portella. They whack up their
drug profits and whack out their enemies. It is
best to be ready. But now, what is on your mind,
my dear Astorre?"

Astorre told them both the information he had
learned and how he had turned Heskow. He told
them about Portella and Cilke and the two
detectives.

"Now I have to go operational," he said. "I
need an explosives guy and at least ten more
good men. I know you two can supply them, that
you can call on the Don's old friends." He carefully skinned the greenish yellow pear he was
eating. "You understand how dangerous this will
be and do not want to be too closely involved."

"Nonsense," Mr. Pryor said impatiently. "We
owe our destiny to Don Aprile. Of course we will
help. But remember, this is not vengeance. It is
self-defense. So you cannot harm Cilke. The
federal government will make our lives too hard."

"But that man must be neutralized," Don
Craxxi said. "He will always be a danger.
However, consider this. Sell the banks and every-
body will be happy."

"Everybody except me and my cousins,"
Astorre said.

"It is something to consider," Mr. Pryor said.
"I'm willing to sacrifice my share in the banks
with Don Craxxi, though I know it will grow to

be an enormous fortune. But certainly there is something to be said for a peaceful life."

"I'm not selling the banks," Astorre said. "They killed my uncle and they have to pay the price, not achieve their purpose. And I can't live in a world where my place is granted by their mercy. The Don taught me that."

Astorre was surprised that Don Craxxi and Mr. Pryor looked relieved by his decision. They tried to hide little smiles. He realized that these two old men, powerful as they were, held him in respect, saw in him what they themselves could never acquire.

Craxxi said, "We know our duty to Don Aprile, may he rest in peace. And we know our duty to you. But one note of prudence: If you are too rash, and something happens to you, we will be forced to sell the banks."

"Yes," Mr. Pryor said. "Be prudent."

Astorre laughed. "Don't worry. If I go down, there will be nobody left."

They ate their pears and peaches. Don Craxxi seemed to be lost in thought. Then he said, "Tulippa is the top drug man in the world. Portella is his American partner. They must want the banks to launder the drug money."

"Then how does Cilke fit in?" Astorre asked.

"I don't know," Craxxi said. "But still, you cannot attack Cilke."

"That would be a disaster," Mr. Pryor said.

"I'll remember that," Astorre said.

But if Cilke was guilty, what could he do?

DETECTIVE ASPINELLA Washington made sure her eight-year-old daughter ate a good supper, did her homework, and said her prayers before putting her to bed. She adored the girl and had banished her father from her life a long time ago. The baby-sitter, the teenage daughter of a uniformed cop, arrived at 8:00 p.m. Aspinella instructed her on the child's medications and said she would be back before midnight.

Soon the lobby buzzer rang and Aspinella ran down the stairs and out into the street. She never used the elevator. Paul Di Benedetto was waiting in his unmarked tan Chevrolet. She hopped in and strapped on her seat belt. He was a lousy night driver.

Di Benedetto was smoking a long cigar, so Aspinella opened her window. "It's about an hour's ride," he said. "We have to think it over." He knew it was a big step for both of them. It was one thing to take bribes and drug money; it was another to perform a hit.

"What's to think over?" Aspinella asked. "We get a half mil to knock off a guy who should be on death row. You know what I can do with a quarter mil?"

"No," Di Benedetto said. "But I know what I can do. Buy a super condo in Miami when I retire. Remember, we're going to have to live with this."

"Taking drug payoffs is already over the line," Aspinella said. "Fuck 'em all."

"Yeah," Di Benedetto said. "Let's just make sure that this guy Heskow has the money tonight, that he's not just jerking us off."

"He's always been reliable," Aspinella said. "He's my Santa Claus. And if he doesn't have a big sack to give us, he'll be a dead Santa."

Di Benedetto laughed. "That's my girl. You been keeping track of this Astorre guy so we can get rid of him right away?"

"Yeah. I've had him under surveillance. I know just the spot to pick him up—his macaroni warehouse. Most nights he works late."

"You got the throwaway to plant on him?" Di Benedetto asked.

"Of course," Aspinella said. "I wouldn't give shit to a shield if I didn't carry a throwaway."

They drove in silence for ten minutes. Then Di Benedetto said in a deliberately calm, emotionless voice, "Who's going to be the shooter?"

Aspinella gave him an amused look. "Paul," she

said, "you've been behind the desk for the last ten years. You've seen more tomato sauce than blood. I'll shoot." She could see that he looked relieved. Men—they were fucking useless.

They fell silent again as both were lost in thought about what had brought them to this point in their lives. Di Benedetto had joined the force as a young man, over thirty years ago. His corruption had been gradual but inevitable. He had started out with delusions of grandeur—he would be respected and admired for risking his life to protect others. But the years wore this away. At first it was the little bribes from the street vendors and small shops. Then testifying falsely to help a guy beat a felony rap. It seemed a small step to accepting money from high-ranking drug dealers. Then finally from Heskow, who, it was clear, acted for Timmona Portella, the biggest Mafia chief left in New York.

Of course, there was always a good excuse. The mind can sell itself anything. He saw the higher-ranking officers getting rich on drug-bribe money, and the lower ranks were even more corrupt. And after all, he had three kids to send to college. But most of all it was the ingratitude of the people he protected. Civil-liberties groups protesting police brutality if you slapped a black mugger around. The news media shitting on the police department every chance they got. Citizens suing cops. Cops getting fired after years of service, deprived of their pensions, even going to jail. He himself had once been brought up for discipline on the charge that he singled out black criminals, and he knew he wasn't racially prejudiced. Was it his fault that most criminals in New York were black? What were you supposed to do—give them a license to steal, as affirmative action? He had promoted black cops. He had been Aspinella's mentor in the department, giving her the promotion she'd earned by terrorizing the same black criminals. And you couldn't accuse her of racism. In a nutshell, society crapped on the cops who protected them. Unless of course they got killed in the line of duty. Then came the tide of bullshit. The final truth? It didn't pay to be an honest cop. And yet—and yet, he had never thought it would come to murder. But after all, he was invulnerable; there was no risk; there was a hell of a lot of money; and the victim was a killer. Still . . .

Aspinella too was wondering how her life had come to such a pass. God knows she had fought the criminal underworld with a passion and relentlessness that had made her a New York legend. Certainly, she had taken bribes, suborned felony. She had only started late in the game when Di Benedetto had persuaded her to take drug money. He had been her mentor for years and for a few months her lover—not bad, just a clumsy bear who used sex as part of a hibernational impulse.

But her corruption had really started her first day on the job after being promoted to detective. In the station-house rec room an overbearing white cop named Gangee had jollied her in a good-natured way. "Hey, Aspinella," he said, "with your pussy and my muscle, we'll wipe out crime in the civilized world." The cops, including some blacks, laughed.

Aspinella looked at him coldly and said, "You'll never be my partner. A man who insults a woman is a small-dick coward."

Gangee tried to keep it on a friendly basis. "My small dick can stop up your pussy anytime you want to try. I want to change my luck anyhow."

Aspinella turned her cold face to him. "Black is better than yellow," she said. "Go whack off, you dumb piece of shit."

The room seemed frozen with surprise. Now she had Gangee blushing red. Such virulent contempt was not permitted without a fight. He started toward her, his huge body clearing space.

Aspinella was dressed for duty. She drew her gun, not pointing it. "Try and I'll blow your balls off," she said, and in that room there was no doubt in anyone's mind that she would pull the trigger. Gangee halted and shook his head with disgust.

The incident, of course, was reported. It was a serious offense on Aspinella's part. But Di Benedetto was shrewd enough to know that a departmental trial would be a political disaster for the NYPD. He quashed the whole thing and was so impressed by Aspinella that he put her on his personal staff and became her mentor.

What had affected Aspinella more than anything else was that there had been at least four black cops in the room and not one of them had defended her. Indeed, they had laughed at the white cop's jokes. Gender loyalty was stronger than racial loyalty.

Her career, after that, established her as the best cop in the division. She was ruthless with drug dealers, muggers, armed robbers. She showed them no mercy, black or white. She shot them, she beat them, she humiliated them. Charges were made against her but could never be substantiated, and her record for valor spoke for her. But the charges aroused her rage against society itself. How did they dare question her when she protected them from the worst scum in the city? Di Benedetto backed her all the way.

There had been one tricky situation when she shot dead two teenage muggers as they tried to rob her on a brightly lit Harlem street right outside her apartment. One boy punched her in the face, and the other grabbed her purse. Aspinella drew her gun and the boys froze. Quite deliberately, she shot them both. Not only for the punch in the face, but to send a message not to try mugging in her neighborhood. Civil-liberties groups organized a protest, but the department ruled that she had used justifiable force. She knew she had been guilty on that one.

It was Di Benedetto who talked her into taking her first bribe on a very important drug deal. He spoke like a loving uncle. "Aspinella," he said, "a cop today doesn't worry much about bullets. That's part of the deal. He has to worry about the civil-liberties groups, the citizens and the criminals who sue for damages. The political bosses in the department, who will put you in jail to get votes. Especially somebody like you. You're a natural victim, so are you going to wind up like those other poor dopes in the street who get raped, robbed, murdered? Or are you going to protect yourself? Get in on this. You'll get more protection from the wheels in the department who are already bought. In five or six years you can retire with a bundle. And you won't have to worry about going to jail for messing up some mugger's hair."

So she had given way. And little by little she

enjoyed socking the bribe money into disguised bank accounts. Not that she let up on the criminals.

But this stuff was different. This was a conspiracy to commit murder, and yes, this Astorre was a Mafia big shot who would be a pleasure to take out. In a funny way, she would be doing her job. But the final argument was that it had so little risk and such a big payoff. A quarter mil.

Di Benedetto drove off the Southern State Parkway and a few minutes later rolled into the parking lot of a small two-story mall. All of the dozen or so shops were closed, even the pizza joint, which displayed a bright red neon sign in its window. They got out of the car. "That's the first time I've seen a pizza joint closed so early," Di Benedetto said. It was only 10:00 P.M.

He led Aspinella to a side door of the pizza joint. It was unlocked. They climbed up a dozen stairs to a landing. There was a suite of two rooms to the left and a room to the right. He made a motion, and Aspinella checked the suite on the left while he stood guard. Then they went to the room on the right. Heskow was waiting for them.

He was sitting at the end of a long wooden table with four rickety wooden chairs around it. On the table was a duffel bag the size of a punching bag, and it seemed to be stuffed full. Heskow shook Di Benedetto's hand and nodded to Aspinella. She thought she had never seen a white man looking so white. His face and even his neck were drained of color.

The room had only a dim bulb and no windows. They sat around the table, Di Benedetto reached out and patted the bag. "It's all there?" he asked.

"Sure is," Heskow said shakily. Well, a man carrying $500,000 in a duffel bag had a right to be nervous, Aspinella thought. But still, she scanned the room to see if it was wired.

"Let's have a peek," Di Benedetto said.

Heskow untied the cord around the neck of the duffel bag and half dumped it out. About twenty packets of bills bound by rubber bands tumbled onto the table. Most of the packages were hundreds, no fifties, and two packets were twenties.

Di Benedetto sighed. "Fucking twenties," he said. "OK, put them back."

Heskow stuffed the packets back into the bag and retied the cord. "My client requests that it be as quick as possible," he said.

"Inside two weeks," Di Benedetto said.

"Good," Heskow said.

Aspinella lifted the duffel bag onto her shoulder. It wasn't that heavy, she thought. A half mil wasn't that heavy.

She saw Di Benedetto shake hands with Heskow and felt a wary impatience. She wanted to get the hell out of there. She started down the stairs, the bag balanced on her shoulder, held with one hand, her other hand free to draw her gun. She heard Di Benedetto following her.

Then they were out in the cool night. They were both dripping with sweat.

"Put the bag in the trunk," Di Benedetto said. He got into the driver's seat and lit up a cigar. Aspinella came around and got in.

"Where do we go to split it up?" Di Benedetto asked.

"Not my place. I have a baby-sitter."

"Not mine," Di Benedetto said. "I have a wife at home. How about we rent a motel room?"

Aspinella grimaced, and Di Benedetto said smilingly, "My office. We'll lock the door." They both laughed. "Check the trunk just one more time. Make sure it's locked tight."

Aspinella didn't argue. She got out, opened the trunk, and pulled out the duffel bag. At that moment Paul turned on the ignition.

The explosion sent a shower of glass over the mall. It was raining glass. The car itself seemed to float in the air and came down in a hail of metal that destroyed Paul Di Benedetto's body. Aspinella Washington was blown almost ten feet away, an arm and leg broken, but it was the pain from her torn-out eye that rendered her unconscious.

Heskow, exiting in the rear of the pizza shop, felt the air press his body against the building. Then he jumped into his car and twenty minutes later was in his home in Brightwaters. He made himself a quick drink and checked the two packets of hundred-dollar bills he had taken out of the duffel bag. Forty grand—a nice little bonus. He'd give his kid a couple of grand for spending money. No, a grand. And sock the rest away.

He watched the late TV news that reported the explosion as a breaking story. One detective killed, the other badly hurt. And at the scene, a duffel bag with a huge amount of money. The TV anchor didn't say how much.

WHEN ASPINELLA Washington regained consciousness in the hospital two days later, she was not surprised to be closely questioned about the money and why it was just forty grand shy of a half million. She denied she had any knowledge of the money. They questioned her about what a chief of detectives and an assistant chief were doing out together. She refused to answer on the grounds that it was a personal matter. But she was angry that they questioned her so relentlessly when she was obviously in such grave condition.

The department didn't give a shit about her. They did not honor her record of achievement. But it ended OK. The department didn't pursue her and set it up so that the investigation of the money came to nothing.

It took another week of convalescence for Aspinella to figure things out. They had been set up. And the only guy who could have set them up was Heskow. And the fact that there was forty grand missing from the payoff meant the greedy pig couldn't resist grafting his own people. Well, she would get better, she thought, and then she would meet with Heskow once again.

CHAPTER 10

ASTORRE WAS NOW very careful of his movements. Not only to avoid a hit but also not to allow himself to be arrested for any reason. He kept close to his heavily guarded home with its five-man round-the-clock security teams. He had sensors planted in the woods and grounds around the house and infrared lights for night surveillance. When he ventured out, it was with six bodyguards in three two-man teams. He sometimes traveled alone, counting on stealth and surprise and a confidence in his own powers if he should meet only one of two assassins. The blowing up of the two detectives had been necessary, but it generated a lot of heat. And when Aspinella Washington recovered she would figure out it was Heskow who had betrayed her. And if Heskow spilled, she would come after Astorre himself.

But by now he knew the enormity of his problem. He knew all the men guilty of the Don's death and the serious problems before him. There was Kurt Cilke, essentially untouchable; Timmona Portella, who ordered the murder; as well as Inzio Tulippa and Michael Grazziella. The only ones he had succeeded in punishing were the Sturzo brothers, and they had been mere pawns.

All the information had come from John Heskow, Mr. Pryor, Don Craxxi, and Octavius Bianco in Sicily. If possible, he had to get all his enemies in one place at the same time. To pick them off singly would surely be impossible. And Mr. Pryor and Craxxi had already warned him he could not touch Cilke.

And then there was the consul general of Peru, Marriano Rubio, Nicole's companion. What was the extent of her loyalty to him? What had she blotted out in the Don's FBI file that she did not want Astorre to see? What was she hiding from him?

In his spare moments, Astorre dreamed of the women he had loved. First there had been Nicole, so young and so willful, her small, delicate body so passionate that she had forced him into loving her. And now how changed she was, her passion absorbed by politics and her career.

He remembered Buji in Sicily, not exactly a call girl, but very close, and with an impulsive goodness that could easily turn into rage. He remembered her gorgeous bed, in the soft Sicilian nights, when they swam and ate olives out of oil-filled barrels. Most fondly of all he remembered that she never lied; she was completely frank about her life, her other men. And her loyalty when he had been shot, how she had dragged him out of the sea, the blood from his throat staining her body. Then her gift of the golden collar with its pendant to hide the ugly wound.

Then he thought of Rosie, his treacherous Rosie, so sweet, so beautiful, so sentimental, who always claimed she truly loved him while betraying him. Yet she could always make him feel happy when he was with her. He had wanted to break down his feeling for her by using her against the Sturzo brothers, and he had been surprised that she relished the role, an adjustment to her make-believe life.

And then flitting through his mind like some ghost came the vision of Cilke's wife, Georgette. What stupidity. He had spent one evening watching her, listening to her talk nonsense he didn't believe, about the pricelessness of every human soul. Yet he could not forget her. How the hell had she married a guy like Kurt Cilke?

ON SOME NIGHTS Astorre drove to Rosie's neighborhood and called her on his car phone.

She was always free, which surprised him, but she explained that she was too busy studying to go out. Which suited him perfectly, since he was too cautious to eat in a restaurant or take her to a movie. Instead he stopped at Zabar's on the West Side and brought in delicacies that made Rosie smile with delight. Meanwhile Monza waited in the car outside.

Rosie would lay out the food and open a bottle of wine. As they ate she put her legs in his lap in a comradely way, and her face glowed with happiness at being with him. She seemed to welcome his every word with a pleased smile. That was her gift, and Astorre knew that she was that way with all her men. But it didn't matter.

And then when they went to bed she was passionate but also very sweet and clinging. She touched his face all over and kissed him and said, "We're really soul mates." And those words would send a chill through Astorre. He didn't want her to be a soul mate with a man like himself. He yearned for classic virtue at these times, yet he couldn't stop himself from seeing her.

He'd stay for five or six hours. At three in the morning he would leave. Sometimes when she was asleep he would gaze down at her and see in the relaxation of her facial muscles a sad vulnerability and struggle, as if the demons she held in her innermost soul were fighting to get free.

One night he left early from a visit with Rosie. When he got into the waiting car, Monza told him there was an urgent message to call a Mr. Juice. This was a code name that he and Heskow used, so he immediately picked up the car phone.

Heskow's voice was urgent. "I can't talk on the wire. We have to meet right away."

"Where?" Astorre said.

"I'll be standing right outside Madison Square Garden," Heskow said. "Pick me up on the fly. In one hour."

When Astorre drove by the Garden, he saw Heskow standing on the sidewalk. Monza had his gun in his lap when he stopped the car in front of Heskow. Astorre pulled open the door, and Heskow hopped into the front seat with them. The cold left watery streaks on his cheeks. He said to Astorre, "You have big trouble."

Astorre now felt a cold chill. "The kids?" he asked.

Heskow nodded. "Portella snatched your cousin Marcantonio and has him stashed some-place. I don't know where. Tomorrow he invites you to a meeting. He wants to trade something for his hostage. But if you're careless, he has a four-man hit team to focus on you. He's using his own men. He tried to give me the job, but I turned him down."

They were in a dark street. "Thanks," Astorre said. "Where can I let you off?"

"Right here. My car is just a block away."

Astorre understood. Heskow was anxious about being seen with him.

"One other thing," Heskow said. "You know about Portella's suite at his private hotel? His brother, Bruno, is using it tonight with some broad. And no bodyguards."

"Thanks again," Astorre said. He opened the door of the car, and Heskow disappeared into the darkness.

MARCANTONIO APRILE was having his last meeting of the day, and he wanted to keep it short. It was now seven in the evening, and he had a dinner engagement at nine.

The meeting was with his favorite producer and best friend in the movie business, a man named Steve Brody, who never went over budget, had great instincts for dramatic stories, and often introduced Marcantonio to up-and-coming young actresses who needed a little help in their careers.

But this evening they were on opposite sides of the fence. Brody had come with one of the most powerful agents in the business, a man named

Matt Glazier, who had a vehement loyalty to his clients. He was there pleading the case of a novelist whose latest book he had turned into an epic, eight-hour TV serial drama. Now Glazier wanted to sell the novelist's three previous books.

"Marcantonio," Glazier said, "the other three books are great but didn't sell. You know how publishers are—they couldn't sell a jar of caviar for a nickel. Brody here is ready to produce them. Now, you've made a shitload of money on his last book, so be generous and let's make a deal."

"I don't see it," Marcantonio said. "These are old books we're talking about. They were never best-sellers. And now they're out of print."

"That doesn't matter," Glazier said with the eager confidence of all agents. "As soon as we make the deal, the publishers will reprint them."

Marcantonio had heard this argument many times before. True, the publishers would reprint, but actually this was not much help to the TV presentation. The TV broadcast would help the publishers of the book more. It was essentially a bullshit argument.

"All that aside," Marcantonio said, "I've read the books. They have nothing for us. They're too literary. It's the language that makes them work, not incident. I enjoyed them. I'm not saying they can't work, I'm just saying it's not worth the risk and the extraordinary effort."

"Don't bullshit me," Glazier said. "You read a reader's report. You're the head of programming—you don't have time to read."

Marcantonio laughed. "You're wrong. I love to read and I love those books. But they are not good TV." His voice was warm and friendly. "I'm sorry, but for us it's a pass. But keep us in mind. We'd love to work with you."

After the two had gone, Marcantonio showered in his executive-suite bathroom and changed his clothes for his dinner date. He said good night to his secretary, who always stayed until he left, and took the elevator to the lobby of the building.

His date was at the Four Seasons, just a few blocks away, and he would walk. Unlike most top executives, he did not keep a car and driver exclusively for himself but just called one when necessary. He prided himself on his economy and knew he had learned it from his father, who had a strong prejudice against wasting money on foolishness.

When he stepped out onto the street, he felt a cold wind and shivered. A black limo pulled up, and the chauffeur got out of the car and opened the door for him to enter. Had his secretary ordered the car for him? The driver was tall, a sturdy man whose cap stood oddly on his head, a size too small. He bowed and said, "Mr. Aprile?"

"Yes," Marcantonio said. "I won't need you tonight."

"Yes, you do," the chauffeur said with a cheerful smile. "Get into the car or get shot."

Suddenly Marcantonio was aware of three men at his back. He hesitated. The chauffeur said, "Don't worry, a friend just wants to have a little chat with you."

Marcantonio got into the backseat of the limo, and the three men crowded in beside him.

They drove a block or two, and then one of the men gave Marcantonio a pair of dark glasses and told him to put them on. Marcantonio did so—and seemed to go blind. The glasses were so dark they screened out all light. He thought that clever and made a mental note to use this in a story. It was a hopeful sign. If they did not want him to see where he was going, that meant they were not planning to kill him. And yet it all seemed as unreal as one of his TV dramas. Until he suddenly thought about his father. That he was finally in his father's world, which he had never completely believed in.

After about an hour, the car came to a stop and he was helped out by two of the guards. He could feel a brick path under his feet, and then he was led up four steps and into a house. Up more stairs to a room, the door closing behind him. Only then were the glasses removed. He was in a small bedchamber whose windows were heavily curtained. One of the guards sat in a chair beside the bed.

"Lie down and take a little snooze," the guard said to him. "You have a tough day ahead." Marcantonio looked at his watch. It was almost midnight.

JUST AFTER FOUR in the morning, with the skyscrapers ghosts in darkness, Astorre and Aldo Monza were let off in front of the Lyceum Hotel; the driver waiting in front. Monza jangled his ring of keys as they ran up the three flights of stairs and then to the door of Portella's suite.

Monza used his keys to open the door to the suite, and they entered the living room. They saw the table littered with cartons of Chinese takeout food, empty glasses, and bottles of wine and whiskey. There was a huge whipped-cream cake, half-eaten, with a crushed-out cigarette adorning the top like a birthday candle. They went to the bedroom, and Astorre flicked on the light from the wall switch. There, lying on the bed, clad only in shorts, was Bruno Portella.

The air was filled with a heavy perfume, but Bruno was alone in the bed. He was not a pretty sight. His face, heavy and slack, glistened with night sweat, and the stale smell of seafood came from his mouth. His huge chest made him appear bearish, and indeed he wore a look of teddy bear sweetness, Astorre thought. At the foot of the bed was an open bottle of red wine, which created its own island of raw fragrance. It seemed a shame to wake him, and Astorre did it gently by tapping on his forehead.

Bruno opened one eye, then the other. He didn't seem frightened or even astonished. "What the hell are you doing here?" His voice was husky with sleep.

"Bruno, there's nothing to worry about," Astorre said gently. "Where's the girl?"

Bruno sat up. He laughed. "She had to go home early to get her kid off to school. I already fucked her three times, so I let her go." He said this proudly, because of both his virility and his understanding of a working girl's problems. He casually reached out a hand to the bedside table. Astorre gently grabbed it, and Monza opened the drawer and took out a gun.

"Listen, Bruno," Astorre said soothingly. "Nothing bad is going to happen. I know your brother doesn't confide in you, but he snatched my cousin Marc last night. So now I have to trade you to get him back. Your brother loves you, Bruno; he'll make the trade. You believe that, don't you?"

"Sure," Bruno said. He looked relieved.

"Just don't do anything foolish. Now, get dressed."

When Bruno finished dressing, he seemed to have trouble tying his shoelaces. "What's the matter?" Astorre asked.

"This is the first time I wore these shoes," Bruno said. "Usually I wear slip-ons."

"You don't know how to tie shoelaces?" Astorre asked.

"These are the first shoes I've had with laces."

Astorre laughed. "Jesus Christ. OK, I'll tie them." And he let Bruno put his foot in his lap.

When he was finished, Astorre handed Bruno the bedside phone. "Call your brother," he said.

"At five in the morning?" Bruno said. "Timmona will kill me."

Astorre realized that it wasn't sleep that dulled Bruno's brain; he was genuinely dim-witted.

"Just tell him I've got you," Astorre said. "Then I'll talk to him."

Bruno took the phone and said in a plaintive voice, "Timmona, you got me in a lot of trouble, that's why I'm calling you this early."

Astorre could hear a roar over the phone, and then Bruno said hurriedly, "Astorre Viola has me and he wants to talk to you." He quickly passed the phone to Astorre.

Astorre said, "Timmona, sorry to wake you up. But I had to snatch Bruno because you have my cousin."

Portella's voice came over the phone in another angry roar. "I don't know anything about that. Now, what the hell do you want?"

Bruno could hear and he shouted, "You got me into this, you prick! Now get me out."

Astorre said calmly, "Timmona, make this swap and we can talk about the deal you want. I know you think I've been bullheaded, but when we meet I'll tell you the reason and you'll know I've been doing you a favor."

Portella's voice was quiet now. "OK," he said. "How do we set up this meeting?"

"I'll meet you at the Paladin restaurant at noon," Astorre said. "I have a private room there. I'll bring Bruno with me, and you bring Marc. You can bring bodyguards if you're leery, but we don't want a bloodbath in a public place. We talk things over and make the exchange."

There was a long pause, and then Portella said, "I'll be there, but don't try anything funny."

"Don't worry," Astorre said cheerfully. "After this meeting we'll be buddies."

Astorre and Monza put Bruno between them, Astorre linking arms with Bruno in a friendly way. They took him down the stairs to the street. There were an additional two cars with Astorre's men waiting. "Take Bruno with you in one of the cars," Astorre told Monza. "Have him at the Paladin at noon. I'll meet you there."

"What the hell do I do with him until then?" Monza asked. "That's hours from now."

"Take him for breakfast," Astorre said. "He likes to eat. That should take up a couple of hours. Then take him for a walk in Central Park. Go to the zoo. I'll take one of the cars and a driver. If he tries to run away, don't kill him. Just catch him."

"You'll be on your own," Monza said. "Is that smart?"

"I'll be OK." In the car Astorre used his cell phone to call Nicole's private number. It was now nearly six in the morning, and light transfixed the city into long thin lines of stone.

Nicole's voice was sleepy when she answered. Astorre remembered it had been like that when she was a young girl and his lover. "Nicole, wake up," he said. "You know who this is?"

The question obviously irritated her. "Of course I know who it is. Who else would call at this hour?"

"Listen carefully," Astorre said. "No questions. That document you're holding for me, the one I signed for Cilke, remember you told me not to sign?"

"Yes," Nicole said curtly, "of course I remember."

"Do you have it at home or in your office safe?" Astorre asked.

"In my office, of course," Nicole said.

"OK," Astorre said. "I'll be at your house in thirty minutes. I'll ring your bell. Be ready and come down. Bring all your keys. We're going to your office."

WHEN ASTORRE RANG Nicole's bell, she came down immediately dressed in a blue leather coat and carrying a large purse. She kissed him on the cheek but didn't dare say a word until they were in the car and she had to give instructions to the driver. Then she continued her silence until they were in her office suite.

"Now, tell me why you want that document," she said.

"You don't have to know," Astorre said.

He saw she was angry with the answer, but she went to the office safe that was part of the desk and produced a file folder.

"Don't close the safe," Astorre said. "I want the tape you made of our meeting with Cilke."

Nicole handed him the folder. "You have a right to these documents," she said. "But you have no right to any tape, even if it existed."

"Long ago you told me you taped every meeting in your office, Nicole," Astorre said. "And I watched you at the meeting. You were a little too satisfied with yourself."

Nicole laughed with scornful affection. "You've changed," she said. "You were never one of those assholes who thought they could read other people's minds."

Astorre gave her a rueful grin and said apologetically, "I thought you still liked me. That's why I never asked what you deleted in your father's file before you showed it to me."

"I deleted nothing," Nicole said coolly. "And I don't give the tape until you tell me what this is all about."

Astorre was silent, then he said, "OK, you're a big girl now." He laughed when he saw how angry she was, her eyes flashing, her lips curled with contempt. It reminded him of how she looked when she confronted him and her father long ago.

"Well, you always wanted to play with the big boys," Astorre said. "And you certainly do that. As a lawyer, you've scared almost as many people as your father."

"He wasn't as bad as the press and the FBI painted him," Nicole said angrily.

"OK," Astorre said soothingly. "Marc was kidnapped last night by Timmona Portella. Not to worry though. I went out and got his brother, Bruno. Now we can bargain."

"You committed a kidnapping?" Nicole said incredulously.

"So did they," Astorre said. "They really want us to sell them the banks."

Nicole almost shrieked, "Then give them the fucking banks!"

"You don't understand," Astorre said. "We give them nothing. We have Bruno. They hurt Marc, I hurt Bruno."

Nicole was looking at him with horror in her eyes. Astorre stared at her calmly, and one hand went up to finger the gold collar around his neck. "Yeah," he said, "I'd have to kill him."

Nicole's firm face broke up into creases of sorrow. "Not you, Astorre, not you too."

"So now you know," Astorre said. "I'm not the man to sell the banks after they killed your father and my uncle. But I need the tape and the document to make the deal go through and get Marc back without bloodshed."

"Just sell them the banks," Nicole whispered to him. "We'll be rich. What does it matter?"

"It matters to me," Astorre said. "It mattered to the Don."

Silently Nicole reached into the safe and took out a small packet, which she placed on top of the folder.

"Play it for me now," Astorre said.

Nicole reached into her desk for a small

cassette player. She inserted the tape, and they listened to Cilke reveal his plan to entrap Portella. Then Astorre pocketed everything and said, "I'll have it all back to you later today, and Marc too. Don't worry. Nothing will happen. And if it does, it will be worse for them than for us."

A LITTLE after noon Astorre, Aldo Monza, and Bruno Portella were seated in a private dining room at the Paladin restaurant in the East Sixties.

Bruno seemed not at all worried about being a hostage. He chatted cheerfully with Astorre. "You know, I lived all my life in New York and I never knew Central Park had a zoo. More people should know that and go see it."

"So you had a good time," Astorre said in a good-humored voice, thinking that if things went badly, Bruno would at least have a pleasant memory before death. The door of the dining room swung open, and the owner of the restaurant appeared with Timmona Portella and Marcantonio. Portella's broad figure with its well-cut suit almost masked Marcantonio behind him. Bruno rushed into Timmona's arms and kissed him on both cheeks, and Astorre was astonished to see the look of love and satisfaction on Timmona's face.

"What a brother," Bruno exclaimed loudly. "What a brother."

In contrast, Astorre and Marcantonio shook hands, then Astorre gave a half hug and said, "Everything is OK, Marc."

Marcantonio turned away from him and sat down. His legs had gone weak partly with relief at his safety and partly because of Astorre's appearance. The young boy who loved to sing, the intense yet joyous youth so carefree and loving, now appeared in his true form as the Angel of Death. The power of his presence dominated Portella in his fear and bluster.

Astorre sat down next to Marcantonio and patted his knee. He was smiling his affable smile as though this were just a friendly lunch. "Are you OK?" he asked.

Marcantonio looked directly into Astorre's eyes. He had never before noticed how clear and merciless they were. He looked at Bruno, the man who would have paid for his life. The man was babbling to his brother, something about the Central Park zoo.

Astorre said to Portella, "We have things to discuss."

"OK," Portella said. "Bruno, get the fuck out of here. There's a car waiting outside. I'll talk to you when I get home."

Monza came into the dining room. "Take

Marcantonio to his house," Astorre said to him. "Marc, wait for me there."

PORTELLA AND ASTORRE now sat alone across from each other at the table. Portella opened a bottle of wine and filled his glass. He didn't offer a glass to Astorre.

Astorre reached into his pocket, pulled out a brown envelope, and emptied its contents onto the table. There was the confidential document he had signed for Cilke, the one in which he was asked to betray Portella.

Then there was the small cassette player with the tape in it.

Portella looked at the document with the FBI logo and read it. He tossed it aside. "That could be a forgery," he said. "And why would you be so dumb to sign it?"

In answer Astorre flipped the switch on the cassette player, and Cilke's voice could be heard asking Astorre to cooperate to trap Portella. Portella listened and tried to control the surprise and rage he felt, but his face had flushed a deep red and his lips moved in unspoken curses. Astorre clicked off the tape.

"I know you worked with Cilke over the last six years," Astorre said. "You helped him wipe out the New York Families. And I know you got

immunity from Cilke for that. But now he's after
you. Those guys who wear badges are never satisfied. They want it all. You thought he was your
friend. You broke omerta for him. You made him
famous, and now he wants to send you to jail. He
doesn't need you anymore. He's going to come
after you as soon as you buy the banks. That's why
I couldn't make the deal. I would never break
omerta."

Portella was very quiet and then seemed to
come to a decision. "If I solve the Cilke problem,
what deal would you make for the banks?"

Astorre put everything back into his attaché
case. "Outright sale," he said. "Except for me—I
keep a five percent piece."

Portella seemed to have recovered from his
shock. "OK," he said. "We can work it out after
the problem is solved."

They shook hands on it, and Portella left first.
Astorre realized he was very hungry and ordered
a thick red steak for lunch. One problem solved,
he thought.

AT MIDNIGHT Portella met with Marriano
Rubio, Inzio Tulippa, and Michael Grazziella at
the Peruvian consulate.

Rubio had been a superb host to Tulippa and
Grazziella. He had accompanied them to the

theater, the opera, and the ballet, and he had supplied discreet beautiful young women who had achieved some fame in the arts and music. Tulippa and Grazziella were having a wonderful visit and were reluctant to return to their natural environments, which were much less stimulating. They were subordinate kings being wooed by an overruling emperor who did everything to please them.

This night the consul general exceeded himself in his hospitality. The conference table was laden with exotic dishes, fruits, cheeses, and huge bonbons of chocolate; beside every chair stood a bottle of champagne in an ice bucket. Small elegant pastries rested on delicate ladders of spun sugar. A huge coffee urn steamed, and boxes of Havana cigars, maduros, light brown, and green were strewn carelessly over the table.

He opened the proceedings by saying to Portella, "Now, what is so important that we had to cancel our engagements for this meeting?" Despite his exquisite courtesy there was a slight condescension in his voice that infuriated Portella. And he knew that he would be lessened in their eyes when they learned of Cilke's duplicity. He told them the whole story.

Tulippa was eating a bonbon when he said, "You mean you had his cousin Marcantonio Aprile, and you made a deal to get your brother released without consulting us." His voice was full of contempt.

"I could not let my brother die," Portella said. "And besides, if I hadn't made the deal, we would have fallen into Cilke's trap."

"True," Tulippa said. "But it was not your decision to make."

"Yeah," Portella said. "Then who—"

"All of us!" Tulippa barked. "We are your partners."

Portella looked at him and wondered what kept him from killing the greasy son of a bitch. But then remembered the fifty Panama hats flying in the air.

The consul general seemed to have read his mind. He said soothingly, "We all come from different cultures and have different values. We must accommodate ourselves to each other. Timmona is an American, a sentimentalist."

"His brother is a dumb piece of shit," Tulippa said.

Rubio shook his finger at Tulippa. "Inzio, stop making trouble for the fun of it. We all have a right to decide our personal affairs."

Grazziella smiled a thin amused smile. "This is true. You, Inzio, have never confided to us your secret laboratories. Your desire to own your own personal weapons. And such a foolish notion. Do you think the government will put up with such a threat? They will change all the laws that now protect us and permit us to thrive."

Tulippa laughed. He was enjoying this meeting. "I am a patriot," he said. "I want South America to be in a position to defend itself from countries like Israel and India and Iraq."

Rubio smiled at him benignly. "I never knew you were a nationalist."

Portella was unamused. "I have a big problem here. I thought Cilke was my friend. I invested a lot of money in him. And now he is coming after me and all of you."

Grazziella spoke directly and strongly. "We must abandon the whole project. We must live with less." He was no longer the amiable man they had known. "We must find another solution. Forget Kurt Cilke and Astorre Viola. They are too dangerous as enemies. We must not pursue a course that could destroy us all."

"That won't solve my problem," Portella said. "Cilke will keep coming after me."

Tulippa also dropped his mask of affability. He said to Grazziella, "That you should advocate such a peaceful solution is against everything we know about you. You killed police and magistrates in Sicily. You assassinated the governor and his wife. You and your Corleonesi *cosca* killed the army general who was sent out to destroy your organization. Yet now you say abandon a project that will earn us billions of dollars. And desert our friend Portella."

"I'm going to get rid of Cilke," Portella said. "No matter what you say."

"That is a very dangerous course of action," the consul general said. "The FBI will declare a vendetta. They will use all their resources to track down his killer."

"I agree with Timmona," Tulippa said. "The FBI operates under legal constraints and can be handled. I will supply an assault team, and hours after the operation they will be on the airplane to South America."

Portella said, "I know it's dangerous, but it's the only thing to do."

"I agree," Tulippa said. "For billions of dollars one must take risks. Or what are we in business for?"

Rubio said to Inzio, "You and I are at minimal risk because we have diplomatic status. Michael, you return to Sicily for the time being. Timmona, you will be the one who must bear the brunt of what follows."

"If worse comes to worst," Tulippa said, "I can hide you in South America."

Portella spread his hands in the air in a helpless

gesture. "I have a choice," he said. "But I want your support. Michael, do you agree?"

Grazziella's face was impassive. "Yes, I agree," he said. "But I would worry more about Astorre Viola than Kurt Cilke."

CHAPTER 11

WHEN ASTORRE RECEIVED the coded message that Heskow wanted a meeting, he took his precautions. There was always the danger that Heskow might turn against him. So instead of answering the message, he suddenly appeared at Heskow's home in Brightwaters at midnight. He took Aldo Monza with him and an extra car with four more men. He also wore a bulletproof vest. He called Heskow when he was in the driveway so that he would open the door.

Heskow did not seem surprised. He prepared coffee and served Astorre and himself. Then he smiled at Astorre and said, "I have good news and bad news. Which one first?"

"Just tell it," Astorre said.

"The bad news is that I have to leave the country for good, and that's because of the good news. And I want to ask you to keep your promise. That nothing will happen to my boy even if I can't work for you anymore."

"You have that promise," Astorre said. "Now, why do you have to leave the country?"

Heskow shook his head in a comical act of sorrow. He said, "Because that dumb prick Portella is going over the top. He is going to knock off Cilke, the FBI guy. And he wants me to be operational chief of the crew."

"So just refuse," Astorre said.

"I can't," Heskow said. "The hit is ordered by his whole syndicate, and if I refuse, I go down the drain and maybe my son does too. So I'll organize the hit, but I won't be in the hit party. I'll be gone. And then when Cilke goes down the FBI will pour a hundred men into the city to solve it. I told them that, but they don't give a shit. Cilke doubled-crossed them or something. They think they can smear him enough so that it won't be such a big deal."

Astorre tried not to show his satisfaction. It had worked out. Cilke would be dead with no danger to himself. And with a little luck the FBI would get rid of Portella.

He said to Heskow, "You want to leave me an address?"

Heskow smiled at him almost scornfully with distrust. "I don't think so," he said. "Not that I don't trust you. But I can always get in touch with you."

"Well, thanks for letting me know," Astorre said, "but who really made this decision?"

"Timmona Portella," Heskow said. "But Inzio Tulippa and the consul general signed off on it. That Corleonesi guy, Grazziella, washed his hands of it. He's distancing himself from the operation. I think he's leaving for Sicily. Which is funny because he's killed practically everybody there.

"They don't really understand how America works, and Portella is just dumb. He says he thought he and Cilke were really friends."

"And you are going to lead the hit team," Astorre said. "That's not so smart either."

"No, I told you when they hit the house I'll be long gone."

"The house?" Astorre said, and at that moment he felt dread over what he was about to hear.

"Yeah," Heskow said. "A massive assault team flies back to South America and disappears."

"Very professional," Astorre said. "When does this all happen?"

"Night after tomorrow. All you have to do is stand aside and they solve all your problems. That's the good news."

"So it is," Astorre said. He kept his face expressionless, but in his mind was the vision of Georgette Cilke, her beauty and goodness.

"I thought you should know about it so that you'll have a good alibi," Heskow said. "So you owe me one, and take care of my kid."

"Damn right," Astorre said. "Don't worry about him."

He shook hands with Heskow before he left. "I think you're being very smart leaving the country. All hell will break loose."

"Yeah," Heskow said.

For a moment Astorre wondered what he would do about Heskow. The man, after all, had driven the hit car in the killing of the Don. He had to pay for that despite all his help. But Astorre had suffered a certain loss of energy when he learned that Cilke's wife and child were to be killed with him. Let him go, he thought. He might be useful later. Then it would be time to kill him. And he looked at Heskow's smiling face and smiled back.

"You're a very clever man," he said to Heskow.

Heskow's face turned pink with pleasure. "I know," he said. "That's how I stay alive."

THE NEXT DAY, at 11:00 A.M., Astorre arrived at FBI headquarters accompanied by Nicole Aprile, who had arranged an appointment.

He had spent a long night pondering his course of action. He had planned all this to have

Portella kill Cilke. But he knew that he could not let Georgette or her daughter be killed. He also knew that Don Aprile would never have interfered with fate in this matter. But then he remembered a story about the Don that gave him pause.

One night, when Astorre was twelve years old and in Sicily with the Don on his annual visit, they were served dinner by Caterina in the garden pavilion. Astorre, with his peculiar innocence, said to them abruptly, "How did you two get to know each other? Did you grow up together as children?" The Don and Caterina exchanged a glance and then laughed at the serious intensity of his interest.

The Don had placed his fingers on his lips and whispered mockingly, "Omerta. It's a secret."

Caterina rapped Astorre's hand with the wooden mixing spoon. "That's none of your business, you little devil," she said. "And besides, it's nothing I'm proud of."

Don Aprile gazed upon Astorre with fondness. "Why should he not know? He's a Sicilian to the bone. Tell him."

"No," Caterina said. "But you can tell him if you like."

After dinner Don Aprile lit his cigar, filled his glass with anisette, and told Astorre the story.

"Ten years ago the most important man in the

town was a certain Father Sigusmundo, a very dangerous man and yet good-humored. When I visited Sicily he often came to my house and played cards with my friends. At that time I had a different housekeeper."

But Father Sigusmundo was not irreligious. He was a devout and hardworking priest. He scolded people into going to mass and even at one time engaged in fisticuffs with an exasperating atheist. He was most famous for giving last rites to victims of the Mafia as they lay dying; he shrived their souls and cleansed them for their voyage to Heaven. He was revered for this, but it happened too often and some people began to whisper, saying the reason he was always so handy was because he was one of the executioners—that he was betraying the secrets of the confessional box for his own ends.

Caterina's husband at that time was a strong anti-Mafia policeman. He had even pursued a case of murder after he had been warned off by the provincial Mafia chief, an unheard-of act of defiance at that time. A week after that threat, Caterina's husband was ambushed and lay dying in a back alley of Palermo. And it so happened that Father Sigusmundo appeared to give him last rites. The crime was never solved.

Caterina, the grief-stricken widow, spent a year in mourning and devotion to the church. Then one Saturday she went to confession with Father Sigusmundo. When the priest came out of the confessional, in full sight of everyone, she stabbed him through the heart with her husband's dagger.

The police threw her in jail, but that was the least of it. The Mafia chief pronounced a death sentence upon her.

Astorre stared wide-eyed at Caterina. "Did you really do that, Aunt Caterina?"

Caterina looked at him with amusement. He was filled with curiosity and not a bit of fear. "But you must understand why. Not because he killed my husband. Men are always killing each other here in Sicily. But Father Sigusmundo was a false priest, an unshriven murderer. He could not give last rites with legitimacy. Why would God listen? So my husband was not only murdered but denied his entrance to Heaven and descended into Hell. Well, men don't know where to stop. There are things you can't do. That's why I killed the priest."

"Then how come you're here?" Astorre asked.

"Because Don Aprile took an interest in the whole affair," Caterina said. "So naturally everything was settled."

The Don said gravely to Astorre, "I had a certain standing in the town, a respect. The authorities were easily satisfied, and the church did not want the public attention of a corrupt priest. The Mafia chief was not so sensitive and refused to cancel his death sentence. He was found in the cemetery where Caterina's husband was buried, with his throat cut, and his *cosca* was destroyed and made powerless. By that time I had grown fond of Caterina, and I made her chief of this household. And for the last nine years my summer months in Sicily have been the sweetest of my life."

To Astorre this was all magic. He ate a handful of olives and spit out the pits. "Caterina's your girlfriend?" he asked.

"Of course," Caterina said. "You're a twelve-year-old boy, you can understand. I live under his protection as if I were his wife, and I perform all my wifely duties."

Don Aprile seemed a little embarrassed, the only time Astorre had seen him so. Astorre said, "But why don't you marry?"

Caterina said, "I could never leave Sicily. I live like a queen here, and your uncle is generous. Here I have my friends, my family, my sisters and brothers and cousins. And your uncle could not live in Sicily. So we do the best we can."

Astorre said to Don Aprile, "Uncle, you can marry Caterina and live here. I'll live with you. I never want to leave Sicily." At this they both laughed.

"Listen to me," the Don said. "It took a great

deal of work to put a stop to the vendetta against her. If we married, plots and mischief would be born. They can accept the fact that she is my mistress but not my wife. So with this arrangement we are both happy and both free. Also, I do not want a wife who refuses to accept my decisions, and when she refuses to leave Sicily I am not a husband."

"And it would be an *infamita*," Caterina said. Her head drooped slightly, and then she turned her eyes to the black Sicilian sky and began to weep.

Astorre was bewildered. It made no sense to him as a child. "Really, but why? Why?" he said.

Don Aprile sighed. He puffed on his cigar and took a sip of anisette. "You must understand," the Don said. "Father Sigusmundo was my brother."

ASTORRE REMEMBERED now that their explanation hadn't convinced him. With the willfulness of a romantic child he had believed that two people who loved each other were permitted any license in the world. Only now he understood the terrible decision his uncle and aunt had made. That if he married Caterina, all the Don's blood relatives would become his enemies. Not that they did not know that Father Sigusmundo was a villain. But he was a brother and that excused all his sins. And a man like the Don could not marry his brother's murderer. Caterina could not ask such a sacrifice. And then what if Caterina believed that the Don had somehow been implicated in her husband's murder? What a leap of faith for both of them, and perhaps, what a betrayal of everything they believed in.

But this was America, not Sicily. During the long night Astorre had made up his mind. In the morning he had called Nicole.

"I'm going to pick you up for breakfast," he had said. "Then you and I are going to visit Cilke at FBI headquarters."

Nicole had said, "This has to be serious, right?"

"Yeah. I'll tell you over breakfast."

"Do you have an appointment with him?" Nicole had asked.

"No, that's your job."

An hour later the cousins were having breakfast together at a posh hotel with widely separated tables for privacy because it was an early-hour meeting place for the power brokers of the city.

Nicole believed in a hearty breakfast to fuel her twelve-hour working day. Astorre settled for orange juice and coffee, which with a basket of breakfast rolls would cost him twenty dollars. "What crooks," he said to Nicole with a grin.

Nicole was impatient with this. "You're paying

for the atmosphere," she said. "The imported linen, the crockery. What the hell is wrong now?"

"I'm going to do my civic duty," Astorre said. "I have information from an unimpeachable source that Kurt Cilke and his family will be killed tomorrow night. I want to warn him. I want to get credit for warning him. He'll want to know my source, and I can't tell him."

Nicole pushed away her plate and leaned back. "Who the hell is that stupid?" she said to Astorre. "Christ, I hope you're not involved."

"Why do you think that?" Astorre asked.

"I don't know," Nicole said. "The thought just came. Why not let him know anonymously?"

"I want to get credit for my good deeds. I get the feeling nobody loves me these days." He smiled.

"I love you," Nicole said, leaning toward him. "OK, here's our story. As we came into the hotel a strange man stopped us and whispered the information in your ear. He was wearing a gray striped suit, a white shirt, and a black tie. He was average height, dark-skinned, could be Italian or Hispanic. After that we can vary. I'll be witness to your story, and he knows he can't screw around with me."

Astorre laughed. His laughter was always disarming; it had the unfettered glee of a child. "So he's more afraid of you than he is of me" he said.

Nicole smiled. "And I know the director of the FBI. He's a political animal, he has to be. I'll call Cilke and tell him to expect us." She took her phone out of her purse and made the call.

"Mr. Cilke," she said into the phone, "this is Nicole Aprile. I'm with my cousin Astorre Viola, and he has important information he wants to give you."

After a pause she said, "That's too late. We'll be there within the hour." She hung up before Cilke could say anything.

An hour later Astorre and Nicole were ushered into Cilke's office. It was a large corner office with Polaroid bulletproof windows that could not be seen out of, so there was no view.

Cilke, standing behind a huge desk, was waiting for them. There were three black leather chairs facing his desk. Behind it, oddly enough, was a schoolroom blackboard. In one of the chairs sat Bill Boxton, who did not offer to shake hands.

"Are you going to tape this?" Nicole asked.

"Of course," Cilke said.

Boxton said reassuringly, "Hell, we tape everything, even our coffee-and-doughnut orders. We also tape anybody we think we may have to put in jail."

"You're a pretty fucking funny guy," Nicole said, deadpan. "On the best day of your life you couldn't put me in jail. Think another way. My client Astorre Viola is meeting you voluntarily to give you an important piece of information. I'm here to protect him from any abuse after he does so."

Kurt Cilke was not quite so charming as he had been in their previous meetings. He waved them into chairs and took his seat behind the desk. "OK," he said. "Let's have it."

Astorre felt the man's hostility, as if being on his own turf didn't require his usual businesslike friendliness. How would he react? He looked directly into Cilke's eyes and said, "I received information that there will be a heavily armed assault on your home tomorrow night. Late. The purpose is to kill you for some reason."

Cilke did not respond. He was frozen in his chair, but Boxton sprang up and stood behind Astorre. To Cilke he said, "Kurt, keep calm."

Cilke rose. His entire body seemed to blow up with rage. "This is an old Mafia trick," he said. "He sets up the operation and then sabotages it. And he thinks I'll be grateful. Now, how the hell did you get such information?"

Astorre told him the story he and Nicole had prepared. Cilke turned to Nicole and asked, "You witnessed this incident?"

"Yes," Nicole said, "but I didn't hear what the man said."

Cilke said to Astorre, "You are under arrest now."

"For what?" Nicole said.

"For threatening a federal officer," Cilke said.

"I think you better call your director," Nicole said.

"It's my decision to make," Cilke told her.

Nicole looked at her watch.

Cilke said softly, "Under executive order of the president, I'm authorized to hold you and your client for forty-eight hours without legal counsel, as a threat to national security."

Astorre was startled. In his wide-eyed, childish way, he said, "Is that really true? You can do that?" He was really impressed by such power. He turned back to Nicole and said cheerfully, "Hey, this is getting more and more like Sicily."

"If you take that step, the FBI will be in court for the next ten years and you'll be history," Nicole said to Cilke. "You have time to get your family out and ambush the attackers. They won't know they've been informed on. If you capture any, you can question them. We won't talk. Or warn them."

Cilke seemed to consider this. He said to Astorre with contempt, "At least I respected your uncle. He would never have talked."

Astorre gave an embarrassed smile. "Those were the old days and that was the old country, and besides, you're not so different, with your secret executive orders." He wondered what Cilke would say if he told him the real reason. That he had saved the man simply because he had spent an evening in the presence of his wife and had romantically and uselessly fallen in love with his idea of her.

"I don't believe your bullshit story, but we'll go into that if there is really an assault tomorrow night. If anything happens, then I lock you up, and maybe you, too, counselor. But why did you tell me?"

Astorre smiled. "Because I like you," he said.

"Get the hell out of here," Cilke said. He turned to Boxton. "Get the commander of the special tactical force in here, and tell my secretary to set up a call to the director."

They were kept another two hours to be interrogated by Cilke's staff. Meanwhile, Cilke in his office talked to the director in Washington over the scramble phone.

"Do not arrest them under any circumstances," the director told him. "Everything would come out in the media, and we'd be a joke. And don't fool with Nicole Aprile unless you have the goods on her. Keep everything top secret, and we'll see what happens tomorrow night. Guards at your house have been alerted, and your family is already being moved out as we speak. Now put

Bill on the phone. He'll run the ambush operation."

"Sir, that should be my job," Cilke protested.

"You'll help with the planning," the director
said, "but under no circumstance will you take
part in the tactical operation. The Bureau operates under very strict rules of engagement to
avoid unnecessary violence. You would be suspect
if things go bad. You understand me?"

"Yes, sir." Cilke understood perfectly.

CHAPTER 12

AFTER A MONTH in the hospital Aspinella Washington was released but still had to heal sufficiently for the insertion of an artificial eye. A splendid physical specimen, her body seemed to assemble itself around her injuries. True, her left foot dragged a little, and her eye socket looked hideous. But she wore a square green eye patch instead of black, and the dark green accentuated the beauty of her mocha skin. She reported back to work wearing a costume of black trousers, a green pullover shirt, and a green leather coat. When she looked at herself in the mirror she thought herself a striking figure.

Though she was on medical leave she would sometimes go in to the Detective Bureau head-quarters and help in interrogations. Her injury gave her a sense of liberation—she felt like she could do anything, and she stretched her power.

On her first interrogation there were two suspects, an unusual pair in that one was white and one was black. The white suspect, about thirty, was immediately frightened of her. But the black partner was delighted by the tall beautiful woman with the green eye patch and the cold level stare. This was one cool sister.

"Holy shit," he cried out, his face happy. It was his first bust, he had no criminal record, and he really didn't know he was in serious trouble. He and his partner had broken into a home, tied up the husband and wife, and then looted the house. They had been laid low by an informant. The black kid was still wearing the house owner's Rolex watch. He said cheerily to Aspinella, without malice, indeed in a voice of admiration, "Hey, Captain Kidd, you gonna make us walk the plank?"

The other detectives in the room smirked at this foolishness. But Aspinella didn't respond. The kid was in handcuffs and couldn't ward off her blow. Snakelike, her truncheon crashed against his face, breaking his nose and splitting his cheekbone. He didn't go down; his knees sagged, and he gave her a reproachful look. His face was a mess of blood. Then his legs folded and he toppled to the ground. For the next ten minutes Aspinella beat him unmercifully. As if from a fresh spring, blood started to flow from the boy's ears.

"Jesus," one of the detectives said, "how the hell do we question him now?"

"I didn't want to talk to him," Aspinella said. "I want to talk to *this* guy." She pointed her truncheon to the white suspect. "Zeke, right? I want to talk to you, Zeke." She took him roughly by the shoulder and threw him into a chair facing her desk. He stared at her, terrified. She realized her eye patch had slipped to one side and that Zeke was staring into that empty orb. She reached up and adjusted the patch to cover her milky socket.

"Zeke," she said, "I want you to listen very carefully. I want to save time here. I want to know how you got this kid into this. How you got into this. Understand? Are you going to cooperate?"

Zeke had turned very pale. He didn't hesitate. "Yes, ma'am," he said. "I'll tell you everything."

"OK," Aspinella said to another detective. "Get that kid into the medical ward and send down the video people to take Zeke's confession of his own free will."

As they were setting up the monitors, Aspinella said to Zeke, "Who fenced your goods? Who gave you information about your target? Give me the exact details of the robbery. Your partner is obviously a nice kid. He has no record and he's not that smart. That's why I took it easy on him. Now, you, Zeke, have a very distinguished record, so I figure you're the Fagin that got him into this. So start rehearsing for the video."

WHEN ASPINELLA LEFT the station house she drove her car over the Southern State Parkway to Brightwaters, Long Island.

Oddly enough, she found driving with one eye was more pleasurable than not. The landscape was more interesting because it was focused, like some futuristic painting that dissolved into dreams around the edges. It was as if half the world, the globe itself, had been bisected and the half she could see claimed more attention.

Finally she was driving through Brightwaters and passing John Heskow's house. She could see his car in the driveway and a man carrying a huge azalea plant from the flower shed to the house. Then another man came out of the shed carrying a box filled with yellow flowers. This was interesting, she thought. They were emptying the flower shed.

While in the hospital she had done research on John Heskow. She had gone through the New York State car-registration records and found his address. Then she checked all the criminal databases and found that John Heskow was really Louis Ricci; the bastard was Italian, though he looked like a German pudding. But his criminal record was clear. He had been arrested several times for extortion and assault but never convicted. The flower shed could not generate the amount of money to support his style of living.

She had done all this because she had figured out that the only one who could have put the finger on her and Di Benedetto was Heskow. The only thing that puzzled her was that he had given them the money. That money had put the Internal Affairs Bureau on her ass, but she had soon gotten rid of their unenthusiastic inquiries, since they were happy to have the money for themselves. Now she was preparing to get rid of Heskow.

TWENTY-FOUR HOURS before the scheduled assault on Cilke, Heskow drove to Kennedy airport for his flight to Mexico City, where he would disappear from the civilized world with fake passports he had prepared years ago.

Details had been settled. The flower sheds had been emptied; his ex-wife would take care of selling the house and put the proceeds in the bank for their son's college expenses. Heskow had told her he would be away for two years. He told his son the same story, over dinner at Shun Lee's.

It was early evening when he got to the

airport. He checked two suitcases, all he needed, except for the one hundred thousand dollars in one-hundred-dollar bills taped around his body in small pouches. He was wallpapered with money for immediate expenses, and he had a secret account in the Caymans, holding nearly five million dollars. Thank God, because he certainly could not apply for Social Security. He was proud that he had lived a prudent life and had not squandered his bankroll on gambling, women, or other foolishness.

Heskow checked in for his flight and boarding pass. Now he only carried a briefcase with his false ID and passports. He had left his car at permanent parking; his ex-wife would pick it up and hold it for him.

He was at least an hour early for his flight. He felt a little uneasy being unarmed, but he had to pass the detectors to get on the flight, and he would be able to get plenty of weaponry from his contacts in Mexico City.

To pass the time he bought some magazines in the bookshop and then went to the terminal cafeteria. He loaded up a tray with dessert and coffee and sat down at one of the small tables. He looked through the magazines and ate his dessert, a false strawberry tart covered with fake whipped cream. Suddenly he was aware that someone was sitting down at his table. He looked up and saw

Detective Aspinella Washington. Like everyone, he was entranced by the square, dark green eye patch. It gave him a flutter of panic. She looked much more beautiful than he remembered.

"Hi, John," she said. "You never did come to visit me in the hospital."

He was so flustered he took her seriously. "You know I couldn't do that, Detective. But I was sorry to hear about your misfortune."

Aspinella gave him a huge smile. "I was kidding, John. But I did want to have a little chat with you before your flight."

"Sure," Heskow said. He expected he would have to pay off, and he had ten grand in the brief-case ready for just such surprises. "I'm glad to see you looking so well. I was worried about you."

"No shit," Aspinella said, her one eye glittering like a hawk's. "Too bad about Paul. We were good friends, you know, besides his being my boss."

"That was a shame," Heskow said. He even gave a little cluck, which made Aspinella smile.

"I don't have to show you my badge," Aspinella said. "Right?" She paused. "I want you to come with me to a little interrogation room we have here in the terminal. Give me some good interesting answers, and you can catch your flight."

"OK," Heskow said. He rose to his feet clutching his briefcase.

"And no funny business or I'll shoot you dead.

Funny thing, I'm a better shot with just one eye."
She rose and took his arm and led him to a stair-
way up to the mezzanine, which held the admin-
istrative offices of the airlines. She led him down
a long hallway and unlocked an office door.
Heskow was surprised not only by the largeness
of the room but by the banks of TV monitors on
the walls, at least twenty screens, monitored by
two men who sat in soft armchairs and studied
them as they ate sandwiches and drank coffee.
One of the men stood up and said, "Hey,
Aspinella, what's up?"

"I'm going to have a private chat with this guy
in the interrogation room. Lock us in."

"Sure," the man said. "You want one of us in
there with you?"

"Nah. It's just a friendly chat."

"Oh, one of your famous friendly chats," the
man said, and laughed. He looked at Heskow
closely. "I saw you on the screens down in the
terminal. Strawberry tart, right?" He led them to
a door in the back of the room and unlocked it.
After Heskow and Aspinella entered the interrogation room he locked the door behind them.

Heskow was reassured now that there were
other people involved. The interrogation cham-
ber was disarming, with a couch, a desk, and three
comfortable-looking chairs. In one corner was a
watercooler with paper cups. The pink walls were

decorated with photographs and paintings of flying machines.

Aspinella made Heskow sit in a chair facing the desk, on which she sat and looked down at him.

"Can we get on with it?" Heskow asked. "I cannot afford to miss that flight."

Aspinella didn't answer. She reached out and took Heskow's briefcase from his lap. Heskow twitched. She opened it and leafed through the contents, including the stacks of one-hundred-dollar bills. She studied one of the false passports, then put everything back in the briefcase and returned it to him.

"You're a very clever man," she said. "You knew it was time to run. Who told you I was after you?"

"Why would you be after me?" Heskow asked. He was more confident now that she had given him back his briefcase.

Aspinella lifted her eye patch so that he could see the wretched crater. But Heskow did not flinch; he had seen much worse in his day.

"You cost me that eye," she said. "Only you could have informed and set Paul and me up."

Heskow spoke with the utmost sincerity, which had been one of his best weapons in his profession. "You're wrong, absolutely wrong. If I did that, I would have kept the money—you can see that. Look, I really have to catch that flight." He unbuttoned his shirt and tore a piece of tape.

Two packets of money appeared on the table. "That's yours, and the money in the briefcase. That's thirty grand."

"Gee," Aspinella said. "Thirty grand. That's a lot of money for just one eye. OK. But you have to tell me the name of the guy who paid you to set us up."

Heskow made up his mind. His one chance was to get on that flight. He knew she wasn't bluffing. He had dealt with too many homicidal maniacs in his line of work to misjudge her.

"Listen, believe me," he said. "I never dreamed this guy would knock off two high-ranking cops. I just made a deal with Astorre Viola so he could hide out. I never dreamed he would do such a thing."

"Good," Aspinella said. "Now, who paid you for the hit on him?"

"Paul knew," Heskow said. "Didn't he tell you? Timmona Portella."

At that Aspinella felt a surge of rage. Her fat partner had not only been a lousy fuck but a lying bastard as well.

"Stand up," she said to Heskow. Suddenly a gun appeared in her hand.

Heskow was terrified. He had seen that look before, only he had not been the victim. For one moment he thought of his hidden five million dollars that would die with him, unclaimed, and the five million dollars seemed a living creature. What a tragedy. "No," he cried out, and huddled his body further into the chair. Aspinella grabbed his hair with her free hand and pulled him to his feet. She held the gun away from his neck and fired. Heskow seemed to fly out of her grasp and crashed to the floor. She knelt by his body. Half his throat had been blown away. Then she took her throwaway gun from its ankle holster, placed it in Heskow's hand, and stood up. She could hear the door being unlocked, and then the two screen men rushed in with guns drawn.

"I had to shoot him," she said. "He tried to bribe me and then he pulled a gun. Call the terminal medical van and I'll call homicide myself. Don't touch anything, and don't let me out of your sight."

THE NEXT NIGHT Portella launched his attack. Cilke's wife and daughter had already been spirited away to a restricted heavily guarded FBI station in California. Cilke, at the director's orders, was at FBI headquarters in New York with his full staff on duty. Bill Boxton had been given the overall command of the special task force and would spring the trap at Cilke's house. The rules of engagement were strict, however. The Bureau didn't want a bloodbath that would cause complaint from liberal groups. The FBI team would not fire unless it was fired upon. Every effort would be made to give the attackers a chance to surrender.

As an assistant planning officer, Kurt Cilke met with Boxton and the special task force's commander, a comparatively young man of thirty-five whose face was set in the rigid lines of command. But his skin was gray and he had a regrettable dimple in his chin. His name was Sestak and his accent was pure Harvard. They met in Cilke's office.

"I expect you to be in constant communication with me during the operation," Cilke said. "The rules of engagement will be strictly observed."

"Don't worry," Boxton said. "We have a hundred men with firepower that exceeds theirs. They will surrender."

Sestak said in a soft voice, "I have another hundred men to establish a perimeter. We let them in but we don't let them out."

"Good," Cilke said. "When you capture them you will ship them to our New York interrogation center. I'm not permitted to take part in the interrogation, but I want information as soon as possible."

"What if something goes wrong and they wind up dead?" Sestak asked.

"Then there will be an internal investigation and the director will be very unhappy. Now, here's the reality: They will be arrested for conspiracy to commit murder, and they will get out on bail. Then they will vanish into South America. So we have only a few days to interrogate them."

Boxton looked at Cilke with a little smile. Sestak said to Cilke in his cultured tone, "I think that would make you terribly unhappy."

"Sure, it bothers me," Cilke said. "But the director has to worry about political complications. Conspiracy charges are always tricky."

"I see," Sestak said. "So your hands are tied."

"That's right," Cilke said.

Boxton said quietly, "It's a damn shame, they can attempt the murder of a federal officer and get off."

Sestak was looking at them both with an amused smile. His gray skin took on a reddish tinge. "You're preaching to the choir," he said. "Anyway, these operations always go wrong. Guys with guns always think they can't be shot. Very funny thing about human nature."

THAT NIGHT Boxton accompanied Sestak to the operational area around Cilke's home in New Jersey. Lights had been left on in the house to make it look like someone was home. Also there were three cars parked in the driveway to give the impression that the house guards were inside. The cars were booby-trapped so that if they were started, they would blow up. Otherwise Boxton could see nothing.

"Where the hell are your hundred men?" Boxton asked Sestak.

Sestak gave him a huge grin. "Pretty good, huh? They're all around here, and even you can't see them. They already have lines of fire. When the attackers come in, the road will be sealed behind them. We'll have a basket full of rats."

Boxton remained at Sestak's side at a command post fifty yards from the house. With them was a communications team of four men who wore camouflage to match the patch of woods they used as cover. Sestak and his team were armed with rifles, but Boxton only had his handgun.

"I don't want you in the fighting," Sestak told Boxton. "Besides, that weapon you carry is useless here."

"Why not?" Boxton said. "I've been waiting my whole career to shoot the bad guys."

Sestak laughed. "Not today. My team is protected by executive order from any legal inquiries or prosecution. You're not."

"But I'm in command," Boxton said.

"Not when we become operational," Sestak

told him coolly. "Then I'm in sole command. I
make all the decisions. Even the director can't
supersede me."

They waited together in the darkness. Boxton
looked at his watch. It was ten minutes to
midnight. One of the communications team
whispered to Sestak, "Five cars filled with men
are on approach to the house. The road behind
them has been sealed. Estimated time of arrival is
five minutes.

Sestak was wearing infrared goggles that gave
him night vision. "OK," he said. "Send the word.
Don't fire unless fired upon or at my order."

They waited. Suddenly five cars raced to the
driveway and men spilled out. One of them
immediately threw a firebomb into Cilke's house,
breaking a pane of glass and sending a thin blaze
of red fire inside the room.

Then suddenly the whole area was flooded
with bright searchlights that froze the group of
twenty attackers. At the same time a helicopter
whirred overhead with glaring lights. Loudspeak-
ers roared a message into the night. "This is the
FBI. Throw away your weapons and lie on the
ground."

Dazzled by the light and the helicopters, the
trapped men froze. Boxton saw with relief that
they had lost all will to resist.

So he was surprised when Sestak brought up

his rifle and fired into the group of attackers. Immediately the attack group started firing back. And then Boxton was deafened by the roar of gunfire that swept the driveway and mowed down the attackers. One of the booby-trapped cars exploded. It was as if a hurricane of lead had completely devastated the driveway. Glass shattered and poured down a silver rain. The other cars sank to the ground so riddled with bullets that their outsides had no color. The driveway seemed to spout a spring of blood that flowed and eddied around the cars. The twenty attackers were blood-soaked bundles of rags looking like sacks of laundry to be picked up.

Boxton was in shock. "You fired before they could surrender," he said to Sestak accusingly. "That will be my report."

"I differ," Sestak grinned at him. "Once they firebombed the house, that was attempted murder. I couldn't risk my men. That will be my report. Also that they fired first."

"Well, it won't be mine," Boxton said.

"No kidding," Sestak said. "You think the director wants your report? You'll be on his shit list. Forever."

"He'll want your ass because you disobeyed orders," Boxton said. "We'll go down in flames together."

"Good," Sestak said. "But I'm the tactical

commander. I can't be overruled. Once I'm called in, that's it. I don't want criminals to think they can attack a federal officer. That's the reality, and you and the director can go fuck yourselves."

"Twenty dead men," Boxton said.

"And good riddance to them," Sestak said. "You and Cilke wanted me to blast them, but you didn't have the balls to come right out with it."

Boxton suddenly knew this was true.

KURT CILKE prepared for another meeting with the director in Washington. He had his notes with an outline of what he would say and a report on all the circumstances of the attack on his home.

As always, Bill Boxton would accompany him, but this time it was at the express wish of the director.

Cilke and Boxton were in the director's office with its row of TV monitors showing reports of activities of the local FBI office. The director, always courteous, shook hands with both men and invited them to sit down, though he gave Boxton a cold, fishy look. Two of his deputies were in attendance.

"Gentlemen," he said, addressing the whole group. "We have to clean up this mess. We cannot allow such an outrageous act to go without answering it with all our resources. Cilke, do you want to stay on the job or take retirement?"

"I stay," Cilke said.

The director turned to Boxton, and his lean aristocratic face was stern. "You were in charge. How is it that all the attackers were killed and we have no one to interrogate? Who gave the order to fire? You? And on what grounds?"

Boxton sat up in his chair stiffly. "Sir," he said, "the attackers threw a bomb in the house and opened fire. There was no choice."

The director sighed. One of his deputies gave a grunt of scorn.

"Captain Sestak is one of our beauties," the director said. "Did he try, at least, for one prisoner?"

"Sir, it was over in two minutes," Boxton said. "Sestak is a very efficient tactician in the field."

"Well, there hasn't been any fuss by the media or the public," the director said. "But I must say I consider it a bloodbath."

"Yes, it was," volunteered one of the deputies.

"Well, it can't be helped," the director said. "Cilke, have you come up with an operational plan?"

Cilke had felt a surge of anger at their criticism, but he answered calmly. "I want a hundred men assigned to my office. I want you to request a full audit of the Aprile banks. I am going into deep background on everyone involved in this business."

The director said, "You don't feel any debt to this Astorre Viola for saving you and your family?"

"No," Cilke said. "You have to know these people. First they get you into trouble, then they help you out."

The director said, "Remember, one of our primary interests is to appropriate the Aprile banks. Not only because we benefit but because those banks are destined to be a center for laundering drug money. And through them we get Portella and Tulippa. We have to look at this as global. Astorre Viola refuses to sell the banks, and the syndicate is trying to eliminate him. So far they've failed. We have learned that the two hired killers who shot the Don have disappeared. Two detectives in the NYPD were blown up."

"Astorre is cunning and elusive, and he isn't involved in any rackets," Cilke told them, "so we can't really put something on him. Now, the syndicate may succeed in getting rid of him, and the children will sell the banks to them. Then I'm sure in a couple of years they will step over the line."

It was not unusual for government law enforcement to play a long game, especially with the drug people. But to do so they had to permit crimes to be committed.

"We've played it long before," the director said. "But that doesn't mean you give Portella carte blanche."

"Of course," Cilke said. He knew that everyone was speaking for the record.

"I'll give fifty men," the director said. "And I'll request a full audit of the banks just to shake things up."

One of the deputies said, "We have audited them before and never found anything."

"There's always a chance," Cilke said. "Astorre is no banker, and he could have made mistakes."

"Yes," the director said. "One little slip is all the attorney general needs."

BACK IN New York Cilke met with Boxton and Sestak to plan his campaign. "We're getting fifty more men to investigate the attack on my home," he told them. "We have to be very careful. I want everything you can get on Astorre Viola. I want to go into the blowing up of the detectives. I want all the dope on the disappearance of the Sturzo brothers and all the information we can get on the syndicate. Zero in on Astorre and also Detective Washington. She has a reputation for bribe taking and brutality, and the story she gives of getting blown up and all that money at the scene is very fishy."

"What about this guy Tulippa?" Boxton asked. "He can leave the country anytime."

"Tulippa is touring the country giving speeches for drug legalization and also collecting his blackmail payment from big companies."

"Can't we nail him on that?" Sestak asked.

"No, Sestak," Cilke said. "He has an insurance company and sells them insurance. We might be able to make a case, but the businesspeople oppose it. They've solved the safety problem of their personnel in South America. And Portella has no place to go."

Sestak grinned at him coldly. "What are the rules of engagement here?"

Cilke said smoothly, "The director ordered no more massacres, but protect yourself. Especially against Astorre."

"In other words, we can leave Astorre for dead," Sestak said.

Cilke seemed lost in thought for a moment. "If necessary," he replied.

IT WAS ONLY a week later that the federal auditors swarmed over the Aprile bank records and Cilke came personally to see Mr. Pryor in his office.

Cilke shook his hand and then said genially, "I always like to meet personally with people I may have to send to prison. Now, can you help us in any way and get off the train before it's too late?"

Mr. Pryor looked at the young man with a benevolent concern. "Really?" he said. "You are completely on the wrong track, I assure you. I run these banks impeccably according to national and international law."

"Well, I just wanted you to know that I'm tracking down your background and everyone else's," Cilke said. "And I hope you are all clean. Especially the Sturzo brothers."

Mr. Pryor smiled at him. "We are immaculate."

After Cilke left, Mr. Pryor leaned back in his chair. The situation was becoming alarming. What if they tracked down Rosie? He sighed. What a shame. He would have to do something about her.

WHEN CILKE notified Nicole that he wanted her and Astorre in his office the next day, he still did not have a true understanding of Astorre's character, nor did he wish to. He just felt the contempt he had for anyone who broke the law. He did not understand the resolve of a true Mafioso.

Astorre believed in the old tradition. His followers loved him not only because of his charisma but because he valued honor above all.

A true Mafioso was strong enough in his will to avenge any insult to his person or his *cosca*. He could never submit to the will of another person or government agency. And in this lay his power. His own will was paramount; justice was what he decreed justice must be. His saving of Cilke and his family was a flaw in his character. Still, he went with Nicole to Cilke's office vaguely expecting some thanks, a relaxation of Cilke's hostility.

It was evident that careful arrangements had been made to receive them. Two security men searched Astorre and Nicole before they entered Cilke's office. Cilke himself stood behind his desk and glared at them. Without any sign of friendliness he gestured them to sit down. One of the guards locked them all in and waited outside the door.

"Is this being recorded?" Nicole asked.

"Yes," Cilke said. "Audio and video. I don't want any misunderstanding about this meeting." He paused for a moment. "I want you to understand that nothing has changed. I consider you a piece of scum I won't allow to live in this country. I don't buy this Don bullshit. I don't buy your story about the informant. I think you engi-

neered this with him and then betrayed your
conspirator to gain more lenient treatment from
me. I despise such trickery."

Astorre was astonished that Cilke had penetrated so near to the truth. He looked at him with
new respect. And yet his feelings were hurt. The
man had no gratitude, no respect for a man who
had saved him and his family. He smiled at the
contradictions within himself.

"You think it's funny, one of your Mafia jokes,"
Cilke said. "I'll wipe that smile off your face in
two seconds."

He turned to Nicole. "First, the Bureau
demands that you tell us the true circumstances
of how you got this information. Not that phony
story your cousin gave. I'm surprised at you,
counselor. I'm thinking of charging you as
coconspirator."

Nicole said coolly, "You can try, but I suggest
you take it to your director first."

"Who told you about the attack on my
house?" Cilke asked. "We want the true informant."

Astorre shrugged. "Take it or leave it," he said.

"Neither," Cilke said coldly. "Let's get this
straight. You are just another dirtbag. Another
murderer. I know you blew up Di Benedetto and
Washington. We're looking into the disappearance of the two Sturzo brothers in L.A. You killed

three of Portella's hoods, and you took part in a kidnapping. We're going to get you in the long run. And then you'll be just another piece of shit."

For the first time Astorre seemed to lose some of his composure, and his mask of affability slipped. He caught Nicole watching him with a sort of terrified pity. And so he permitted some of his anger to escape.

"I don't expect favors from you," he said to Cilke. "You don't even know what honor means. I saved the lives of your wife and daughter. They could be lying underground if it wasn't for me. Now you invite me here to abuse me. Your wife and daughter are alive because of me. Show me respect for that at least."

Cilke stared at him. "I'll show you nothing," he said, and he felt a terrible anger at being in Astorre's debt.

Astorre rose from his seat to walk out of the room, but the security guard pushed him down.

"I'm going to make your life miserable," Cilke said.

Astorre shrugged. "Do what you like. But let me tell you this. I know you helped put Don Aprile on the spot. Just because you and the Bureau want to get hold of the banks."

At this the security man moved toward him, but Cilke waved him off. "I know you can stop the attacks on my family," he said. "I'm telling you now that I make it your responsibility."

From the other side of the room, Bill Boxton looked at Astorre and drawled, "Are you threatening a federal officer?"

Nicole broke in. "Of course not, he is just asking for his help."

Cilke now seemed more cool. "All this for your beloved Don. Well, obviously you haven't read the file I gave to Nicole. Your beloved Don was the man who killed your father when you were only two years old."

Astorre flinched and glanced at Nicole. "Is that the part you tried to erase?"

Nicole nodded. "I didn't think that part was true, and if it was, I didn't think you should know. It could only hurt you."

Astorre felt the room begin to spin, but he kept his composure. "It doesn't make any difference," he said.

Nicole said to Cilke, "Now that everything is clear, can we go?"

Cilke had an overpowering build, and as he came out from behind the desk he gave Astorre a playful slap on the head. Which surprised Cilke as much as Astorre, for he had never done such a thing before. It was a blow to show his contempt, which masked true hatred. He realized that he could never forget Astorre saving his family. As for Astorre, he looked steadily into Cilke's face. He understood exactly how Cilke felt.

NICOLE AND ASTORRE went back to Nicole's apartment, and Nicole tried to show her sympathy for Astorre in his humiliation, but this angered him even more. Nicole prepared a light lunch and then persuaded him to lie down on her bed for a nap. In the middle of his nap, he was conscious that Nicole was on the bed beside him, hugging him. He pushed her away.

"You heard what Cilke said about me," he said. "You want to get mixed up in my life?"

"I don't believe him or his reports," Nicole said. "Astorre, I really do think I still love you."

"We can't go back to when we were kids," Astorre said gently. "I'm not the same person, and neither are you. You're just wishing we were kids again."

They lay in each other's arms. Then Astorre said sleepily, "Do you think it's true what they say about the Don killing my father?"

THE NEXT DAY Astorre flew out to Chicago with Mr. Pryor and consulted with Benito Craxxi. He brought them up to date and then asked, "Is it true that Don Aprile killed my father?"

Craxxi ignored the question and asked Astorre, "Did you have anything to do with inspiring the attack on Cilke's family?"

"No," Astorre lied. He lied to them because he did not want anyone to know the depth of his cunning. And he knew that they would have disapproved.

"And yet you saved them," Don Craxxi said. "Why?"

Again Astorre had to lie. He could not let his allies know he was capable of such sentimentality, that he could not bear to see Cilke's wife and daughter killed.

"You did well," Craxxi said.

Astorre said, "You haven't answered my question."

"Because it is complicated," Craxxi said. "You were the newborn son of a great Mafia chief in Sicily, eighty years old, and head of a very powerful *cosca*. Your mother was very young when she died in childbirth. The old Don was in extremis, and he summoned myself, Don Aprile, and Bianco to his bedside. The whole of his *cosca* would tumble at his death, and he was worried about your future. He made us promise to look after you and chose Don Aprile to take you to America. There, because his wife was dying and he wanted to save you any more suffering, he placed you with the Viola family, which was a mistake, because your foster father turned out to be a traitor and had to be executed. Don Aprile took you into his home as soon as his trouble had passed. The Don had a macabre sense of humor, and so he arranged to have the death labeled suicide in the trunk of a car. Then, as you grew older, you showed all the traits of your real father, the great Don Zeno. And so Don Aprile made the decision that you would be the defender of his family. So he sent you to Sicily to be trained."

Astorre was not really surprised. Somewhere in his memory was a picture of a very old man and a ride on a funeral hearse.

"Yes," Astorre said slowly, "and I am trained. I know how to take the offensive. Still, Portella and Tulippa are well protected. And I have to worry about Grazziella. The only one I could kill is the consul general, Marriano Rubio. Meanwhile, I have Cilke hounding me. I don't even know where to start."

"You must never never strike at Cilke," Don Craxxi said.

"Yes," Mr. Pryor said. "That would be disastrous."

Astorre smiled at them reassuringly. "Agreed," he said.

"There is some good news," Craxxi told him. "Grazziella, in Corleone, has requested Bianco in Palermo to arrange a meeting with you. Bianco will send you word to come within a month. He may be your key."

TULIPPA, PORTELLA, and Rubio met in the conference room of the Peruvian consulate. In Sicily, Michael Grazziella expressed his profoundest regret that he was unable to attend.

Inzio opened the meeting without his usual South American charm. He was impatient. "We must solve the question: Do we get the banks or not? I've invested millions of dollars, and I am very disappointed in the results."

"Astorre is like a ghost," Portella said. "We can't get at him. He won't take more money. We have to kill him. Then the others will sell."

Inzio turned to Rubio. "You're sure your little love will agree?"

"I will persuade her," Rubio said.

"And the two brothers?" Inzio asked.

"They have no interest in vendetta," Rubio said. "Nicole has assured me."

"There is only one way," Portella said. "Kidnap Nicole and then lure Astorre out to rescue her."

Rubio protested, "Why not one of the brothers?"

"Because now Marcantonio is heavily guarded," Portella said. "And we can't fuck around with Valerius because army intelligence will come down on us, and they are a vicious bunch."

Tulippa turned to Rubio. "I will not hear any more of that bullshit from you. Why should we risk billions of dollars to go easy on your girl-friend?"

"It's just that we tried that trick before," Rubio said. "And remember, she has her bodyguard." He was being very careful. It would be disastrous for Tulippa to be angry with him.

"The bodyguard is no problem," Portella said.

"Well, I'll go along with you as long as Nicole doesn't get hurt," Rubio said.

MARRIANO RUBIO set things up by inviting Nicole to the annual Peruvian ball at the consulate. On the afternoon of the ball, Astorre came to visit her to tell her he was going to Sicily for a brief visit. As Nicole bathed and dressed Astorre picked up a guitar that Nicole kept for him and crooned Italian love songs with his hoarse but pleasant voice.

When Nicole came out of the bathroom, she was completely naked except for the white bathrobe over her arm. Astorre was nearly over-whelmed by her beauty, which was hidden in her everyday dress. When she reached him, he took the bathrobe and draped it around her.

She moved into his arms and sighed. "You don't love me anymore."

"You don't know who I really am," Astorre said, laughing. "We're not kids anymore."

"But I know you're good," Nicole said. "You saved Cilke and his family. Who is your informant?"

Astorre laughed again. "None of your business." Then he went into the living room to avoid any more questions.

THAT NIGHT Nicole attended the ball accompanied by her bodyguard Helene, who had a better time than she did. She understood that Rubio, as host, could not pay her special attention. But he had arranged for a limo for the night.

After the ball, the limo took her to the front of her apartment. Helene got out first. But before they could enter her building, four men surrounded them. Helene bent down to her ankle holster, but she was too late. One of the men fired a bullet into her head, forcing her crown of flowers to bloom into blood.

At that moment another group of men came out of the shadows. Three of the attackers fled, and Astorre, who had discreetly followed Nicole to the ball, had her behind his back. The shooter of Helene had been disarmed.

"Get her out of here," Astorre said to one of the men. He held the gun on the killer and demanded, "OK, who sent you?"

The killer seemed unafraid. "Fuck you," he said.

Nicole saw Astorre's face go cold just before he fired a bullet into the man's chest. He strode closer and grabbed the man by the hair as he fell, then fired another bullet into his head. At that moment she saw what her father must have been. She vomited over Helene's body. Astorre turned to her with a regretful smile on his lips. Nicole could not look at him.

Astorre brought her up into her apartment. He instructed her on what to tell the police, that she had fainted as soon as Helene was shot and had seen nothing. When he left, she called the police.

THE NEXT DAY, after arranging an around-the-clock bodyguard for Nicole, Astorre flew to Sicily to meet with Grazziella and Bianco in Palermo. He followed his usual route, flying first down to Mexico and there boarding a private jet to Palermo, so there would be no record of his journey.

In Palermo he was met by Octavius Bianco, now so well groomed and elegant in the Palermo style that it was hard to remember him as a bearded and ferocious bandit. Bianco was delighted to see Astorre and embraced him with affection. They were driven out to Bianco's villa at the seashore.

"So you're in trouble in America," Bianco said in the villa's courtyard, which was decorated with statues of the old Roman Empire. "But I have some good news for you." Then he digressed to ask, "Your wound. Does it give you trouble?"

Astorre touched the gold chain. "No," he said. "It just ruined my singing voice. Now I'm a croaker instead of a tenor."

"Better a baritone than a soprano," Bianco said, laughing. "Italy has many tenors anyway. One less won't hurt. You are a true Mafioso, and that's what we need."

Astorre smiled and began to think of that day so long ago when he went swimming. Now, instead of the sharp sting of betrayal, he only remembered how he felt when he woke up. He touched the amulet at his throat and said, "What's the good news?"

"I have made peace with the Corleonesi and Grazziella," Bianco said. "He was never involved in the killing of Don Aprile. He came into the syndicate afterward. But now he feels dissatisfied with Portella and Tulippa. He thinks they are too rash and bunglers besides. He disapproved of the attempt on the federal agent. And he also has enormous respect for you. He knows you from your service with me. He sees you as a remarkably hard man to kill. Now he wants to drop any previous vendettas with you and help you."

Astorre felt relief. His task would be easier if he did not have to worry about Grazziella.

"Tomorrow, meet us here at the villa," Bianco said.

"He trusts you that much?" Astorre asked.

"He must," Bianco said. "Because without me here in Palermo, he cannot rule Sicily. And we are more civilized today than when you were here last."

THE NEXT AFTERNOON Michael Grazziella arrived at the villa, and Astorre noted he was dressed in the ultrarespectable mode of a Roman politician—dark suit, white shirt, and dark tie. He was accompanied by two bodyguards dressed in a similar fashion. Grazziella was a small man, courteous, with a very soft voice—you would not have guessed he was responsible for the murders of high-ranking anti-Mafia magistrates. He gripped Astorre's hand and said, "I have come here to help you as a token of my deep esteem for our friend Bianco. Please forget the past. We must begin again."

"Thank you," Astorre said. "It is my honor."

Grazziella motioned to the guards, and they walked out onto the beach.

"So Michael," Bianco said. "How can you help?"

Grazziella looked at Astorre and said, "Portella and Tulippa are too reckless for my taste. And Marriano Rubio is too dishonest. Whereas I find you a clever man and qualified man. Also, Nello is my nephew, and I learned you spared him, no small thing. So there are my motives."

Astorre nodded. Beyond Grazziella, he saw the black-green waves of the Sicilian sea and, glinting off them, the dull deadly rays of the Sicilian sun. He had a sudden feeling of nostalgia, and a pang because he knew he had to leave. All this was familiar to him as America could never be. He longed for the streets of Palermo, the sound of Italian voices, his own tongue in a language more natural to him than English. He returned his attention to Grazziella. "So what can you tell me?"

"The syndicate wants me to meet with them in America," Grazziella said. "I can inform you as to the whereabouts and the security. If you take drastic action, I can then give you refuge in Sicily, and if they try to extradite you, I have friends in Rome who can stop the process."

"You have that kind of power?" Astorre asked.

"Certainly," Grazziella said with a little shrug.

"How could we exist otherwise? But you must not be too rash."

Astorre knew he was referring to Cilke. He smiled at Grazziella. "I would never do anything rash."

Grazziella smiled politely and said, "Your enemies are my enemies, and I pledge myself to your cause."

"I assume you will not be at the meeting," Astorre said.

Grazziella smiled at him again. "At the last moment I will be detained: I will not be present."

"And when will this be?" Astorre asked.

"Within a month," Grazziella said.

AFTER GRAZZIELLA left, Astorre said to Bianco, "Really, tell me, why is he doing this?"

Bianco smiled at him in appreciation. "How easily you understand Sicily. All the reasons that he gave were valid. But there is a primary motive he did not mention." He hesitated. "Tulippa and Portella have been cheating him out of his correct share of the drug money, and he would soon have to go to war over that in any case. He could never tolerate that. He thinks highly of you, and it would be perfect if you wiped out his enemies and became his ally. He's a very clever man, Grazziella."

That evening Astorre walked along the beach and thought about what he should do. Finally the end was coming.

MR. PRYOR had no worries about controlling the Aprile banks and defending them against the authorities. But when the FBI flooded New York following the assassination attempt on Cilke, he became a little concerned about what they would dig up. Especially after Cilke's visit.

In his early youth Mr. Pryor had been one of the prized assassins of the Palermo Mafia. But he had seen the light and gone into banking, where his natural charm, intelligence, and criminal connections ensured his success. In essence, he became a Mafia banker to the world. He was soon an expert in currency-rate storms and the stashing of black money. He also had a talent for buying legitimate businesses at good prices. Eventually he had emigrated to England because the fairness of the English system could better protect his wealth than the bribery in Italy.

However, his long arm still stretched out to Palermo and the United States. And he was the prime banker for Bianco's *cosca* in their control of construction in Sicily. He also was the link between the Aprile banks and Europe.

Now, with all the police activity, he was

reminded of a possible danger point: Rosie. She could link Astorre to the Sturzo brothers. Also, Mr. Pryor knew Astorre had a weak spot and still took some comfort in Rosie's charms. This did not make him respect Astorre any less; this weakness in men had existed since the beginning of recorded time. And Rosie was such a Mafioso girl. Who could resist her? But as much as he admired the girl, he did not think it wise to have her around.

So he decided to take a part in this affair as he had once done in London. He knew he would not win Astorre's approval for such an act—he knew Astorre's character and did not underestimate his dangerousness. But Astorre was always a reasonable man. Pryor would persuade him after the fact, and Astorre would recognize the sagacity behind the deed.

But it had to be done. So Mr. Pryor called Rosie one evening. She was delighted to hear from him, especially when he assured her he had good news. When he hung up the phone he let out a sigh of regret.

He took his two nephews with him as drivers and bodyguards. He left one in the car outside the building and took the other up with him to Rosie's apartment.

Rosie greeted them by running into Mr.

Pryor's arms, startling his nephew, who made a motion inside his jacket.

She had made coffee and served a dish of pastries that she said were specially imported from Naples. They tasted nothing like it to Mr. Pryor, who considered himself to be an expert in such matters.

"Ah, you're such a sweet girl," Mr. Pryor said. To his nephew he said, "Here, try one." But the nephew had retreated into a corner of the room and sat in a chair to watch this little comedy his uncle was playing.

Rosie thumped Mr. Pryor's homburg lying beside him and said mischievously, "I like your English bowler better. You didn't look so stuck-up then."

"Ah," Mr. Pryor said with great good humor, "when one changes one's country, one must always change one's hat. And, my dear Rosie, I'm here to ask you a great favor."

He caught her slight hesitation before she clapped her hands in glee. "Oh, you know I will," she said. "I owe you so much." Mr. Pryor was softened by her sweetness, but what had to be done had to be done.

"Rosie," he said, "I want you to arrange your affairs so that tomorrow you can leave for Sicily, but just for a short time. Astorre is waiting for you there, and you must deliver some papers to him from me, in the strictest confidence. He misses you and wants to show you Sicily."

Rosie blushed. "He really wants to see me?"

"Of course," Mr. Pryor said.

The truth was that Astorre was on his way home from Sicily and would be in New York the following night. Rosie and Astorre would cross paths over the Atlantic Ocean in their separate planes.

Rosie now became businesslike as a form of coyness. "I can't get away so quickly," she said. "I'd need to get reservations, go to the bank, and a lot of other little things."

"Don't think me presumptuous," Mr. Pryor said. "But I've arranged everything."

He took a long white envelope from inside his jacket. "This is your plane ticket," he said. "First-class. And also ten thousand American dollars to do some last-minute shopping and for travel expenses. My nephew, sitting there dazzled in the corner, will pick you up in his limousine tomorrow morning. In Palermo you will be met by Astorre or one of his friends."

"I have to be back after a week," Rosie said. "I have to take some tests for my doctorate."

"Don't concern yourself," Mr. Pryor said. "You will not have to worry about missing your tests. I promise. Have I ever failed you?" His voice was sweetly avuncular. But he was thinking, what a pity that Rosie would never see America again.

They drank coffee and ate the pastries. The nephew again refused refreshments though Rosie begged him prettily. Their chat was interrupted when the phone rang. Rosie picked it up. "Oh, Astorre," she said. "Are you calling from Sicily? Mr. Pryor told me. He's sitting right here having coffee."

Mr. Pryor continued to sip his coffee calmly, but his nephew rose from his chair and then sat down again when Mr. Pryor gave him a commanding look.

Rosie was silent and looked questioningly at Mr. Pryor, who nodded at her reassuringly.

"Yes, he was arranging for me to meet you in Sicily for a week," Rosie said. She paused to listen. "Yes, of course I'm disappointed. I'm sorry you had to come back unexpectedly. So you want to talk to him? No? OK, I'll tell him." She hung up the phone.

"What a shame," she said to Mr. Pryor. "He had to come back early. But he wants you to wait here for him. He said about half an hour."

Mr. Pryor reached for another pastry. "Certainly," he said.

"He'll explain everything when he gets here," Rosie said. "More coffee?"

Mr. Pryor nodded, then sighed. "You would have had such a wonderful time in Sicily. Too bad." He imagined her burial in a Sicilian cemetery, how sad that would have been.

"Go down and wait in the car," he told his nephew.

The young man rose reluctantly, and Mr. Pryor made a shooing motion. Rosie let him out of the apartment. Then he gave Rosie his most concerned smile and asked, "Have you been happy these last years?"

ASTORRE HAD ARRIVED a day early and been picked up by Aldo Monza at the small airport in New Jersey. He had, of course, traveled by private jet under a false passport. It was only on impulse that he had called Rosie, out of a desire to see her and spend a relaxing night with her. When Rosie told him that Mr. Pryor was in her apartment, his senses raced with the signals of danger. As for her trip to Sicily, he understood Mr. Pryor's plans immediately. He tried to control his anger. Mr. Pryor had wanted to do the right thing according to his experience. But it was too big a price to pay for safety.

When Rosie opened the door, she flew into his arms. Mr. Pryor rose from his chair, and Astorre went to him and embraced him. Mr.

Pryor concealed his surprise—Astorre was not usually so affectionate.

Then, to Mr. Pryor's astonishment, Astorre said to Rosie, "Go to Sicily tomorrow as we planned and I'll join you there in a few days. We'll have a great time."

"Great," Rosie said. "I've never been to Sicily."

Astorre said to Mr. Pryor, "Thanks for arranging everything."

Then he turned to Rosie again. "I can't stay," he said. "I'll see you in Sicily. Tonight I have some important business to do with Mr. Pryor. So start getting ready for your trip. And don't bring too many clothes; we can go shopping in Palermo."

"OK," Rosie said. She kissed Mr. Pryor on the cheek and gave Astorre a long embrace and a lingering kiss. Then she opened the door to let them out.

When the two men were out in the street, Astorre told Mr. Pryor, "Come with me to my car. Tell your nephews to go home—you won't need them tonight."

It was only then that Mr. Pryor felt a little nervous. "I was doing it for your own good," he said to Astorre.

In the backseat of Astorre's car, Monza driving, Astorre turned to Mr. Pryor. "Nobody appreciates you more than I do," he said. "But am I the chief or am I not?"

"Without question," Mr. Pryor said.

"It was a problem I have been meaning to address," Astorre said. "I recognize the danger and I'm glad you made me act. But I need her. We can take some risks. So here are my instructions. In Sicily, supply her with a luxurious house with servants. She can enroll at Palermo University. She will have a very generous allowance, and Bianco will introduce her to the best of Sicilian society. We will make her happy there, and Bianco can control any problem that may arise. I know you don't approve of my affection for her, but that's something I can't help. I count on her faults to help her be happy in Palermo. She has a weakness for money and pleasure, but who doesn't? So now I hold you responsible for her safety. No accidents."

"I'm very fond of the girl myself, as you know," Mr. Pryor said. "A truly Mafioso girl. Are you going back to Sicily?"

"No," Astorre said. "We have more important business."

CHAPTER 13

ONCE NICOLE gave the waiter her order, she focused intently on Marriano Rubio. She must deliver two important messages on this day, and she wanted to be certain she got both of them right.

Rubio had chosen the restaurant, a classy French bistro where waiters hovered nervously with tall varnished pepper mills and long straw baskets of crusty fresh bread. Rubio disliked the food, but he knew the maître d', so he was assured a good table in a quiet corner. He brought his women there often.

"You're quieter than usual tonight," he said, reaching across the table for her hand. Nicole felt a shiver run through her body. She realized that she hated him for having that power over her, and she pulled her hand away. "Are you all right?" he asked.

"It's been a difficult day," she said.

"Ah," he said with a sigh, "the price of working with snakes." Rubio had no regard for Nicole's law firm. "Why do you put up with them? Why don't you let me take care of you instead?"

Nicole wondered how many other women had fallen for his line and then thrown away their careers to be with him.

"Don't tempt me," she said flirtatiously.

This surprised Rubio, who knew Nicole was devoted to her career. But this was what he had hoped. "Let me take care of you," he repeated. "Besides, how many more corporations can you sue?"

One of the waiters opened a cold bottle of white wine, offered Rubio the cork, poured a small amount into an elegant crystal wineglass. Rubio tasted it and nodded. Then he turned his attention back to Nicole.

"I'd quit right now," she said, "but there are some pro bono cases I want to see through." She sipped her wine. "Lately, I've been thinking a lot about banking."

Rubio's eyes narrowed. "Well," he said, "lucky for you that banks run in the family."

"Yes," Nicole agreed, "but unfortunately my father didn't believe women were capable of running a business. So I have to stand by and watch my crazy cousin screw things up." She raised her head to look at him when she added,

"By the way, Astorre thinks you're out to get him."

Rubio tried to look amused. "Really? And how would I accomplish this?"

"Oh, I don't know," Nicole said, annoyed. "Remember, this is a guy who sells macaroni for a living. He's got flour on the brain. He says you want to use the bank for money laundering and who knows what else. He even tried to convince me that you were trying to kidnap me." Nicole knew she had to be careful here. "But I can't believe that. I think Astorre is behind everything that's been happening. He knows that my brothers and I want to control the banks, so he's trying to make us paranoid. But we're tired of listening to him."

Rubio studied Nicole's face. He was proud of his ability to separate truth from fiction. In his years as a diplomat, he had been lied to by some of the most respected statesmen in the world. And now, as he looked deeply into Nicole's eyes, he determined she was telling him the absolute truth.

"Just how tired are you?" he asked.

"We're all exhausted," Nicole said.

Several waiters appeared and fussed over them for long minutes in order to deliver their main course. When the waiters had finally retreated, Nicole leaned toward Rubio and whispered,

"Most nights my cousin works late at his warehouse."

"What are you suggesting?" Rubio asked.

Nicole lifted her knife and began to slice her main course, dark medallions of duck swimming in a light shimmery orange sauce. "I'm not suggesting anything," she said. "But what is the controlling shareholder of an international bank doing spending all his time at a macaroni warehouse? If I had control, I'd be at the banks constantly, and I'd make sure my partners were getting a better return on their investment." With that, Nicole tasted her duck. She smiled at Rubio. "Delicious," she said.

ALONG WITH all her other qualities, Georgette Cilke was a very organized woman. Each Tuesday afternoon she volunteered exactly two hours of her time at the national headquarters of the Campaign Against the Death Penalty, where she helped answer the phone and reviewed pleas from lawyers of prisoners on death row. So Nicole knew exactly where to deliver her second important message of the day.

When Georgette saw Nicole walk into the office, her face brightened. She rose to embrace her friend. "Thank goodness," she said. "Today has been dreadful. I'm glad you're here. I can use the moral support."

"I don't know how much help I'm going to be," Nicole said. "I've got something troubling that I have to discuss with you."

In the years they had worked together, Nicole had never confided in Georgette before, though they maintained a warm professional relationship. Georgette never discussed her husband's work with anyone. And Nicole never saw the point in talking about her lovers with married women, who always thought they had to offer advice on how to get a man to the altar, which was not what she wanted. Nicole preferred talking about the raw sex, but she noticed that this made most married women uncomfortable. Maybe, Nicole thought, they didn't like hearing about what they were missing.

Georgette asked Nicole whether she wanted to talk in private, and when Nicole nodded, they found a small empty office down the hall.

"I've never discussed this with anyone," Nicole began. "But you must know that my father was Raymond Aprile—the one known as Don Aprile. Have you heard of him?"

Georgette stood up and said, "I don't think I should be having this conversation with you—"

"Please sit down," Nicole interrupted. "You need to hear this."

Georgette looked uncomfortable but did as Nicole asked. In truth, she had always been curious about Nicole's family but knew she couldn't bring it up. Like many others, Georgette assumed Nicole, through her pro bono work, was trying to make up for the sins of her father. How frightening childhood must have been for Nicole, growing up in the shadow of criminals. And how embarrassing. Georgette thought of their own daughter, who was embarrassed to be seen with either of her parents in public. She wondered how Nicole had survived those years.

Nicole knew Georgette would never betray her husband in any way, but she also knew Georgette was a compassionate woman with an open mind. Someone who spent her free time as an advocate for convicted murderers. Now Nicole looked at her with a steady gaze and said, "My father was killed by men who have a close relationship with your husband. And my brothers and I have proof that your husband accepted bribes from these men."

Georgette's first reaction was shock, then disbelief. She said nothing. But it was only seconds before she felt the first clear flush of anger. "How dare you," she whispered. She looked Nicole squarely in eyes. "My husband would rather die than break the law."

Nicole was surprised by the intensity of Georgette's response. She could see now that Georgette truly believed in her husband. Nicole continued: "Your husband is not the man he seems to be. And I know how you feel. I just read my father's FBI file, but as much as I love him, I know he kept secrets from me. Just as Kurt is keeping secrets from you."

Then Nicole told Georgette about the million dollars Portella had wired into Cilke's bank account and about Portella's dealings with drug kingpins and hit men, who could only do their work with the tacit blessing of her husband. "I don't expect you to believe me," Nicole said. "All I hope is that you'll ask your husband whether I'm telling you the truth. If he's the man you say he is, he won't lie."

Georgette betrayed no hint of the turmoil she was feeling. "Why are you telling me this?"

"Because," Nicole said, "your husband has a vendetta against my family. He's going to allow his associates to murder my cousin Astorre and take over control of our family's banking business. It's going to happen tomorrow night at my cousin's macaroni warehouse."

At the mention of macaroni, Georgette laughed and said, "I don't believe you." Then she got up to leave. "I'm sorry, Nicole," she said. "I know you're upset, but we have nothing more to say to each other."

• • •

THAT NIGHT, in the sparsely decorated bedroom of the furnished ranch house where his family had been moved, Cilke faced his nightmare. He and his wife had finished dinner and were sitting across from each other, both of them reading. Suddenly, Georgette put down her book and said, "I need to talk to you about Nicole Aprile."

In all their years together, Georgette had never asked her husband to discuss his work. She didn't want the responsibility of keeping federal secrets. And she knew this was a part of his life Cilke needed to keep to himself. Sometimes, lying in bed next to him at night, she would wonder how he did his job—the tactics he used to get information, the pressure he must have to put on suspects. But in her mind she always pictured him as the ultimate federal agent, in his neatly pressed suit, with his thumbed-over copy of the Constitution tucked into his back pocket. In her heart she was smart enough to know this was a fantasy. Her husband was a determined man. He would go far to defeat his enemies. But this was a reality she never chose to examine.

Cilke had been reading a mystery novel—the third book in a series about a serial killer who raises his son to become a priest. When Georgette asked her question, he immediately closed the book. "I'm listening," he said.

"Nicole said some things today—about you and the investigation you're conducting," Georgette said. "I know you don't like to talk about your work, but she made some strong accusations."

Cilke felt the rage rising within him, until he was in a blind fury. First they had killed his dogs. Then they had destroyed his home. And now they had tarnished his purest relationship. Finally, when his heart stopped racing, he asked Georgette in the calmest voice he could manage to tell him exactly what had happened.

Georgette repeated her entire conversation with Nicole and watched her husband's expression carefully as he absorbed the information. His face betrayed no hint of surprise or outrage. When she was finished, Cilke said, "Thank you, sweetheart. I'm sure it was very difficult for you to tell me. And I'm sorry you had to do it." Then he rose from his chair and walked toward the front door.

"Where are you going?" Georgette asked.

"I need some air," Cilke said. "I need to think."

"Kurt, honey?" Georgette's voice was questioning; she needed reassurance.

Cilke had sworn he would never lie to his wife. If she insisted on the truth, he would have to tell her and suffer the consequences. He was hoping she would understand and decide it was better to pretend these secrets did not exist.

"Is there anything you can tell me?" she asked.

He shook his head. "No," he said. "I would do anything for you. You know that, don't you?"

"Yes. But I need to know. For us and for our daughter."

Cilke saw there was no escape. He realized she would never look at him the same way again if he told her the truth. At that moment, he wanted to crush Astorre Viola's skull. He thought of what he could possibly say to his wife: I only accepted the bribes the FBI wanted me to? We overlooked the small crimes in order to focus on the big ones? We broke some laws to enforce more important ones? He knew these answers would only infuriate her, and he loved and respected her too much to do such a thing.

Cilke left the house without saying a word. When he returned, his wife pretended to be asleep. He made up his mind then. The following night he would confront Astorre Viola and reclaim his own vision of justice.

ASPINELLA WASHINGTON did not hate all men, but she was repeatedly surprised by just how many of them turned her off. They were all so . . . useless.

After she had taken care of Heskow, she was briefly interrogated by two officers in airport security, who were either too dumb or too intimidated to challenge her version of events. When the cops found $100,000 taped to Heskow's body, they figured his motive was obvious. They decided it was appropriate to reward themselves with a service fee for cleaning up the mess she'd made before the ambulance arrived. They also gave Aspinella a clump of blood-stained bills, which she added to the $30,000 Heskow had already given her.

She had only two uses for the money. She locked all but $3,000 in her safe-deposit box. She had left instructions with her mother that if anything ever happened to her, all of the money in the box—over $300,000 in payoffs—should be put in a trust for her daughter. With the remaining $3,000, she took a cab to Fifth Avenue and Fifty-third Street, where she entered the fanciest leather-goods store in the city and took an elevator to a private suite on the third floor.

A woman wearing designer glasses and a navy pin-striped suit took her payment and escorted her down the hall, where she bathed in a tub filled with fragrant oils imported from China.

She soaked herself for about twenty minutes and listened to a CD of Gregorian chants while she waited for Rudolfo, a licensed sexual-massage therapist.

Rudolfo received $3,000 for a two-hour session, which, he was delighted to point out to his very satisfied customers, was more than even the most famous lawyers received per hour. "The difference," he said with a Bavarian accent and a sly grin, "is that they just fuck you over. I fuck you over the moon."

Aspinella had heard about Rudolfo during an undercover vice investigation she conducted in the city's elite hotels. One concierge was worried that he might be asked to testify, so in exchange for not being summoned, he gave her the tip about Rudolfo. Aspinella thought about making the bust, but once she met Rudolfo and experienced one of his massages, she felt it would be an even bigger crime to deny women the pleasure of his extraordinary talents.

After several minutes he knocked on the door and asked, "May I come in?"

"I'm counting on it, baby," she said.

He walked in and looked her over. "Great eye patch," he said.

During her first session, Aspinella had been surprised when Rudolfo entered the room naked, but he had said, "Why bother getting dressed just to get undressed?" He was an extraordinary specimen, tall and taut, with a tattoo of a tiger on his right biceps and a silken mat of blond on his chest. She particularly liked the chest hair, which separated Rudolfo from those magazine models who'd been plucked, shaved, and greased so carefully you couldn't tell whether they were male or female.

"How have you been?" he asked.

"You don't wanna hear about it," Aspinella said. "All you need to know is that I need some sexual healing."

Rudolfo began with her back, pressing deep, honing in on all her knots. Then he gently kneaded her neck before turning her over and lightly massaging her breasts and stomach. By the time he began to caress between her legs, she was already moist and breathing hard.

"Why can't other men do this to me?" Aspinella said with a sigh of ecstasy.

Rudolfo was about to begin the premium part of the service, his tongue massage, which he did expertly and with remarkable stamina. But he was struck by her question, which he had heard many times. It always amazed him. It seemed to him that the city was exploding with sexually undernourished women.

"It's a mystery to me, why other men can't do it," he said. "What do you think?"

She hated to interrupt her sexual reverie, but she could tell Rudolfo needed pillow talk before the grand finale. "Men are weak," she said. "We're the ones who make all the important decisions. When to get married. When to have kids. We rein them in and hold them accountable for the things they do."

Rudolfo smiled politely. "But what does that have to do with sex?"

Aspinella wanted him to get back to work. "I don't know," she said. "It's just a theory."

Rudolfo began to massage her again—slowly, steadily, rhythmically. He never seemed to tire. And each time he brought her to great heights of pleasure, she imagined the terrible depths of pain to which she would bring Astorre Viola and his gang of thugs the following night.

THE VIOLA Macaroni Company was located in a large brick warehouse on the Lower East Side of Manhattan. More than one hundred people worked there, unloading giant burlap bags of imported Italian macaroni onto a conveyor belt, which then automatically sorted and boxed it.

A year before, inspired by a magazine article he'd read about how small businesses were improving their operations, Astorre had hired a consultant straight out of Harvard Business

School to recommend changes. The young man told Astorre to double his prices, change the brand name of his macaroni to Uncle Vito's Homemade Pasta, and fire half of his employees, who could be replaced by temporary help at half the price. At that suggestion Astorre fired the consultant.

Astorre's office was on the main floor, which was roughly the size of a football field, lined with shiny stainless-steel machines on both sides. The back of the warehouse opened to a loading dock. Video cameras had been placed outside the entrances and inside the factory, so he could keep track of visitors and monitor production from his office. Normally, the warehouse closed down at 6:00 P.M., but on this night Astorre had retained five of his most qualified employees and Aldo Monza. He was waiting.

The night before, when Astorre had told Nicole his plan at her apartment, she was adamantly opposed to it. She shook her head violently. "First of all, it won't work. And second, I don't want to be an accessory to murder."

"They killed your assistant and they tried to kidnap you," Astorre said quietly. "We're all in danger, unless I take action." Nicole thought of Helene, and then she remembered her many dinner-table arguments with her father, who would certainly have sought vengeance. Her father would have said that she owed this to the memory of her friend, and he would have reminded her that it was reasonable and necessary to take precautions to protect the family.

"Why don't we go to the authorities?" she asked.

Astorre's response was curt: "It's too late for that."

Now Astorre sat in his office, live bait. Thanks to Grazziella, he knew that Portella and Tulippa were in the city for a meeting of the syndicate. He couldn't be sure that Nicole's leak to Rubio would force them to pay a visit, but he hoped they might try one last attempt at persuading him to turn over the banks before resorting to violence. He assumed they would check him for weapons, so he didn't arm himself, except for a stiletto, which he stored in a special pocket sewn into his shirtsleeve.

Astorre was carefully watching his video monitor when he saw a half dozen men enter the back of the building from the loading dock. He had given his own men instructions to hide and not to attack until he gave them the signal.

He studied the screen and recognized Portella and Tulippa among the six. Then, as they faded off the monitor, he heard the sound of footsteps approaching his office. If they had already decided to kill him, Monza and his crew were at the ready and would be able to save him.

But then Portella called out to him.

He didn't answer.

Within seconds Portella and Tulippa paused at the door.

"Come in," Astorre said with a warm smile. He stood to shake their hands. "What a surprise. I hardly ever get visitors at this hour. Is there something I can do for you?"

"Yeah," Portella cracked. "We're having a big dinner and we ran out of macaroni."

Astorre waved his hands magnanimously and said, "My macaroni, your macaroni."

"How about your banks?" Tulippa asked ominously.

Astorre was ready for this. "It's time we talked seriously. It's time we did business. But first I'd like to give you a tour of the plant. I'm very proud of it."

Tulippa and Portella exchanged a confused look. They were wary. "OK, but let's keep it short," Tulippa said, wondering how such a clown had been able to survive this long.

Astorre led them to the floor. The four men who had accompanied them were standing nearby. Astorre greeted them warmly, shaking hands with each of them and complimenting them on their dress.

Astorre's own men were watching him carefully, waiting for his command to strike. Monza had stationed three shooters on a mezzanine overlooking the floor, hidden from view. The others had fanned out to opposite sides of the warehouse.

Long minutes passed as Astorre showed his guests through the warehouse. Then Portella finally said, "It's clear that this is really where your heart is. Why don't you let us run the banks? We will make you one more offer and cut you in for a percentage."

Astorre was about to give his men the signal to shoot. But suddenly he heard a rattle of gunshots and saw three of his men fall twenty feet from the mezzanine and land facedown on the concrete floor in front of him. He scanned the warehouse, looking for Monza, as he quickly slipped behind a huge packaging machine.

From there he saw a black woman with a green eye patch sprint toward them and grab Portella by the neck. She jabbed him in his protruding belly with her assault rifle, then she pulled out a revolver and threw the rifle to the ground.

"OK," Aspinella Washington said. "Everybody drop your weapons. Now." When no one moved, she did not hesitate. She turned Portella around and fired two bullets into his stomach. As he doubled over, she slammed her revolver down on his head and kicked him in the teeth.

Then she grabbed Tulippa and said, "You're

next unless everybody does what I say. This is an eye for an eye, you bastard."

Portella knew that without help, he would only live for a few more minutes. His vision was already beginning to fade. He was sprawled across the floor, breathing heavily, his florid shirt soaked with blood. His mouth was numb. "Do what she says," he groaned weakly.

Portella's men obeyed.

He had always heard that being shot in the stomach was the most painful way to die. Now he knew why. Every time he took a deep breath, he felt like he had been stabbed in the heart. He lost control of his bladder, his urine making a dark stain on his new blue trousers. He tried to focus his eyes on the shooter, a muscular black woman he didn't recognize. He tried to utter the words "Who are you?" but couldn't find the breath. His final thought was an oddly sentimental one: He wondered who would tell his brother, Bruno, that he was dead.

It took Astorre only a moment to figure out what had happened. He had never before seen Detective Aspinella Washington, except in newspaper photos and on TV news shows. But he knew if she had discovered him, she must have gotten to Heskow first. And Heskow must certainly be dead. Astorre did not mourn for the slippery bagman. Heskow had the great flaw of being a man who would say or do anything to stay alive. It was good that he was now in the ground with his flowers.

Tulippa had no idea why this angry bitch was holding a gun to his neck. He had trusted Portella to handle the security and given his own loyal bodyguards the night off. A stupid mistake. America is such a strange country, he thought to himself. You never know where the next violence is coming from.

As Aspinella dug the nozzle of the gun deep into his skin, Tulippa made a promise to himself that if he escaped and could return to South America, he would speed up production of his nuclear arsenal. He would personally do everything he could to blow up as much of this America as possible, especially Washington, D.C., an arrogant capital of lazy bullies in armchairs, and New York City, where they seemed to breed crazy people like this one-eyed bitch.

"All right," Aspinella said to Tulippa. "You offered us half a mil to take care of this guy." She pointed to Astorre. "It would be my pleasure to accept the job, but since my accident I've had to double my fee. With only one eye, I have to concentrate twice as hard."

· · ·

KURT CILKE had been staking out the warehouse throughout the day. Sitting in his blue Chevy with nothing but a pack of gum and a copy of *Newsweek,* he waited for Astorre to make his move.

He had come alone, not wanting to involve any other federal agents in what he believed might be the end of his career. When he saw Portella and Tulippa enter the building, he felt the bile rising in his stomach. And he realized what a clever foe Astorre was. If, as Cilke suspected, Portella and Tulippa attacked Astorre, Cilke would have a legal duty to protect him. Astorre would be free and would clear his name without breaking his silence. And Cilke would blow years of hard work.

But when Cilke saw Aspinella Washington storm into the building toting an assault rifle, he felt something different—cold fear. He had heard about Aspinella's role in the airport shooting. It sounded suspicious to him. Just didn't add up.

He checked the ammunition in his revolver and felt a distant hope that he would be able to count on her for help. Before leaving the car, Cilke decided it was time to inform the Bureau. On his cell phone, he dialed Boxton.

"I'm outside Astorre Viola's warehouse," Cilke told him. Then he heard the sound of rapid gunfire. "I'm going in now, and if things go wrong, I want you to tell the director I was acting on my own. Are you recording this call?"

Boxton paused, not sure whether Cilke would appreciate being taped. But ever since Cilke had become a target, all of his calls were being monitored. "Yes," he said.

"Good," Cilke responded. "For the record, neither you nor anyone else within the FBI is responsible for what I'm going to do now. I am entering a hostile situation involving three reputed organized-crime figures and one renegade New York City cop who is heavily armed."

Boxton interrupted Cilke. "Kurt, wait for backup."

"There isn't time," Cilke said. "And besides, this is my mess. I'll clean it up." He thought of leaving a message for Georgette, but he decided that would be too morbid and self-indulgent. Better to let his actions speak for themselves. He hung up the phone without saying anything more. As he left the car, he noticed he was illegally parked.

The first thing Cilke saw when he entered the warehouse was Aspinella's gun digging into Tulippa's neck. Everyone in the room was silent. No one moved.

"I am a federal officer," Cilke announced, waving his gun upward. "Lay all your weapons down."

Aspinella turned to Cilke and spoke with derision: "I know who the fuck you are. This is my bust. Go collar some accountants or stockbrokers or whatever the hell it is you suits spend your pansy-ass time on. This is an NYPD matter."

"Detective," Cilke said calmly, "drop your weapon now. If you don't, I will use force if necessary. I have reason to believe you are part of a racketeering conspiracy."

Aspinella had not counted on this. From the look in Cilke's eyes and the steadiness of his voice, she knew he would not back down. But she was not about to give in, not as long as she had a gun in her hand. Cilke probably hadn't fired on anyone in years, she thought. "You think I'm part of a conspiracy?" she yelled. "Well, I think *you're* part of a conspiracy. I think you've been taking bribes from this piece of shit for years." She jabbed Tulippa again with the gun. "Isn't that right, *señor*?"

At first Tulippa didn't say anything, but when Aspinella kneed him in the groin, he folded and nodded.

"How much?" Aspinella asked him.

"Over a million dollars," Tulippa gasped.

Cilke controlled his fury and said, "Each dollar they wired into my account was monitored by the FBI. This is a federal investigation, Detective Washington." He took a deep breath, counting down, before he told her, "This is my final warning. Put down your weapon or I'll fire."

Astorre coolly watched them. Aldo Monza was standing unnoticed behind another of the machines. Astorre saw a twitch in Aspinella's face. Then, as if it were happening in slow motion, he saw her slip behind Tulippa and fire at Cilke. But as soon as she fired, Tulippa broke free and dove to the ground, pushing her off balance.

Cilke had been hit in the chest. But he fired once at Aspinella and saw her stagger backward, blood spurting from below her right shoulder. Neither had been shooting to kill. They were following their training to the very end, aiming for the widest part of the body. But as Aspinella felt the searing pain of the bullet and saw its damage, she knew it was time to forget procedure. She took aim between Cilke's eyes. She fired four times. Each bullet hit its mark until Cilke's nose was a flattened pulp of cartilage and she could see chunks of his brain splattered on what was left of his forehead.

Tulippa saw that Aspinella was wounded and reeling. He tackled her and elbowed her in the face, knocking her out cold. But before he had a chance to grab her gun, Astorre came out from behind the machine and kicked it across the room. Then he stood over Tulippa and gallantly offered his hand.

Tulippa accepted it and Astorre pulled him up. Meanwhile, Monza and the surviving members of his team rounded up the rest of Portella's men and tied them to steel support beams of the warehouse. No one touched Cilke and Portella.

"So," Astorre said, "I believe we have some business to finish."

Tulippa was puzzled. Astorre was a mass of contradictions—a friendly adversary, a singing assassin. Could such a wild card ever be trusted?

Astorre walked to the center of the warehouse and signaled Tulippa to follow. When he reached an open space, he stopped and faced the South American. "You killed my uncle and you tried to steal our banks. I should not even waste my breath on you." Then Astorre pulled out the stiletto, its silver blade flashing, and showed it to Tulippa. "I should just slice your throat and be done with it. But you are weak, and there is no honor in butchering a defenseless old man. So I'll give you a fighting chance."

With those words and an almost imperceptible nod toward Monza, Astorre raised both of his hands, as if in surrender, dropped his knife, and took several steps back. Tulippa was older and bulkier than Astorre, but he had carved rivers of blood in his lifetime. He was an extremely qualified man with a knife. Still, he was no match for Astorre.

Tulippa picked up the stiletto and began to move toward Astorre. "You are a stupid and reckless man," he said. "I was ready to accept you as a partner." He lunged at Astorre several times, but Astorre was quicker and evaded him. When Tulippa stopped momentarily to catch his breath, Astorre removed the gold medallion from his neck and threw it to the ground, exposing the purple scar in his throat. "I want this to be the last thing you see before you die."

Tulippa was transfixed by the wound, a shade of purple he had never seen. And before he knew it, Astorre kicked the stiletto out of his hand and with rapid precision kneed Tulippa in the back, put him in a headlock, and snapped his neck. Everyone heard the crack.

Without pausing to look at his victim, Astorre picked up his medallion, placed it back on his throat, and left the building.

Five minutes later a squadron of FBI cars arrived at the Viola Macaroni Company. Aspinella Washington, still alive, was taken to the intensive care unit of the hospital.

When the FBI officers had completed their study of the silent videotape recorded by the cameras Monza had run, they determined that Astorre, who had raised his hands and dropped his knife, had acted in self-defense.

EPILOGUE

NICOLE SLAMMED down the phone and yelled to her secretary, "I am sick of hearing about how weak the damn Eurodollar is. See if you can track down Mr. Pryor. He's probably on the ninth hole of some golf course."

Two years had passed, and Nicole had taken over as head of the Aprile banks. When Mr. Pryor was ready to retire, he had insisted she was the best person for the job. She was a skilled corporate fighter who wouldn't fold under pressure from bank regulators and demanding customers.

Today Nicole was frantically trying to clear her desk. Later that night she and her brothers would fly to Sicily for a family celebration with Astorre. But before she could go, she had to deal with Aspinella Washington, who was waiting to hear whether Nicole would represent her in an appeal to avoid the death penalty. The thought of it filled her with dread, and not just because she had a full-time job.

At first, when Nicole had offered to run the banks, Astorre had hesitated, remembering the Don's final wishes. But Mr. Pryor convinced him that Nicole was her father's daughter. Whenever a big loan was due, the bank could count on her to deploy a potent combination of sweet talk and veiled intimidation. She knew how to get results.

Nicole's intercom buzzed, and Mr. Pryor greeted her in his courtly manner: "What can I do for you, my dear?"

"We're getting killed on these exchange rates," she said. "What do you think of moving more heavily into deutsche marks?"

"I think that's an excellent idea," Mr. Pryor said.

"You know," Nicole said, "all of this currency trading is about as logical as going to Vegas and playing baccarat all day."

Mr. Pryor laughed. "That may be true, but baccarat losses aren't guaranteed by the Federal Reserve."

When Nicole hung up, she sat for a moment and reflected on the bank's progress. Since taking over, she had acquired six more banks in booming countries and doubled corporate profits. But she was even more pleased that the bank was providing larger loans to new businesses in developing parts of the world.

She smiled to herself as she remembered her first day.

As soon as her new stationery had arrived, Nicole had drafted a letter to Peru's finance minister demanding repayment of all of the government's overdue loans. As she expected, this produced an economic crisis in the country, resulting in political turmoil and a change of government. The new party demanded the resignation of Peru's consul general to the United Nations, Marriano Rubio.

In the months that followed, Nicole was delighted to read that Rubio had declared personal bankruptcy. He was also involved in fighting a series of complicated lawsuits with Peruvian investors who had bankrolled one of his many ventures—a failed theme park. Rubio had vowed it would become "the Latino Disneyland," but all he had been able to attract was a Ferris wheel and a Taco Bell.

THE CASE, which the tabloids dubbed the Macaroni Massacre, had become an international incident. As soon as Aspinella Washington recovered from the wound inflicted by Cilke's gunshot—a punctured lung—she had made a series of pronouncements to the media. While awaiting her trial, she portrayed herself as a martyr on the scale of Joan of Arc. She sued the FBI for attempted murder, slander, and violation of her civil rights. She also sued the New York Police Department for back pay she was owed while under suspension.

Despite her protestations, it had taken the jury only three hours of deliberation to convict her. When the guilty verdict was announced, Aspinella fired her attorneys and petitioned the Campaign Against the Death Penalty for representation. Demonstrating further flair for publicity, she demanded that Nicole Aprile take her case. From her cell on death row, Aspinella told the press, "Her cousin got me into this, so now she can get me out."

At first Nicole refused to meet with Aspinella, saying that any good lawyer would recuse herself from such an obvious conflict of interest. But then Aspinella accused Nicole of racism, and Nicole—not wanting bad blood with minority lenders—agreed to see her.

The day of their meeting, Nicole had to wait twenty minutes while Aspinella greeted a small congress of foreign dignitaries. They hailed Aspinella as a brave warrior against America's barbaric penal code. Finally Aspinella gave Nicole the signal to approach the glass window. She had taken to wearing a yellow eye patch stitched with the word FREEDOM.

Nicole launched into all of her reasons for wanting to turn down the case and concluded by pointing out that she had represented Astorre in his testimony against her.

Aspinella listened carefully, twirling her new dreadlocks. "I hear you, she said, "but there's a lot you don't know. Astorre was right: I am guilty of the crimes I've been convicted of, and I will spend the rest of my life atoning for them. But please, help me live long enough to begin to make whatever amends I can."

At first Nicole figured this was just another one of Aspinella's ploys to gain sympathy, but there was something in her voice that moved Nicole. She still believed that no human being had the right to condemn another to death. She still believed in redemption. She felt Aspinella deserved a defense, just as every death row inmate did. She just wished she didn't have to handle this one.

Before Nicole could make a final decision, she knew there was one person she had to face.

AFTER THE FUNERAL, at which Cilke had received a hero's burial, Georgette had requested a meeting with the director. An FBI escort picked her up from the airport and took her to Bureau headquarters.

When she entered the director's office, he wrapped her in a hug and promised that the Bureau would do everything necessary to help her and her daughter cope with their loss.

"Thank you," Georgette said. "But that's not why I came. I need to know why my husband was killed."

The director paused quite a while before speaking. He knew she had heard rumors. And those rumors could pose a threat to the Bureau's image. He needed to reassure her. Finally, he said, "I'm embarrassed to admit that we even needed to mount an investigation. Your husband was a paragon of what an FBI man should be. He was devoted to his work, and he followed every law to the letter. I know he never would have done anything to compromise the Bureau or his family."

"Then why did he go to that warehouse alone?" Georgette asked. "And what was his relationship with Portella?"

The director followed the talking points he had practiced with his staff prior to the meeting. "Your husband was a great investigator. He had earned the freedom and respect to follow his own leads. We don't believe he ever took a bribe or crossed the line with Portella or anyone else. His results speak volumes. He's the man who broke up the Mafia."

As she left his office, Georgette realized that she didn't believe him. She knew that in order to find any peace, she would have to believe the truth she felt in her heart: that her husband, despite his zeal, was as good a man as she would ever know.

AFTER THE MURDER of her husband, Georgette Cilke continued to volunteer at the New York headquarters of the Campaign Against the Death Penalty, but Nicole had not seen her since their fateful conversation. Because of her responsibilities at the bank, Nicole had said she was too busy for the Campaign. The truth was, she could not bear to face Georgette.

Even so, when Nicole walked through the door, Georgette greeted her with a warm embrace. "I've missed you," she said.

"I'm sorry I haven't been in touch," Nicole responded. "I tried to write you a condolence letter, but I couldn't find the words."

Georgette nodded and said, "I understand."

"No," Nicole said, her throat tightening, "you don't understand. I deserve some of the blame for what happened to your husband. If I hadn't spoken to you that afternoon—"

"It still would have happened," Georgette cut in. "If it hadn't been your cousin, it would have been someone else. Something like this was bound to happen sooner or later. Kurt knew it and so did I." Georgette hesitated only a moment before she added, "The important thing now is that we remember his goodness. So let's not talk any more about the past. I'm sure we all have regrets."

Nicole wished it were that easy. She took a deep breath. "There's more. Aspinella Washington wants me to represent her."

Though Georgette tried to hide it, Nicole saw her flinch at the mention of Aspinella's name. Georgette was not a religious woman, but at this moment she was certain God was testing her powers of conviction. "OK," she said, biting her lip.

"OK?" Nicole asked, surprised. She had hoped Georgette would object, forbid it, and that Nicole would be able to refuse Aspinella out of loyalty to her friend. Nicole could hear her father telling her, "There would be honor in such loyalty."

"Yes," Georgette said, closing her eyes. "You should defend her."

Nicole was amazed. "I don't have to do this. Everyone will understand."

"That would be hypocritical," Georgette said.

"A life is sacred or it isn't. We can't adjust what we believe just because it causes us pain."

Georgette became silent and extended her hand to Nicole to say good-bye. There was no hug this time.

After replaying that conversation in her mind all day, Nicole finally phoned Aspinella and, with reluctance, accepted the case. In one hour Nicole would be leaving for Sicily.

THE FOLLOWING week Georgette sent a note to the coordinator of the Campaign Against the Death Penalty. She wrote that she and her daughter were moving to another city to start a new life and that she wished everyone well. She did not leave a forwarding address.

ASTORRE HAD KEPT his vow to Don Aprile, to save the banks and ensure the well-being of his family. He had avenged the death of his uncle and brought honor to Don Zeno's name. In his own mind he was now free of any obligations.

The week after he had been cleared of all wrongdoing in the warehouse murders, he met with Don Craxxi and Octavius Bianco in his warehouse office and told them about his desire to return to Sicily. He explained that he felt a longing for the land itself, that it had insinuated itself into his dreams for many years. He had many happy memories of his childhood at Villa Grazia, the country retreat of Don Aprile, and he had always hoped to return. It was a simpler life but a richer one in many ways.

It was then that Bianco told him, "You do not have to return to Villa Grazia. There is a vast property that belongs to you in Sicily. The entire village of Castellammare del Golfo."

Astorre was puzzled. "How can that be?"

Benito Craxxi told him of the day the great Mafia chief, Don Zeno, had called his three friends to his bedside as he lay dying. "You are the young boy of his heart and soul," he said. "And now you are his only surviving heir. The village has been bequeathed to you by your natural father. It is your birthright."

"When Don Aprile took you to America, Don Zeno left provisions for all those in his village, until the day you would come to claim it. We provided protection for the village after your father's death, according to his wishes. When the farmers suffered a bad season, we offered the means to purchase fruits and grains to plant—a helping hand," Bianco said.

"Why didn't you tell me before?" Astorre asked.

"Don Aprile swore us to secrecy," Bianco said.

"Your father wanted your safety and Don Aprile wanted you as part of his family. He also needed you to protect his children. In truth, you had two fathers. You are blessed."

ASTORRE LANDED in Sicily on a beautiful sun-filled day. Two of Michael Grazziella's bodyguards met him at the airport and escorted him to a dark blue Mercedes.

As they drove through Palermo, Astorre marveled at the beauty of the city: Marble columns and ornate carvings of mythic figures made some buildings Greek temples, others Spanish cathedrals with saints and angels carved deep into the gray stone. The trip from Palermo into Castellammare del Golfo took over two hours on a rocky, single-lane road. To Astorre as always, the most striking thing about Sicily was the beauty of the countryside, with its breathtaking view of the Mediterranean Sea.

The village, in a deep valley surrounded by mountains, was a labyrinth of cobblestone, lined with small, two-story stucco houses. Astorre noticed several people peeking through the cracks of the painted white shutters pulled shut against the scorching midday sun.

He was greeted by the mayor of the village, a short man in gray baggy pants held up by black suspenders who introduced himself as Leo DiMarco and bowed with respect. *"Il Padrone,"* he said. "Welcome."

Astorre, uncomfortable, smiled and asked in Sicilian, "Would you please take me through the village?"

They passed a few old men playing cards on wooden benches. On the far side of the piazza was a stately Catholic church. And it was into this church, Saint Sebastian's, that the mayor first took Astorre, who had not said a formal prayer since the murder of Don Aprile. The mahogany pews were ornately carved, and dark blue votives held holy candles. Astorre knelt, head bowed, to be blessed by Father Del Vecchio, the village priest.

Afterward, Mayor DiMarco led Astorre to the small house in which he would stay. Along the way, Astorre noticed several *carabinieri*, or Italian National Police, leaning against the houses, with rifles at the ready. "Once night falls, it is safer to stay in the village," the mayor explained. "But during the days, it is a joy to be in the fields."

For the next few days Astorre took long walks through the countryside, fresh with the scent of the orange and lemon orchards. His primary purpose was to meet the villagers and explore the ancient stone-carved houses built like Roman villas. He wanted to find one he could make his home.

By the third day he knew he would be happy

there. The usual wary and solemn villagers greeted him in the street, and as he sat in the café in the piazza, the old men and children teased him playfully.

There were only two more things he must do.

THE FOLLOWING morning Astorre asked the mayor to show him the way to the village cemetery.

"For what purpose?" DiMarco asked.

"To pay my respects to my father and my mother," Astorre replied.

DiMarco nodded and quickly grabbed a large wrought-iron key from the office wall.

"How well did you know my father?" Astorre asked him.

DiMarco quickly made the sign of the cross on his chest. "Who did not know Don Zeno? It is to him we owe our lives. He saved our children with expensive medicines from Palermo. He protected our village from looters and bandits."

"But what was he like as a man?" Astorre asked.

DiMarco shrugged. "There are few people left who knew him in that way, and even fewer who will speak to you about him. He has become a legend. So who would wish to know the real man?"

I would, Astorre thought.

They walked through the countryside and then climbed a steep hill, with DiMarco stopping occasionally to catch his breath. Finally, Astorre saw the cemetery. But instead of gravestones, there were rows of small stone buildings. Mausoleums, all surrounded by a high, cast-iron fence, which was locked at a gate. The sign above read: WITHIN THESE GATES, ALL ARE INNOCENT.

The mayor unlocked the gate and led Astorre to his father's gray marble mausoleum, marked by the epitaph VINCENZO ZENO: A GOOD AND GENEROUS MAN. Astorre entered the building and on the altar studied the picture of his father. It was the first time he'd seen a picture of him, and he was struck by how familiar his face looked.

DiMarco then took Astorre to another small building, several rows away. This stone was white marble, the only hint of color a light blue raiment of the Virgin Mary carved into the arch of the entrance. Astorre walked in and examined the picture. The girl was not more than twenty-two years old, but her wide green eyes and radiant smile warmed him.

Outside, he said to DiMarco, "When I was a boy, I used to dream of a woman like her, but I thought she was an angel."

DiMarco nodded. "She was a beautiful girl. I

remember her from church. And you're right. She sang like an angel."

ASTORRE RODE bareback across the countryside, only stopping long enough to eat the fresh goat-milk cheese and crusty bread that one of the village women had packed.

Finally, he reached Corleone. He could no longer put off seeing Michael Grazziella. He owed the man at least that courtesy.

He was tan from all his time in the fields, and Grazziella greeted him with open arms and a crushing bear hug. "The Sicilian sun has been good to you," he said.

Astorre struck the proper note of gratitude: "Thank you for everything. Especially your support."

Grazziella walked with him toward his villa. "And what brings you to Corleone?"

"I think you know why I'm here," Astorre replied.

Grazziella smiled. "A strong young man like yourself? Of course! And I will take you to her right away. She is a joy to behold, this Rose of yours. And she has brought pleasure to everyone she has met."

Knowing of Rosie's sexual appetite, Astorre

wondered for just a moment if Grazziella was trying to tell him something. But he quickly caught himself. Grazziella was far too proper to say such a thing, and too Sicilian to allow such impropriety to occur under his watchful eye.

Her villa was only minutes away. When they reached it, Grazziella called out, "Rose, my dear, you have a visitor."

She was wearing a simple blue sundress with her blond hair tied back at the neck. Without her makeup, she looked younger and more innocent than he remembered.

She stopped when she saw him, surprised. But then she cried out, "Astorre!" She ran to him, kissed him, and began talking excitedly. "I've already learned to speak the Sicilian dialect fluently. And I've learned some famous recipes, too. Do you like spinach gnocchi?"

He took her to Castellammare del Golfo and spent the next week showing her around his village and the countryside. Each day they swam, talked for hours, and made love to each other with the comfort that only comes with time.

Astorre watched Rosie carefully to see if she was getting bored with him or restless with the simple life. But she seemed truly at peace. He wondered if, after all they'd been through together, he could ever really trust her. And then he wondered whether it was smart to love any woman so much that you would trust her completely. He and Rosie both had secrets to protect—things he did not wish to remember or share. But Rosie knew him and still loved him. She would keep his secrets, and he would keep hers.

There was only one thing that still troubled him. Rosie had a weakness for money and fancy gifts. Astorre wondered if she would ever be satisfied with what any one man could offer her. He needed to know.

On their last day together in Corleone, Astorre and Rosie rode their horses through the hills, flying over the countryside until dusk. Then they stopped in a vineyard, where they picked grapes and fed each other.

"I can't believe I've stayed so long," Rosie said as they rested together in the grass.

Astorre's green eyes glistened intensely. "Do you think you could stay a little longer?"

Rosie looked surprised. "What did you have in mind?"

Astorre got down on one knee and extended his hand. "Maybe fifty or sixty years," he said with a sincere smile. In his palm was a simple bronze ring.

"Will you marry me?" he asked.

Astorre looked for some sign of hesitation in Rosie's eyes, some mild disappointment with the quality of the ring, but her response was immediate. She threw her arms around his neck and showered him with kisses. Then they fell to the ground and rolled together in the hills.

ONE MONTH LATER, Astorre and Rosie were married in one of his citrus groves. Father Del Vecchio performed the ceremony. Everyone from both villages attended. The hill was carpeted with purple wisteria, and the smell of lemons and oranges perfumed the air. Astorre was dressed in a white peasant suit, and Rosie wore a pink gown of silk.

There was a pig on a spit roasting over red coals and warm ripe tomatoes from the fields. There were hot loaves of bread and freshly made cheese. Homemade wine ran like a river.

When the ceremony was over and they had exchanged vows, Astorre serenaded his bride with his favorite ballads. There was so much drinking and dancing that the festivities lasted until sunrise.

THE FOLLOWING MORNING, when Rosie awakened, she saw Astorre readying their horses. "Ride with me?" he asked.

They journeyed all day until Astorre found

what he was looking for—Villa Grazia. "My uncle's secret paradise. I spent my happiest times here as a child."

He walked behind the house to the garden, with Rosie following. And finally they came upon his olive tree, the one that had grown from the pits he planted as a young boy. The tree was as tall as he was now, and the trunk was quite thick. He took a sharp blade from his pocket and grabbed one of the branches. Then he cut it from the tree.

"We will plant this in our garden. So when we have a child, he will have happy memories too."

One year later, Astorre and Rosie celebrated the birth of their son, Raymonde Zeno. And when it came time to baptize him, they invited Astorre's family to join them at the Church of Saint Sebastian.

After Father Del Vecchio had finished, Valerius, as the eldest of the Aprile children, lifted a glass of wine and made a toast. "May you all thrive and live joyfully. And may your son grow up with the passion of Sicily and the romance of America beating in his heart."

Marcantonio lifted his glass and added, "And if he ever wants to be on a sitcom, you know who to call."

Now that the Aprile banks were so profitable, Marcantonio had established a twenty-million-dollar line of credit to develop his own dramatic properties. He and Valerius were working together on a project based on their father's FBI files. Nicole thought it was a terrible idea, but they all agreed that the Don would have appreciated the idea of receiving large sums of money for dramatizing the legend of his crimes.

"*Alleged* crimes," Nicole added.

Astorre wondered why anyone still cared. The old Mafia was dead. The great Dons had accomplished their goals and blended gracefully into society, as the best criminals always do. The few pretenders who remained were a disappointing assortment of dim, second-class felons and impotent thugs. Why would anyone want to bother with the rackets when it was much easier to steal millions by starting your own company and selling shares to the public?

"Hey Astorre, do you think you could be our special consultant on the movie?" Marcantonio asked. "We want to make sure it's as authentic as possible."

"Sure," Astorre said, smiling. "I'll have my agent get back to you."

LATER THAT NIGHT, in bed, Rosie turned to Astorre. "Do you think you'll ever want to go back?"

"Where?" Astorre asked. "To New York? To America?"

"You know," Rosie said hesitantly. "To your old life."

"This is where I belong, with you, here."

"Good," Rosie said. "But what about the baby? Shouldn't he have the chance to experience everything America has to offer?"

Astorre pictured Raymonde, running through the hills of the country, eating olives from barrels, hearing tales of the great dons and the Sicily of old. He looked forward to telling his son those stories. And yet he knew that those myths would not be enough.

One day his son would go to America, a land of vengeance, mercy, and magnificent possibility.

ACKNOWLEDGMENTS

Very special thanks to Carol Gino; my literary agents, Candida Donadio and Neil Olson; my attorneys, Bert Fields and Arthur Altman; my brother, Anthony Cleri; my editor at Random House, Jonathan Karp; and my children and grandchildren.

ABOUT THE AUTHOR

Mario Puzo was born in New York and, follow-ing military service in World War II, attended New York's New School for Social Research and Columbia University. His bestselling novel *The Godfather* was preceded by two critically acclaimed novels, *The Dark Arena* (1955) and *The Fortunate Pilgrim* (1965). In 1978, he published *Fools Die,* followed by *The Sicilian* (1984), *The Fourth K* (1991), and the second installment in his Mafia trilogy, *The Last Don* (1996), which became an international bestseller and the highest-rated TV miniseries of 1997. Mario Puzo also wrote many screenplays, including *Earth-quake, Superman,* and all three *Godfather* movies, for which he received two Academy Awards. He died in July 1999 at his home on Long Island, New York, at the age of seventy-eight.